WITHDRAWN

# A Tale of
# Two Murders

# A Tale of
# Two Murders

## HEATHER
## REDMOND

**KENSINGTON BOOKS**
www.kensingtonbooks.com

Library of Congress Control Number: 2018932842

ISBN-13: 978-1-4967-1715-3
ISBN-10: 1-4967-1715-5
First Kensington Hardcover Edition: August 2018

eISBN-13: 978-1-4967-1718-4
eISBN-10: 1-4967-1718-X
First Kensington Electronic Edition: August 2018


10 9 8 7 6 5 4 3 2 1

Printed in the United States of America

For Andy

# Cast of Characters

Charles Dickens*            A journalist

Kate Hogarth*              The daughter of George Hogarth, Charles's editor at the *Evening Chronicle*

Fred Dickens*              Charles's younger brother and room-mate

Mr. George Hogarth*        Charles's editor at the newspaper, and Kate's father

Mrs. Georgina Hogarth*     Kate's mother

Mary Hogarth*              Kate's younger sister

William Aga                Charles's fellow journalist at the *Evening Chronicle*

Lady Lugoson               Baroness and mother of the victim

Lord Theodore Lugoson      Baron and brother of the victim

The late Lord Lugoson      Deceased

Christiana Lugoson         The victim

Marie Rueff                Deceased. Another victim?

| | |
|---|---|
| Angela Acton | Lady Lugoson's sister, an actress |
| Percy Chalke | Angela's partner, an actor |
| Julie Saville | A young actress and assistant to Miss Acton |
| Mrs. Ellen Carley | Whig hostess and neighbor of the Lugoson family |
| Mr. Eustace Carley | Member of Parliament, married to Ellen Carley |
| Beatrice Carley | Christiana's best friend, and daughter of Mr. and Mrs. Carley |
| Bertram Carley | A handsome young man, son of the Carleys |
| Lady Holland* | A famed hostess |
| Mrs. Marian Decker | A wealthy Whig patroness |
| Émile Dubois | A dance master |
| Horatio Durant | A young man of wealth and connection |

*Real historical figures

The water of the fountain ran, the swift river ran, the day ran into evening, so much life in the city ran into death according to rule, time and tide waited for no man . . .

Charles Dickens, *A Tale of Two Cities*, Chapter 13

It has been observed, and I am apt to believe it is an observation which will generally be found true, that before a terrible truth comes to light, there are certain murmuring whispers fly before it, and prepare the minds of men for the reception of the truth itself.

William Harrison Ainsworth, *Rookwood*

# Chapter 1

*Brompton, outside of London, January 6, 1835*

"Epiphany is truly the best of times," Charles Dickens exclaimed as his hostess carried a beautiful jam tart over from the sideboard. The enormous dessert, decorated traditionally for the holiday with star-shaped pastry and thirteen different-colored kinds of jam marking the six points, enticed with fruit and sugar scents.

Mrs. Hogarth's large family applauded as she set her creation in the center of the dining table, on top of an embroidered cloth depicting the Three Kings visiting the Christ child. Candlelight glittered over the egg-wash pastry, making Charles's mouth water, despite the tasty meal of roast, potatoes, and cabbage they had already finished. At the head of the table, George Hogarth hefted a clean knife, almost slicing off his bushy side whiskers.

"No, sir, it is the worst," teased his daughter, pretty Kate Hogarth, seated at Charles's side. "For, Father must bring home guests with whom we have to share my mother's lovely tart."

"You shall have your favorite jam," Charles promised, staring into the bright blue eyes of the nineteen-year-old daughter of the house. He'd been talking business with the coeditor of his newspaper all through the meal, but his eye kept alighting upon this fair maiden, despite the dozen other adults and children in the room. "Which one is it?"

"Gooseberry," she said with a blush. "But you must have your first choice. Why, you are Father's guest."

"I am only a new employee of the *Evening Chronicle*," declared Charles, "scarcely worth noticing."

"Fie," George Hogarth said, settling his free hand across his waistcoat. "Ye are our most promising journalist. To be so accomplished at a mere twenty-two years of age. Gives me hope, my lad."

"How exciting," Kate Hogarth said, eyes sparkling. "You must tell us what you've been writing about, Mr. Dickens."

When the initial sounds of approval from her children had diminished, the matriarch, Mrs. Hogarth, a decade younger than her graying husband, slid the tart down the table to him. Charles regaled them with the tale of a recent parliamentary debate he had reported upon, complete with a falling-down drunk Member of Parliament, a sneezing man-at-arms, and a speech that went on for three hours, until one poor elderly statesman, napping away, fell off the bench, after snoring so loudly that half the crowd was in hysterics.

By the time he had finished his tale, Miss Hogarth had clutched his sleeve to keep herself upright through her convulsive giggles. He was proud of his tailcoat with its black velvet collar. His gaze moved between her fingers, sliding on the new fabric, and the toothsome sight of the pie being sliced.

He turned guiltily toward his host, his dining companion on the opposite side. His stares were improper, but such a tempting morsel had never yet been set before a young man on the rise.

"What would ye like, Charles?" asked Mrs. Hogarth.

"One of the red ones, please," he enthused. "Miss Hogarth would love the green."

"Same as her mother," Mr. Hogarth said comfortably. "She does make an excellent gooseberry."

"Did you have a good Christmas, Mr. Dickens?" Miss Hogarth asked. Her Scottish accent was less pronounced than that of her parents. "Did you see your family?"

Charles took his plate of tart. The red jam was tucked inside a triangle of pastry. "My father is out beyond Hampstead, but the rest of the family is nearby. My brother Fred lives with me, in fact. I'm to supervise his education. My mother has her hands full with my two sisters and the two youngest, both boys."

"How nice to have family with ye," Mr. Hogarth said, as a child, perhaps four years old, climbed into his lap and burped loudly. "How old is Fred?"

"Fourteen." Charles grinned. "We had an excellent meal for my mother's birthday just before Christmas. But mostly I worked through the Twelve Days. I write for more than one newspaper, and since I am not a family man, it seemed best to take all the work I could, and relieve those with little children at home."

"Very decent of ye, sir," Mrs. Hogarth said, from the opposite end of the table, where she bounced a babe with enormous dark eyes on her knee. "But I am so glad ye could be with us tonight."

"Thank you for having me," Charles said, before turning irresistibly to the girl at his side. "Tell me, Miss Hogarth, when did you come here from Edinburgh?"

"About four years ago," she said. "I don't seem to have lost any of the Scottish in my voice."

"I find it charming," Charles declared. "It is easy to see that your family is a musical one, with the sweet tones of your voice and those of your sisters."

"We should have music when we are finished," Mr. Hogarth

said, removing the child from his leg and finishing his dividing of the tart. "But you have a long walk home, I know."

"Where do you live?" Miss Hogarth asked, as her father passed out the final plates.

Charles watched the tart spread across the table. He had nothing like this in his bachelor lodgings, and his mother didn't have the money to prepare such treats either, with her husband on the run from his financial difficulties. "I live in Holborn, at Furnival's Inn. It's a quiet, rather gloomy place, nothing like here, with all the gardens and orchards surrounding your house. We live in close contact with our fellow man."

"As do we," Miss Hogarth said, pulling at a red ribbon that had come untied on the sleeve of her green dress. "See how many brothers and sisters I have?"

"My family is not small either," Charles said. "But how wholesome is it to feed your family from your own plot?"

"That is why I can make such lovely jam," Mrs. Hogarth said. "With Kate's help, of course."

Her daughter's lips curved with her mother's praise, but then her eyebrows went up and her mouth rounded into shocked surprise.

Charles heard the disturbance as well. It came from outside the snug house. "What was that?" He swiveled around toward the heavily curtained windows.

"Sounded like a scream." Mr. Hogarth set down his knife and rose.

He, Charles, and Miss Hogarth went to the window. Mr. Hogarth tied back one side of the winter-weight curtain so they could see. Charles cupped his eyes with his hands, trying to peer into the gloom, but mist had risen, undulating over the fallow vegetable beds. He couldn't see anything but the ghostly branches of distant, leafless apple trees, waving in the breeze.

Another scream. Miss Hogarth jumped and shivered.

"Who lives in the next house?" Charles asked.

Mr. Hogarth frowned. "It's a fine mansion. Lady Lugoson, a baron's widow, returned from France with her two children a few months ago."

"A widow alone?" Charles's voice sharpened. These houses were spread apart. Any amount of mischief might take place with no one noticing.

Mr. Hogarth nodded, his expression concerned.

"We must go to them," Miss Hogarth said, with an admirable sense of purpose.

"Mrs. Hogarth, will you light us a couple of lanterns?" her father suggested.

"Of course." Mrs. Hogarth tucked a stray lock of brown hair behind her ear and hurried away.

The younger children chattered as Charles and Miss Hogarth went to find his outer coat and her mantle. She pulled off her evening slippers, and he stealthily admired her small, narrow feet in the moment it took her to find her boots and pull them on. How perfectly made she was, and how far above him. This girl had never experienced a moment's want, never had a father in debtor's prison or seen her brothers forced out of their education into warehouse jobs.

Charles recognized Mr. Hogarth's coat on a hook, along with their hats, and brought them back to the dining room. As soon as Mrs. Hogarth had delivered the lit lanterns, they walked through the green baize door leading to the kitchen, startling a young kitchen maid, and made their way out of the door closest to the garden.

Across the field floated more cries, dampened and spread by the mist. "Are they being murdered?" cried Miss Hogarth.

"I can differentiate between three different females," her father said.

Charles knew the man was a musical genius and trusted in his abilities. "Are they in pain?"

"Distress, certainly." Mr. Hogarth pulled a stout walking stick away from the stone wall.

Charles and Miss Hogarth followed the older man as he walked around vegetable beds and pools of rainwater, mist nipping at their ankles. Only Miss Hogarth had appropriate footwear, though Charles, with necessary economy, had shoes suitable for long walks. The polish he'd painstakingly applied the previous evening would never survive this damp walk.

They reached the edge of the garden and moved into the orchard, all dirt underfoot, encrusted with the decaying leaves of fruit trees.

"May I?" Charles asked, pointing at a branch just barely attached to an apple tree.

Mr. Hogarth coughed and nodded. "Of course. I should have thought more of weapons."

"Oh, Father," Miss Hogarth exclaimed. "Surely we don't need any."

Charles tore the branch from the tree. As long as his arm, it might hold up in a fight. When he saw another branch a few feet away, already on the ground, he handed it to her.

"Goodness," she said, her eyes wide. But she took it, stouthearted, and carried the makeshift weapon the rest of the way.

When they had moved past the orchard mists, light from the mansion came into view. They stepped into a formal garden from the Hogarths' apple grove. A gravel path was set among boxed hedges. Charles tried to imagine the shape of them, wishing he could see from an overhead perspective.

He had viewed the front of the house earlier as he'd walked by with Mr. Hogarth, and had examined it carefully, always cataloguing information he might be able to use in an article. The house, formed in the shape of an E, had been built in the Elizabethan age, though it had been added on and modified over the years with stone. In excellent condition, it spoke of wealth if not taste.

Now, however, they walked onto a paved terrace along the side of the house. Through glass-paned doors they could see a number of people moving around frantically in the room beyond, black-dressed maids carrying towels, footmen in formal evening livery moving toward a fixed point out of sight. Charles viewed the modern carpet and pale apple-green paint, though the newer, robust furnishings were mixed in with late Georgian pieces from the turn of the century. Mr. Hogarth opened one of the French doors.

On a sofa, Charles saw a richly dressed elderly lady, seated next to a bespectacled gentleman about ten years younger.

The middle-aged gentleman peered over his glasses and offered a polite "Good evening."

# Chapter 2

After all the screaming they had heard, the polite, German-accented phrase seemed utterly out of place.

As Mr. Hogarth greeted the man, Charles was distracted by a raised voice. In front of a second fireplace lay a young girl, perhaps a couple of years younger than Miss Hogarth. Her head rocked from side to side, as if she was coming out of a faint. Towels covered something on the floor next to her, and he could smell ill-favored scents wafting from that part of the room. The girl must have been sick before collapsing.

Miss Hogarth put her hand to her nose as the odor assaulted her senses.

A slender woman, about a decade older than Charles, knelt at the girl's side. She matched the drawing room paint in her dropped-shoulder gown of white silk embroidered with green leaves, but as she moved, he saw her skirt was marked with cinders at the knees. Her hands gestured above the girl, as if imploring her to rise.

Two female companions stood by the woman, one in a dinner dress that was out of style, its ruffled skirt a dead giveaway for fashion of the previous decade, the color an unflattering shade of yellow. The woman on the right, who had the familial look of an adolescent girl Charles's gaze had passed over in the middle of the room, made more of a concession to fashion and feminine appeal in her dress, with a lower-cut bodice and tightly fit waistline.

Given the tableau, he expected the woman kneeling was the baron's widow. The girl, now blinking her eyes, had blond hair the shade of angels' wings. Along the wall to the right of the fireplace leaned a boy in mid-adolescence, looking more confused than anxious. The kneeling lady was also blond and Charles recognized that the slanted nostrils of her nose matched the boy's. This then, was likely to be young Lord Lugoson, for some reason not away at school.

Miss Hogarth did not pause but, admirably, went straight to the kneeling woman after setting her stick against the wall. "My lady, I am Miss Hogarth from next door. We heard the screams from our house."

As the woman lifted her gaze and blinked at Miss Hogarth, Charles noted her wide-spaced gray eyes and high cheekbones, along with an elfin chin. A lovely lady, he suspected she would not be a widow long.

In contrast, the other two women were a bit older, with skin just starting to sag at the jawline and under the chin. The less fashionable of them seemed to be in a near faint herself, but the other watched two footmen closely as they stepped to the head and feet of the young girl. The maids they had seen through the terrace doors had already vanished.

"Can you rise, Miss Lugoson?" Miss Hogarth asked. "Or do you need these men to help you?"

"Oh, she mustn't try herself," Lady Lugoson said. "She fainted dead away." She gestured vaguely toward the towels.

"Hit the floor before anyone could catch her." Young Lord

Lugoson spoke in tones of admiration. His limbs looked too spindly to carry the minimal weight of the girl.

The footmen seemed afraid to touch the girl. Impatient, Charles went to one knee on the other side of the lady, letting his branch fall to the carpet. "I'll be happy to carry her, my lady, if your men will not."

At a nod from Miss Hogarth, Charles gently slid his arm under the girl's knees while Miss Hogarth helped her sit up. Charles slowly stood with his burden. He wasn't a large man himself, but the girl was slight.

One of the young footmen seemed to come to his senses then. He took a three-pronged candelabrum from the mantelpiece and led the procession away from the foul-smelling floor. Miss Hogarth walked next to Charles and her father joined them, trailed by Lady Lugoson and the second footman.

"Please, my lady, take my arm," Mr. Hogarth said, solicitous. She leaned heavily on him, a bent reed, as Charles followed the footman into the passage. The girl relaxed in his arms, seeming mostly unconscious still.

"Would you mind taking her to her chamber?" Lady Lugoson asked. "She'll be more comfortable there."

"Of course," Miss Hogarth assured her. "Mr. Dickens won't mind, I'm sure."

Charles felt his awkward burden instantly lighten under Miss Hogarth's affectionate gaze. The girl in his arms was calm. She smelled of cloying floral perfume and sweat.

They went up the grand staircase to the first floor, and then continued up to the second. The carpet on this floor was a dusty rose color and few candles were lit to guide the way, unlike downstairs.

The third door on the right was open. Inside was an unadorned chamber, mostly taken up with a large bed. Charles noted an ancient, blackened chest and a washbasin on a simple table. A woman, who must be Miss Lugoson's lady's maid, sat in a hard-backed chair next to the chest, sewing lace onto a handkerchief's edge. She was a plain creature of about thirty years and her eyes widened in alarm as the crowd entered.

Miss Hogarth rushed from Charles's side to pull back the blankets. When she stepped aside, Charles set the girl on the mattress. The young lady tossed her head from side to side and then settled.

Instead of pulling away, Lady Lugoson clutched Mr. Hogarth's arm even more tightly, dragging him toward the bed and the girl upon it, still in her white evening dress, as tightly cinched as her mother's.

"I will help her maid ready her for bed," Miss Hogarth said. "With your permission, my lady? I am used to caring for my younger sisters."

The woman smiled faintly and nodded. "Agnes will assist you."

Mr. Hogarth nodded in his kindly way at the distressed baroness. "Then we shall return to your guests. Perhaps you should post a footman outside the door to be ready to bring messages or whatever they might require?"

"An excellent notion," Lady Lugoson said after a pause. She nodded at the first footman. He placed his candles on the table next to the bed, then led most of the group out of the door.

Charles smiled in the direction of Miss Hogarth, but the efficient little nurse had not even taken off her mantle, much less noticed him, as she bent over her charge.

"Such a capital girl, your daughter," he said to Mr. Hogarth.

"She's an excellent child. Never any trouble to her mother or me." He turned to the distressed girl's mother. "I hope your daughter doesn't suffer so often, my lady."

"No." Lady Lugoson put a small handkerchief to her eyes. "This is very strange."

They returned downstairs to find the elderly lady and her German companion in the hall. Lady Lugoson's butler helped them into furs and cloaks.

"Thank you so much for coming, Lady Holland," the hostess said.

Charles did a double take. This was Lady Holland? Why, she was famous, both in political circles and for her naughty past. Charles and Mr. Hogarth waited until the guest departed, then followed Lady Lugoson back into the drawing room.

He counted five people still gathered there. Lady Lugoson walked across the room to the second fireplace. "Mr. Hogarth, may I present my son? I am afraid I do not know the name of this young man who has been so kind."

"Of course, my lady," Mr. Hogarth said. "This is Charles Dickens, an employee of ours at the *Evening Chronicle*. Perhaps ye know that I am coeditor there."

Charles bowed his head, happy to see the towels and whatever they had covered had vanished in their absence from the room, along with their makeshift weapons.

"A pleasure. Yes, I did know your profession, Mr. Hogarth," Lady Lugoson said. "I have met your wife and two of your daughters. They called here one afternoon when I was at home." Lady Lugoson held out her hands to her son. With a sulky air, the boy set aside a scrapbook in his lap and stood. Charles saw the scrapbook was thick with clippings, and on the cover was an engraving of a theater's interior. Drury Lane, most likely.

"Lord Lugoson," the lady began speaking to the boy. "May I present the distinguished journalists Mr. George Hogarth and Mr. Charles Dickens. Mr. Hogarth is our new neighbor. And gentlemen," she addressed Charles and Mr. Hogarth, "that was my daughter, Miss Christiana Lugoson, whom you aided."

"You are interested in the theater?" Charles asked, after they greeted the young lord.

"Oh yes," Lord Lugoson said, his expression animated for the first time. "We have a relative who has a theatrical calling."

Charles kept his eyebrows in a neutral position with difficulty. While a couple of formerly theatrical ladies had married into the aristocracy, rarely would such a family advertise any relationship to the theater.

"Yes," Lady Lugoson said, in a faded tone very different from before. "The children do love the theater. They collect paper sets of famous productions."

"I like the opera best, especially Mozart," the boy said eagerly, his voice cracking. He had a wide mouth and rather large teeth set in a narrow jaw. "But Christiana prefers Shakespeare."

"I share your interests," Charles said. "But tell me, what happened here tonight? From the screams, we were afraid murder was afoot."

"Christiana lurched through the room like a figure out of a play," Lord Lugoson announced. "Then she cast up her accounts and collapsed to the floor. Rather thrilling, really."

His mother stared at the lad, her mouth pulling down, aging her face. He cleared his throat awkwardly and went back to his scrapbook.

"I am Eustace Carley," said a man who had been in the middle of the room earlier, coming toward them. Carley, a man with overblown salt-and-pepper hair and a grizzled moustache, wore a waistcoat straining at the buttons. He had the arm of the better-dressed woman in his meaty clasp. While Mr. Carley appeared to be around fifty, his wife still had the tiny waist and brown hair of a younger woman, perhaps in her very late thirties.

"A Member of Parliament, if I am not mistaken." Mr. Hogarth nodded to him.

"Yes." Mr. Carley inclined his head. "We are near neighbors, as my wife prefers our country residence to our home in Grosvenor Square, and were invited for the Epiphany meal."

"My daughter is a particular friend of Miss Lugoson's," said Mrs. Carley. The gems in her gold drop earrings sparkled with the firelight.

"Is she much better now?" squeaked Miss Carley, the couple's daughter, whom Charles had seen standing in the middle of the room earlier. She had taken the seat next to a harp, and her hands moved restlessly in her lap, fingers clutching and unclutching. Her gown fit her poorly, as if someone had merely pinned her into one of her mother's castoffs. Despite her creamy skin and pink cheeks, she was not pretty, and her hair color could not be described by any term more accurate than "mousey."

"Oh yes, my dear. She needs only to rest." Lady Lugoson's smile was gentle.

"I cannot imagine what happened," said the less fashionable woman in yellow, moving toward them. She was slightly older than Mrs. Carley, and had silver streaks in her black hair. "She seemed quite herself when we first arrived."

"This is Mrs. Decker." Lady Lugoson gestured in the woman's direction. "Another neighbor, beyond the Carleys' house. I know your husband had to be away this evening."

"He is in New York," Mrs. Decker said, pride marking her voice. "A cousin of his died and he is sorting out the poor man's affairs."

Lady Lugoson nodded. "If you'll forgive me, I must speak to Panch and order fresh tea. We all need a restorative." She rushed off, looking flustered.

"Lady Lugoson was a well-known political hostess, as I recall," Mr. Hogarth said.

"She was during the late Lord Lugoson's day," Carley said. "But he shuffled off this mortal coil nearly two years ago now and she took the children to live with her aunt in France for some time. They have only recently returned."

They spoke of the past glories of the House of Lugoson, Charles wondering all the while why the Hogarths hadn't been invited to this gathering when the other neighbors had been. Not high enough in the instep, he supposed, despite their nearby home.

Lady Lugoson returned and begged everyone to seat themselves in a squared-off area in front of the first fireplace, furnished abundantly with sofas and chairs, leaving her son near the second fireplace. The Carley girl whispered in her mother's ear, then left the room.

"I am only just reentering society." Lady Lugoson's tone was musing as a maid brought fresh tea. "I am sorry to have my first party end like this."

"Are you as concerned about social reform as your late husband?" Mr. Hogarth asked.

"Oh, yes." She put her hands to her cheeks. "I'm particularly inclined against the workhouse system. So dreadful, the new Poor Law Amendment Act of last year. I keep my son in London so he can see things as they really are, instead of locked away with other boys of his class."

The butler, some forty years older than the footmen, entered the room, looking even more distant than before. Lady Lugoson frowned. "Excuse me." She stood and walked toward her servant as the man didn't seem to want to come closer.

The butler lowered his head on its long stalk of neck and spoke into her ear. Her eyes widened and her face went pale. Charles read some calamity on her expressive face.

Instinctively, he rose and went to her side. "What has happened, madam? May I be of some assistance?"

"Christiana has taken ill again," she whispered, fingering her garnet pendant necklace. "Oh, Mr. Dickens, I must go to her."

She took a step, but then seemed to falter.

"I'll go with you," Charles said. "We must not delay." Had the girl fainted again, while lying on the bed? Or had she risen and paid the consequences of ill health?

Lady Lugoson took Charles's arm as she had taken Mr. Hogarth's before. Panch led them, trailed by Miss Carley, who was sobbing loudly, back to Miss Lugoson's room. The footman had disappeared, and the door was open. Charles peered inside the room.

"What happened?" he demanded, taking in the pale, panting face on the bed as he stepped in. He glanced back. Miss Carley followed him in, wringing her hands, tears dripping off her nose. Miss Hogarth leaned over Miss Lugoson on the opposite side, dotting her forehead with a square of cambric. She lifted her face and joined her gaze to Charles's, then a moan returned her attention to the wretched figure on the bed.

Charles pulled his arm away from Lady Lugoson, and pointed his finger at Agnes.

"I went to the WC, sir." The maid, frizzy hair in disarray, let out a sob. "When I returned Miss Christiana was like this."

"Call for a doctor," he said.

No one moved. He turned around, hoping the butler was still in the room, but he had vanished. Taking the maid's cold, callused hand in his, he stared into her eyes. "Fetch a doctor. Miss Lugoson needs medical attention."

# Chapter 3

An hour passed. The butler had come and gone after receiving orders to call for more doctors. Charles sat in the corner, as unobtrusive as the maid, wincing at the sight of the girl writhing on the bed, complaining about stomach pains and nausea. He felt unable to leave, as the household seemed generally indecisive. Miss Hogarth stayed at the bedside, sponging sweat from Miss Lugoson's brow and praying with her. Charles admired her steadfast support, even as he mentally composed an article for the *Chronicle* about the tragic scene.

Eventually the situation worsened. Miss Lugoson lost the contents of her stomach repeatedly, weakening with each blow to her fragile frame. One doctor came, then another. None of the remaining guests appeared ill. The Deckers and Carleys went home during the second hour of the ordeal, after Mrs. Carley sent up a maid to call mousy and hysterically sobbing Miss Carley from the room.

At some point, Lady Lugoson retired to her bedchamber. She returned after half an hour in a different dress, simple and black, something out of her mourning wardrobe. She gestured to Charles and together they knelt at the side of the bed to pray.

He could ill afford the time to stay at the bedside, but he knew it was his duty, both to this distressed girl and to the valiant Miss Hogarth.

Eventually a footman came with a note for him. Charles excused himself and read the missive from Mr. Hogarth. He was returning home to his family, and entrusting his daughter Kate to Charles's care. A promise to notify his editors at both papers with the reason for his next day's absence cleared his mind.

Candles burned around the bed, keeping the room illuminated despite the utter blackness outside. As the hours passed, he committed the sight to memory, as he'd done with anything he'd found interesting since he was about eight years old. The sad sight of the girl on the bed, the bouncy curls spread across her sweat-stained pillow a testament to a young woman who should be healthy and strong, pulled him to her, a partner in her dance with death. His pulse seemed to slow with every sign of her deterioration.

Death was what he feared, though the dawn brought a blessed cessation of symptoms. Miss Hogarth helped Miss Lugoson drink a little beef broth. A sense of relief cut through his half-dreaming state and he realized his clothes were sticky and clung to his body after a night by the constantly stoked fire.

"Oh," Miss Hogarth cried. The broth dropped from her grip, spilling its contents on the rug.

He shifted to stand from his kneeling position, but a deep moan from the bed startled him and he went down, hitting his head on the hard wood bed frame. Recovering himself, he helped Lady Lugoson to her feet, just in time to reach for the girl as she cast up her accounts yet again.

Miss Hogarth dabbed at Christiana's temples with a cloth while Lady Lugoson dropped her head into her hands. The maid went for towels to clean up the latest mess.

Charles's shoes squelched in the broth soaking into the rug

as he moved to Miss Hogarth's side. "You must have the kitchen thoroughly cleaned before anyone else takes sick," he said to Lady Lugoson from the other side of the bed. "Throw away all your stores and bring in new food."

"Do you think something was wrong with the broth?" The lady wrung her hands.

Charles gestured to the bed. "She had been somewhat recovered for more than an hour. I had thought to return Miss Hogarth to her family."

"You've been everything that is kind," Lady Lugoson said. "Will you wait while I have the doctor called again?"

"Of course." Miss Hogarth caught his eye. Her stricken face had him wishing he could squeeze her hand to offer her comfort.

"Is there anything more we can do, Mr. Dickens?" she asked.

"We are not so far into the countryside. The family will bring more doctors. Someone must know what to do," he said soberly.

Over the course of the morning, three doctors came and fretted over Christiana. One of them brought a bloodletter, but Lady Lugoson stopped his labors abruptly when Christiana fainted. The man bandaged the girl's arm and stalked off with his bowl of blood. Crimson droplets dotted the white sheets, the vibrant color in sharp contrast to the pale, still girl. The smell of beef broth and blood commingled with the general air of sickness in the room.

Of young Lord Lugoson, Charles saw no sign.

"Your son?" he asked Lady Lugoson suddenly, after an hour of silence, late that morning. Miss Hogarth sat across from him, her ribbons trailing along the edge of the stained counterpane. "Has he taken ill as well?"

"No, sir, he's with his tutor. I don't want him to be exposed further to whatever has taken Christiana. What if it is contagious?"

He stared at Miss Lugoson again. That slight, slight figure. "I still would consider the food, given her reaction to the broth."

Lady Lugoson nodded. "I have given orders to clear the kitchen and clean it."

Charles considered if he was thinking food poisoning in the hopes whatever was plaguing Miss Lugoson would not affect himself or Miss Hogarth. He felt his throat, no sign of the lumps that often presaged illness, and Lady Lugoson, though drawn and looking every minute of what he now knew was her thirty-three years, did not look ill either.

"I thought the cream sauce served with the potatoes had gone off," her ladyship fretted. "Perhaps that was it."

"You should find out who ate it and have your guests monitored for symptoms," Charles said.

"I will write letters when I can," Lady Lugoson said in a small voice. She sank to her knees on the carpet next to the bed and began to pray again, holding the unbandaged arm of her daughter, who had yet to fully regain consciousness since the bloodletting. He knelt next to her on the damp rug and joined her prayer.

The maid's keening was the first sign something was wrong. "The rattle," she cried. "The rattle."

They both struggled to their feet and stared at the girl. Miss Lugoson's head was back, the tendons of her neck sharply delineated. Miss Hogarth touched her shoulder, calling her name. Lady Lugoson threw herself onto the bed, half covering her daughter. Miss Lugoson wheezed gently, then went silent.

"A mirror," Charles called.

The doctor in attendance opened his bag and found one, then held it up to the girl's mouth for a couple of minutes. "I am sorry, but there is no sign of life."

Some fifteen hours after Lady Lugoson had been called to her daughter's bedside, perhaps seventeen hours since her dinner party had commenced, Christiana Lugoson's soul had fled her mortal form.

Charles walked through the apple orchard with Miss Hogarth an hour later, blinking in the weak January sunlight. She held her bonnet strings, attempting to keep the sides closely around her cheeks despite the brisk wind. They had refused the offer of the Lugoson family carriage for the brief journey, but his hat had already flown off once and in consequence bore a fresh streak of dirt along the brim. His clothes were stained with sweat and broth. Altogether, he looked and smelled like a man who had been cooped up in a death chamber for most of a day.

Across the road he could see workers in the market gardens, planting dormant fruit trees and pruning the hedges that squared off the orchards. The ten bells in the tower of St. Luke's Church, a couple of streets away, tolled the late morning hour in sonorous fashion.

"I'd prefer to address remarks to you about pruning your family's apple trees," Charles remarked. "Anything but the dreaded subject." He dared to take Miss Hogarth's arm as they traversed a particularly muddy dip under a tree.

She thanked him. "But it does not seem appropriate."

"I'm afraid not. Had you ever seen anything like Miss Lugoson's demise?" Charles asked. The Hogarth family's home came into view on the other side of the tree. A chill, not just from the wind, blew through him as he realized this private moment with Miss Hogarth might not come again.

"No. I've seen babies die, poor darlings," Miss Hogarth said from behind the protection of her bonnet. He could scarcely see more than her nose. "But nothing like that. When my time comes, I sincerely hope it is more peaceful."

"And not so sudden," Charles agreed, letting go of her arm as she took half a step away, reminding him of propriety. "Do you feel ill?"

"Not at all, but I find that illnesses take a couple of days to spread within a household. As it is Tuesday . . ." she trailed off.

"Wednesday now," he said gently.

"Goodness," she said, stopping at the edge of the herb garden and turning to face him. "I've quite forgotten. I have never stayed up an entire night before."

He smiled at the silly expression she made, though he was too tired to laugh. "Friday, then. We must check in with each other on Friday. Do write me, will you, so that I can be certain you are well?"

She put her gloved fingers over her mouth. "Oh, do you think Mother would approve?"

"You can give a message to your father on Friday morning," he said. "To bring to the office."

"Very well," she said, taking a step in the direction of the house. "As long as my parents approve. Will you come in?"

"No, I had best be on my way, so that I can work at least a little today."

"I hope you aren't going to walk into London, after being awake all night."

"It is far from the first time," he said cheerily. "If I come across an inn with a short-stage ready to go I promise to climb aboard, but I can walk at least as quickly."

"Oh, very well. If only I weren't certain that Father had long since departed. Would you like anything to eat first?"

He would, very much, but dawdling would not impress the father of this pretty girl, and he would know how long Charles had relaxed in his family home if he entered. "No, thank you. That can be managed along the way, as well."

"Then, this is farewell." She pushed a trailing sprig of herb off the path back into its allotted spot.

He inclined his head. "As tragic as the night was, Miss Hogarth, please be sure that my regard for you is of the highest. You were a true angel to the Lugosons during their ordeal."

"I wish it had made a difference." She clasped her hands together. Her bonnet strings loosened and flew around her face, as if adding punctuation. She smiled suddenly. "You were an angel too, Mr. Dickens."

He watched, bemused, as the slim figure dashed across the herb garden and went through the kitchen door. Only then, feet wet, entire body aching, he retraced Mr. Hogarth's route of the night before, going east toward the city.

The closer Charles came to the *Chronicle*'s offices, the more his head ached, the more the old pain in his side flared. He remembered Miss Hogarth's wise words about illness taking time to develop, but he had drunk the tea the Lugosons had provided during the night. If their kitchens had been befouled, he might have contaminated himself merely by drinking the beverage. Or if Miss Lugoson had a contagious disease, he might have contracted it.

These worries must be ignored, for he had a parliamentary debate to write up, and he was eager to begin on sketches for Mr. Hogarth's new paper, his portrait musings about London. He stumbled into the reporters' workroom and found his desk. Through a haze of pain, he assembled ink, pen, and paper. An under-editor, Thomas Pillar, came by some time later.

"I need that debate article, Charles," Thomas said, depositing a slice of bread and butter next to his arm.

"Thank you." Charles handed his papers to the kindly, late-middle-aged man and picked up the bread. "Though laudanum might have been more effective. I'm half dead today."

"I didn't want to say anything," William Aga said from the chair behind him. His fellow reporter, a few years older, who received choice theater and crime assignments as well as the political, had turned his seat around. "What's wrong with you? Did a stagecoach break down? You look like you spent the night walking home from Dover."

Charles pushed away from his desk, devouring his bread while the under-editor sifted through his article. "The worst happened."

"What do you mean?" William asked. He had the kind of mouth that always looked ready to tell a joke, and had an appealing, easygoing manner. Added to a straight, wide-shouldered frame and innate dress sense, it was no wonder he attracted glances and made new friends everywhere he went.

Charles's voice had turned into a croak. "A girl died. I watched her life flee."

"Where, on the street?" William asked as Thomas looked up from the article.

"No, in her bed. She is—was—a neighbor of Mr. Hogarth. Just seventeen. Struck down after dinner." He described the course of the illness.

"I'm sorry to hear that," Thomas said, a little green from the deathbed description. "But you have managed a decent article despite it all. I need to make a few changes, then send it to the printers."

After the under-editor moved away, William pulled a flask from a hidden pocket in his coat and unscrewed the cap. "Gin. It will help."

Charles took the flask and downed a mouthful. "I need about three of these."

"Did the doctors have any theories?" William asked.

"I do not know. Why?" Charles drank again, the cheap spirits clawing against the back of his throat.

William sucked at his teeth. "It's odd, but I've heard the same death described. I remember, it was the same day, too. Epiphany, a year ago. I followed the case for the *Chronicle*."

Charles handed William the flask. The spirits couldn't be going to his head already. "Have I heard you correctly?"

William nodded and drained the flask. "A seventeen-year-old girl, dead after a long night of mortal struggle, one year ago last night."

Charles let his arms drop limply to his sides, a thought striking him in the strongest manner. "Two angels, gone to their reward, and it is our duty to know why."

"Whatever can you mean?" William asked, secreting away his empty flask.

"The deaths of Christiana Lugoson and the girl you wrote about might be related." Charles stared through the workroom, unseeing, despite the parade of reporters, editors, and secretaries moving around the space. "They might be."

"It was pronounced heart failure, that death a year ago. A well-born girl, as I recall. Died in her bed somewhere out in Kensington."

"Not so far from the Lugoson house. I thought it might be bad food, or some kind of contagious illness." Charles tilted his head from side to side, and heard a popping noise in his neck. "Not a heart problem. Did you see the body?"

"Yes, she was beautiful." William clicked his tongue. "A waste."

Charles stretched his legs and his arms, trying to loosen his stiff and exhausted body. "Lady Lugoson said the potato sauce tasted bad. I wonder if anyone else at her dinner party became ill."

"You were invited to a titled lady's dinner?" William asked, more than a touch of envy in his voice.

"No. I was at the Hogarths'. We heard screams across the orchard between the houses," Charles explained, sitting upright again. "And went to investigate."

"You have yet to stop investigating," William said. "But Parliament calls. You have too much work to do to worry about this further. Maybe you can write a sketch about this girl's life."

"Yes," he said enthusiastically. "I shall suggest it to Mr. Hogarth. A capital notion. I'll write him a note and have one of the boys deliver it to his office, then get to work on my next article."

"That is all? From you?" He laughed. "No plan for a crusade against the ills of aristocrats feeding their children sauce? Or a new bill to be introduced banning the deaths of all pretty young girls?"

"There must be some reform in the food supply or something similar I can write an article about," Charles mused, pretending he hadn't picked up on William's sarcasm. "Something that can be fixed."

William laughed. "Now there is the Dickens I know. Always with an angle."

The conviction of truth made his voice ring out. "Lady Lugoson took us to Miss Lugoson's death chamber for a reason. I must do this."

# Chapter 4

❧

A couple of hours later, Charles still sat, his quill scratching busily on paper as he wrote up a review of a play he had seen a couple of days before, featuring a most unnatural murderer, a mother of three who had pushed her husband off the Battersea Bridge about fifteen years ago, back before the iron railings were added to the notoriously dangerous bridge. His brain only half minded the grisly material, puzzling unceasingly over the death of Christiana Lugoson. He'd found his sketch in progress tending very dark. It was time to give in to his impulse to find closure for the dreadful event at Lugoson House.

Setting his sketch aside, he took up a fresh piece of paper and began to detail the death scene he'd witnessed. When he had relived each excruciating detail, he went back and underlined the items that might lead to a decision on the cause of death. The truth was, he knew almost nothing about what Miss Lugoson had done before taking ill.

Next, he detailed what little he had heard about the death William had mentioned. What *did* he know? Both girls had been seventeen. They had died in their own beds, with family present. The progression of their illness was similar. None of this should excite him. Yet, something had struck William as so alike.

He pushed back his chair and rose to his feet, his ink-stained fingers disordering his hair. While he couldn't trouble the Lugosons in their fresh grief, he could try to recover William's old articles from last year. When he turned around, though, William had vanished, and he realized the workroom was nearly dark. Nothing but candles lit the space.

George Hogarth came in through the door as a couple of Charles's fellow reporters departed for the night.

"Still here?" he asked, buttoning his thick winter coat. "Ye have the stamina of a soldier at the front."

"Better, I hope," Charles joked. "I am well fed. Mrs. Hogarth outdid herself last night."

"I am glad ye think so." Mr. Hogarth peered down at him. "Are ye well, Charles?"

"No, I have a dreadful headache." He lifted his candle. "I think I have done enough for today."

"Why don't you come home with me?" the older man suggested. "We'll give ye a good dinner."

"I haven't washed," Charles demurred. "I'm not fit to be around your family."

"Kate, ye mean?" Mr. Hogarth chuckled in a conspiratorial fashion. "Well, given what ye both experienced last night, she'll expect you to be a bit wan. Let the girl nurse ye."

Charles brightened at the name. "As you wish."

They caught a short-stage that would take them most of the way. The fresh air stroked Charles's headache away from his temples as they walked down Fulham Road an hour later, washing the scent of horse and unwashed coachman from his nostrils. At this hour, Lugoson House should have been brightly lit, as it had been the night before, but instead it had an air of doom and disuse.

"Poor family," Mr. Hogarth said, as they passed.

Charles nodded. "Had you heard that another girl died similarly a year ago? William Aga reported on the case. He even saw the body."

"What was the name?" Mr. Hogarth asked, his forehead creasing.

"I don't know yet. I need to have the articles pulled from the archives."

The Hogarths' front door opened as they came up the walk. "If it isn't Mr. Dickens," Mrs. Hogarth said, her face creasing with pleasure. Her hair had fluffed up around her face. She must have been working over the fire or stove. "I'm so pleased to see ye again."

"I am a stray dog brought home by your husband once more," he joked.

"Well, come in. What a day ye've had. We'll fix ye a nice meal, the girls and me, and ye will feel better."

"I hope Miss Hogarth isn't feeling the effects of the night too keenly," Charles said. "How is she?"

"Very well indeed. She and Mary did the shopping this afternoon and left me to my babies."

Miss Hogarth must have stamina equal to or even greater than his. He hadn't paid much attention to her younger sister at Epiphany, other than to notice Miss Mary Hogarth had the identical rosebud lips of her sister but considerably darker hair. "Have you learned anything more about the Lugosons?" Charles asked. "Any contact with the household today?"

Mrs. Hogarth took their coats, mufflers, and hats. "I had a chat with our maid. She recalled that the late Lord Lugoson was a political man. Very active in the House of Lords."

"I believe so. My impression is that his widow wants to be a political hostess again," Mr. Hogarth added, as he replaced his shoes with slippers.

"Last night wouldn't have put her back on the right footing," Charles said.

Mrs. Hogarth pointed them into the dining room. "They aren't a literary family, or a musical one. I canna imagine any connection will strengthen between us."

"A theatrical family," Charles recalled, as a number of children came into the room. One of the younger ones tumbled against a violoncello leaning against the wall in a precarious position. Last was Miss Hogarth, holding one of the babies, followed by her younger sister, Mary, with the twin.

Today, her ribbons were lemon yellow, freshening her face, though her gown was gray and worn and rather tight, as if she'd almost outgrown it. She obviously hadn't been expecting outside visitors, but she smiled with generous ease when she saw him.

"I've brought our friend home again," Mr. Hogarth declared. "Too scrawny. Needs another good meal in him."

"Then come to the table, Mr. Hogarth, and let us all dine. We've waited for you." Mrs. Hogarth took the baby from her eldest's arms.

Charles's eyes widened. Hadn't Mrs. Hogarth fed the children yet? They ought to have dined long before now, but the entire large family came to the long table, as they had the night before, and they supped well on Scotch broth, cold beef, and potatoes. "Delicious," Charles praised.

"Unlike what they must have eaten next door last night," Mrs. Hogarth said with a shudder.

"I asked at the butcher's today." Miss Hogarth leaned forward. "And we don't use the same one."

"It was the potato dish's sauce that was bad," Charles said. "Isn't that what Lady Lugoson said? So it would be bad cream, or butter."

"Or flour." Mrs. Hogarth rubbed her chin. "Flour can go bad."

"I suppose ye could speak to everyone who was at the party, to see if anyone else became ill, but what good would it do? If they have a lazy cook or bad suppliers, it is no business of yours," Miss Mary Hogarth added pertly.

"Not so," her father chided. "We are newspapermen, always on the look for a story."

"Will you ever be a lawyer again, Father, do you think?" the oldest Hogarth son, Robert, asked. He was just about a year younger than Miss Kate Hogarth, and seemed bright enough, though Charles wasn't sure about his level of education.

"No, the news has been good to me," Mr. Hogarth said. "What do ye say, Charles? Ye were busily working when I came to check on ye."

Charles's heart thumped at the sudden attention. He'd been musing over the fascinating way the tight fabric of Miss Hogarth's bodice illuminated her assets. "I had murder on my brain," he said.

Mr. Hogarth sat forward on his chair. "Ye think Christiana Lugoson was murdered? By whose hand?"

Charles blinked. "No, sir, I meant that I had been writing up a review of a murder play."

"Could she have been murdered?" Miss Hogarth asked tentatively. "It was such a dreadful death. What if she was poisoned?"

"Good heavens, Kate," the older man said. "She was a blameless lass. You must excuse my daughter. She is such a great reader that fanciful notions fill her head at times."

"We don't know much about Miss Lugoson's character." Even gently reared girls could be less than perfect. "Honestly, I would like to know more. Still, I want to suspect food poisoning."

"And that other girl, Charles? Food poisoning there as well?" Mr. Hogarth said, echoing the main point of his concerns.

"What other girl?" Miss Hogarth demanded.

Charles recounted what William Aga had told him about the first Epiphany death. "Is it not suspicious? Another young girl? The same night?"

"Do find those articles," Miss Hogarth said, leaning over the table until Charles fancied he could see the dark shadow of her cleavage. "I'm fascinated."

Gallantry forced the words from his mouth. "I will endeavor to please you," he said. "I almost hope Miss Lugoson was murdered to keep you so intrigued."

He did wish it in that moment, too.

"I will have to think on it," Mr. Hogarth declared. "If others became ill, then surely it is some contaminant of the food, and nothing like murder. But Charles can investigate the matter."

"How might the two deaths be tied together?" Miss Hogarth mused aloud. "Where did the other girl reside?"

"Not far from here. Could there be some actual person at fault for the death of these innocents, through unhygienic habits creating another catastrophe?" Charles asked. "A kitchen maid both households employed?"

Mr. Hogarth raised a finger. "Very clever, Charles. A very clever thought indeed. It seems ye have multiple paths of investigation available to ye."

# Chapter 5

The next day, Charles was scratching away at his desk, catching up on yet another theatrical review, when a boy came trotting through the newsroom and came to a stop behind him, at William Aga's desk. Charles ignored the exchange and finished the last paragraph of his review, but was forced to put down his pen when William exclaimed behind him.

"What is it?" Charles asked.

"You will soon see. Attend one of the minor theaters with me tomorrow evening. The Garrick."

"I always enjoy attending the theater," Charles admitted, "but if you are assigned the review, I will beg off. I have been at the Hogarths these past two evenings, and will be up half the night as it is, working on a sketch. I'm finishing up a comic piece about the hackney-coach stand below my window."

"No, you must come." William stood and peered over him. "I cannot allow you to scratch away."

Charles attempted to turn his chair around without hitting his friend's toes. "Why? Is one of your friends having a play produced there?"

William lowered his voice mysteriously. "No, but you shall find the experience illuminating."

"Then I had better go," Charles said, hearing the fulsome tone of mischief. "Are the chorus girls unusually pretty?"

William chuckled. "Even better than that."

"It will be dark soon," Charles said. "Did you have time to find those articles about the Epiphany death for me?"

"I do apologize," William said. "You know what a mess the *Chronicle*'s files are in. I promise I shall have the archivist commence the search tomorrow."

Charles saw his chance of delighting Miss Hogarth with new information regarding his redoubtable murder case diminish. "Do you recall her name? Where she lived?"

"Not the name," William said, unscrewing his flask. "But she lived near St. Luke's."

"That's not far. These two dead girls must have lived mere streets away from each other." Charles dipped his pen back into his ink, and pulled out one of the papers he'd used to make lists about Christiana Lugoson's death. A very important piece of information, indeed.

The next evening, in full darkness except for the street lamps, Charles and William walked down a narrow street on the edge of the West End. The foul animal stench of many generations of men relieving themselves along the dark cobblestones had Charles breathing shallowly. When he saw the playbills glued along an old stone wall, he knew they were almost to the theater. He hadn't been to the Garrick before. They didn't produce quality new work; rather, they did as best they could for a lower class of patron, bits of this and that to excite and entertain an assortment of laborers, clerks, and shopgirls.

"What are we in for?" he asked, stopping in front of a crisp new playbill. He tore it from the wall and attempted to hold it to catch the brightness of the gaslight a couple of feet away.

William leaned over his shoulder. He smelled of ironing and the stew they'd dined upon in Aga's rooms, a welcome change from the street's effluvia. "Pantomime, farce, tragedy. A full bill."

"I don't see anything unusual. What is here to interest me?"

"It's not the bill." William rapidly blinked his eyes.

"Then what is it? Do we have time for the public house before the night begins? We might need fortification." Charles pointed across the street. Though mist was slowly rolling in, they could still see that far.

"Looks like a crowd tonight," William said, after turning to face the theater. Loud conversations between patrons still outside blocked the sound of carriages on the street beyond. "I think we had better go in. We don't want to sit in the gallery."

Charles shuddered and pressed his hands down his pristine outer coat. "I hope we can get a box."

They found their place in line and shuffled along, entertaining themselves with recollections of performances at the Adelphi and other favorite theaters.

"I have an idea for a theatrical piece myself," Charles said. "I considered becoming an actor at one time, but now I think I might become a writer of plays."

"Yes, your brand of humor might be a success. I'm sure you will find interest," William agreed as they reached the ticket taker, a middle-aged woman wrapped in a molting brown shawl and a bonnet lined in some sort of animal fur.

After they secured a box, which would allow them to use a separate staircase and keep away from the crowd of noisy young clerks who seemed to comprise most of the audience, they went upstairs and found their seats to the right of the stage. The box had seats for six so they were quite comfortable, though they had paid dearly for the privilege.

They sat through a pantomime, then a farce. Intermittently, Charles pulled the playbill from his pocket, mentally ticking off the players and the performances. While there was some amusement to be had, and good performers among the company, he could not see what William had intended to be revealed. Eventually, after an intermission, came extracts from Shakespeare's *Richard III.* From the rapturous applause from the pits, he understood this performance was the highlight of the night.

Indeed, Percy Chalke, the Garrick's resident troupe manager, was a compellingly oily Richard. When he gave the opening speech, even Charles's jaded flesh crawled. From there, they skipped along through the best bits, ignoring all the confusing politics and generational unrest of the War of the Roses. Though they did include Queen Margaret's monologue, spoken in appropriately witchy tones by a girl not much more than a child, her tender years obvious despite the robes and makeup. When they came to the Lady Anne scenes, which ought to be played by a girl of tender years, a different actress appeared, a more mature lady, in a modern mourning dress and an old-fashioned veil. Her face was obscured, but her form had some thickening to it, making her look closer to forty than twenty.

They included the full exchange of the scene over the king's bier. At first, Charles thought the female parts had been miscast, due to the ages of the characters, but the interchange rang thrillingly. Both Percy Chalke and the mature actress, Angela Acton, were excellent performers with the diction of upper-class Londoners. Charles listened to the dialogue closely.

The actress playing Lady Anne spoke her lines. "Would it were mortal poison, for thy sake!"

The actor playing Gloucester, so bent over with his assumed hunchback that his nose nearly touched the actress's cleavage, hissed, "Never came poison from so sweet a place."

Lady Anne spun away. "Never hung poison on a fouler toad. Out of my sight! Thou dost infect my eyes."

Charles overturned the words that had so struck him during

the scene. Was this what William had wanted him to hear? Had he meant to make Charles think of poison? Had Christiana Lugoson, assuredly a blameless innocent, been poisoned? And that other girl, too?

"Hell and damnation!" Charles cried when the playacting had come to an end. He put his hand on William's solid shoulder. His head ached from the smell of the gaslights by the time the players came onstage to take their bow.

"What?"

"Is that what you wanted me to think?" Charles bent to his friend's ear. "That the dead girls were poisoned?"

The crowd cheered and called for an encore. William blinked slowly as he turned his attention from the stage to Charles. "What nonsense."

"Then what?" Charles demanded above the roar of the pit.

William lifted his brows. "That woman playing Lady Anne."

"What about her?" Charles flourished the playbill. "Angela Acton. Quite good, I thought. Above the usual class of actress."

The players came back on stage in a long line, enough of their costumes removed so that the audience could see what they really looked like.

"Well, she ought to be. I have it on good authority that she is Lady Lugoson's younger sister."

Charles's mouth dropped open. "You don't say." He stared at the players. Angela Acton, having removed the headgear that obscured some of her face, did indeed look to be about the same age as Lady Lugoson. "Did Lady Lugoson marry up?"

"I wrote Lord Lugoson's obituary when he died. Lady Lugoson was Sarah Acton before her marriage," William said. "A second wife. Her husband was some twenty-five years older, but he didn't have children from his first marriage."

Charles perused the rest of the players. Without her widow's veil and crown, and the false beak of a nose besides, the girl playing Queen Margaret was indeed a lass of about fifteen, with carrot-red hair and a pointed, animated face, and behaved nothing like blond Angela Acton. Their manner was opposite, Acton cool and composed, the girl grinning like it was the first time she'd heard a crowd's applause. "Was Lady Lugoson on the stage?" he asked.

"No, the Actons were wool traders, very prosperous. I think Angela has come down in the world a bit and Lady Lugoson went up, courtesy of a large dowry."

"What happened to Angela's dowry?"

"She has never married, but I believe she owns this theater. Or at least that is the rumor."

So her dowry might have gone to this building, or even been the building from the start. "She and this Percy Chalke must be aligned in some fashion."

"Precisely."

"Julie!" went up a shout from the pit. Several young men cheered as the redheaded girl blushed.

"Methinks the Acton-Lugoson family might be more colorful than I might have surmised," Charles mused, as Percy Chalke pointed his players offstage. The girl Julie tripped on a bit of scenery, then twirled gracefully out of a near fall. The pit roared.

"That means nothing in regard to the girl's death," William said, chuckling at the girl's antics.

"Of course not. It's probably just coincidence that my dead girl and your dead girl died the same night a year apart in the same general neighborhood."

"No doubt."

Julie paused at the stage's end. The lads in the pit shouted again. She kicked up a heel in her overlong costume dress, tossed her head, and walked off to the thunder of the pit's approval.

"I did think about who the servants might have been. Could a cook from the dead girl's house have gone to Lugoson House?"

"Are you so certain that anything is suspicious about either death?" William asked.

"Both girls were the picture of health, and then were dead within a day. Surely no young girl ought to die so mysteriously." Charles listened to the catcalls of the lads below, and thought of how neither girl would ever receive the attentions of a youth like the actress Julie just had, how that special light they brought to the world had been so cruelly extinguished.

"It does happen," William chastised. "We cannot see the dishumor lurking inside the mortal form."

Charles grunted. "I feel I must keep investigating Miss Lugoson's death. My reporter's instincts are tingling."

"So you will write to someone at Lugoson House about the servants?"

He shifted on his chair, ready to leave the theater and return home to his comfortable, warm bed. "Yes, and speak to Miss Lugoson's doctors."

William nodded. "It always troubles me when things are not quite as they seem."

Charles detected snobbery in his fellow reporter. "Meaning the family is not as high in the instep as I thought?"

"The impression of Lugoson House is so ancient, yet the family honor rests on one spindly fifteen-year-old boy, the son of a wool merchant's daughter, no less. And Lady Lugoson seems so very elevated with her beautiful diction and reform leanings, yet she has a sister likely living in sin with an actor."

"Something is outside of the norm, but then most families have their black sheep and certain secrets." An image of Charles's father flashed into his head, and the embarrassments and privations that had ended his childhood and damaged his education.

"You have the instincts of a dramatist," William said. "And therefore may see connections and intrigue where there are none. However," he continued.

"What?"

"You may, in your feverish imaginings, find material for a new sketch," William said. "After all, I read your draft of your Mr. Watkins Tottle short story. You made him a suicide. Why not write a story about a possible murder next?"

On Friday morning, Charles and his younger brother Fred ate together, a meal of bread and butter at a small table in front of the parlor fire in their rooms. He poked through his mail, and found a note from Mrs. Hogarth, inviting him to attend St. Luke's with her family on Sunday morning.

"Good news?" his brother asked, seeing his satisfaction.

Sometimes it seemed Fred was a mirror image of himself. Same chin, though his brother's was dimpled, same thick eyebrows and wavy dark hair frothing out from a widow's peak at the center of his expressive forehead. His nose was developing differently, though, losing the soft form of childhood. It seemed to be planning to hook decisively at the tip. What character difference did that augur? "It seems the Hogarths approve of me. I'm to see them again in two days."

"The family of a journalist is much less proud than that of a banker."

"But Mr. Hogarth is also a lawyer," Charles said, not enjoying the reminder of his past romantic failure, three years of wasted effort courting a banker's daughter. "And an intimate of Sir Walter Scott."

"Everything you desire is contained in his life story," Fred joked. "You must have his daughter to wife."

"I don't know," Charles mused, setting down his letter opener. "Maria Beadnell broke my heart, and Kate Hogarth can be flirtatious. She could be toying with my affections, as Miss Beadnell did."

"Or she might genuinely like you," Fred insisted. "You've only just met her, and Miss Beadnell took three years to break your heart."

"I would not let the situation stretch out as it did then. No, the Hogarths like me more than the Beadnells ever did. They might be better than some of our relatives, but I'm ambitious enough to transcend Father's difficulties, and Mr. Hogarth likes me very well."

"You'll make your decision quickly?" Fred asked.

"Yes, I have steady work. Four years have passed. No lady I'm courting will ever have cause to call me a boy again."

His brother poked at the crumbs on his plate. "What is your plan for the day?"

"I need to write a couple of letters, then attend a meeting, and then go to the office and write about the meeting," Charles said. "To school for you."

Fred made a monstrous face, all bulging eyes and thrust-out tongue, as Charles rose. His writing box was on the mantelpiece since he did not yet possess a desk. He wrote a note to Mrs. Hogarth, accepting her kind offer, then moved on to Lady Lugoson, begging her pardon but asking if he could know the names of her servants so he could do some checking on them. After asking Fred to post both items, he found his top hat and coat, and went out into the chilly January day.

On Saturday, Charles and Fred walked to George Street, where Charles had housed his mother and siblings after his father's most recent arrest for debt. The suite of rooms was near the Adelphi Theater, chosen by Charles so that his older sister Fanny could be close to her singing engagements, which brought needed money into the household. Mr. Dickens had fled out to the hamlet of North End, past Hampstead, to avoid his creditors, upon his release late the previous year.

Fred sneezed. Charles tilted his younger brother's hat so that the rain dripped to the pavement instead of down his collar. "Do you think Mother finished our laundry?" Fred asked.

"If she had time to dry it. I need to engage a laundress at the inn and spare her the trouble. She's already doing the laundry for five. That's hard in the limited space she has." The thought of laundresses made Charles wince. When he reflected that his father was staying with a woman in that lowly trade, it made him all the more determined to distance himself from his father's failures and make sure he succeeded in his endeavors, whatever the future might hold. Poverty and disease held back so many. He must stay strong and avoid disaster.

"Do you think there will be cake at this party?" Fred asked.

"I don't know. The vicar's mother is turning seventy. Do elderly people want cake?" Charles asked.

"I hope so," Fred said in an outraged voice.

Mrs. Dickens met them at the door to her apartment. "Hello, hello, my dears!" She'd just turned forty-five, but her dark curls were still nearly free of silver strands, and her long nose remained the same as Charles remembered from earliest childhood. A pleasant, engaging woman always ready to socialize, the corners of her mouth were wreathed with laugh lines, emphasizing her narrow jaw. Never one to mope, she wore three strings of bright beads and a secondhand gown of russet silk. She kissed Charles on the cheek first, then Fred as Charles passed through the door.

Inside, Charles could hear his youngest sister Letitia, a pretty eighteen-year-old, fretting about her shoes again as she sat on the cottage piano bench.

"What's wrong?" Charles asked his sister, wiping the damp from his cheeks.

"I found another hole, and in this weather, the newsprint I stuff in doesn't keep the cold out," she explained, shaking out her skirt. "It gets damp and hurts my toes."

"I'm sorry, dearest," he said gently. "We all need new shoes. Not one of us has a pair free of holes."

"I have to walk past Hampstead in my dancing pumps," complained his brother Alfred, who was almost two years younger than Fred. "Carrying messages for Father."

"Things will get better," Charles insisted. "At least he has managed to stay out of debtor's prison this time."

"Time for the party," his mother sang. "Fanny, and Boz, dear, please join us."

His sister, older by a year, and his youngest brother, seven-year-old Augustus, known as Boz, emerged from a back room, already dressed in cloaks. Charles went to Fanny, who was not just his sister but a dear friend, and kissed her on the cheek. Her hair, lighter than his, fell naturally into the same ringlets, and tickled his lips where he had kissed her. His mother nodded her satisfaction, pleasure evident in having her brood together, and went to her hook to gather her own cloak.

"I miss Father," Letitia said. "He's ever so jolly. On a dreary day like this, I would love to hear one of his jokes."

"How about a song?" Charles asked, pulling a comical face. "One of his old favorites?"

"None of that now," his mother said. "The vicar won't like us being late. His mother keeps a very strict schedule."

# Chapter 6

On Sunday afternoon, Miss Hogarth agreed with Charles's suggestion to walk in the burial ground next to St. Luke's after services. Trailed by her younger sister Mary, they walked, warmly bundled in coats and cloaks, hats and gloves, in the spaces between graves. He attempted to keep the conversation light and flirtatious but it was clear she had more serious thoughts on her mind.

"I have been wondering," Miss Hogarth said, turning her rosy-cheeked face to his as they passed a weeping cherub protecting a child's grave.

"What?" Charles asked, his heart thumping harder than before.

"I've wondered if that girl who died last year is slumbering right here." She stopped on the gravel path and spread her arms. "Our maid said Miss Lugoson will be buried here sometime this week."

"I don't see any new graves being dug," Miss Mary Hogarth said, catching up to them. A slyer creature than her older sister, Charles thought she'd be much more difficult to manage, though he enjoyed her impish humor. At fifteen, her character was still being formed, while Miss Hogarth had already proven herself to be a stout-hearted, self-sacrificing creature, in her unending care of Miss Lugoson in her final hours.

"There should be some record of the funeral," Charles said. "This isn't a slapdash parish. Why, the Duke of Wellington's brother was the rector here." He stared up at the Gothic tower, built of Bath stone and assuredly impressive.

"A few years ago, I've been told," Miss Hogarth agreed. "We can speak to the curate or the verger. At least one of them is probably still here."

They tramped through the burial ground with more purpose, making their way back toward the church. Charles nearly stepped on the tail of an enormous black tabby slinking around the edge of a tall, narrow gravestone, its engraving too weather-damaged to read.

"I'd believe in ghosts in a setting like this," he muttered, staring at the spiky winter-stripped branches of trees around them, and all the lonely graves.

"There's George Small," Miss Mary Hogarth exclaimed, waving her arm.

"The curate," Miss Hogarth explained, hooking her hand around Charles's upper arm. "Let's catch up with him."

Charles felt a jolt of pleasure at her touch. Were they to be so friendly already? Of course, he had taken her arm in the mud, but that was for safety. He wasn't sure how her parents would feel about her taking his arm, but they weren't there to see.

George Small, a short, thin figure in a large gray overcoat, blended against the lower windows of the church.

"Your sister has excellent eyes," Charles commented.

Miss Hogarth laughed and propelled him forward. "We've known Mr. Small since we moved to Brompton. Mother has made a pet of him."

Miss Mary had already engaged the curate in spirited conversation by the time the others had reached them.

"Why Miss Hogarth," the curate lisped. "Come to invite me to Sunday dinner?"

Charles watched, amused, at the mental calculations going on behind Miss Hogarth's eyes. Could they stretch dinner far enough? Also, she'd dropped his arm as soon as they'd come in sight of the older man. Though he wasn't so old as to hide the light of interest in his eyes when he looked at Miss Hogarth.

"Of course," she said, just as Charles had opened his mouth.

He spoke over her, irritated by the thought of a rival suitor. "When is Miss Lugoson's funeral?"

"Wednesday, I believe," the curate returned, spittle dotting his lip as he reached the sibilant. "Were you acquainted?"

"Yes. Slightly, though I did speak to her brother. He isn't at school," Charles said, attempting to lead the curate to more information.

"No, they've just returned from France. The young lord is delicate, I believe."

"Was the weather better in France?"

"It can be, in the south. I do not know very much about them, though they are one of the great families of the neighborhood."

"Perhaps the rector ministers to them directly?"

"Yes, I suspect so," Mr. Small sputtered. "They do not seem to know any bishops, but they were out of the country for some two years."

Lady Lugoson had not been raised in an upper-class family, though he had no idea if anyone at St. Luke's knew what he did about her. "I wonder if I might trouble you with one more question?"

"Of course," Mr. Small said, leading the way through the edge of the burial ground to the street. Apparently, he'd determined he would be at dinner, no matter how tepid the offer.

"Do you remember a girl who died on Epiphany night in 1834?" Charles asked. "Or the next morning. Aged seventeen, I believe."

"Yes," the curate said. "I'd just arrived. My first funeral."

"What was her name?" Miss Hogarth asked, the tremble in her voice betraying her excitement.

"Marie Rueff, she was," Mr. Small told them. "And a fetching little thing she must have been in life, though I only saw her in her coffin."

Charles and the Hogarth sisters exchanged horrified glances. Miss Mary put her hand over her mouth, to hide the laughter that bubbled up.

Charles cleared his throat. "You found her attractive, then?"

"Flaxen hair, still a child's color," Mr. Small said with enthusiasm. "A doll's face, neat little body. They put her in her aunt's wedding dress, as the aunt had already had twins twice and would never wear the dress again."

"Goodness," Miss Mary said. "Two sets of twins."

"A blessing to the family," the curate pronounced. "All those children to help the family through their pain."

"Was there any question that the death was unnatural?" Charles asked.

The curate paused, seeming genuinely surprised by the question. "The body, the face, you understand, was peaceful. I do remember whispers about the suddenness of it. But I don't know the family well."

Charles took that to mean that the parish didn't pander to the Rueff family as much as they might have to the Lugosons, given the opportunity. He gave Miss Hogarth a significant glance and she fell behind the curate and Miss Mary a few steps.

"No acquaintance with that bereaved family?" he said in a low voice.

"Indeed, I scarcely knew Miss Rueff," Miss Hogarth said. "Only to see her at services. She was a quiet girl. But if they are still in the parish I'll be able to find them. If there is any society or charitable organization I can join where there are Rueffs involved, I shall do so."

"What a project we have embarked on," Charles said. "It may still be revealed that the deaths were due to some normal cause."

"Yet neither of us quite believe that," replied Miss Hogarth.

"Yet Lady Lugoson has not contacted the authorities, as far as I know," Charles said.

"She has not," Miss Hogarth said decisively. "How could the police help, with no evidence of a crime?"

"True. I have a theory about the servants," Charles admitted. "I've written to Lady Lugoson. Also, I thought I would call on Dr. Keville. He seemed very impressive, but young enough not to be pompous. I'm trying to discover if someone might have contaminated food."

"I liked him best of all the doctors who attended Miss Lugoson," Miss Hogarth agreed. "Yes, you should speak to him. I wish I could join you."

Charles smiled at her. "I wish it as well, but it was so kind for your mother to invite me today. It gives me hope."

Miss Hogarth colored and looked away. In that instant, Charles knew she'd manufactured the invitation somehow. He felt positively elated.

On Monday afternoon, between a parliamentary session and returning to his office to write up his articles, Charles walked to Marylebone, where Dr. John Keville had rooms on Harley Street. From conversation that fateful Epiphany night, he knew Dr. Keville had attended the late Lord Lugoson, and had been the family's trusted physician for some fifteen years.

Indeed, he seemed to be a prosperous sort, having rooms in a building three deep in consulting offices. A pleasant woman in a clean white apron ushered Charles into a spotless study. An anatomical etching was framed on one wall, but otherwise it could have been any distinguished man's sanctum, with its bookshelf and comfortable chairs. The woman brought tea, and then the doctor himself came into the room a couple of minutes later.

Charles rose to greet him, appreciating the signs of care in his tailored clothing, well-groomed fingers, and the mature hints of gray at the doctor's temples. He looked vigorous and trustworthy.

"Mr. Dickens, what a pleasure to see you again," Dr. Keville said, shaking his hand. "What can I do for you today? A minor complaint, I trust?"

"I am too busy to notice my own health," Charles said, as they took their seats. "No, I was concerned enough to consult with you regarding Miss Lugoson. My employer is her near neighbor, you understand. Tell me, did you hear of any other illness attributed to Lady Lugoson's party?"

Dr. Keville demurred. "Not in the digestive area, nothing more than the passing complaint of that evening. I have seen Lady Lugoson since, for other reasons."

"She is suffering from grief?" suggested Charles.

The doctor exhaled. "Indeed. The loss of one's only daughter is a crushing blow. But, Mr. Dickens, you are a reporter, are you not? I don't wish to be a party to sensationalizing a girl's death in the press."

Charles tapped his fingers over his heart. "I report on Parliament in the main. Anything else I write is free of names. So then, to the best of your knowledge, Miss Lugoson was the only one taken ill that night?"

Dr. Keville nodded, pulling off his spectacles and wiping the lenses with a soft cloth.

Charles came to the point of his visit. "If I may be blunt, sir, I am very troubled by the girl's death. What do you think was the cause?"

"It is impossible to know," the man said, replacing his spectacles.

Charles checked off the symptoms on his fingers. "Nausea, sweating, vomiting, pain, chills."

"Could be influenza, cholera, a reaction to bad food," the doctor said.

"Poison?" Charles asked.

The doctor steepled his fingers under his chin. "Poison is possible. There is always a risk of ingesting something fatal, whether meat has turned, or someone thought they were gathering herbs when they were gathering something poisonous."

"Such as?"

The doctor opened a desk drawer and pulled out an old journal, then referred to a page. "Early in my career, I treated an old woman, rather barmy anyway, who thought she had drunk comfrey tea, but had mistaken that plant for foxglove."

"Did she survive?"

"No," Dr. Keville said, warming to his topic. "Some girls have been known, foolishly, to take small amounts of foxglove to suppress appetite."

Connections sparked to life in Charles's brain. Now he could see a path forward. "Has anyone attempted to trace what Miss Lugoson ate or drank that day outside of the party?"

"Whatever happened, I must tell you, as a physician, that the kernel of her distress might have been contracted, or even digested, up to five days before her mortal pains began," the doctor said.

"I understand," Charles persisted, "but has anyone tried to retrace her last days?"

The doctor shook his head. "I do not know. Her mother has been prostrate with grief, her father is deceased, and her brother is a fifteen-year-old boy. Who is going to look into her last days, and why is it necessary?"

Charles leaned forward. "Does the name Marie Rueff mean anything to you?"

The doctor shook his head. "No."

"She was a seventeen-year-old girl, of the same parish as

Miss Lugoson, who died in similar fashion, on Epiphany night, one year ago."

The doctor's mouth widened as he broke into a chuckle. "Dear me, sir, you reporters have quite the imagination. Surely you don't think some lunatic is out murdering seventeen-year-old girls each Epiphany?"

"It was so alike," Charles said, irritated at the man's humor. "Two blameless girls, dying so similarly."

"Did they know each other?" the doctor asked. "There could be some habit of possible mortality, such as foxglove tea, passed on."

Charles considered. "At this time I do not know if the girls knew each other."

"The Lugoson family was in France this time last year."

Charles nodded. "What about bad jam in an Epiphany tart? I would dearly like to know if any servants had switched households, or if they had a peddler in common, or a shop merchant."

The doctor's smile vanished. "Could be anything, given they lived in the same parish. The same merchants, for instance. Are there any medical records?"

"A colleague is attempting to find the reports from last year," Charles explained.

"A habit of tisanes? An interest in plants?" The doctor smoothed his moustache. "If you cannot find a dietary issue, something like that in common between the girls might answer your question."

"What should I look for at the start of my investigation?"

"Often digestive problems are set in motion by previous meals some hours or even days before," the doctor commented.

"I had never met Miss Lugoson or any member of her family before," Charles said. "Thank you for helping me to puzzle this out. One thing striking me is that Miss Lugoson was a very slender girl. Perhaps she did drink a preparation of foxglove."

Dr. Keville pressed his lips together before speaking. "Unlikely, though I take the blame for mentioning it. She didn't seem to hallucinate, or have vision problems, as would be expected. Often sufferers complain of yellow or green vision disturbances. May I ask something?"

"Of course," Charles said.

"What is your goal in sorting this out?"

"I cannot help but think the cause is the same, whether it is the same bad food, or a tea, or if I must say the terrible thing, poison." Charles paused. "My employer has young daughters. I would hate for whatever befell Miss Lugoson or Miss Rueff to happen to them."

"I cannot imagine anyone wanting to murder Christiana Lugoson," the doctor said. "A respectable family, a girl whose mother had yet to plan a come-out ball. Lady Lugoson was quite troubled by that. She had intended for the ball to be next spring. Raved about it, in fact."

"That must have been after I left."

"Yes, a day or so later. I'm sure that if there is some exact cause, other than illness, it will be found to be an accident, in both cases."

There was a knock on the door. When Dr. Keville said, "Enter," the woman opened the door.

She smiled pleasantly. "Your next patient has arrived, Doctor."

Charles stood immediately, smoothing his coat over his bottle-green waistcoat. "Thank you for your time, and I do appreciate you listening to my meanderings."

Dr. Keville shook his hand. "I do not blame an intelligent man for making inquiries. I cannot deny the coincidences you have raised. Two girls, exactly a year apart. But I think it is just that, a coincidence."

Charles nodded and forced a smile. "I sincerely hope you are right. It is probably just my reporter's mind at work, seeing parallels and points of connection that do not exist."

"Lady Lugoson is a reasonable woman, but I do not know

that she would want you questioning her servants and such. She is private."

"Of course she is, and I have no right to invade her home. Yet," Charles said thoughtfully, "it was she who invited me into her daughter's private chamber, and I must continue to offer my support as needed."

"As your conscience dictates, of course."

Charles took his leave and departed the building, full of notions of how to proceed. He needed to consult with William on one or two points as soon as possible.

# Chapter 7

Charles called in at William's bachelor lodgings that evening. He lived at Furnival's Inn as well and had not been in the office that day since he'd been covering a meeting in Blackheath. Charles could smell the coal when William opened the door. His friend had a low fire going, his rooms always being chilly due to the direction the windows faced.

William pointed to his quill on a deal table near the fire. "I had just sent you a note to see if you would like to attend Lady Holland's salon this evening."

"Are you serious? You can get us in?" He took a seat in a faded red velvet armchair. His friend took the opposite chair, this one more of a dusty gray color, next to the coal scuttle.

"I can. You may recall Lord and Lady Holland are great admirers of Napoleon, and my modest little tract about Alexandre Walewski, his illegitimate son, and his time as diplomatic envoy to the Court of St. James on behalf of the Polish, brought me to their attention."

"One never knows what will bring us to the attention of our betters," Charles mused.

"True. What further thoughts have you had about our discussion on Thursday night?"

"I have written Lady Lugoson about her servants." Charles rubbed at the stained nap on the chair's arm. William needed to do some scrubbing or have someone in. "Then I went to see Dr. Keville. You didn't meet him that night, but he was the first doctor called and has known the family for years."

"Did he have any conclusion?"

"He certainly doesn't suspect murder, even suggested a very fast-moving influenza or cholera or such, but he did have one interesting thought."

"What was that?"

"The cause of death could be some kind of preparation a young girl would take in order to stay slender."

"Like a quack preparation?"

"Certainly could be," Charles agreed, noticing that the stain went down the inside of the chair's arm. He poked at it. Smelled like cheese sauce but at least it was dry. "The doctor suggested foxglove tea before retracting the notion. The other option would be a food adulterant, as I suspected from the first, whether something had gone bad, or a poison accidentally got into something."

"It does happen." William rubbed his chin. "I've given up on the archives for now, and I'm trying to find my notes on that other dead girl for you, but I may have burned them."

Charles leaned away from the fire and pulled off his gloves. "A pity, but I have the name now."

William bent forward. "Yes?"

"Marie Rueff," Charles said in portentous tones.

"Ah," said William thoughtfully. "That should help the archivist at the newspaper. I asked him for assistance. Surely the blasted man has some kind of filing system."

"I would hope so. Now, on to the more recent business. My understanding is no one else in the Lugoson family took ill."

"But plenty of others were present."

Charles nodded. "That leaves the three members of the Carley family, Mrs. Decker, and Lady Holland. I do not know any of them, unlike you, apparently."

William took on a superior air. "Any points of inquiry?"

"The cream sauce on a potato dish was off, according to Lady Lugoson. She said she'd write her guests and check on their health. Not everyone would have eaten the potatoes. If they had been poisoned, how? The servants?"

"An excellent question. Assuming no one else became ill that night, Miss Carley is likely to be the font of knowledge about anything else regarding Miss Lugoson."

Charles shifted again. He'd managed to sit in the one overly warm part of the room. No wonder William preferred the other chair. "I agree, but I have no reason to speak to her. For now, let us raise the question of the food with the guests who were there. It might create questions in their minds, as it has done in my own."

"Excellent. I shall dress for the evening." William stuck his tongue in his cheek. "I take it you'd like to walk to Holland House for the salon?"

"It is too fine of a night not to," Charles joked, though William's windows were already coated with ice.

"As much as I appreciate your lack of regard for the elements, we shall never make it in time. We will have to pool our shillings and visit that hackney-coach stand below your window. Go dress in your rooms. I'll send a boy down to fetch a coach and join you shortly."

When they arrived at the venerable red brick mansion in Kensington, Charles mentally calculated the distance between it and Lugoson House, and figured it must be less than two miles, depending on the route. Once known as Cope Castle, the scale of Holland House was majestic indeed, as was the influence of the baron and his lady on the nation. Lord Holland had offered his services in various capacities for decades though he was out of office at the moment.

Charles could not help but feel shock at the luxury of the great estate as they followed a footman to the gathering. The height of the rooms, ceiling decorations, pillars, and columns were of a scale of grandeur no ordinary man could ever hope to attain in his lifetime, no matter his success. In his twenty-two years Charles had never seen anything like it in a private home. Did all the wealthy live like this? If so, he'd never met anyone more than merely comfortable before.

This family had built an impressive collection of friends and supporters over the decades, and one could always come to their home in order to speak to the great men of the day, whether it be Byron or Sir Walter Scott in their era, or politicians like former prime minister Earl Grey or Lord Lansdowne now. These were the powerful people who could effect social change more assuredly than any piece of sentimental journalism.

Tonight, however, Charles was less interested in politics and more in the guests. He did spot Mr. Carley in a corner, speaking to another Member of Parliament, but, not wanting to interrupt such important men, he decided to look for Lady Holland's attention first.

A footman, more expensively dressed in his livery than Charles in his evening clothes, answered his inquiry. "Lady Holland is in her private rooms, sirs," he said.

"Is Lord Holland still ailing?" William asked, with a knowing air.

"She does intend to come down this evening," the footman said, then pretended to be called away from them.

"I'm going to take a look around," Charles said.

"I will ask if Mrs. Decker is present," William said. "And keep an eye on Mr. Carley so we can speak to him after he finishes his political conversation."

Charles wandered through a couple of rooms filled with guests. He overheard someone say, "Have you seen the Gilt Chamber yet?"

The other man shook his head and his companion pointed to the far end of the room. Charles followed them, craning his neck around the side of the one at the door. He saw a room covered in shimmering gold, with a carpeted floor, fancifully decorated walls, and ornate ceilings. While the fireplace had been constructed from stone of black and sienna, and some figures were painted the color of flesh, the rest of the room was gilt, even the columns. His dazzled eyes eventually understood that some work at the base of the walls was dressed in white, but the overall effect was luxurious, mesmerizing. Sinful.

"Difficult to describe, even if you're trying," said a man at his elbow.

Charles recognized the curly haired, fleshy-faced young man as the one who'd been told about the room a few moments before.

"Description is my business," Charles said. "I work for the *Morning Chronicle*."

"I am an illustrator," the other man returned. "Daniel Maclise."

Charles took in the dark, intent eyes, strong nose, and Irish accent. "We should know each other, then, we men of words and pictures. Who do you illustrate for?"

They talked about their different journal experiences. While Maclise worked primarily for a Tory journal he seemed a liberal sort. By no means a hack, he showed his intelligence in a discussion of the merits of the marble busts in the room.

When he saw Mr. Carley walking by the open double doors of the room, Charles said, "If you'll excuse me, I must catch that politician."

He moved with purpose, reaching the Member of Parliament before he reached his destination. "Mr. Carley. A moment of your time?"

"Mr. Dickens," Carley said, exposing a mouthful of irregular, oversize teeth. "How very good to see you, sir."

The words sounded right, but Carley was looking over his shoulder, as if looking for bigger prey than a mere journalist.

"It is fine to see you looking hearty, sir," Charles said. "And how are your wife and daughter?"

"Very well." The politician drained his glass.

"No ill effects from the dinner last week?"

Carley frowned. "No, other than sorrow, of course. My daughter, Beatrice, and Miss Lugoson were close friends from childhood."

"I am not surprised, they seemed very close. Is Miss Carley your only child?"

"No, I have a son as well, older than Beatrice. Younger than yourself, however."

"Have you spoken to anyone else who was at Lugoson House that night? I have wondered if anyone else became ill."

"I don't believe Lady Holland had any cause for concern, and I do not really know Mrs. Decker, though my wife might. If you'll excuse me, my good man, I see Charles Greville. I wanted to ask him about a horse." Mr. Carley tightened his fingers around his glass and strode off.

The man had more interest in horseflesh than the guests at Lady Lugoson's party. Just when Charles thought the evening had been unhelpful in the matter of the mysterious death of Christiana Lugoson, though of great interest in terms of how the wealthy and titled lived, Lady Holland appeared, walking in his direction, so glittering in her gems that one almost missed her own fading beauty.

"My lady," Charles begged, as soon as he could get her attention. "May I have a minute of your time?"

"You may have more than one, my dear Mr. Dickens," she declared, taking his arm and guiding him to a sofa at the far end of one drawing room. "I have heard how kind you were to poor Christiana Lugoson."

"I believe you hear everything, madam, and I wondered what you might know about Lady Lugoson's dinner?"

"I believe I saw Mr. Carley here," the lady said, employing her fan to sweep away a flying creature that hovered around her nose.

"I did speak to him. He said that none of his family had taken ill. Lady Lugoson thought the potato sauce had gone off. I wonder if anyone else ate the potatoes?"

"I don't imagine anyone except the footman who served would have any hope of remembering that," Lady Holland said. "But I know I ate potatoes myself, in a white sauce?"

"Yes," Charles agreed.

She patted her décolletage. "Not a moment's indigestion, my dear Mr. Dickens. So I do not think they played any role in poor Miss Lugoson's demise."

"Thank you for clearing my suspicions on that account. Have you heard any news of the others? Your German acquaintance? Mrs. Decker?"

"I had a note from my dear Professor Klemme and he didn't mention anything but sorrow for the Lugoson family. I do not know Mrs. Decker well. Mr. Decker is in shipping and they often travel." She patted her jewelry, then gave him a speculative glance. "I don't understand your concern, Mr. Dickens. Did the medical men not understand why the girl perished?"

"Not in any decisive manner." Charles moved a scant inch closer to the lady. "You may recall, strangely enough, that another young girl died on Epiphany night in the same neighborhood, one year before Miss Lugoson. I cannot remove the coincidence from my thoughts."

"The same illness?" she inquired. "The random, unexceptional death of one girl would not come to my notice ordinarily."

"That is my understanding," Charles said. "Not the way you expect a young girl to die."

"Is there any point of commonality?" the lady asked shrewdly.

"They were both seventeen at the time of death. Both worshippers at St. Luke's. I am trying to learn more."

"It is odd," Lady Holland agreed. "But of course, there are so many rumors about the Lugoson family. Now, I can't say anything against the Lugoson girl herself."

"But?" Charles prodded, his senses pricking up. Was this about the actress sister, or something else?

Lady Holland leaned her head closer, her expression avid in her timeworn face. Charles was reminded that Lady Holland was not a character without controversy herself, between her divorce, her rumored affairs, and the illegitimate son she shared with her husband, born during her divorce.

"Do you know about Lady Lugoson's sister?" Lady Holland asked.

"Angela Acton," Charles confirmed. "Yes, my friend William Aga told me. Is that important?"

"She is Lady Lugoson's younger sister," Lady Holland confirmed, "and the rumor is that she is really Christiana's mother."

The room seemed to dim as he focused entirely on Lady Holland. "Who was the rumored father?"

"I cannot speak to that, but you understand that Lady Lugoson had no children then, so it was quite a scandal. Christiana might have been a great heiress undeservedly, if Lady Lugoson had not given birth to the present Lord Lugoson."

Charles rubbed his lower lip with his thumb. "Any question about his parentage?"

"No. I remember the baroness during that time. I have no doubt that she had expectations and that her husband was pleased with her."

"I don't see what any of this would have to do with Miss Lugoson's death," he mused. Fascinating though it was.

Lady Holland chuckled. "There was still quite a bit of money settled on her, and not just from the Actons. The late Lord Lugoson had property that wasn't entailed and left it all to Christiana's dowry. She was much wealthier than her supposed brother."

"That is unusual," Charles agreed. *Very unusual.* "He must have thought he was her father."

"I didn't know them well until shortly before the present Lord Lugoson's birth. The mother and children lived mostly at their country estate before they all moved to France for a time. I had understood it to be a matter of Lady Lugoson's lungs, but she shows no sign of delicacy these days."

Charles considered that night. Could Christiana have been struck down by an inherited lung ailment? But no, any wheezing had come late in the process, when her entire body was shutting down. Meanwhile, any inquiry he might make now must take Lady Lugoson's possible capacity for falsehood into account.

"Will you be attending the funeral?" asked Lady Holland, changing the subject. "It is on Wednesday."

"Of course," Charles said.

"I shall give you some advice, young man," Lady Holland said. "While this is a house without a father, no family wants their secrets uncovered. As a reporter you are used to uncovering the truth, but remember that the truth has its cost. Given that you have no connection to this matter, it might be best to leave the gossip alone."

"Her death is an injustice, my lady," Charles said. "If there is a cause, something in the neighborhood, something that could affect the Hogarth girls, I must know the answer."

"Ah, the Hogarths," Lady Holland said shrewdly. "Now I

understand your interest. But if a young man like yourself can uncover the secrets of a girl's life, I should be very surprised."

Charles smiled. "Better that I put myself at risk than Miss Hogarth."

Lady Holland looked over Charles's shoulder. "If it isn't Mr. Aga."

William inclined his head as a footman brought him a chair. Charles settled back, happy to listen as the two discussed Napoleonic minutiae.

# Chapter 8

The previous Sunday, Charles had had the happy experience of traversing the St. Luke's burial ground with the Hogarth sisters under weak sunlight. Now, on Wednesday afternoon, a brisk wind blew tiny, stinging snowflakes in his eyes as he stood with Mr. Hogarth, Mr. Carley, young Lord Lugoson, and a dozen other men around the short iron gate squared around the stone vault of the Lugoson family.

The rector read the burial service, his damp shoes sunk into the soaking grass, taking frequent pauses for a phlegmy cough. "Blessed are those who mourn, for they will be comforted," he intoned.

Charles's gaze passed over the pine coffin inside the open gate and looked across. Lord Lugoson represented his family, since women rarely attended funerals. He recognized Lord Holland and his wife's friend Professor Klemme. Next to the German stood another familiar face, the man who had played Richard III, Percy Chalke. Charles supposed he represented Angela Acton, Miss Lugoson's aunt. Or her mother, if the rumors were true.

He glanced away, but something niggled at the back of his mind. Casually, his gaze roved over Chalke's narrow-shouldered frame again, and then he realized what had caught his eye. Under his top hat, shaggy fringe surrounded the actor's face. He had blond hair. To play Richard III, he had either darkened his hair or worn a wig. The thought struck Charles. Could Percy Chalke be Miss Lugoson's real father?

The actor had light eyes, probably blue. While both the hair and eyes of Miss Christiana Lugoson had been mimicked in Lady Lugoson, it did not hurt the evidence to find Mr. Chalke had the same physical characteristics. His hands, too, were long-fingered and delicate, like Miss Lugoson's. Charles had spent too many hours watching over the girl to forget. He wondered if she would be buried with the ruby ring she had worn on her right hand, or if someone had taken it as a keepsake.

The wind groaned loudly, and a gust of mold-scented air blew directly into Charles's nose. He sneezed, and turned away, fumbling for a handkerchief. Half hidden by a large cross, he saw a large young man with bright pink circles of cold on his cheeks. Perhaps older than Charles, his overall appearance was a handsome one, with curling hair and fashionable attire.

When Charles put his handkerchief away and turned back, Mr. Carley was glaring, but he realized that the man wasn't looking at him, but over his shoulder at the youth. Was the timid figure young Mr. Carley, his son?

"We have entrusted our sister Lugoson to God's mercy, and we now commit her body to the ground: earth to earth, ashes to ashes, dust to dust: in sure and certain hope of the resurrection to eternal life," the rector continued.

Punctuated by coughs, the rector completed the main part of the service, commending Miss Lugoson to God. The verger and a church warden, who'd been standing behind the rector, stepped forward. The rector opened the door of the vault and then gestured to Lord Lugoson and Lord Holland, who took places at the foot of the small coffin. The quartet lifted the coffin and carried it through the door into the final resting place of the Lugoson family.

Mr. Hogarth pulled out his handkerchief and blew his nose loudly into it. His eyes were reddened around the lower lashes. "Her poor mother," he murmured. "I have never decided if it is cruel or sympathetic to keep women from burials."

Charles wondered if the Hogarths had lost any of their children. Common enough, but the tender age of Christiana Lugoson would still make any man despair.

Before the participants left, he did his best to memorize every face, wondering if any of them might be a member of the Rueff family. At least half a dozen were unknown to him.

When the men returned from the vault, the rector blessed them all, then went to Lord Lugoson to tend to him.

"Why don't you eat with us, Charles?" Mr. Hogarth asked. "It's late enough, and Mrs. Hogarth has a nice mutton stew for dinner tonight."

"Delightful," Charles said. He could do with the cheerful smiles of the Hogarth girls after such a sad scene, and the thought of being able to put his feet in front of a fire for a while was glorious. His toes felt frozen despite thick shoes and wool socks.

They said their good-byes to the men they knew, then made their way across the wintery streets toward Fulham Road. Charles shared what little he'd learned about the Lugosons with Mr. Hogarth. It left the older man shaking his head.

"No wonder Lady Lugoson took the family off to France when she could," he said. "I have no idea if the stories are rubbish or not, but trouble found them sure enough when they returned home."

"Do you think I am imagining murder?" Charles asked bluntly, as they walked up the front walk of the Hogarth home.

"As a reporter, I would not give up the story until I knew more about Marie Rueff. Young girls can be verra foolish, and Christiana Lugoson was a fatherless girl newly returned home. What might she have done?"

"So you think Miss Lugoson poisoned herself?"

"Upon reflection, though I know I was a skeptic at first, this had the look of poison to me," Mr. Hogarth said. "From what little I saw. A strange pagan ritual? Something local girls do on Epiphany night?"

"A ritual." Charles shivered. "What an interesting line of inquiry. I shall have to do some research."

The front door opened. Charles's side clenched when he saw the pure, smiling face of Miss Kate Hogarth, her hair twisted into red ribbons. Some emotion upon seeing her wrought a physical reaction upon him. "Such a delight, your daughter," he murmured.

"Kate is a credit to me," Mr. Hogarth agreed, lifting his bushy eyebrows. "And a help to her mother."

"Father!" Miss Hogarth cried. "And Mr. Dickens."

She kissed her father's cheek, seeming not to notice how the damp wool of his coat left a wet square on the skirt of her dark tartan dress, then took Charles's hand and gave it an affectionate little pat. "How are ye? Was the service terribly sad?"

Charles could scarcely feel the press of her sweet little hand on his cold glove, yet his palm began to sweat underneath.

Mr. Hogarth shook his head. "Let us drip dry in front of the fire, lass, before we catch our death."

She stepped back, releasing Charles, and helped her father with his coat while Charles removed his snow-dusted outer layer. "The warmest room is the dining room," she said.

He followed the Hogarths down the hall into the noisy, musical instrument– and family-filled space where he had shared Epiphany with them more than a week ago. Much could be said for the bachelor lifestyle but these homey touches of handmade rugs, warm little bodies dancing around, and cheerful smiles on every face made him long for a more domestic comfort.

If only he felt secure enough to manage the costs, as his father had not. Never did he want to put his innocent children through what he'd suffered in his childhood.

He took a step back to balance as a young boy collided with his legs. Gently, he disentangled the lad. "You'll get wet," he chided. He set the child on a piano bench.

Mrs. Hogarth came into the room, holding a platter of bread, followed by a maid with the stew pot. Mr. Hogarth ushered everyone to their seats. Charles picked up the little boy, remembering that the youngest didn't have their own chairs, and managed to seat himself next to Miss Hogarth.

"I believe you are a great reader," he said to her, after the food was served. "Have you read anything about pagan rituals?"

"Goodness, what a question." Her rosebud mouth pursed. "I might have done. Why?"

"What if some kind of ritual brought on these deaths?" he said.

"I can't think of anything that might occur on January sixth," she said. "Solstice would be the time for pagan rituals. We had a queer old neighbor in Edinburgh who celebrated Yule for eleven days, but that wouldn't last until Epiphany."

Charles took up his spoon. "A dead line of inquiry, then. Unfortunate."

She looked into his eyes, and he had the certain notion that she wanted to please him. "What about the saints? Father has a book of the Roman Catholic saints in his study, and we still venerate those from before the sixteenth century."

"And our more modern heroes," Charles said, "but I can't think of anyone relevant."

"May we be excused, Father?" Miss Hogarth asked. "I wish to consult a book in your library."

Mr. Hogarth gave her an indulgent smile and nodded. Charles followed her out of the dining room. She took a lamp off a table by the door and led him down a chilly passageway, into a little room set off on the main floor.

"Quite a nice collection," Charles said, staring at the packed bookshelf on one wall. "My father had books when I was young, but nothing like this display."

She smiled and handed him the candle, then knelt on the rug and ran a finger along the second shelf. "Here it is. *Lives of the Saints.*" She rose, holding a little, battered, blue leather–bound book.

"Anything?" Charles asked after she opened the volume and ran her finger down a page.

"There is a Feast Day list, but I don't recognize any of these names. Most of them are men, anyway. Diman?" She turned a page. "No, that's a man, too. I was hoping for some strange female saint ritual."

"It was worth a try. It makes sense that the girls died due to something they had in common."

She bent down to return the book to its spot on the shelf. Charles admired the suppleness of her movements. "Any other ideas about, well, being a seventeen-year-old girl in Brompton, or a St. Luke's parishioner?"

"No, and Miss Lugoson hadn't been returned to this area for very long. I never even met her. She was ill the day we called, and they didn't return the call."

"I don't know much about the etiquette of the upper classes."

"We aren't the upper classes," Miss Hogarth said with a sly grin that reminded Charles of her younger sister. "What will you do now?"

His smile matched hers. "My dear Miss Hogarth, we need to pay a call on Lady Lugoson."

Her eyes widened. "Oh, we couldn't."

"Fortune favors the bold," he declared. "She hasn't returned my letter. The funeral is over now, and I am sure she wants to know what happened to her daughter."

"Does she?" Miss Hogarth said.

Charles pushed doubt aside. "How could she not? Besides, you might be older than Miss Lugoson, and may be out of any danger that might befall a young girl, but what about Mary, just fifteen? Or the younger girls, Georgina and Helen? Might they in turn befall whatever killed her and Miss Rueff?"

Miss Hogarth nodded. "You are so right, Mr. Dickens. We must learn enough to protect my sisters."

# Chapter 9

❧

Charles had to report on a meeting being held at a church in Knightsbridge on Thursday morning, so he was already well on his way to Brompton by late that morning. He went to the Hogarths' home as soon as the meeting had ended, attempting to write his article in pencil as the bus jolted along the crowded road. Miss Hogarth and her mother were waiting for him when he arrived, ready to pay their call on Lady Lugoson.

"Such a treat to see you again, Mr. Dickens," Miss Hogarth said, dressed today in gray with blue ribbons darker than her bright eyes. Her eyelids lowered, giving her a sultry look.

He wanted to take her hand but they were both in view of her mother. While her parents seemed to approve of him, even encourage him, there were very firm limits on their tolerance.

"Do you really think she will be at home?" Mrs. Hogarth asked, taking her cloak off its hook.

"I left a note with one of her footmen last night," Charles said, handing Miss Hogarth her cloak, recognized from their previous interactions. "If she wants to see us she will be prepared."

Mrs. Hogarth called out some instructions to her maid regarding the younger children, then opened the front door. Charles had hoped for a quick cup of tea before they departed, but his toes hadn't even had time to warm before they were back in the cold.

As they walked across the orchard, Miss Hogarth, just ahead of him, tripped on a fallen branch. Charles leapt forward and caught her, one hand on her arm and the other on her back.

"Thank you," she whispered, her face flushed.

Mrs. Hogarth hadn't noticed, and still walked steadily ahead of them. He kept his hand on Miss Hogarth's back since their chaperone wasn't watching. Miss Hogarth's lips curved in a small, mischievous grin in response to his forward behavior. He could smell smoke in her cloak, mud and leaves as well.

What a contrast, this daylight walk, to the eerie experience of passing through nighttime fields filled with mist on that fateful night more than a week before. The graveyard weather of Wednesday's funeral service had passed into something like sunlight, and the wind had gone for now. He felt almost cozy in his heavy coat and hat.

Miss Hogarth's blue bonnet accentuated her eyes. Her mother did not have her style, but she was a respectable woman, and Charles appreciated the fact that she'd left her children to give them the right air of concern for their call.

"You should always wear blue," he said in a low voice. "It suits you well."

"Thank you, Mr. Dickens," Miss Hogarth said gravely. "You should always wear a checkerboard pattern on your trousers for you are a most complex young man."

He grinned widely, stifling his chuckle as her mother turned at the edge of the orchard, staring at them quizzically. His hand dropped from Miss Hogarth's back, hidden by the folds of her cloak.

When they arrived at the front door of Lugoson House, the

butler opened it quickly and greeted them by name. "Her Lady-ship is expecting you in the south parlor."

"How kind," Mrs. Hogarth said, as they gave their wraps to a footman before the butler led them down the hall.

"She does want to see us," Miss Hogarth said in Charles's ear as they walked across creaking boards in a back hall. "But we are going to a part of the house we didn't see before."

Indeed, Panch opened the door into a pleasant morning room with small but numerous windows. A large fireplace, framed with wood instead of the marble in the main reception room, blazed cheerily with a well-set coal fire. A round table was set with a tea service a couple of feet away from the grate. Lady Lugoson, alone except for a maid and seated in an arm-chair, lifted her hand to them.

"My poor, dear Lady Lugoson," said the sympathetic Mrs. Hogarth, rushing to her with concern in her eyes. She took the lady's hand and pressed it between her own, speaking words too low for Charles to hear.

After a few moments, Lady Lugoson gestured to him and to Miss Hogarth. They too were privileged with clasping the noble lady's hand before being invited to sit at the table.

"I do not know how I have survived the past ten days," Lady Lugoson said tearfully, as she poured the tea. Grief had aged her, etching lines of pain and exhaustion onto her beautiful face. "I have relived those hours of my darling's suffering over and over again."

"Have you come to any conclusions?" Charles asked. At a sharp glance from Miss Hogarth, he amended, "Any resolution or peace, I mean?"

"My dear Mr. Dickens, I am without rest," the lady con-fessed. "What happened? She was perfectly healthy until that evening."

Charles's gaze was drawn to the fireplace. Above it hung a portrait of Lady Lugoson and her two children. It must have been painted a decade ago. He could well believe the children were about age five and seven. Lord Lugoson wore a black velvet jacket and his sister was in white. They both had pale curls and sweet, childish expressions. Charles felt utterly saddened. Someday a portrait of that little girl, grown with children of her own, should have hung here. Instead, nothing but the grave.

"Do you wish to discuss the matter plainly?" he asked, throat tight with emotion. "As you may recall, I am a journalist, and while I do not wish to be unkind, I would be happy to help you unravel this situation."

"I welcome your thoughts," admitted the lady, handing around the plate of seedcake.

"I sent you a note about your servants," Charles said, happy to take the largest slice. "There was another girl who died in the area last year, and I did wonder if you had taken on a servant from the Rueff household."

"Why would it matter?" the lady asked, returning the plate to the table.

"Someone incompetent in the kitchen?" Miss Hogarth suggested. "Someone who put some poison into the food?"

"Into her food, you mean? And murdered my poor girl?" Lady Lugoson made a choking sound and buried her red nose in a cambric handkerchief.

Charles and Miss Hogarth shared a glance. At least the lady herself had been the one to raise the specter of murder.

"It doesn't mean murder for certain," Charles said, as Mrs. Hogarth passed him the butter dish and knife. "Simple incompetence. Letting food spoil. Cream, for instance, in the potato sauce."

"I have wondered if my sister might have bribed someone to hurt my daughter," Lady Lugoson said, ignoring Charles's calm words. "But I have no knowledge of this other girl. Was she a friend of my daughter's?"

"Who is your sister?" Mrs. Hogarth asked with a frown.

"An actress," Charles said softly, shocked by the lady's words. "Lady Lugoson, the other girl's name was Marie Rueff, and she would have been a year older than Miss Lugoson."

"You mean Jacques Rueff's daughter?" Lady Lugoson tucked her handkerchief into her apron pocket. "I did not know she had died. Some correspondence did not reach me in France, but I must confess I was terribly inadequate with my letter writing. Since my husband died it has been so hard."

"So you did know her," Miss Hogarth prompted.

Lady Lugoson nodded. "Yes, she and my daughter were bosom friends when they were young, but we were in France, of course, and I do not think she and Christiana corresponded."

Charles decided to leave the specifics of that relationship alone for now, and learn more about Lady Lugoson's most troubling accusation. "Why do you think your sister, Miss Acton, might wish to harm your daughter? Have you spoken to the police about this matter?"

"Of course not, this is my family. I cannot burden my son's future with a scandal." Lady Lugoson sniffed. "To be honest, Christiana expressed an interest in treading the stage herself."

"I see. She wanted to be an actress." Charles understood how unrespectable the profession was. He finished spreading a thick layer of butter over his cake and picked up his fork. "Please continue."

"Angela claims to be twenty-two, though she is really thirty-one," the lady said.

"Goodness," Mrs. Hogarth exclaimed. "There's a wee difference."

"If Christiana joined Mr. Chalke's theatrical company and it was known that she was family, it might expose Angela's true age." Lady Lugoson crumbled the bit of cake on her plate. None went past her lips.

"Is that worth murdering for?" Charles asked.

"It might be to her," the lady said in a glum voice. "Angela has sunk every penny she had into that theater, yet never seems to see any profit. She needs to act, yet she is already more than twice the age of some of the other girls."

"Would you have let your daughter perform? The daughter of a baron?" Mrs. Hogarth inquired.

"Not under her real name, of course," Lady Lugoson said, "but she was so very talented. She could have played at it for a few months, before joining the fashionable world. Or even returned to France to marry. There are a couple of young men there most eager to seek her hand, but I would not hear of it at just seventeen, and she herself was not ready to wed." She sighed, the barest hint of a smile on her lips.

"Is that why you returned to England? So that Christiana could join her aunt's theatrical troupe?" Miss Hogarth asked, setting the butter knife back in the dish and moving it to the center of the table.

"I had hoped to seek an English husband for her." Lady Lugoson shuddered. "I cannot feel it is entirely safe to be a person of noble birth in France, even now. But children do not take life seriously."

"I can see why you would choose not to wed in France yourself," Charles said, injecting a note of sympathy. "Would you like me to speak to your sister, and to Mr. Chalke? I can attempt to uncover their state of mind for you, so that you do not have to involve the police."

"I would like that very much," Lady Lugoson said, turning her face toward him.

The sight of all that beseeching loveliness would have overset a young man whose thoughts were not already enchanted by a much younger lady. But still, Charles could not help feeling pity for the woman, who had married so young herself. "I shall accept your commission with all the severity it requires," he said. "I ask only one thing."

"Name it, Mr. Dickens."

"I would like your permission to speak to your butler about your dinner party that night."

"Of course, if you think it will help. I shall call Panch for you immediately." She reached for the bellpull as Charles managed a third and fourth bite of his cake. It scarcely filled the empty space in his belly, but it was better than nothing.

Five minutes later, Charles had pled for and received a second slice of cake and butter, feeling hypocritical for his concern that someone in the Lugosons' kitchen might be adulterating the food while partaking of it so liberally. Miss Hogarth's eyes danced with amusement.

When Panch entered the room, bowing to his lady and reminding Charles yet again of a long-stemmed flower on a stalk, Lady Lugoson told him that he needed to answer some questions.

Panch looked down his nose at Charles. "Yes, sir?"

"Have you hired any staff from the Jacques Rueff residence into this establishment, since Lady Lugoson and her children returned?"

The butler's eyelids drooped to half-mast before opening again. "No, sir."

"Did Miss Lugoson partake of anything at dinner that last night that no one else ate?"

"I thought of that myself at the time," the butler drawled. "And the answer is no."

"Did she eat the potatoes in cream sauce?"

"A large portion, sir."

That seemed to sharpen Lady Lugoson's intellect. "Did she eat more than anyone else?"

"No, I believe Mr. Carley and Mrs. Decker also partook, liberally. We had to refresh the dish."

"Is it possible that Miss Lugoson therefore ate the first dish, or the refreshed one?" Charles asked.

"It all came from the same cooking pot."

"I made the seating plan myself," Lady Lugoson said. "Mr. Carley would have been served last."

"Therefore your daughter couldn't have had a version of the potatoes that no one else did," Charles said. "Very well, then."

"That broth she drank in the morning made her ill again," Miss Hogarth said thoughtfully.

"With all due respect I must disagree," the butler said. "I have seen many fatal illnesses in my eight-and-sixty years, and often the body gathers its strength for a time before continuing its fatal journey. It is as if we save some small amount of strength with which to give our final good-byes."

Miss Hogarth nodded politely. "Thank you for that information, Panch. I will remember it."

"If there is nothing else, my lady, I was supervising some intricate polishing."

"Thank you, Panch, you may go." Lady Lugoson looked down at her folded hands. "I should write Monsieur Rueff a condolence note, reminding him of happier times, since I have only just learned of poor Marie's death."

"We shall leave you to it, my lady," Mrs. Hogarth said. "Mr. Dickens will send you a note after he interviews your relations."

A dozen more questions prickled on Charles's tongue, but he recognized that Mrs. Hogarth desired to leave this house of mourning, and it would be bad manners to attempt to stay one minute longer.

In the orchard on the walk back, Miss Hogarth put her hand delicately on Charles's sleeve. His heart skipped a beat and he stopped, letting her mother gain a few footsteps on them before he began to walk again, more slowly.

"What were your impressions?" Miss Hogarth asked in a low voice.

"Not a servant, not the potatoes," Charles said, impressed that she was so keen on the mystery. "But still a possible connection to Marie Rueff."

"I was utterly shocked that Lady Lugoson herself suspected foul play," said the girl. "Why, it gave color and form to your own suspicions, Mr. Dickens."

Charles nodded soberly. "So it did, my dear Miss Hogarth. We must continue our lines of inquiry."

Her nod matched his. "I share the same resolve. I will help in any way I can."

# Chapter 10

Charles didn't have any meetings the next morning. He'd meant to spend the time working on one of his sketches, but instead he went to the Garrick Theater, to fulfill his promise to Lady Lugoson.

He'd dressed in his best checked trousers and black frock-coat, and carefully brushed his hat and coat while his brother Fred polished his shoes, with some idea of looking like a possible investor. Barring that, he could always claim to be a budding playwright, which indeed he was, or at least a hopeful one.

When he reached the cobbled street, he went down a side road and turned into the alley, looking for the stage door. At that time of day most actors might well still be abed, but he suspected that actor-managers and actress–building owners did not have the luxury, but instead would be in meetings with workmen or someone of that sort.

Indeed, as Charles walked in through the back, he saw a rush of activity. A trio of paint-stained men were carrying buckets and brushes, a seamstress rushed by with a bolt of fabric in her arms, and some other man, whom Charles suspected had some-thing to do with the gas, bustled by, his belt jangling with tools. He heard shouting behind a tall partition that hid the alley door from a more businesslike part of the theater.

As he peered around the partition, made of freshly sawn wood that still smelled like a tree, he heard one of the men's voices rise into a powerful rant. Percy Chalke pointed at the other man, his strong tone mesmerizing, even if the words didn't make much sense. Charles had a sense that the other man was a painter and he'd made an error on the backdrop.

The man raised his fist and shook it at Chalke, then pushed his way through a narrow opening to the stage and disappeared. Chalke huffed out a breath and put his hands on his narrow hips.

"Mr. Chalke?" Charles said in a deferential tone.

The actor-manager seemed to go on point like a hunting dog, his nose quivering, his lean form greyhoundlike. After a mo-ment in that pose, he turned slowly, sighting Charles.

"Yes?" He pushed his straggly blond locks out of his eyes.

"I am Charles Dickens, reporter at the *Morning Chronicle* and an, er, friend of Lady Lugoson."

Arrogantly, Chalke's gaze went up and down Charles. He held his ground, as befitted a man who claimed friendship to a baron's widow.

"What do you want?" Chalke growled.

"I'd like to pay my respects to Miss Acton."

"She isn't seeing anyone. Death in the family."

"I know, Mr. Chalke. I was at the funeral. I stood right across from you, if you remember."

"Doesn't matter."

"I've come with a message from Lady Lugoson."

Chalke grunted. "Give it here, then."

Charles stepped forward. He could see the lines around the

other man's eyes. They put him close to forty, some years older than Miss Acton. "It's a verbal message. Where is Miss Acton?"

"Not your business, sir. If Lady Lugoson wants to see her sister, she sends a note, not a lackey."

Charles drew himself up. "I am no lackey."

"I don't know who you are," Chalke said, with an oily sneer that reminded Charles of the actor's portrayal of Richard III. "But I'm not bothering Miss Acton with your nonsense. She has to go on tonight, despite her pain and grief, and I won't disturb her preparations."

"She lost her niece, whom she must not have known very well," Charles said. "Given that the girl had only recently returned to England. Or is perhaps Miss Acton's grief more that of a mother's?"

Chalke's eyes narrowed. Two workmen entered the space from the stage side of the partitions, and moved into place behind him, muscular arms crossed over beefy chests. Charles wondered what he had said that had sent the workmen toward them. Ex-boxers, from the look of them, one with a badly repaired nose and the other with a cauliflower ear.

"I shall speak to Lady Lugoson about this insult," Charles said, ignoring the blood rushing through his ears, making a humming sound. "I will fulfill my commission to her." He held Chalke's gaze for a long moment, then hurtled himself through the narrow opening back into the large backspace area.

He was almost to the alley door when he heard light, rapid footfalls. Glancing back, he saw a girl. She followed him out the door, then put a finger to her lips and gestured to him to follow her.

Back in the daylight, he could not see the girl's hair under her bonnet, but he recognized the freckles. This was Julie, the girl actress who had so enchanted the lads in the pit.

When they reached the wall where he had pulled down the

playbill some days ago, she paused and turned to him. "You said you were a friend of Lady Lugoson's?"

"Yes. You are Julie?"

"Julie Saville. I was a friend of Miss Lugoson's."

"You were?" Surprised, he wondered if Miss Lugoson had envied this girl's life and had cultivated her friendship as a result.

"Yes, I'm not just an actress. I help Miss Acton with her scripts and letters. If you need to get a message to her, I can take it."

"I see. Thank you." He considered her. "Could you answer some questions for me? It may do just as well."

"Of course." Her eyebrows rose, giving her an expectant air. "Miss Lugoson and I are, were, the same age, you see. She and her brother liked to visit the theater."

"I thought you were younger."

"It's the freckles," she said, pointing ruefully to the brown dots that crossed her nose and spread across the top of her cheeks. "But I'm seventeen."

"Did Miss Lugoson ever speak of her parentage?"

Julie frowned. "I don't know what you mean, but she only spoke about one thing to me. Obsessed, she was."

"What?"

"She had a dance instructor. Practicing for her come-out, like ladies must."

"And she talked about dancing?"

"No, about him. The instructor. French, you see. She'd just come from France, and they spoke French together. She was in love with him."

Charles's eyebrows lifted. "I see. Do you think she might have done herself harm, in grief over him rejecting her?"

Julie's mouth rounded into an O. "No, she didn't kill herself. But did she die of a broken heart? Maybe he rejected her. I don't know."

He found it hard to believe that an aristocrat would confide her deepest longings to a mere actress. Even more, he doubted the theory. Christiana Lugoson had not perished from a broken heart. "When did you see her last?"

"They came for the pantomime just before Christmas."

*Aha.* "So you hadn't seen her in weeks before she died?"

"No, she didn't come into London, then, but I know she was still taking her lessons."

"Do you think this instructor took advantage of her?" He paused, then pursued a forbidden subject. After all, this was an actress, not a lady of quality. "Could there have been expectations of a child?"

"She was much more of a child than me," Julie said frankly. "Not wise in the ways of the world. I don't think she'd have recognized the signs."

"But you think this man was her lover," Charles said flatly.

Julie bit her lip. "She spoke of him very loverlike, but what that meant to her, I really don't know. She still had dolls."

He came to the heart of Lady Lugoson's concerns at last. "Do you think Miss Acton or Mr. Chalke would have meant her harm?"

Julie glanced around, as if looking for spies. "I don't like them," she confessed. "Rather desperate, they are, worried about money. Theaters are a hard business. It's easier for her, she owns the building, but he's always trying to lower the rent. They fight about it."

The painter Charles had seen arguing with Percy Chalke came out of the alley, a pipe in his hand. His gaze roamed over Julie as he made a show of lighting his pipe. Charles knew the man couldn't hear them, but still, the girl could still be scolded for speaking to him.

"Thank you." He wanted to offer her some money for speaking to him, but not in front of a witness. "I'm Charles Dickens, of the *Morning Chronicle*. You can send me a note at the newspaper if you have more to tell me." He turned away and strode down the street in the opposite direction, many thoughts crossing his mind.

He had the direction of the Carley house from another parliamentary reporter. Mr. Carley was an MP for the City of London and must indeed be a very wealthy man, for his home on Grosvenor Square could be included as one of the most fashionable addresses in London.

The house, when Charles found it, was not one of the best buildings arranged around the large central park. It had not been updated with a top story the way many of the houses had. In fact, it had not likely been touched in the hundred or so years since it had been initially built. Still, the address impressed, and the neighbors were among the highest the aristocracy and government had to offer.

When a footman opened the door, he offered his card, mentioning Lady Lugoson's name, and was sent to wait in a small parlor.

"At least I wasn't turned out on my ear," Charles muttered, as he glanced around the room. Like the outside, it had seen better days. It held furnishings likely purchased around the turn of the century, mostly carved with marine motifs, and an occasional crocodile. The purple-and-gold wallpaper border included shells and pearls in its decorations and must have been a good twenty years old. Given that public rooms would have the best furnishings, he could only imagine the state of the upstairs.

He wandered around the room for twenty minutes memorizing the furniture, hoping someone would arrive with a tea tray, but no one did. So he imagined the day where he wouldn't be a mere parliamentary reporter, when houses like this would be pleased to offer him entry, and pretty parlormaids would fall over themselves offering him the finest cake the household had to offer. Perhaps he would become a famous solicitor, or a playwright with a theatrical run so outstanding that his play would travel through the provinces for years to come.

Some minutes into these fanciful musings, the door finally opened, and Mrs. Carley came in. Old enough to be his mother, though quite a young one, she wore a brown-and-white dress with pronounced sleeves, very fashionable, with lace cuffs and collar. Her brown hair was well curled and her figure displayed just as spectacularly as he remembered. The household funds must be diminished in favor of the lady's dresses. He recalled she was the more fashionable lady on Epiphany night as well.

"Mr. Dickens," Mrs. Carley said, touching the ringlets drooping down her temples. The hairstyle further elongated her narrow face and the rouge she wore did not disguise the sallowness of her cheeks. For all that, she moved like a younger woman, and the smile that flashed across her thin lips was flirtatious.

"Mrs. Carley."

"Please, have a seat." She gestured toward an armchair next to the fire, and seated herself opposite. "Lady Lugoson sent you?"

He thought quickly. "Lady Lugoson wants to trace the movements on her daughter in her final days of life."

"Whatever for?" She pulled the bellpull on the wall next to the fireplace.

"Sentimentality, I suppose. She must have visited your daughter in those last days."

"I believe Beatrice saw her at our country house," Mrs. Carley said carelessly. "They were often together."

"Did Miss Carley share a dance master with Miss Lugoson?"

"Why?"

"I believe there was such a person," Charles said. "Or so I've been told."

"There is such a person, of course," she said.

A maid appeared in the doorway, and the lady ordered the tea Charles had so wished for before the fire had warmed him. Now the room seemed too hot, and he could smell rosewater radiating from the lady's clothing.

"Do you know his name? Did the young ladies take lessons together?"

"He is called Émile Dubois, and no, their lessons were separate." She picked up a piece of embroidery and pulled the needle from the cloth.

"A Frenchman?"

"Yes, in fact, I believe the Lugosons knew the dance master in France." The needle hung from red silk. The lady stabbed it in and out of the cloth with great competence.

"Where did they live in France? I have never heard."

"Fontainebleau, as I recall. I have never been to France, myself."

"Nor I," Charles said. "I would like to travel. The French Revolution fascinates me."

"That is because you are far from the gates of power, Mr. Dickens. I am certain you would not like your neck to be at risk."

Charles felt the hairs on the back of his neck rise at the thought of the guillotine's kiss. They both sat in quiet contemplation, until the maid returned with a tray. The four-piece silver set, shaped like gourds, gleamed with freshly polished flair.

Charles smiled when he saw the teacups were hand painted with yellow shells and red and blue flowers. "Very in keeping with the room."

Mrs. Carley nodded as the maid poured. "My mother's china. I remember it being unpacked from crates when I was very young."

"Did she decorate this room?"

"Yes. This was her home. She departed this earth just two years ago, and I have not yet had the heart to redecorate." She tied off the silk, removed the needle, and set her cloth aside.

"You must have been very close," Charles said.

"Indeed." Mrs. Carley handed him a cup and saucer. "The loss has made my children all the more dear to me."

"Might Miss Carley be called downstairs?" Charles asked. "I'm sure Lady Lugoson would be delighted to hear anything of her final interactions with Miss Lugoson."

"Lady Lugoson can expect us to call on her personally, as soon as she is able to receive guests," Mrs. Carley said, eyeing him over her cup rim.

Charles had the uncomfortable idea that Mrs. Carley was afraid he had designs on her daughter. He cast about for some way to inject Miss Hogarth into the conversation, but as the Carleys were no doubt in close relation to the titled, despite not having titles themselves, he knew Miss Hogarth would not be likely to be favored in their acquaintance. He'd only accessed the house using Lady Lugoson's name himself.

"Delicious tea," he commented. "A special blend?"

"Yes, Jacksons of Piccadilly makes it for me. Do you like the bergamot?"

"It is strong, but I do like it."

"Try it with a dot of cream," she urged. "I am famous for my tea."

He allowed her to doctor his cup, and they spent a pleasant half hour discussing her committee work in the temperance movement, before she suddenly seemed to realize that she was talking to a mere journalist, and not someone of her own class.

He admired the progress of the shell she was embroidering, then departed with good grace, warmed by the delicious tea and genteel surroundings. As he walked into the midafternoon mist, Charles realized his interview with Mrs. Carley might have gone better if Miss Hogarth had been present. Surely Miss Carley might have been invited downstairs, with proof that he wasn't attempting to court her.

He walked south toward Piccadilly, returning himself to the *Chronicle*'s offices on the Strand, in order to ask Mr. Hogarth if he might include his daughter in the next step in his investigation. He also planned to write to Lady Lugoson to have her arrange an interview with Émile Dubois, the dance master. With any luck, she might answer him this time.

# Chapter 11

On Monday, Charles was finishing an article about a parliamentary debate in the *Chronicle* offices when the post arrived. He found a note from Lady Lugoson, inviting him to call that afternoon. She indicated that Monsieur Dubois would be on the premises, as she'd made arrangements to settle his account.

Charles jumped up from his desk. He didn't have a moment to waste if he was to reach Brompton in time.

"What's the rush?" William inquired as Charles wiped ink from his fingers and cleaned his pen.

"I'm going to interview the dance master," Charles said. He'd caught his fellow reporter up on his investigation the night before, over a little dinner he'd hosted in his apartment.

"Folly with a foppish frog," William alliterated.

"We shall see. Do the French like poison?" He waved at a boy and handed his article over, instructing him to take it to Thomas Pillar, the under-editor.

"Medici, Borgia," William mused. "No, they were Italian. The French just like to cut." He mimed a slicing motion at the back on his neck.

"A kinder way to die," Charles said, remembering Miss Lugoson's agony.

Mr. Hogarth appeared in the doorway. "Charles. A word."

"Yes, sir." Charles grinned at William, then grabbed his outerwear and walked across the floor to greet his mentor.

Mr. Hogarth handed him a messy sheath of papers. "Here ye go. I made some notes on yer sketch."

"Thank you. Anything in particular I should pay attention to?"

"I would make sure to give the characters in these pieces their dignity. Ye can poke fun, but allow them something. The little, dumpy bride, for instance. Give her some positive attribute."

Charles nodded. "Leave the reader with an overall positive impression?"

"Indeed. Ye will do very well, Charles. Not everything needs to be a tragedy."

"Yes, sir. Speaking of tragedy, I am to go to Lugoson House this afternoon." He cleared his throat. "May I call upon Miss Hogarth and ask her to accompany me? I am to interview Miss Lugoson's dance master."

Mr. Hogarth crossed his arms. "What is the story there?"

"Lady Lugoson thinks her sister might have poisoned her daughter. I went to the theater and was unable to see Miss Acton, but I did meet her young assistant, and she suggested Miss Lugoson could be dead of a broken heart. I had the sense that she had known her dance master in France, or at least, she pined for France."

"If Lady Lugoson did not turn off the dance master, I cannot imagine he broke the girl's heart or dishonored her."

Charles shrugged. "A man of principle?"

"Or a hired killer." The editor tilted his head. "Miss Acton could have paid him to poison the girl."

Charles pulled on his gloves. "Anything is possible. I do wish we knew if she really had been poisoned."

"Impossible to know. Someday I'm sure medical men will be able to determine such things."

The light went on in Mr. Hogarth's eyes just as Charles had, no doubt, the same thought. "I could write about the state of medicine in light of poison."

Mr. Hogarth nodded. "Not yer area of expertise, but an interesting path of inquiry."

"It gives me an excuse to speak to doctors."

"I recall there is some way to detect arsenic," Mr. Hogarth said, his gaze drifting to the ceiling. "We reported on complaints in the House of Lords about the high cost of a trial in Kent some time back, and the expense was for arsenic testing."

"I'll see if I can recover the article," Charles promised. "But I had better leave for Brompton now."

"Must be a treatise on poisons you can access," Mr. Hogarth mused, turning away. He began to whistle.

"I'll add that to my list," Charles called.

When Charles arrived at the Hogarth home, he presented his letter from Lady Lugoson to Mrs. Hogarth.

"I am too busy to join ye, Mr. Dickens," she said at the door with an air of exhaustion. She had an apron with a damp streak down it over a dress with frayed cuffs. "Mondays are washing days."

He leaned toward her. "Would Miss Hogarth be able to come? It's just across the orchard and Mr. Hogarth is aware I was going to visit here."

She handed him the letter. "It's her duty to watch the bairns while Mary helps me with the wash, this time." Mrs. Hogarth sighed.

"I am sorry." He thought quickly. "But how often will a fine lady ask me to call? Surely it does your daughter good to claim one such as her as an acquaintance."

Mrs. Hogarth gazed at him and chuckled. "Very well." She left Charles in the hall.

He could hear her calling for Kate, telling her to tidy herself and accompany him to Lugoson House. He pulled off his hat and attempted to straighten his flattened hair. Settling himself onto the bench above the boots, he whiled away the time considering the situation at the Garrick. How could he get to Miss Acton? Would a letter of introduction from Lady Lugoson suffice, given that he was already known to her supposed paramour?

Miss Hogarth appeared twenty minutes later, in a fresh white wool dress patterned with blue flowers. She clapped her hands when she saw him. "Tea at Lugoson House? What a treat."

She gave him a wink, with a decidedly conspiratorial air.

Charles came to his feet grinning, his arms already full of her cloak. "We had better hurry. I can see the clouds through the window and we don't have long before another rainstorm hits." Not to mention her mother's tolerance would be low for a long excursion.

She fastened her cloak securely while he rebuttoned his coat and handed her her gloves and bonnet. "You have a cheerful air about you today, Mr. Dickens."

"When I can spend time with you it makes for a very good day." Their gazes met for an instant before she shyly turned away. He opened the front door while she called her good-byes back into the house; then they were alone under lowering skies.

"What is our intent?" she asked, as they walked down the road so they could access the front entrance of Lugoson House.

He told her about Julie Saville's suggestions about Dubois, the dance master.

She pursed her lips. "Dance lessons are one of the few ways a girl like Miss Lugoson can be alone with a man. Miss Saville could be correct."

"But even she considered Miss Lugoson a child," Charles argued.

She chuckled gaily. "Girls are very capable of deception."

Charles knew that to be true, given his long, unsuccessful courtship of Maria Beadnell. "Are you? A girl capable of deception?"

"Goodness, Mr. Dickens, such a question," Miss Hogarth said in a musing tone. "I should hope not. I have never had reason to lie."

He liked her answer. "You have a most happy family. I like that."

She touched his arm, but didn't linger. "Is your family not happy?"

"It is complicated," he said. "My father is a difficult man, but my mother does support him. We do have some good relatives."

"Oh?"

"Yes." He spoke of his extended family, everyone who might impress her and her parents, until they came to the outside of Lugoson House. It had an air of disuse today, if not neglect, like Carley House.

Panch let them in, then informed them that Monsieur Dubois was already closeted with his ladyship. They were brought to a formal parlor, rather chilly, with no tea service in sight. Another family portrait hung over the fireplace in this room, of a constipated-looking young man in the fashion of Beau Brummell's heyday. He had a Caesar haircut forming his blond hair to his thick skull, which was the only feature tying him to Lord Lugoson or the late Miss Lugoson. Still, the era of his attire made him likely to be their father, now deceased.

Charles reflected that he'd rather be at Mrs. Carley's dilapidated mansion, drinking her tea, than in this grander house with no sign of warmth or comfort. Miss Hogarth tried to control her shivers, but the tip of her nose went very pink and she said little while Charles paced.

"I am sorry for the chill," he apologized.

Her hands rubbed up and down her shoulders. "It is of no matter."

"I wish I could take you in my arms," he said daringly.

Despite the cold, her cheeks colored. "Mr. Dickens."

"Well?" he demanded. "Don't you wish the same thing?"

"Only if our thoughts were the same on certain matters," she said delicately. Before she could say more, the butler returned and brought them to the room in the back.

The dance master stood upon their entrance, and bowed rather vaguely in Miss Hogarth's direction. Charles was conscious of the insult toward the dashing girl, but they greeted Lady Lugoson and were introduced to the instructor in turn.

Émile Dubois was a starvation-shaped man in his late twenties, with very tight clothing. While clean and manicured, he had an air of genteel desperation that Charles often saw in his own mother, and a Continental dash that marked him as a foreigner. Perhaps he had no energy to be polite to anyone not likely to put bread on his table.

Charles was disappointed. How could he get to the heart of the matter with Christiana Lugoson's mother present? He didn't want to slander the girl, but they needed the truth.

When they were all seated around an empty deal table, Charles took the lead, knowing he couldn't keep Miss Hogarth there long. "Are you from Fontainebleau, monsieur?"

Dubois nodded.

"Had you taught Miss Lugoson for many years?"

"*Oui*, since she was a girl of twelve. Very graceful girl." Lady Lugoson smiled faintly at this praise of her daughter. She was as pale as Dubois, and her neck appeared thinner than ever. Had she been eating?

"Was she in love with you?" Charles asked bluntly.

Next to him, Miss Hogarth squeaked. He shot a glance at her, then realized he might have been more graceful in his questioning.

"*Mais non,*" Dubois protested, with a glance at Lady Lugoson.

"Really?" that lady said. "I rather thought she was. It gives me comfort now, to think she had experienced calf love, at least."

Monsieur Dubois cleared his throat, his eyes darting from side to side. "I am sorry to say, my lady." He paused to clear his throat again. "Miss Lugoson was secretly engaged."

"What?" said the other three all together.

"To whom?" Lady Lugoson asked.

"Not me," he said, with a quick Gallic wave of his hands. "I know my place and I have a wife already. I do not know the gentleman in question. She said she liked to dance, but she would never need to go to balls and find a husband." Dubois finished his heavily accented speech with a flush.

"What clues do you have about this gentleman's identity?" Charles asked.

"None," Dubois insisted in injured tones.

Lady Lugoson drew herself up, as if coming out of a trance. "I have paid you your fees, monsieur. I would suggest, for your future, not to hide young girls' secrets from families." She sniffed. "Or something terrible might be the result."

Dubois stood, and bowed, then quickly left the room before Charles could press him. He'd lost control of the interview to Lady Lugoson.

"If the goal of every young girl is to find a husband, is it not a good thing to find one, even if she isn't officially out?" Charles asked.

Lady Lugoson let out a short bark of laughter. Or despair. "It depends on the gentleman. The family must know. There can be no secrets, as a girl's parents are likely to know a great deal more about gentlemen than young girls. Finances, character, all the things of which they know nothing."

"I think it unwise," Miss Hogarth agreed. "While a girl might think she knows best, most parents have their best wishes at heart. Assuming her family does not have financial or moral difficulties."

Charles considered her words, guessing she meant them as a warning to him as well as relevant to the situation. Was the Lugoson family in financial or moral difficulty? There was no sign of financial hardship. Staff seemed sufficient, and no expense had been spared on doctors that terrible day, when he'd given instructions for help. But morality was another issue, not perhaps in Lady Lugoson herself, but in her sister. Also, there were the rumors about Miss Lugoson's parentage. How had such an innocent-looking girl lived such a complicated life? He glanced up at the portrait, looked again on that sweet young child she had been.

"Do you believe the dance master?" Charles asked.

Lady Lugoson sighed, her gaze returning to the door. "If this man my daughter considered herself engaged to was attached to the theater, I would well believe it."

"So you do not think it was Dubois?"

"I didn't have the sense he liked my daughter very well," Lady Lugoson admitted. "And a wife tucked away somewhere? I did not know that either."

"Then who? Someone like Percy Chalke?" Charles asked, wondering about the dance master's true character.

Lady Lugoson shook her head. "No, he'd have been much too old. Christiana was a girl. She liked girlish things."

"Why would Julie Saville have thought Dubois was the one?"

The lady straightened. "You are telling me that someone else thought my daughter was secretly engaged?"

"Something like that," Charles said, not wanting to admit

the bald facts. "An employee of your sister's, who, incidentally, I was unable to see, due to Mr. Chalke's refusal."

"He controls her," Lady Lugoson said. "Poor Angela." She glanced around. "Shall I order tea? There is a chill in the air."

"I must return home," Miss Hogarth said gently. "My mother needs me."

Charles clenched his fists. He knew she had to go, but they needed more time. And food. "We might be able to figure out the gentleman's identity if we can trace your daughter's last day or so," Charles said. "Do you think you could write down what you know? We could return tomorrow for another interview."

Lady Lugoson nodded. "We called on Mrs. Decker. Poor woman, alone for the holidays with her husband gone."

"Would you give me your card again? I will call on her before I return home," Charles said. "Since I am in the neighborhood. Then I will return for your list of your daughter's activities tomorrow."

"Very good."

Charles glanced around the richly furnished though uncomfortable room. A house like this might contain a well-filled library. "Was your husband a book collector? Did he have many volumes?"

"Certainly," she responded.

"Could I use the library tomorrow? To see if there are any books on natural history or medicine that might be of use to me?"

Lady Lugoson blinked. "For what purpose?"

"I believe arsenic is the only poison currently detectable in the body. But that doesn't mean observations regarding other poisons haven't been made. Maybe I can find something in a book."

"Very well." She rose and yanked the bellpull. "I will have my calling card brought to you, and speak to the servants about my daughter's movements on Epiphany when she wasn't with me. Please do visit Mrs. Decker. She might remember something I do not. She did see my poor girl twice that day, after all."

"Thank you, my lady." Charles and Miss Hogarth rose as well.

They followed her into the hall, and waited while their outerwear and the calling card were delivered. Then, before they knew it, they were back on Fulham Road, in the cold.

# Chapter 12

⚛

"Can you see Mrs. Decker?" Charles asked once they were outside.

Miss Hogarth's exasperated expression mimicked that of her mother's. "Briefly. I really must go back soon."

"What do you think of this secret engagement business?" Charles asked, as they walked toward the more modest but still palatial Decker home.

"I am against secrets. A young woman should have a good relationship with her parents, and respect them enough to not hide such things. It is the path to ruin."

"What about a young man who is destined for great things, but the girl's parents don't believe it?" Charles spoke from bitter experience.

"Everyone can have their little prejudices, but where can a secret engagement lead?" Miss Hogarth asked. "No young man should wed until he can afford a wife, after all."

Charles smiled a secret little smile. Now, with his double income from the *Chronicles*, he could afford a wife. Unlike his past courtship of Maria Beadnell, he knew well that Miss Hogarth's parents liked and respected him.

So, instead of pursuing her remarks from that cold room some forty-five minutes before, he asked, "So you would say Christiana Lugoson was on the path to ruin?"

"Between the theater obsession and a possible lover, I would say yes. Her mother had no control over her. The Lugosons have all but died out, and with only a younger brother, she had no one watching over her." Miss Hogarth sighed. "But poison? Why? If only we could know for certain."

"Suicide? Perhaps the man jilted her?"

"Life is not a play."

"Maybe it was to her. All of those toy theaters she shared with her brother."

"Perhaps."

"What did you think of Dubois?"

"A weak character, basically," Miss Hogarth said. "I do not think he would have been involved. Especially with a wife already. He couldn't have been engaged to Miss Lugoson. She was no threat to him."

"I shall take your word for it and move on to other ideas. We need to speak to Beatrice Carley. There is likely to be no one else than her reported best friend who might know her secrets."

Miss Hogarth inclined her head. "There is the Decker home now. Let us try to hold on to Lady Lugoson's card. We might be able to use it to good effect with Miss Carley."

He admired her good sense. "Her mother will block me."

"Maybe I can see her," Miss Hogarth said. "I want to do my part to protect my sisters."

Charles knocked on the door of the gracious three-story home and it was answered by a parlormaid. They reluctantly placed the calling card on a silver tray and watched it disappear into the inner recesses of the house. However, the maid returned swiftly and they were led into a drawing room about half the size of Lady Lugoson's. Mrs. Decker, one of the last women to spend time with Christiana Lugoson the day before her death, was already in place in front of her fireplace, a tea tray in front of her. Silver winked at her temples, where the black strands of her hair had taken on the tarnish of age, and she wore a slightly yellowed lace cap. Two other ladies, of similar age and dowdy appearance, were together on a settee to her right, but they were murmuring words of departure.

"How lovely," Mrs. Decker exclaimed upon seeing the fresh influx of visitors.

"We have found you at home," Miss Hogarth said. "I wish my mother had been free to come with us."

Mrs. Decker smiled at the departing ladies, then said, "Lady Lugoson sent you?"

"Yes, ma'am," Miss Hogarth said. "I just live next door to her. Mr. Dickens works for my father so my parents allowed us to cross the orchard to speak to her, but then she sent us here."

"I can keep an eye on one courting couple," Mrs. Decker said, settling comfortably into her chair with a wink. She gestured to a sofa. "What did Lady Lugoson hope I could tell you?"

"We are trying to retrace Miss Lugoson's last day," Charles explained, taking a seat and looking longingly at the teapot while Miss Hogarth blushed and sat next to him.

"Aha. She and her mother were here that day," she exclaimed.

The maid appeared with a set of fresh teacups and a pot of steaming water. She refreshed the pot.

"We'll just let that steep," Mrs. Decker said.

"Miss Lugoson is presenting herself as a rather complicated young individual," Charles said. "Did you know her well?"

"I am afraid not. We lived in New York for a time so I only knew her as a child, and then again these past few months. I am older than her mother and was not privileged with her confidences, but I liked them both. Lady Lugoson took one of our footmen to be her son's valet. He was ready for the promotion."

Now Charles could identify the city scenes richly filling the walls. They were all of American locations. "Have your servants heard of any irregularities in the household?"

"Goodness me, what a question," Mrs. Decker said, handing around a tray of iced buns.

Charles's stomach gurgled with relief, and when he passed the tray to Miss Hogarth he saw her scarcely suppressed smile. "We have heard any number of strange stories about both the girl herself and the family."

"And Lady Lugoson herself sent you here to hear gossip about her own family?"

Miss Hogarth winced. Charles said, "I apologize, Mrs. Decker. I am a journalist by trade and do tend to get ahead of myself."

"The rough world of politics. I understand," Mrs. Decker said. Her upper lip pulled away from her gums slightly, exposing the gold bracket of her false teeth. "Lord Lugoson is of course a decade or so away from looking for a wife, but Miss Lugoson's actions would reflect on his family. Of course, he is the last of his line, so he needs to find a good bride."

"Do you think she might have been murdered as a result?" Miss Hogarth whispered.

Mrs. Decker let out a sigh, her bosom deflating as she bent to pour the tea. "It is what everyone is thinking, is it not?"

"Are they? Tell us," Charles urged, a secret thrill in his heart. The maid poured fresh tea into everyone's cup.

"The way she died made it seem she was poisoned," Mrs. Decker said. "And poison is very popular these days. Ridding oneself of an unpopular or inconvenient relative is all the thing."

"You think Lord or Lady Lugoson poisoned her?" Miss Hogarth gasped, then put her hand over her mouth.

She and Charles exchanged a horrified glance.

"I would not have thought either of them had the backbone for it, but if they are casting about for blame, it may be to deflect their own actions," Mrs. Decker said primly. "For myself,

I dearly wish I had returned to New York with my husband and had not had to witness such ghastly suffering."

Charles ate his bun, stale, and drank his tea, much too weak, in a matter of two minutes. He wanted to leave this house. Why had he not considered Lady Lugoson or her son as the responsible party? Between her possible secret engagement and her planned theatrical career, she was a disgrace in the making to an aristocratic family. He felt such a fool, but also knew that Beatrice Carley would be the best source of information about the relationships within her best friend's family. "Any final thoughts for us, Mrs. Decker?" he inquired. "How did the ladies seem that afternoon?"

"I can remember nothing out of the ordinary. Miss Christiana Lugoson was sullen, as she often was on calls. I do not think she liked it here because there are no young people in my household. I have been at Mrs. Carley's gatherings, with the children present, and she presented herself in a much more pleasant fashion."

"Interesting," Miss Hogarth murmured. "I wish I had known them."

Mrs. Decker clicked her false teeth together. "Return to Mrs. Carley. She will be reasonable if you explain that you must retrace Christiana's last day, since clearly she was given some kind of poison that does not cause immediate death, if indeed poison is the cause of her demise."

"Such a terrible thought," Miss Hogarth said.

"I am glad I do not have any young daughters," Mrs. Decker said. "Another young girl died mysteriously in the parish just last year."

Charles sat forward, his attention focused entirely on her. "Marie Rueff?" Or would it be another?

Mrs. Decker nodded. "I do wonder if it is some kind of French influence. Monsieur Rueff is French, and Lady Lugoson had a French mother."

"Really?" Charles exclaimed. "I had not heard that before."

"Oh, yes. French mother, merchant father."

"We did know about that," Miss Hogarth said. "And her sister."

Mrs. Decker's eyelids fluttered closed. "Some people simply do not belong. Marrying above oneself can cause so many troubles."

Charles glanced at Miss Hogarth uneasily, but she seemed serene as she finished her last sip of tea. Mrs. Decker's teapot was silver, like Mrs. Carley's, though not quite so freshly plated. Her teacups and saucers were hand painted with pink and gold abstract designs, and looked quite new. "I feel there is a lot you are not saying," Charles said.

"Not everything is fit for Miss Hogarth's ears, Mr. Dickens. All I can say is that I do not believe Miss Lugoson succumbed to entirely natural causes."

"Murder," Miss Hogarth pronounced with a defiant air.

Mrs. Decker did not respond, just made a humming sort of noise.

"I had better return you to your mother," Charles said to Miss Hogarth after a minute of silence.

Miss Hogarth and Mrs. Decker both nodded their agreement, and not five minutes later they were back on the street, some ten minutes' walk from the Hogarths' home.

"The situation becomes blacker," Charles said, peering up at the clouds, which had similarly blackened.

"No one seems to doubt that Miss Lugoson met a bad end, but for so many possible reasons," Miss Hogarth exclaimed, rubbing her mitten-clad hands together. "It is difficult to wrap one's mind around all the possibilities."

Featherlight, he clasped his hands around hers. "Our next step is to see Lady Lugoson again tomorrow, though now we have to view her as a suspect as well."

She pulled her hands away with an admonishing stare into

his eyes. "What time will you come? I will have to make arrangements with Mother."

"Late morning, I hope." Charles let his hands drop to his sides, but stepped closer, until his breath puffed on her cheek. "Do you look forward to seeing me?"

"Of course, Mr. Dickens." Her head lifted. "And what other plans do you have?"

"I have to attend the theater tonight but no meetings are on my schedule for tomorrow. However, I have a great deal of work to do. I will make my mark."

She nodded thoughtfully and began to walk again. They stopped on the street in front of the path to her door. "I have enjoyed this, in a strange way," she said, turning to him.

He smiled at her. "I am glad you could come with me."

She nodded. "Until tomorrow."

He watched the neat figure trot up the path to her door, and saw the light shine through the entryway when another girl opened it to welcome her sister. A cozy home. He would have a similar establishment one day, and he and his family would be regularly received in homes like these.

Charles walked to Brompton directly from the cobbler the next morning, as he was quickly wearing out his shoes with all these trips to Fulham Road. He collected his smiling Miss Hogarth, still very well aware of the honor of her parents' trust in him and her willingness to let him pursue her. They walked across the apple orchard to the baroness's house.

"I feel increasingly strange about this," Miss Hogarth confessed. "After yesterday's conversation."

His side clenched. Had she decided she didn't want to be courted? "In what way?"

"It had never occurred to me to treat Miss Lugoson's own family as potential murderers," she said. "Yet, who is more likely to poison than an intimate?"

He felt a sinking in his knees, from the sheer relief that she had only referred to their quest. "Yet, Lady Lugoson could have argued against us treating her daughter's death as suspicious. She could have barred us from her door," Charles said. "There is no way to know."

"Unless someone confesses," Miss Hogarth said somberly. "Do you know why I have agreed to keep paying calls and considering the matter, which after all does not concern me?"

"Why?"

Miss Hogarth stopped walking, and turned to him. "You, Mr. Dickens," she said simply. "It gives me time with you."

Charles looked at her shining face, pink-cheeked from the wind, blond tendrils flying around her shoulders that had come loose from her bonnet, and his heart seemed to expand. He pressed her hand between his. "What a lovely thing to say."

She glanced at a pile of blackened leaves, piled into a depression at the base of one of the trees. "It is very forward of me, but I should like to know you better, and you don't live nearby."

"I am honored by your interest. I feel the same," he said, then realized how close they were to the house already. "I wish we had to go on a longer journey."

"Alas," she said merrily. "We should go around to the front."

Before she could speak again, the French doors along the Lugosons' drawing room opened. He dropped her hand. He could see Lady Lugoson herself gesturing at him.

He and Miss Hogarth walked toward her. At least she wasn't the sort to report on his inappropriate closeness to a young woman.

"Oh, I have such a headache," Lady Lugoson whispered, putting a hand to her head, when they reached her. "I must go upstairs, but I wanted to make you welcome first."

"I am sorry you are unwell, my lady," Miss Hogarth said, frown lines appearing on her forehead.

Charles peered at the older beauty, looking for signs of Miss Lugoson's mortal affliction in her mother. Could Lady Lugoson have been poisoned as well?

Lady Lugoson moaned low in her throat. She'd gone pale. "My maid has my drops. When I am like this sleep is the only solution."

"You have terrible headaches?" Charles asked, concern that she'd been poisoned diminishing.

"For many years now," Lady Lugoson said, pressing her fingers to her temples. "I had a bad fall from a horse about a decade ago."

"Would you like me to ring for your maid?" Miss Hogarth asked, once again proving her essential kindness.

Lady Lugoson moaned again. Charles took her arm, leading her to a sofa, while Miss Hogarth went for the bell.

"Let me tell you," Lady Lugoson said faintly. "That last day, Christiana took breakfast with her brother and me. We paid the call on Mrs. Decker, then she went to tea with her friend Beatrice Carley. She saw the dance master in between."

"Does that account for most of the time?"

The lady closed her eyes. "No. She would have been alone for over an hour or so in the morning, a few hours in the early afternoon. But after that she dressed for my party. I'm sure she was with her maid because she mentioned having to repair the dress she wore that night."

Panch came into the room. Miss Hogarth asked him to fetch Lady Lugoson's maid.

"You will still allow us to spend time in your late husband's library?" Charles asked.

"Why did you want to use it? I don't remember."

"I want to look for herbals, attempt to identify poisons that would fit the situation," Charles explained.

She rubbed along her cheek, as if to dispel some muscular

tightness. "He might have had some volumes. I have no interest in such things, but his mother did. Look for journals, too."

"Thank you. When you're better, I might beg you to contact Mrs. Carley and ask her if Miss Hogarth can see her daughter, Miss Carley?"

Before she could answer, Lady Lugoson's maid came into the room. The woman, of a similar age to Lady Lugoson, made encouraging French noises in the back of her throat as she helped the lady to her feet. She leaned heavily on the maid's arm, reminding Charles of the night her daughter had died. When Panch returned, he told the butler that they had permission to investigate the library.

Panch looked down his nose at Charles, but gestured them to the doorway. They formed a procession up the stairs to the first floor and down a long corridor toward the back of the house. The late Lord Lugoson's library was not the cigar-scented, dark-walled aristocratic male sanctum that Charles had expected. Instead, the windows were large and exposed the vista of the rear garden, little more than green and brown at this time of year. The walls were hung with light blue silk cloth, old-fashioned but beautiful.

"Don't the bindings become sun-damaged?" Charles asked Panch.

"The curtains are drawn unless a member of the household is in the room," he said officiously.

Charles and Miss Hogarth shared a glance. No one had been here and yet the curtains were open. Not that the light was excellent this day.

"Will you require lamps?" Panch asked grudgingly.

"Yes, please," Charles said, moving to the bookshelves closest to the light.

Panch lit two lamps that were on the mantelpiece and then went around the room lighting table lamps. Miss Hogarth went to the opposite end of the room and began to look there. After the butler had departed, she approached Charles with two bound volumes.

"These look promising," she said. "Handwritten."

"A woman's handwriting?" he asked, leaving his finger on the binding he'd reached on the second shelf.

She glanced at them. "No. They must be the wrong ones. I'll keep looking."

"Panch shut the door."

She was still looking at the books. "What?"

"The butler, he shut the door. We're alone in here."

The old journals slipped through her fingers, and landed on the shelf with a thud. "I should—" Her pupils moved from side to side.

"What? Don't you trust me?"

"You brought the matter to my attention," she demurred. "What am I to say if my mother asks? I cannot deny I noticed we were alone."

"So you want to be with me?" he suggested.

She stepped toward him until her face, pore-less and china smooth, was fully in the lamplight. "You know I do, Mr. Dickens, but without some statement of intention to my parents, I will not dabble in impropriety. I am not some actress, or a spoiled, lonely aristocrat."

"No."

She drew herself up to her full, diminutive height. "I am a member of a family privileged to be in the world. I meet people. Father brings them home. Sometimes I even go to his office."

His lips twisted. "I have rivals for your affection?"

"I am saying that you will not be my only choice. If you let me down, there will be others."

"How could I let you down?"

"By talking only of lovemaking, and never of anything else," she said. "I want to know what happened to Miss Lugoson and Miss Rueff. Give me a mystery, Mr. Dickens, and a solution, and I will follow you into places I should not." She gestured around the room, with a significant nod at the door.

The hair on the backs of Charles's forearms had risen during her speech. Here was not just a girl who could make a sweet home, and who would enjoy it, but an inquiring mind. Utterly fascinated, he managed to hold back everything he wanted to say, everything that smacked of romantical banter, and only said, "I hear you, Miss Hogarth. I hear and obey."

After ten minutes of searching at the opposite end of the room from his spirited companion, Charles found a couple of volumes of Culpepper and sat down at a large round table in the center of the room with these old herbals. A globe, perhaps an antique from the age of the Stuarts, rested in the center, but plenty of space existed along the perimeter.

Miss Hogarth appeared at his side some twenty minutes later with a thick journal. "What does Culpepper have to say?"

He glanced up at her, schooling his expression. "Lots of treatments for poison. Haven't found a mention of a poison itself."

"I think this is the right journal." Her dust-and-lemons scent made his nose twitch. "It has the name Mary, Lady Lugoson, inscribed on the flyleaf and the date is about right. 1775."

"Much too early for the current Lady Lugoson to have known her."

"She might have started it then and kept updating it all her life. If Lord Lugoson was much older than our Lady Lugoson, his mother was probably a young woman in 1775."

"True. See if you can read the handwriting."

She opened the book. "It isn't too faded, just dusty."

Charles stood and pulled back the chair next to his. "Please, make yourself comfortable."

She smiled, her gaze still downcast, and sat in the chair. He pushed it closer to the table, then returned to his seat, distracted by the scent of lavender he now discovered in her hair. When he glanced up a couple of minutes later, he saw she was smiling. A more perfect moment could not have been. All they needed were tea and buns.

"Do you like to bake, Miss Hogarth?"

"I like all forms of cookery," she said lightly. "For I like to eat."

He grinned, then turned his head back to his volume.

Miss Hogarth was just saying, some twenty minutes later, "Fascinating diary, but certainly no mention of poison," when the door opened without warning. The gangly form of Lord Lugoson appeared in the doorway.

His slanted nostrils were pinched and had a reddish hue. While he had been dressed in the finest fabrics, inexpert hands had tied his cravat and he had a dusting of fluffy, boyish whiskers on his face. He looked like fifteen trying to be older and failing miserably.

Coming toward them, he pointed at the books. "My mother told me you were here. Why are you reading about poison?" he asked, and then turned down his mouth in a fair imitation of a turtle.

"We aren't, my lord," Charles explained. "We were trying to read about it, however."

The lordling pulled out an inlaid enamel snuffbox and opened it. The medallion portrait in the center appeared to be the actress Sarah Siddons.

As he took a pinch of snuff, Charles said, "That must be from the same era as this journal. Was Mary your grandmother?"

Miss Hogarth closed the journal so Lord Lugoson could see the cover. He sneezed dramatically, not bothering to cover his nose with a handkerchief, spraying the journal and Miss Hogarth's hand with the contents of his nose.

"That is what I think of my family," he said dramatically, before turning on his heel and stomping through the room.

"Come back, please, my lord," Miss Hogarth called. She set down the journal and pulled a handkerchief from a hidden pocket in her skirt.

Lord Lugoson hesitated at the doorway. "Why? No one ever wants to speak to me. Just come to pay court to Mother. Expect he wants to marry her." His stare reminded Charles of the butler, Panch.

*Good Lord.* Surely *Panch* wasn't Lord Lugoson's father?

"I'm a bit young for your mother, no matter how beautiful she is," Charles demurred. "No title, either, I'm afraid."

"My sister used to pour over Debrett's," he said in a scathing tone. "Planning for her time in the marriage market."

"Isn't that a good thing to do?" Miss Hogarth asked as Charles wondered why Miss Lugoson would do that if she were secretly engaged.

"As if she was worthy," he sneered.

"Why do you say that?"

"Common," the boy spat. "Just as common as Aunt Angela."

"You didn't like her because of what she had in common with your aunt?" Miss Hogarth asked. "If your sister was looking for a husband, surely she wasn't truly about to become an actress."

The boy's hands went to his hair. He pulled at the blond locks, disordering them mightily, then stormed from the room.

"My stars," Miss Hogarth said. "He obviously didn't like his sister."

"Or whatever she was," Charles said. His suspicions about Miss Lugoson's parentage increased. Lord Lugoson seemed to know something, despite his tender years. The air of despair troubled him.

"What do you mean, Mr. Dickens?"

"The details are rather lurid," Charles admitted.

"Oh?" Miss Hogarth closed the library door and took her seat next to Charles. "You must tell me, otherwise I might miss something important."

"Your mother might disagree."

"Father wouldn't and ye work for him. Besides, ye already know I want to be engaged in the mystery."

"Well played." Charles leaned close, amused by the Scottish that had turned up in her usually careful speech. "You are your father's daughter. Rumor has it that Miss Lugoson could actually be Angela Acton's daughter, father unknown."

"Oh, my," Miss Hogarth breathed.

"Too scandalous for you?"

She tossed her head. "Not at all."

He cleared his throat. "Apparently, no one believed Lady Lugoson was expecting. One of those situations where a lady went away for a time, then returned with a baby that no one knew was coming."

Miss Hogarth's hands went to her scarlet cheeks. "Why? Why would Lord Lugoson have wanted that?"

"As he is deceased, we shall never know."

"I suppose fashionable people don't think as respectably as we do," Miss Hogarth said. "The mere idea of passing off my sister's child as my own. I would never."

"I am sorry to put such indelicate thoughts in your head."

"Oh, don't worry about that." She dismissed the thought with a wave. "I've assisted at my mother's lyings-in. And I'm coming to the time of life when such things will be my world as well. It's the deceit that troubles me."

"If indeed it happened," Charles cautioned.

"The young lord and Miss Lugoson did look so much alike, but if they are cousins it stands to reason."

"I did not have the impression that any other mother was suspected," Charles said. He set Culpepper aside and went back to the shelves for more fruitless searching.

Miss Hogarth shivered. "I don't like this house. Ours is so pleasant, so homey and fun."

And untidy, compared to the austerity of Lugoson House. It did not truly feel peopled, unlike the rambunctious Hogarth abode. "I will take you home. I glanced over all the shelves and did not find much. If the poisoner comes from here, I doubt they found any ideas in the library."

"Unless those volumes have been removed."

He tapped his finger alongside his nose. "Now you are thinking like a villain, my dear Miss Hogarth, but for now, I think we are done here."

# Chapter 13

After Charles returned Miss Hogarth to the care of her mother and arrived home himself, he felt too restless to stay in his rooms, scratching away at his sketches while Fred attempted to memorize some of Lord Byron's poetry. Charles went to see William Aga, in order to take his tormenting thoughts off Kate Hogarth and the sensual fire in her eyes when she'd demanded her amusement. In his sitting room, William was whittling a piece of driftwood cast up by the Thames into an obscene bust.

"Ach. You made me cut off a nipple," William cried, shaking his fist at Charles. He set down his knife and patted the breast of his carving.

"You'll have to take them down a size and re-create," Charles said.

"Where is the fun in that?" William pushed back his chair. "We can always find another piece of wood. What do you say? A mudlark evening?"

"By all means," Charles agreed. "Low tide should be around midnight. We won't be able to see anything, mind."

"I just want a piece of wood thick as my leg," William said. "Don't need to see much for that."

"Change your clothes," Charles suggested. "I'm in my oldest rags but you still have the whiff of journalist about you."

"Very well, maestro." William stood and pointed at a small table by the door, where he tossed his key and mail. "I finally acquired those articles for you about Marie Rueff. Bring them to the lamp and take a look while I refresh my wardrobe."

Charles yawned as he sat down with the yellowing newspapers. He'd be better off with a cup of coffee than reading material. He scanned through the articles. Words jumped out at him like *Fontainebleau*, *poison*, *age seventeen*.

"Find anything?" William asked, coming back into the room as he knotted a thick muffler around his neck.

"Yes," Charles said, forcing his jaw closed around another yawn. "Very suspicious. Much to consider."

"A walk shall clear our heads."

"I agree." Charles put his hat back on.

They went out into the darkened court and moved toward the street. Most of the lights were out in surrounding buildings. Even the watermen for the stagecoach stop had found their beds at this hour. They headed south toward Fleet Street, then south again, to the worksite that was Blackfriars Bridge.

"I wonder when they will give it up," Charles said, staring at the old Portland stone bridge with its eight stone arches. Wooden structures were built around the base of the closest pilings, ready to reinforce the old wood. Out on the river, a wherry passed underneath one of the central arches, lanterns dappling the water as it sliced through the river.

"Devil it," William swore, and moved his boot. "Foot went right through an icy patch."

"Spring must be coming," Charles joked. "But I don't see how we're going to find a good piece of wood for your new lady in all this muck."

Dark shapes moved from behind the closest piles. He counted four of them, all smaller than the two men, stick figures dressed in rags. Friends or foes?

William pulled his boot from the puddle and went toward them, fearless, holding up his lantern to his face. "It's me, lads."

"Old William," called a girl.

"Give us sixpence," begged another.

"Or a shilling," suggested the third, cocky as a rooster.

Charles moved behind William, ready to block any attempts at pickpocketing.

"These are proper men of business," William said, glancing back at him, amused. "My mudlark friends. Little Ollie, Poor John, Lucy Fair, and Brother Second."

The boys, ranging from the size of a five-year-old to an eight-year-old but probably older, nodded solemnly at him in turn, little more than shining eyes in the moonlight. The girl, whom he judged to be the mother hen of the group at about twelve, curtsied with grave dignity.

Charles crossed his arms and rubbed his gloves down his coat, feeling chilled, perhaps in sympathy for their less than adequate clothing. Lucy Fair had a ragged shawl, but the boys only had thin jackets. They must be used to being wet all the time, but January was such a cruel month. "How do you know these fine gentlemen and lady?"

"They learn all kinds of interesting tidbits," William said. "Why, there isn't a drowning victim or a suicide that escapes their notice."

"We finds the bodies," said little Ollie, exposing his missing front teeth.

"Good pickings," said the oldest boy, Poor John. Cold breath wreathed his bare head when he spoke.

"I want another proper piece of wood," William said. "Have you saved me a good one?"

"It will cost you a shilling," Brother Second said, holding out his hand.

"I'll see it first," William said jovially, but his eyes belied his air of trust.

Brother Second nodded to Little Ollie and he dashed back to the pilings, his holey boots trailing water. Charles saw something glinting a foot ahead in the muck and stepped carefully around an icy patch.

"Wot is it?" asked Lucy Fair, following him.

These sharp-eyed children weren't going to let anyone take their treasures away. Charles didn't blame them, but he still bent down and pulled his glove off and stuck his hand straight into the muck. His fingers found a sharp point and a long rectangle of something hanging off it.

With a squelching sound, the item came free. Ignoring the girl's protest, he moved closer to a puddle that was too large to be completely frozen over and dipped the item in, before reaching in his pocket for a handkerchief. He set the item in it, then began to clean it off.

"Silver," the slim girl said, ducking under his elbow. "Not completely tarnished."

"I must have seen a stray corner," he said, exposing a lady's comb, or what remained of it, as some of the tines were missing. A long, tarnished rectangle of silver centered the piece, with a fancy feather detail floating off the top. "An attractive piece."

"Worth a bit," the girl said bitterly. "And you the one to find it, lucky devil."

He could see a streak of dirt on her face as the moon passed out of a cloud. She had round cheekbones that seemed too large for her face and chapped lips. Her hair was knotted into a braid flung over her shoulder on top of her shawl, and tied at the bottom with a piece of unbraided rope.

"Might be a piece of history," Charles said.

"Oh, that. It's no older than me mother." She flipped her braid to the other shoulder.

"I'll make a bargain with you," Charles said. "I'll give this to you, but only if you promise to treat me the way you do William. We work together, you see, at the newspaper."

"You want us to tell you things before we tell him?" she said, eyeing him.

"No, but I want to be safe when I'm down here, and have my questions answered fairly when I ask them. Do we have a bargain?" He held out his chilled, bare hand, muck-free courtesy of the puddle.

She nodded. "I'll tell the others."

"Here you go, then." He handed her the silver comb.

She broke into motion, running toward the boys, her braid flying behind her, a rare moment of childish exuberance.

By the time Charles had stretched his glove over his aching, damp fingers and returned to the little group, William had obtained a nice stout column of oak, about two feet long.

"A good prize," Charles observed.

"I want to get this home to dry," William said. He inclined his head. "Gentlemen."

The boys didn't take much notice of them, too excited by Charles's find. He detailed it to William as they walked away.

"Must have been pulled out of some lady's hair by the wind," William said.

"No one goes out on the river without covering their head," Charles said. "Maybe it fell out of the hair of a suicide."

"You should write fiction," William said, clapping him on the shoulder.

"I don't know when I would find the time," Charles said, as they found the street again. "But I'm sure there will be quite a tale in Christiana Lugoson's death, whenever I get to the bottom of it."

"Did my Marie Rueff articles make you any more certain about your theories?"

"Her father came here from Fontainebleau, where the Lugosons lived as well," Charles said. "I didn't read the details of her death yet."

"Do you think the poison came from France?"

"If so, why did she survive four months after coming here? What triggered the murder? I'm only just coming to terms with the idea that Lady Lugoson or her unpleasant son may have had a part to play in her death."

"You can get arsenic easily enough. Any rat catcher or apothecary would have it."

"The symptoms don't match arsenic poisoning," Charles said, as their strides quickly ate up the short distance back to the inn. "What other options are there?"

"Anyone who had a garden could grow many poisonous substances," William suggested, his breath blowing smoky plumes into the chilly air.

"The Lugosons have one, but most people in Brompton would as well. Anyone who knew plants could probably find what they needed in a graveyard." Both girls had attended St. Luke's.

"Or even a park. What will you do now?"

"I need to speak to her dear friend. Try to get to the truth of her supposed romance." Charles still wasn't sure about that. Miss Lugoson seemed a contradictory creature.

"Ah, romance. Not enough of that in my life lately." William sighed.

"A wooden breast is not the same as a real one."

"Very true."

They turned left on Fleet Street and walked toward St. Dunstan-in-the-West, the recently finished church rebuilt on the graveyard of the medieval structure.

"My romancer friend," Charles teased. "Why don't you attempt to work your wiles on Beatrice Carley? Not a pretty girl, but her father is an MP."

"Wealthy?" William inquired.

"Hard to say. I found their London house to be run-down, but they also own a home in Brompton."

"Far above my touch."

"Clearly, but if her friend was willing to be romanced by a French dance master, who can say what mischief Miss Carley may accept? Still, her mother is a dragon."

William made an amused noise. "Not like the Hogarths."

Charles drew himself up. There were no finer people than the Hogarths. "Not at all. Miss Hogarth has been trusted into my care a couple of times now."

"I believe you shall wear the romancer's cornet now. Have you kissed her?"

Charles shook his head. "But she has touched me. You know, those little touches, on my arm, my hand and such."

William hummed in singsong fashion. "She likes you."

"I think she does. But also, she likes our endeavor. She's quite captivated by our hunt for her neighbor's killer."

"It's hard for women. If they have brains how do they get to use them?"

"By teaching others. Running a pleasant, comforting home," Charles said promptly. "Not as simple as it seems, to run a household on a budget."

Ahead of them, alongside the neo-Gothic façade of the new church, they saw a trio of women pass under a streetlight. One of them dropped her shawl to her shoulders, exposing a flash of red before rearranging it over her hair again. The other two women crossed the street, carrying baskets.

"They look much too respectable to be out at this hour," William observed.

Charles had stopped, as the third woman, shorter than the

others, turned around. Moonlight shone down on her, exposing features he recognized. "Julie Saville."

"Who?" William asked, peering into the streetlight.

"The actress. Remember her? From *Richard III*?"

"Ah yes, the pretty one."

Julie came toward them, almost passing, but then she saw Charles and stopped. "You are out late, sirs."

"As are you," Charles answered. "Quite a way from the Garrick."

"It happens," she said saucily. "When you work for a manager it is hard to find time to rest."

"I thought you worked for Miss Acton."

"It is the same thing."

"Then, what business would Percy Chalke have at a church?"

"Never you mind."

Irritated at her superior manner, Charles poked into her basket, and pulled out a handful of bright silk skeins. "Smuggled?"

Julie tugged them out of his unresisting hand and stuffed them back into her basket. "I do what I'm asked. I'm taking them to a weaver."

"Aren't you ever allowed to sleep?" William asked.

She grinned. "I'll sleep when I'm dead. For now, I need to earn my bread."

"You're a lively one, girl," William said. "If you ever need a place to nap, come see me at Furnival's Inn."

Charles pulled his friend away from the laughing girl. "Speaking of beds, let us find our own. I think I'm finally weary enough to sleep."

At his desk at the *Chronicle* the next afternoon, Charles went through the stack of mail the postboy had placed on the edge of his desk. He hoped to hear from Lady Lugoson, if her headache had cleared enough for her to function, but instead, he found a note from Mrs. Carley. Had Lady Lugoson convinced her to let him see her daughter, Miss Carley?

He pulled the sealing wax away and opened it. "Blasted woman."

"What?" William asked, coming over to lean against his desk.

"Mrs. Carley claims Beatrice is ill and can't be seen."

"Do you believe it?"

"I would imagine she was prostrate with grief in the immediate aftermath of Miss Lugoson's death, but it's been over two weeks now. Lady Lugoson did as asked and still the mama bear refuses me access."

"Does Miss Carley have a weak chest? Illness is rampant at this cold time of year."

"I have no idea." Charles flourished the letter. "It is obvious from this note that Lady Lugoson did do as we asked. In fact, she must have sent her request yesterday. But she cannot budge Mrs. Carley. I have no greater weapon."

"There is Lady Holland."

"A peripheral figure," Charles said. "I have half a mind to some subterfuge."

"Oh?"

Charles winked. "What could we do with Julie Saville?"

"She could sneak in as a housemaid, swinging those saucy hips of hers."

"Or claim to be a friend, come to call. She's the right age."

"She played a queen," William said. "And all that hair." He mimed combing through it. "I wonder if she's as fiery below."

"Come to the theater with me tonight," Charles said impulsively, ignoring the crude question. "We can challenge her to find a way to get to Beatrice. Miss Lugoson was supposedly her friend, after all. She's bound to want to help."

"What's on the playbill?" William said, folding his arms.

Charles laughed. "Quit playing hard-to-catch, you rogue. I know you want another look at her."

Accordingly, they met at the Garrick Theater that evening. The Garrick wasn't one of those theaters that did a long run of a popular show. Instead, they had several rotating amusements. Even their pantomime was still running, though according to the bill pasted to the low stone wall down the street, it was to be finished at the end of the month, until Christmastime came again.

"Panto tonight?" William complained. "We won't even be able to see Julie amidst all the spectacle."

"I don't know how much spectacle Percy Chalke can afford, if he's going to smugglers for supplies," Charles said. "It isn't fifty years ago. Who goes in for smuggling these days?"

"It's still rampant in Kent, my lad," William said. "You have a lot to learn."

"I'll have to go there and investigate myself," Charles said, out of curiosity. "Let's see if we can make it through another night at the Garrick."

The grand spectacle amused the audience wholeheartedly. Percy Chalke had spared no expense, as it happened. He and Angela Acton played Harlequin and Columbine, the star-crossed lovers, and in yet another age-traded role against Miss Acton, Julie Saville played the fairy godmother. Charles noticed William's gaze was glued to the stage during the girl's lithe acrobatic feats. He knew what delights his friend imagined.

"Glorious," William gushed, when the performance had ended. "Takes me back to my childhood."

"The theater was only three-quarters full."

"Panto is on the decline," William said, "but when done like that I remember how popular it was. My father took me to the Covent Garden theater as a child, to see Grimaldi play."

"That must have been quite a show. I have no idea who played the Clown tonight."

"My eyes were only for Miss Saville," William confessed.

They left the theater and went to the backstage door. A cluster of men were grouped around it, hoping for a chance of making one of the chorus girls their own, but Charles and William used their newspaper credentials to get past the door manager. They found Julie backstage, still in her fairy godmother gown, though she'd taken off her stage makeup. Thankfully, there was no sign of Percy Chalke.

"You again?" she said. "Looking for Miss Acton?"

"Wanted to see you," William said, his voice muffled.

Charles glanced at his worldly friend to see the man was blushing. He mentally brushed away Julie's worldly indifference. "Can you play an upper-class girl?" he asked brusquely.

"Why?" Julie brushed at her net skirt overlay. A sequin fell to the floor, the glitter extinguished.

"I've had no luck speaking to Miss Lugoson's friend Beatrice Carley," Charles explained.

Julie lifted her eyebrow and pursed her lips slightly. The mere slant of her head changed something indefinable. Charles forgot about the silly old-fashioned dress, the red hair.

"How do you do this evening?" she asked.

"You're imitating Lady Lugoson," Charles snapped. "Obviously, you know her."

Julie inclined her chin gracefully, a tiny movement. Her face seemed thinner, more refined. Sucking in her cheeks, perhaps. Charles was fascinated by performers. He'd wanted to be one himself before he found himself in a well-paid position as a journalist.

Before their eyes, Julie's wide mouth transformed with a grin. She laughed merrily, and William clapped.

The deceptive creature might be useful to further their search for the truth about Christiana Lugoson.

As William ceased his clapping, and Julie's laugh died away, Charles saw Angela Acton approach. With Percy Chalke nowhere in sight backstage, would Lady Lugoson's sister finally speak to him?

The actress still wore her white shepherdess costume and full stage makeup, though her towering wig had disappeared. Red paint smeared her lips, adding a curved bow to her thin upper lip, and circles of rouge dotted her cheeks. Underneath lay a pallor that couldn't be denied.

"An epic performance," Charles said with enthusiasm, shifting on the worn floorboards. "Bravo."

Miss Acton stopped next to Julie. "Are these your friends?"

"I am Charles Dickens from the *Morning Chronicle* and this is my colleague William Aga," Charles said, finding it hard to believe she didn't know of them when they knew so much about her.

"If you were here to review our performance you'd have come a month ago," she said in a languid voice.

The gaslight did not quite illuminate enough for Charles to see her eyes, but he suspected her pupils would be pinpricks. She had the air of a laudanum drinker. Had Julie and Percy Chalke not told her anything, or had she forgotten?

"We are here upon a mission from your sister," Charles said.

"Is she hoping to have me admit to strangers that Christiana was my daughter?" Miss Action said with a strange laugh.

William's mouth dropped open as Julie made an inarticulate noise. Charles asked, "Was she?"

Miss Acton's head lowered in a nod, then rose again, her expression one of quiet anguish. "If you are Mr. Dickens, then you were there for her last moments in this world."

"I was," he agreed, satisfied that she knew his role.

"Was her suffering as bad as my sister claims?"

"I cannot lie to you," Charles said. "I am sure Lady Lugoson told the truth. But her pain was not continuous."

Her voice dropped to a whisper. "Did she ask for me?"

"Not in a way I would recognize," he said. "But I did not know the story then."

She let out a very long sigh, as if a snake hissed. "I refuse to believe my daughter was murdered."

"On what basis?"

She clasped her hands prayerfully. "She was a child. An innocent child."

Charles's gaze slid to Julie as Miss Acton made her statement. Julie's attention had focused on William. They seemed to be communicating without words. "Then you don't believe she had any inappropriate relationships with men, like her dance master or others?"

"I have complete faith in my sister," Miss Acton whispered. "I must. I cannot bear it, otherwise."

"I am sorry for your loss," Charles said formally.

"Why must my sister persist in this delusion?" Miss Acton asked. "Christiana must not have been murdered." Her tortured eyes filled with tears.

One sister was deluded, but which one? "Did you know Jacques Rueff or his daughter, Marie? He came from Fontainebleau, and his daughter died on Epiphany night, 1834."

Her hands went to her cheeks, a gesture reminiscent of her sister. "In the same manner?"

"Yes."

She licked her lips. "I did not hear the details."

A number of the *Evening Chronicle* staff members were still at the office late the next night. Charles, mindful that he had yet to host a dinner for the group, impulsively invited the men to dine at Furnival's Inn. William ducked into a wine shop for him on the walk and he chose a roast from a cook shop. The merry group settled around Charles's deal table, teasing Fred, the youngest in the room, while William and a couple of their friends went to fetch all of his chairs.

Ten minutes later, Charles held his newly purchased knife over the roast and sliced away. "The food may be nothing special, but I have a bottle of truly exceptional claret," he announced to the cheer of the half dozen men.

"But he won't let me have any," Fred groused, inciting more laughter.

After they had eaten their meager repast, Mr. Hogarth opened his instrument case and pulled out a violin. William improvised some lyrics to sing along while a couple of the others clapped their hands and Fred danced a hornpipe with a solicitor who lived across the hall.

Charles watched the merry group, drinking steadily from his claret cup. John Black, the *Morning Chronicle*'s editor, about the same age as Mr. Hogarth, sat down next to him, twin cup in hand. "You've made fast friends with this group of blackguards after only a few months," he observed.

"We roam so much, chasing after political speeches, that it is nice to find everyone at home in London."

"How are your sketches coming along?"

"Very well, thank you. I cannot tell you how sincerely I appreciate the opportunities you have provided me. Why, I was just thinking I now made enough to support a wife." He emptied his cup.

"Marriage is a difficult undertaking," Black warned. "You may have heard of my marital disaster."

"You married a friend's mistress, did you not?" He winced. Drink had lowered his caution.

The editor was cup-shot enough not to mind. "To my shame. Dreadful woman. Never make a decision based on lust," the editor advised. "She's done nothing but demand money since."

Meanwhile, Charles knew, Black supported yet another

woman, along with his wife and child. But he still managed to find the money to be known as one of the largest book collectors in the industry.

"Where does your family come from?" he asked, curious about this complex man.

"Up north. Simple farm people, were Ebenezer and Janet, my parents. They all died when I was young, and I was taken up by my uncle, no better educated or employed than they were."

"How did you escape the drudgery?" Charles asked.

"I see you in myself," Black told him. "My uncle gave me a bit of education, and opportunities to work with my mind, instead of just my back, but mostly I read."

"I have wondered what might have become of me, without my father's library," Charles said.

"Ebenezer Black had no such thing," Black said. "But the local subscription library was my dearest friend. I owe a great deal to my uncle." He fell silent.

Charles refilled both their glasses, as Mr. Hogarth shifted from "Maggie Lauder" to a less lively air, "Loch Lomond." The mood darkened as John Black began to sing.

Charles sniffed back emotion as Black reached the part in the song about true loves never meeting again. He saw his brother had tears running down his face. Who had Christiana Lugoson been in love with, and was the man mourning her now in secret?

He could stand it no more and held up his hand imploringly, until Mr. Hogarth set down his bow and drew attention to Charles in his chair.

"No wee birdies for you?" Black asked.

"Your song reminded me that there might be a man out there who loved a girl who died in front of me," Charles said feelingly. He stood up, setting his cup on the table, and went to stand next to the fire. "I pose a question to all of you, gentle-men."

His dramatic pause caused even William to set down his cup and center his attention on Charles's face.

"Was Christiana Lugoson murdered or not?" Charles asked the group.

"What have ye learned?" asked Mr. Hogarth.

"That she was an actress's daughter, not a lady's. That she died in the same manner as a girl whose father came from the same village in France where she once resided. That her brother hated her. If he truly was her brother, even a half brother. That she may have had a lover." Charles paused for breath.

"Then what is the verdict?" asked Black.

"That anything might be going on behind the gilded doors of the aristocracy," called one of the senior *Chronicle* men.

"It's all about the money for them," said the solicitor. "Follow the money."

"The girl was supposedly a great heiress," Charles said.

"What about the other dead girl?" asked the solicitor.

"Good question," William said. "I remember she had a dowry."

"I did read that," Charles said. "Her fortune went to a French cousin."

"There you go," said the senior journalist.

"I can't chase these deaths to France," Charles said. "Besides, they occurred here, and the only French person I've met in the course of following this story was the dance master, who is an unlikely candidate for lover."

"Was he the other dead girl's dance master?" Thomas Pillar asked.

William chuckled. "Good question. Blame the Frenchman, whenever possible."

"What is our verdict?" Charles asked. "Am I wasting my time?"

"Inconclusive," said John Black. "But certainly something is rotten in the Lugoson family."

"Who receives Christiana's money? Does it return to France?" Mr. Hogarth asked.

"It was Acton money, and Lord Lugoson's personal fortune," Charles said. "So I shouldn't think so."

The men lost interest at that, and returned to drinking and discussing the general election presently being polled. There was still most of a week to go before the final poll. Fred yawned in the corner, ready to fall asleep now that the music was done.

Charles took the empty platter that had held the meat and placed it in his washbasin, then, with Fred's help, returned for plates and a few stray cups. Mr. Hogarth met him on his return journey to the parlor.

"I need to ask ye something, Charles," said the older man.

"Anything," Charles said, thinking it was about one of his sketches.

"What are yer intentions toward my daughter?"

"What is your concern?" Charles countered.

"We have given ye a great deal of latitude to pay calls with her in the neighborhood, but ye must remember ye are pursuing a possible murderer. Mrs. Hogarth has expressed a concern for Kate's safety."

"I am certain I can keep Miss Hogarth safe." He paused. "Though admittedly, the secrets we are uncovering are not always appropriate for a young lady's ears."

"Should I forbid her to continue paying calls with ye?"

"Until we know for sure what happened, I cannot be easy in my mind about the fate of other young girls in Brompton," Charles said. "Most assuredly there is a tie to France here, but all the money does not go to France. If we follow the money?"

Mr. Hogarth nodded. "It goes to relations. My Kate does not come with the money of an aristocrat."

"No, but she comes with a good mind, a stout heart, and the best of connections," Charles said with feeling. "I would keep her safe by solving this mystery."

"I'm not worried about her being hurt by this amorphous murderer," Mr. Hogarth said. "But I am worried about the expectations that may grow where ye are concerned. All this talk of a wife, Charles. I have faith in yer talents, but ye've only had a steady income for a few months. If the evening paper fails, ye'll be back to yer old salary."

"I will not fail," Charles said, staring his mentor in the eye. "You can count on me."

Mr. Hogarth nodded. "I well believe it, as I must, but ye must promise me that ye will treat my daughter's heart with tenderness, and not make promises that are less than disinterested."

"Her well-being is paramount to me," Charles promised. "I assure you I have been everything that is proper in my dealings with her."

"Very well then. Shall we call it a night? There are a great many speeches to attend on the morrow."

"Yes," Charles agreed, though as the claret wore off he could feel himself coming back to life. This would be a night for one of his rambles, yet again.

After everyone had left, Charles sat next to the freshly stoked fire to fully read William's stories about Marie Rueff for the first time. Fred clattered away at the washbasin in the other room, cleaning up the rest of the dishes.

The first story featured more about Miss Rueff's father and his business interests in Jamaica. It seemed that her French father had married an English sugar plantation heiress. The mother, long dead, had left a substantial fortune for the daughter. She'd grown up as a grand heiress, but then the Baptist War had hit their plantation hard. Though the slaves hadn't been emancipated until after Miss Rueff had died last year, their plantation had essentially been destroyed three years before. The fortune had been used to restore the plantation, leaving the girl essentially penniless and the father still in possession of his late wife's lands. These French relations would not have received much.

Charles turned to the second article. William had continued investigating, obviously concerned by some aspect of the story. He'd discovered that Jacques Rueff had a fiancée. Had she wanted the girl dead so that her future children would inherit everything that the family had left?

Monsieur Rueff himself appeared to be a murky figure, rising out of France to marry an heiress, but no hint of a previous profession existed in the articles.

Charles read the description of Miss Rueff's death carefully. Described by her maid to William, it sounded exactly the same as Miss Lugoson's end. The maid wasn't named, but William might remember her. Her words about her mistress seemed tender and genuine.

Charles set down the papers and dropped his chin into his hand. Marie Rueff had lost most of her fortune, but was still her father's heir. Christiana Lugoson, a double heiress, through both her mother's family, and her supposed father's. In the Rueff case, the father seemed to have taken her fortune to advance the family's business interests. In the Lugoson case, the family may have wanted the money back in the control of the male heir.

Could Jacques Rueff or his fiancée have trained Lord or Lady Lugoson on the means they had used to kill Miss Rueff?

Charles stood, a little unsteady on his feet, and stirred the fire. Fred came out of the kitchen, wiping his reddened hands on a towel.

"Going to bed?" Charles asked.

A yawn split his face. "Yes. You?"

"Taking a walk. I need to order my thoughts."

"Bitter night." Fred pointed at the ice forming outside the window.

"I never mind that," Charles said. "I'll bundle up warmly."

Fred blinked in his wake while he fetched sturdy shoes, thick coat, muffler, and gloves.

"See, I'll even cover my nose," Charles said, but Fred had gone bleary-eyed. "Go to bed," he instructed, opening the door.

He walked into the crisp air. Wind blew, seemingly right through him, but no rain or snow marred his way. All was gray and black and dreary, just like the state of his mind, filling in the blanks of William's prose about the Jamaican slave revolts and Marie Rueff's final hours.

He walked toward Gray's Inn, thinking to suit his mood to damp grass and leafless trees. Treading the paths there, he could free his mind and imagine himself, however improbably, out in the countryside if he narrowed his vision.

As he walked north, his footsteps made squelching noises on the pavement. The city, never entirely silent, seemed sleepier than usual, the thick clouds overhead dampening the sound. Ahead, a fat tomcat paraded past him, followed by a thin dog, unlikely friends. At least he didn't see any children about. They were always the hardest sight, ragged little beggars, attempting to survive the cold.

He heard sharper footsteps, behind him now. Some lawyer, going back to his rooms after a night's revelry? But the shoe impressions didn't seem heavy enough to be a man's.

Walking faster to stay warm, he turned left, ancient buildings hovering on either side, keeping silent secrets in the night. Behind him, the steps continued, matching his pace. He didn't like the feeling of being followed in the dark. Clouds moved swiftly, covering and uncovering the moon, and the gaslight only offered yellow pools around their lamp bases.

A narrow opening, the entrance to some Georgian building, offered a solution. He ducked in, waiting for the other night-time trespasser to pass.

# Chapter 14

Twenty seconds later, a figure passed, hesitating in the doorway. He saw a slim body under a voluminous, tattered cloak, a shawl wrapped over the head.

"Julie?" he called, recognizing her. "Are you following me?"

"Mr. Dickens," she said, pulling off her shawl so that he could catch a glimpse of red hair in the moonlight.

"What do you want?" he asked.

"I was coming to your door, but then I saw you leave."

Her expression indicated she saw nothing out of the norm about her behavior, but he found it very odd. "You behave like a spy."

"I was curious about where you were going."

"Curiosity killed the cat."

She stepped closer to him. "Yes, but at least the cat found out the truth."

"What do you want?" he repeated as he stepped out of the dark space.

She huddled against one side of the entryway, and pulled up the shawl again, tucking the edges into her cloak. "Mr. Chalke wants to see you."

"In the middle of the night?"

"The theater is quiet, and you never seem to sleep."

"What bad thoughts are keeping Mr. Chalke awake tonight?"

"You'll have to ask him," she said solemnly. "Will you come to the Garrick with me?"

He thought of Kate Hogarth, their walks through the daylight, pursuing murder with teatime calls and plates of seedcake. Then arrived this girl in the night, all cold, frost-breath and eyes burning from a face just a little too thin.

"Of course I'll go with you, but I wish he'd let you sleep," he said, suddenly feeling cross, and restless.

"Are you drunk?" she asked.

"Not very." His toes, chilled and blocky, demanded movement. He took one step, then another, heading onto a grassy space, dotted with large trees.

Julie followed him. "You, Charles Dickens, need a wife to put you warmly to bed, instead of sending yourself into the streets to do ever more thinking. It is bad for your constitution."

"I thank you not to concern yourself with me," he snapped.

She drew back. "I'm only concerned. You will burn out. I can see it in your eyes."

"I have ambitions that cannot be bound solely to the daylight," he said stiffly.

"Yet, unlike me, you have a position that pays well, in the daylight. No one sends you out on moonlight errands."

"You didn't have to follow me," Charles said, moving under a tree as two men passed on the dirt path, one humming a rowdy tune. "You are playing a game in your own head, wandering behind me, attempting to frighten me. You should have been honest, stopped me right at the hitching posts."

She stepped closer to him. He smelled onions and greasepaint. "But where would be the fun in that?"

"You chase dramatics like a fool."

"Don't be harsh, Mr. Dickens." Her voice had lowered to a purr. She lifted her hand, gracefully, like a siren.

He glanced away. He would not be moved. "Miss Acton should be more of a mother to you. You are of tender years, yet."

"She is even less motherly than her sister," Julie said with a bitter laugh. "Oh, yes. Think about that while I take you to Mr. Chalke."

Charles turned away. He saw a glint out of the corner of his eye, despite the lack of gas lamps nearby. But the moon had picked something out. He bent down, seeing the edge of something next to an exposed tree root. Taking off his glove, he dug in the dirt with one finger, until he pulled out a lump.

"What is it?" Julie asked.

He rubbed the lump against damp, mushy grass until the shape emerged. "An old coin."

"How old?"

"I won't know until I can get it in the light. People have lived in this area for six hundred years or more."

"It's hard to imagine. Our lives are so small in comparison." Her breath warmed his cheek as she tried to look at the coin.

"They aren't," Charles said, rising. "We have a duty to ourselves, and to those shoulders we stand on, to make life better." He tucked the coin into his pocket and pointed to the path.

"I've never had much interest in history."

"You perform Shakespeare. Surely you want to know what is behind the plays."

She shrugged. "I just like the attention from the pit. That tells me what is worthy. It doesn't matter what the ancient story is behind the words."

Charles wanted to be baffled by her attitude, but he knew far too many people thought much the same. If his sketches, or the plays he wanted to write, made some feel differently, he would consider his time well spent.

They passed a corner gin shop. The old seventeenth-century

building that had stood on the corner had been pulled down, something that had perhaps been there when Shakespeare's plays had first been performed, and instead, the new shop was all light and large windows and imposing signs. Charles paused, forgetting himself, wondering who the patrons were of such an exalted space.

Julie shook his arm. "Come on, then. We are taking too much time."

She was right, for the Garrick was utterly dark when they arrived. "Now what?" he asked, still feeling the sparks of nervous energy rushing through his veins.

"He'll be at the public house on the corner," said Julie with an air of confidence. "Angela kicked him out of the house."

"Is that normal, or is Miss Lugoson's death still making waves?"

"Theater people are always volatile, as are drunks," Julie said. "I rarely see the difference."

"Then why don't you change professions?"

"Maybe I will." She turned with a snap of her cape and marched down the street. "Here we go. The Baited Bear."

Charles could see firelight through the windows, illuminating the shadowy outlines of the patrons. He pulled open the door underneath the wooden sign with a leashed bear burned into it. The public house was one he'd attempted to drink in before, not one of the new upscale shops, but there hadn't been time before the performances began. Inside, which was surprisingly well lit, a number of men sat at tables, probably theatergoers who found the warm rooms and the companionship within more comfortable than their lonely, damp beds.

Julie led him unerringly toward the best spot in the public house, a table directly in front of the vast fireplace. Percy Chalke, wrapped in a woolen shawl, sat at the table, slumping a bit, and alone. He hadn't washed his hair recently, and grease made the blond go brown.

Charles judged the light to be excellent for the time of night, and sat down next to the actor-manager. Julie disappeared as he took off his coat and unwound his muffler. He set the coin on the table.

Chalke yawned and gave a gentle burp, no hint of hostility in his manner. "What's that?"

"Found a coin over by Gray's Inn. Looks old."

"Set it here." Chalke moved a plate, empty but for bread crumbs, in between them.

Charles placed the coin on it and the other man dumped the dregs of his ale over the coin. They pushed it around with their fingers, then Charles fished it out and dried it with his handkerchief.

"It's a woman," he said with surprise.

"With a crown," Chalke grunted. "May I?"

Charles nodded and Chalke held it up to the firelight. "Letters around the outside. Some of it is worn away but I think it's Elizabeth."

"Silver," Charles said.

Chalke nodded. "You could pawn it."

"Make a necklace out of it, for a lady," he countered.

"Julie seems fond of you," Chalke said.

"She's not for me. Too young."

"How old are you?"

"Almost twenty-three."

Chalke chuckled. "You think you're quite a man of the world, I suppose." His eyes were pocketed in deep wrinkles.

"Why don't we hold off on the insults," Charles said, the warmth starting to make his eyes feel heavy. "Why did you want to see me? I don't care to have actresses accosting me on the street all hours."

"Now I know you don't fancy her," Chalke said. "I might have thought I was doing you a favor, though you are fair enough of face to find your own."

"I'll thank you to keep your opinions to yourself."

"Listen, Dickens," Chalke said, bending his head toward Charles. "I do believe Christiana was murdered."

"Oh? I thought the pendulum was swinging the other way."

"Not at all."

He decided to be blunt. "Miss Acton said the girl was her daughter."

"Yes."

"And yours?"

Julie returned with two half-pints of ale. As she set the tankard down in front of Charles, froth overflowed onto the coin. "Oh, you cleaned it," she said with a delighted smile. She bent over it. "A woman? How lovely. May I have it?"

Charles closed his hand over the coin. "No, you may not."

She sniffed and flounced off.

"You have another young lady in mind," Chalke observed. "That is why our Julie doesn't move you."

"None of your business," Charles rejoined. "Now, as to the question. Was Miss Lugoson your daughter?"

"No," Chalke said, in a tone so disinterested that Charles believed him.

"Then who was Miss Acton's lover before you?"

Chalke's bland tone increased the shock of his words. "I believe he was the late Lord Lugoson."

Charles had been about to pick up his mug, but his fingers faltered around the handle.

To disguise his tremble, Charles slid the Elizabethan coin off the public house's sticky table and tucked it into his waistcoat pocket, to make sure no light-fingered young actress liberated it from his possession.

"What is the time line?" he asked. "One sister bears a child, the other marries the man."

Chalke drummed his fingers on the table. "Lady Lugoson is the elder by two years."

"How old is Julie?" Charles's gaze wandered over to the actress, flirting with a couple of sturdy young men who apparently had nothing to do but drink and play after midnight.

"About sixteen."

He frowned as he did the math in his head. "Miss Acton must have been little more than a child when she bore Christiana."

"Thirteen or fourteen."

"And a merchant's daughter?" He was frankly confused. "How did this happen?"

"Lord Lugoson was a friend of Mr. Acton's." Chalke raised his tankard to his lips and drained half the vessel, leaving a foamy moustache on his upper lip.

Charles's mind whirled with several possibilities, all disgusting. "Miss Acton must have had expectations before Lord Lugoson married her sister, then."

"He couldn't marry such a child, so they sent her away. He married the elder daughter, and then passed off Christiana as theirs. I doubt she had much of a say in the matter."

"Leaving Miss Acton to what?"

Chalke drained his tankard. "What you see."

"An actress, not a woman who would attract minor nobles."

"She wasn't left penniless, at least. Her family behaved honorably."

"Why haven't you married her?"

"If there had been a child of mine, I would have offered, but it has never happened."

Charles pushed his tankard to the man. He wasn't thirsty. As Chalke nodded his thanks, Charles inquired, "I assume something in this sad history leads to why you think the girl was murdered."

"Everything in this world comes down to money. Lady Lugoson wants her own child to inherit all the family money, and so much of it was in Christiana's hands."

"So you think she killed her daughter?"

"Poison?" Chalke sipped from the fresh tankard. "That is a family weapon, a womanish weapon."

Charles had a sense of more unsaid thoughts tumbling through Chalke's brain. "Do you think she's done it before?"

Chalke gave a phlegmy sniff. "I am amazed Lord Lugoson lasted as long as he did. She must have loathed him, and once she secured an heir for the family, he had the mark of death on him."

Now, in his cups, Charles saw the thespian emerge. He suspected the conversation would descend to one long monologue. "Were these deaths the same?"

"I would not know. You were not an eyewitness to the first. I believe he died at home after a short illness." Chalke sneered. "Tended by his loving wife, who then vanished almost overnight to France. Didn't even stay past the funeral. Couldn't stand to wear mourning for a man she loathed."

"Not uncommon, but not rare, either," Charles observed.

"Not at all. All the servants are new these past few months. Nothing but the house remains from before. Not that we are allowed inside. It is as if the lady has forgotten her sister's sacrifice gave her all this luxury." He burped and drank more.

Charles was reminded that this man bought from smugglers to keep his costs down. He was probably a jealous man. "Do you have a poison in mind?"

Chalke's head tilted in a thoughtful anger. *"Thoughts black, hands apt, drugs fit, and time agreeing, Confederate season, else no creature seeing; Thou mixture rank, of midnight weeds collected, With Hecate's ban thrice blasted, thrice infected, Thy natural magic and dire property, On wholesome life usurp immediately."*

"*Hamlet*," Charles said, recognizing the quotation. "Midnight weeds? Some natural substance."

Chalke snorted. "Something grown in France, probably. A poisonous place. But it doesn't matter what it was."

"Did you know the Rueff family? The other girl who died a year ago?"

"The lady practiced," Chalke suggested.

"No, Marie Rueff died in Brompton, not in Fontainebleau."

"Then maybe the first death gave her the idea for the second," Chalke snapped.

"But Lord Lugoson's death was more than two years ago. That was the first death."

Chalke's head lolled on his chest. A faint snore escaped his lips.

He had lost the man to drunken sleep. But no matter, as he made little sense with his time line of death. Here, at least, was motive. Hatred of her husband, of his dead daughter. Was that angry boy in her house in danger as well?

The next evening, at the close of the work day, Mr. Hogarth invited Charles home to Brompton for dinner. He accepted eagerly, though he had been close to nodding off at his desk before his editor came to him. Nothing sounded better than the innocent laughter of a pleasant, wholesome family after the unsavory conversations of the wee hours.

As soon as they walked in the house, they were greeted by an almost overwhelmingly cheerful group of children, fussing over Mr. Hogarth as he discarded his winter layer of clothing.

Mrs. Hogarth patted her husband's hand, then greeted Charles. "My Kate had been feeding one of the babies, and as a result, has to make minor repairs on her wardrobe."

"One of my brothers never kept anything down once he started walking. I thought he'd grow dreadfully thin, but something nourished him," Charles said, handing her his coat and gloves.

"There is an age where the wee ones live on little but air," Mrs. Hogarth opined. "But as they have such a sweet tooth, these bairns, I suspect they are secretly stealing biscuits. I can never keep any in the house."

Mr. Hogarth winked and patted his belly.

Mrs. Hogarth ushered her husband and their visitor into the dining room and pulled chairs away from the table so they could sit in front of the fire. Charles stuck his feet as close as he could, wishing he could take off his shoes and dry his socks.

"William complained you'd been particularly quiet today, when you came back from that debate," Mr. Hogarth said, plumping the cushion his wife had placed behind him in the chair. "Something troubling you?"

"Not at all," Charles said. "Just working out a new sketch in my mind."

"What's it about?"

"The new gin shops," he said, taking a hot cup of cider from Mary Hogarth with a smile.

"What's to write about in them?"

"Have you seen the new style? I walked past one last night, near Drury Lane, and then stopped in at another between the debate and the office this afternoon. Such a world of contrast."

"Oh?"

"Yes? You have the sporting gentleman, and the faded ladies, and the ladies of, er, business, and then, in the corners, the most wretched. The starving Irish, the miserable men who starve their children for a few drops of forgetfulness. What need have they of signs they cannot read, plate glass to look out upon an unforgiving landscape, snooty young ladies to serve them?"

"I see."

Charles persisted. "It is a new fashion. I have seen it before. Different businesses take their turns improving their land-scapes, until their lust for upgrading leads them down the path to bankruptcy. It is a peculiar habit in the lifestyle of a trade."

"Something for our readers to be reminded of," Mr. Hogarth

said, warming his hands with his glass. "The cyclical nature of these things."

"Dinner, Mr. Hogarth," his wife called. "I don't want the soup getting cold."

"Something stodgy tonight, I'm afraid," Mr. Hogarth confided. "Bean, perhaps."

Charles didn't care, especially when he saw Miss Hogarth appear at the doorway. She wore her gray dress with green ribbons, and her hair looked damp and consequently darker than usual. Maybe one of her siblings had thrown porridge in it and she'd had to rinse it out. Her eyes were sleepy-tired, but her smile was as bright as ever when she saw him. He greeted her politely, mindful that while she might be a bit daring, even demanding, in private, her father expected total propriety in public.

Mr. Hogarth had been wrong about the dinner, for instead the lady of the house served a delicious pea-and-ham soup. Charles had his mouth primed for a roast after that, but Mr. Hogarth's prediction came true, as the next course was beans on toast. However, Mrs. Hogarth had added interest with the sauce, some kind of curry, and it was much better than anything he and Fred might have made for themselves over the fire.

After they finished, the younger girls helped their mother clear away, while Miss Hogarth led him and her father into his study. Charles stood against a bookcase while she picked sheet music off the chairs and put it on her father's desk. Mr. Hogarth took the first emptied chair.

"Have you learned anything more?" she asked, straightening the rest of her father's chairs. "It feels an age since I've seen you, Mr. Dickens."

He had remembered to bring William's articles for her, and in the flush of pleasure he received at her artless words, he pulled them out of his frock coat pocket for her. "This is the information about Marie Rueff, but the most interesting experience I've had this week was my conversation with Percy Chalke."

"He believes Lady Lugoson killed Miss Lugoson," Mr. Hogarth interjected, shivering in the chilly room. He lit a lamp on his desk to add to the candle they'd brought with them.

Miss Hogarth's jaw dropped as she looked up from the papers. "Never!"

"He's following the money," Charles explained. "Christiana Lugoson wasn't Lady Lugoson's child. With her gone, Lord Lugoson inherits. And he *is* Lady Lugoson's child. It's a very twisted story."

Miss Hogarth flourished the papers, nearly catching the edge of one in the open flame. "Goodness, what a strange family. Then Marie Rueff's death is mere coincidence?"

"Read for yourself," Charles said, moving the candle to the center of the desk. "You were there. Doesn't the death described sound so very much the same?"

As she read, leaning close to the lamp, Mr. Hogarth lit his pipe with the candle and settled into his chair. "I think they both died the same way. Monsieur Rueff and Lady Lugoson somehow came to the same poison, something grown in France. They are not the same as us, these Frenchmen. You only have to look at the revolution to see that." He shuddered.

"I don't recognize this doctor's name," Miss Hogarth said, setting the papers in her lap a few minutes later. "Father, could we call on him tomorrow? Maybe he has a suspicion about what happened. We could even suggest he write to Dr. Keville about Miss Lugoson's demise."

"Your mother needs you here, Kate," Mr. Hogarth chided.

"But I was there, sir," Miss Hogarth pleaded. "I remember Miss Rueff from services. She was very shy, but very sweet, and lovely, too. I don't remember her dying, but then, I had that terrible influenza last year after Christmas."

"It seemed the entire household was laid up in succession," Mr. Hogarth remembered. "Charles, what do you think?"

He kept his countenance calm while strategizing this chance to have Miss Hogarth to himself again. "I'm happy to escort her. If you bring her in with you to the *Chronicle*, we can find this doctor's offices."

"Very well. Have you learned anything else useful?" Mr. Hogarth asked.

Charles rubbed his chin. "There was a maid. I don't know that we can find her after a year. Of course, the late Lord Lugoson might have been poisoned, as well."

"No way to uncover that truth now." Mr. Hogarth glanced at the top sheet of music on his desk, then turned over the stack. "Not that I canna imagine."

"If Miss Rueff had a mother, Mama and I could pay a condolence call," Miss Hogarth suggested. "But she is deceased. We had better focus on the doctor, for now."

"What about Lord Lugoson?" Mr. Hogarth asked.

Charles winced. He wasn't eager to leave any questions uninvestigated, but he couldn't see how to follow up in this case. "All the servants have been changed. No one will know exactly how he died."

# Chapter 15

Dr. Claude Manette had his business on the old turnpike road. Several new and fragile-looking two-story buildings had sprouted on the north side, and a group of ragged boys were chasing an old wheel down the side of the road. Peering through the Saturday afternoon gloom from the trap, Miss Hogarth at his side, Charles saw lit lamps in the window of the center building. It appeared the doctor was open for business.

Charles jumped to the ground and called to the boys, offering each a penny to watch the horse. They struck a deal, and he returned to the trap, followed by a trio of them.

"Dr. Manette practices very close to where the Rueff family lives," Miss Hogarth said, as Charles helped her alight from the conveyance he had rented, so they didn't have to walk in the swirling snow that had plagued traffic that day.

"We should visit the house after we see the doctor." At her horrified look, he pressed her hand and said, "Not to pay a call, of course, just to get an idea of the family."

"They are on Pelham Crescent. Quite new houses, I think. Very exclusive." Miss Hogarth slid her hand from his and straightened her bonnet.

"I'd expect them to have money if they associated with Lady Lugoson's family. Hold on for a second."

"What?" she asked.

He made his voice calm, though he was in an agony of discomfort. "You seem cool with me today. Is something the matter?"

"Only that my parents have cautioned me to be more careful with you."

He threw up his hands. "What on earth do they think we have been up to? Our investigation is forever leaping forward."

"I might have been too secretive, Mr. Dickens. My sister asks me questions about you and I refuse to offer." Her lips turned up. "I prefer to keep what I think of you close to my heart."

He could scarcely breathe. "Do you?"

She nodded. "Let us get on with our business, before we prove my parents to be correct."

"Very well." Letting the subject go, Charles glanced back at the boys, hoping the trap and the horse would survive their tender ministrations, then ushered Miss Hogarth up the front step. He rapped the door with the knocker. It was opened promptly by a girl about Mary Hogarth's age.

"Would the doctor be able to see us for a few minutes?" Charles asked. "I'm Mr. Dickens from the *Chronicle*, and this is Miss Hogarth of St. Luke's Parish."

"Please come into the parlor," the girl said very politely, though she didn't offer to take their coats. They followed her into a long, narrow room, well warmed by a fire. A portrait of a very forbidding-looking elderly woman in a white lace cap and wide panniers hung over the fireplace.

"French costume," Miss Hogarth whispered.

"Manette does sound French," Charles agreed. "His grandmother?"

"*Tante* Antoinette," said a voice from the door.

Charles saw a man in a black tailcoat and striped white-and-black trousers in the doorway. His silk waistcoat attempted to hold in a round belly. "Are you Doctor Manette?"

"That is correct," he said, rolling his *R*s in that particular French manner.

"Charles Dickens." He held out his hand, then introduced Miss Hogarth.

"Why do I have the honor of being addressed by a journalist?" the doctor asked, ushering them to a sofa and taking the chair opposite.

"We wanted to ask you about one of your patients."

"Former patient," Miss Hogarth murmured.

"Who?" Doctor Manette asked.

"Marie Rueff," Charles answered. "William Aga, my fellow reporter, wrote about the case for our newspaper last year."

"Of course." The doctor chewed his lip for a moment before continuing. "A very sad death. I had known her from childhood. In fact her father paid my passage to come here to London, to care for our countrymen."

"You did not care for the Lugoson family?"

"Ah, but they are not French," he said, exposing teeth yellowed by pipe smoke.

"Lady Lugoson is half French. We were at Christiana Lugoson's deathbed," Charles said. "When I told Mr. Aga about the dreadful experience, he remembered what he had written about, especially since it was Epiphany night in both cases."

"That is odd," the doctor agreed, taking his pipe out of his pocket.

They waited politely while he went about the work of filling and lighting it.

"I'm concerned that the young girls of the neighborhood might be in danger," Charles said. "That was your daughter at the door?"

"Yes," the doctor agreed. "But she does not have the habit, as Miss Rueff did, of foraging."

"Foraging?" Miss Hogarth asked.

"Yes. Miss Rueff grew up near Fontainebleau Forest. Every

autumn she would forage for wild mushrooms. Every spring, for wild greens. It takes a careful eye and a bit of luck to manage not to poison yourself."

"Oh?" Charles said.

"Not everything evil is bright red and decayed-looking," the doctor said. "I have some samples of French mushrooms if you would like to see them."

"Certainly," Charles agreed. "But you are saying Miss Rueff died in January from something she had foraged for herself? When? The previous autumn?"

"It is possible she dried something to drink as a tea," the doctor said. "Not likely to be a mushroom at that time of year. By the time I saw her she could no longer speak, I am afraid."

He stood, and they followed him out. Down the corridor was the doctor's study, complete with hanging skeleton and a shelf full of jars. He pulled down a trio of small jars, all holding various mushrooms in sickly shades.

"This is Satan's Boletus," he said, holding one up to Miss Hogarth. "You can see the white cap, the disgusting red tinge of the stalk, but sadly, some of this variety do not look so dangerous."

"And these kill?" Charles asked.

"If you eat enough, yes," the doctor said.

"Is this what you suspect killed her?" Miss Hogarth asked.

"No, there was no yellow slime in her vomit," the doctor said. "No French mushroom that I can think of would cause exactly this death, which is why I expect some tea did it."

Charles frowned. "You believe she did, what, kill herself, accidentally or on purpose?"

"Accidentally, of course," the doctor insisted, setting his glass jar on the desk. "No, she was a happy girl, Miss Rueff."

"She seemed withdrawn to me," Miss Hogarth said. "So very shy."

"You knew her?" Manette asked.

"By sight," she said. "From St. Luke's."

"Ah, yes. Well, there was nothing wrong with her life. Her father's only daughter, and he doted on her. A very quiet, simple girl."

"Quiet, yes," Miss Hogarth agreed.

"A hard death," the doctor said, taking off his spectacles and rubbing them clean. "Not an entirely natural one. Very good health, until then."

"Did you tell her father about your suspicions regarding her foraging?" Miss Hogarth asked. "Did he have any of her home-made teas examined?"

"He did not care about that, or anything else. Jacques was heartbroken. For a time I was afraid he would follow his beloved child into the grave."

Charles didn't want to ask about money. He could tell the doctor would not cast any aspersions on the father so he didn't ask about the Rueff finances either. "Thank you very much for your time."

"Did it do you any good, Mr. Dickens?"

"It was the same death," he said. "Which tells us that we are not wrong in treating Miss Lugoson's death as unnatural."

"But not necessarily murder," Dr. Manette countered.

Charles ticked items off on his fingers. "We need to discover what happened to Miss Rueff's foraging journals if she kept them, her homemade tisanes and such. I'd like to understand better if the youthful friendship between the girls continued."

"Miss Lugoson was an heiress," Miss Hogarth interjected, asking what Charles had not. "Was Miss Rueff?"

"Oh, yes," the doctor said, lifting his brows in a very Gallic expression. "Her mother's fortune settled upon her only child."

"Where did the fortune go?" Charles blurted. *What was left of it.*

"To Miss Rueff's cousin, I believe. The daughter of the Madame Rueff's younger sister."

Charles's and Miss Hogarth's gazes collided. They needed to find out who that was.

"Thank you for your time, Doctor," Charles said. He helped Miss Hogarth rise.

"Of course. I am sorry to hear of the death of your neighbor. Perhaps I shall write a short tract on the dangers of foraging," Dr. Manette said.

"I would read it most carefully," Miss Hogarth said. "And be grateful for the information."

They took their leave, and retrieved the trap from their trio of helpers. "Pelham Crescent?" Charles asked, as they settled themselves in the vehicle.

"Absolutely," Miss Hogarth agreed at his side, tightening the ribbon at the top of her cloak.

Charles set the horse on its way, then settled the reins into a more comfortable position in his hands. He wasn't terribly easy with his driving skills, as he didn't do it often enough. "What are your thoughts after that interview?"

"Murder," she said promptly, staring straight ahead. "Miss Lugoson liked the theater, and dancing. She was not a girl to go about foraging. She hadn't been back in Brompton long enough anyway. She was only here from sometime in September."

"Long enough to find a lover, not long enough to find some wild teas or mushrooms?" Charles asked.

"Simply the wrong season for it," Miss Hogarth said.

"But something that has a short season, right around Christmas?" Charles suggested. "I don't know what. Holly berries or something like that?"

"Or even an Epiphany treat that only comes out that night."

"Then we are right back to a bad jam," Charles said.

"I know." She folded her hands into her lap. "That they were both heiresses seems suspicious."

"I agree. Let us see what we can learn about her." He turned the horse onto a street of elegant, cream stucco–fronted terraced houses with lots of decorative iron grating.

"Absolutely lovely," Miss Hogarth breathed.

"I agree. Though I must admit I prefer stand-alone villas to terraced houses, but these are in the first stare of fashion, to be sure."

"Knightsbridge," she said. "I love our dear, rambling house, and the orchards, but you are really somebody if you live in a place like this."

"You will have to choose your husband very carefully to find yourself here," Charles said, the words coming out more harshly than he meant them to be.

"Indeed," she said crisply. "But for now, I am more interested in a dead heiress than my future prospects."

She did like a mystery. While Charles had an interest in Kate Hogarth's future prospects as well, that puzzle could be set aside for now. "Did she seem well cared for, this Miss Rueff?" Charles asked. "Dressed appropriately? That sort of thing."

"She wore half-mourning every time I saw her. For her mother, perhaps?"

Charles jumped down, casting about for the usual sort of boys who might keep the horse walking for him, but the truth was, they had no excuse to call on the dead girl's father. He stared up at Miss Hogarth. "Could we pretend you don't know that she's died? Go to the door and call on her?"

Miss Hogarth tilted her head, her pretty curls brushing the black wool of her coat.

"Who are you looking for?" said a woman in a practical black dress, approaching them with a market basket on her arm. Her speech was fairly distinguished, and her age made her likely to be one of the house's cooks or housekeepers.

"Marie Rueff. A parishioner at St. Luke's," Charles said.

"Why?"

"A mutual friend has died," Charles said, thinking fast. "Miss Christiana Lugoson. We wanted to tell her, but our acquaintance is both slight and long ago."

"Miss Rueff died herself more than a year ago," the woman said. "I am Mrs. Appleby, and I work at the house next door."

"Goodness," Miss Hogarth said, her hand going to her throat as she playacted alarm. "I had wondered why I never saw her at St. Luke's anymore."

"It was very sudden," the woman said.

"She was such a dear, quiet girl."

Mrs. Appleby snorted. "You wouldn't have thought that if you lived here. Such doings in the wee hours. Horses in the street, shouts."

"Marie Rueff?" Miss Hogarth said. "I shouldn't think so. Why, she was practically a mouse."

"Had a man," the servant said, tapping the skin around her left eye. "Tried to run away with him. Father caught her."

"And the man?" Charles asked.

"Unmarked phaeton. Got away clean," she said, betraying a hint of Yorkshire in her voice for the first time.

"My stars," Miss Hogarth said. "I'd never have had any clue of such a thing. How could she have met a man?"

"Any pretty girl from a good family with money will attract men," Mrs. Appleby said. "Monsieur Rueff married an English heiress."

"We'd understood Miss Rueff to be the heiress now," Charles said.

"I don't know about any of that. Just that there was a scandal."

"How long before she died?"

"Shortly before Christmas. They must have thought they could get away because Monsieur Rueff had a holiday party. Lots of Frenchies about, all those foreign tongues wagging, but someone saw her leaving, trying to sneak out of the tradesman entrance, and told her father."

"He had already been suspicious," Miss Hogarth said wisely.

A curtain twitched in the next house and Mrs. Appleby snapped to attention. "I must go. I am sorry for your loss."

Charles let her dash down the basement steps. She was unlikely to have known Marie Rueff personally and would be of no use regarding her foraging habit. With a sigh, he climbed back into the trap and snapped the reins.

"That was not Marie Rueff as described by William in the *Chronicle*," Charles said. "He made her sound so housebound."

"Likely someone she knew from her intimate family circle," Miss Hogarth said. "Whether here or in France. A girl in love can always find a way, and a determined fortune hunter will aid her."

"What do you think about such a scenario?"

"It is poison to marry where family has not consented," she said. "I would never do it. I trust my parents to help me make a good choice."

"Otherwise you will never rise to Pelham Crescent?" he asked, turning them back to Fulham Road.

"Very true." She tossed her head.

Charles's stomach rumbled uneasily. Miss Hogarth seemed to have the spirit of a fortune hunter herself. She would never look at him as a suitor, if he were poor.

# Chapter 16

Charles set down his pen late that night in his parlor, his thoughts on money and how to get it. He pulled the Elizabethan coin he'd found two nights ago out of his pocket and examined it. It had to be worth something, and what if there were more, turned up by those tree roots?

He leapt from his chair, startling Fred out of his doze in front of the hearth, and went into the kitchen. After he fetched the largest spoon he could find, he threw on his outer clothes and called for his brother.

"Light the lantern. We're going treasure hunting!"

"You must be mad," Fred said, but he gathered his coat and the lantern with alacrity.

Charles straightened his brother's collar and pulled his muffler over the dimple in his chin. "A bitter night, but no one will be out to watch us dig."

"What are we going to do? Rob a grave?" Fred asked, pulling on green mittens that their sister Letitia had knitted for him.

"I hope not." He squinted in mysterious fashion. "But I found that coin in tree roots. It just struck me that there might be more. Who knows what the root might have pushed up?"

"What kind of coins did they have, hundreds of years ago?"

"I have never forgotten learning one was called an angel," Charles said, lighting the lantern. "But I don't know what I found. I should ask someone."

"An angel," Fred said, following Charles out the door. "Were all the coins different?"

"I don't think so. Mostly the same." They walked down the dark stairs, lighting the way with the lamp.

"Do I get a spoon?"

"I forgot to take another one," Charles said. "But we'll trade turns with the lamp."

When they reached the street, Fred began to whistle, a jaunty tune that did not fit any notion of dark deeds. Charles shrugged and added his own whistle.

When they reached the edge of the field where he'd found the treasure tree, he heard another whistle join theirs.

"Bother," Fred said, breaking off. "Sorry."

Charles pulled him into the shadow of the closest tree and shuttered the lantern. The other whistle continued for a moment, then faltered. He heard the footsteps, those light ones that had begun to signify trouble to him.

Stepping away from the tree, he called, "Julie?"

The steps didn't speed up, but kept moving forward. Some thirty seconds later, the moon revealed the girl, her red hair down, no bonnet on her head. Not like Julie Saville to take no lack of care with her appearance. Charles opened the lantern. And gasped.

"What happened?" He handed the lantern to his brother and tilted Julie's chin, exposing the bruise on her cheek. "Who hit you?"

"Miss Acton," she said, pulling away.

"It's all right," he said to his brother. "I know her. She's an actress. Who likes to follow me."

Julie rolled her eyes at him.

A tree branch caught at the back of his coat. He pulled away. "Why did Miss Acton hit you?"

"She beat me for questioning Lady Lugoson's parenting skills."

"You made such remarks to her face?" Charles asked.

"No. I assume you told her." She sniffed and tucked in her chin.

"I don't wish you any sort of harm. I'd never have done that," Charles protested. "No, someone else said something."

"Why would anyone want to cause problems between them?"

He felt drips on his hat. Moving out from under the tree, he said, "They've had a very domestic tragedy on their hands. All kinds of accusations are going to occur."

"I don't want to pay for that. I had nothing to do with it. I didn't hurt Christiana." Her voice had lost some of its crispness.

"She's in pain," Fred said. "Should we escort her home?"

Charles ignored his brother's suggestion. "Keep your mouth shut," he advised. "Don't offer any more opinions. You don't know anything more, correct?"

"She was my friend," Julie whined.

Bluntly, he asked, "Do you think your mistress killed her? Or Mr. Chalke?"

She stared at him, then her eyes went to Fred for a moment before returning. "I don't know what to think," she said, in a small voice. Then she stood up straight. "But I don't want to be the next victim."

"A slap is hardly a dish of poison," Charles said. "Poison is sneaky and political. A slap is rage."

"So you don't think Miss Acton did it?" she asked.

"To kill Miss Lugoson merely to keep her age a secret is silly," he declared. "After all, she has you onstage with her. That never made any sense."

"She isn't the sort to do very much," Julie said. "After having a baby meant she'd never marry well, she found herself in the theater because her parents gave her the building. I don't think she's ever really tried to make anything of herself."

"Isn't she a well-known actress?" Fred asked.

"In a third-rate theater?" Julie sniffed. "Watch me go higher than that, and soon."

"If you aren't arrested and transported," Charles snapped. "For falling in with Chalke's illegal doings."

"What about you?" she demanded. "Out all hours of the night?"

"I was going to look for more coins. I need a fortune, same as anyone else." He put his hands on his hips.

"Can I help?" she asked.

"No and no," he said. "I have my brother to help me. Stop following me. Get some sleep for a change."

"I don't sleep much."

"Neither do I, but we don't want you here."

She sniffed again, theatrically this time, and swanned off in a gliding kind of walk that made her feet scarcely touch the earth.

"She's going to get herself killed or raped, wandering around at night like this," Fred said. "Shouldn't we have made sure she arrived home safely?"

"She knows how to take care of herself," Charles said. "Actresses aren't respectable, but they do have the freedom to go places by themselves." They couldn't afford to get mixed up with her. The next thing he knew he might be offering her a place in front of his fire and if Mr. Hogarth found out he'd been harboring a pretty little actress like some novelist instead of a respectable family man, he'd lose the man's good opinion, which was everything at this stage of his career.

"But she was hurt!" Fred protested.

"Her mistress did that, not some blackguard. She has a place to go, and she isn't badly hurt." Charles put his finger to his lips, and closed the lantern again. When all was silent, he pulled his brother across the field toward the correct tree, then went to his knees on the cold earth next to the root, opened the lantern, and began to scrape with the spoon.

Fred sat on the thickest of the roots and poked around on the opposite side. Charles could tell the boy was still pouting, but he ignored it. If Fred had his own establishment, then he could house wounded actresses. He convinced himself that Julie had been acting hurt more than really hurt, anyway.

While they worked, Charles thought about the case. Or at least he tried. His thoughts kept meandering to bright blue eyes and dancing curls. Of Kate Hogarth, not Julie Saville. The girl who wanted to live at Pelham Crescent someday.

By God, he did have ability to rise to a place like that, with hard work and diligence, and yes, forgoing many nights of sleep. Not only that, he would solve Miss Lugoson's murder. For now, that would impress Kate Hogarth.


While no postmen came on Sundays, Charles found a note had been pushed under his door when he and Fred arrived home from visiting their family on Sunday afternoon.

"William Aga proposing a flare-up?" his brother asked, pulling off his hat.

"Don't forget that bread and cheese," Charles said, fluffing Fred's hair back from his widow's peak. Their dinner was in his pocket.

"Right-o," Fred said cheerfully, pulling out the wrapped packet before he went to stir up the fire. "I hope those coins are done soaking." He went into the kitchen to check on their tree root findings of the night before. In the dark, and with frozen fingers, they'd been unable to do more than soak some interesting lumps in a pan of water. Then they'd both slept over-late and had to dash for services the next morning, so as not to upset their mother. Charles had found a little extra money for the resoling of Fanny's and Letitia's shoes. Fanny had paid for Boz's new secondhand pair, so he was out of his dancing pumps now.

Charles pulled off his gloves and opened the note. He whistled when he saw the signature and went to his letter box to prepare a response.

"What have you got?" Fred asked, returning with a lumpy handkerchief.

"It's a letter from Mrs. Carley saying I can now interview her daughter, Miss Carley," he said. "I never thought the day would come, but I'd still better bring Miss Hogarth. I'll write her and walk the letter right to the General Post Office on St. Martin's Le Grand so that she receives it before I arrive."

"Don't the Carleys live in London?"

"They are at their Brompton house right now. I expect she's making this as difficult for me as possible. She's that sort of woman."

"Politicians." Fred's dimples popped out as he grimaced. "On your way back, can you get some sausages? There must be something open at Smithfield Market."

"You know I detest that place. Terrible hygiene."

"I need more than bread and cheese," Fred pleaded. "If my stomach growls all night you won't be able to sleep either."

Charles laughed. "Fine. I'd tell you to stop growing but you have a few years to go yet. Let me write my note and you can show me our coins while the ink dries."

"Yes. I just need to polish them up and light the lamps so we can see." Fred sat down at the table, intent over his handkerchief while Charles carefully composed his note. He wondered how filthy the cloth was, since their laundry had been in a terrible state when they delivered a bundle to their mother to be washed before they met the family for church.

After he blotted his note, he rose from his chair and pushed the curtains as far back from the window as he could, allowing for the maximum light. "What have we got?"

Fred straightened out the grayish cloth and displayed three flat disks. "We really did find three coins."

"Like the first one I found?" Charles plucked it from the mantelpiece and placed it on the cloth next to the others.

"No."

"They are all silver, though, whatever they are," Charles said.

"Metal's worth something," Fred agreed.

Charles picked one up. All three coins were battered, but some lettering survived around the edges, and the queen was evident. "We must have found the remains of someone's lost coin purse."

Fred handed him another coin. "This one is in the best shape. There is still some beadwork around the edge."

"We'll go out hunting again as soon as the rain stops," Charles vowed. "Then we'll take the coins to a dealer and get what we can for them."

Fred clapped his hands together. "What will we do with the money?"

"Maybe some crockery," Charles said, hoping the money would stretch so far. "Lamps?"

"Furniture," Fred said with a laugh. He spread his arms wide and twirled. "Way too much room to move around in here. I can hear an echo!"

"Exactly," Charles said. He turned slowly, imagining the room full of plump furnishings and interesting trinkets, a portrait or two on the wall. Maybe a seascape, to remind him of his childhood in Portsmouth. And their feet, well, he and Fred would have fine new shoes. Warm slippers, too. Possibly embroidered by some soft, girlish hand.

"Now what?" Fred asked. "What are you smiling about?"

Charles felt embarrassment heating his cheeks. "Little domestic pleasures. Why don't you finish cleaning the coins, then lock them into my box? I'm going to take my letter to the post office and fetch those sausages. We've earned them."

"Think it will stop raining tonight?"

They both heard the clap of thunder. With a shudder, Charles went to pull the curtains. The sky was too cloud-filled to allow much light. "Doubtful. But even Julie doesn't know quite where our cache is. It will keep."

On Sunday night, Charles remembered he had to attend a political meeting out near Putney late the next morning. Accordingly, he traveled by water the next morning to dutifully record the happenings of the meeting before making his weary way to Brompton late that afternoon. At least there could be no doubt of Miss Hogarth's having received his message by now.

"Ye are soaked tae the bone!" exclaimed Mrs. Hogarth when he arrived at her door. Her son had to help him take off his thoroughly damp coat. His muffler had become a sponge.

"Can ye feel yer feet?" she asked.

Charles stared down at his discolored shoes. "I think I'd prefer snow."

"Get them off. Let's get them and ye tae the fire," she scolded.

Five minutes later, he had a cup of tea in his hand and a pair of Mr. Hogarth's slippers on his frozen feet. "They won't allow us entry if we delay much longer," he pleaded. "Mrs. Carley has been very difficult."

Miss Hogarth entered the room, looking lovely in pale blue wool, her hair tied back with matching ribbons. Charles forgot his aches and pains and gave her his brightest smile.

"You poor thing," she cooed, rushing over to pat his shoulder. "At least your clothes stayed dry."

His trousers hadn't. He pointed to the circles of damp around his knees. "The fire will soon mend me, and we can be on our way."

She blushed and turned away. He shouldn't have teased her so, making her look at his limbs. "I don't mind the wet, but my feet were sliding around in my shoes."

She looked doubtfully at his shoes and socks, drying over

the fender. "It will take too long to dry them. I'll find you some of Father's."

She rushed away. Charles closed his eyes, pleased to be so cared for. Miss Mary brought him a slice of bread with butter and a comb for his hair, and he was quite set to rights by the time Miss Hogarth reappeared with a pair of thick, rather clumsily knitted socks, and boots.

"Father wears them over his shoes," she explained. "They will work, I think." She held up the socks.

"Did you knit those?"

"I did." Miss Mary giggled. "Terrible job, but I'm better now. Father never wears them."

The heels were turned in such a manner that they did not look like they would fit comfortably on a human foot, but Charles struggled into them, grateful that his feet were too frozen to feel bulky seams.

"I wish we kept a carriage," Miss Hogarth fretted as she caught Charles limping slightly as they went to the door a few minutes later.

"I am built for hard use," Charles said, smiling at her. "You needn't worry. But I cannot wait for spring."

"It is too bad you needed to go to one of your meetings just when Mrs. Carley wrote," she said, opening the door.

"Yes, but I need to earn a living, so I don't mind. Still, let us go before it is full dark. I don't want to give Mrs. Carley another chance to turn us away."

Thankfully, they arrived after just a quarter-hour walk in the rain. Miss Hogarth had been so warmly bundled that water only marked the bottom inch of her skirt.

The Carleys' Brompton house displayed itself in less dilapidated fashion than the city abode. A newer building, part of a line of terraced houses that some speculator had built at the start of the century, the furnishings were simpler, though there were still some grand works of art, probably too large to fit on the walls of the London establishment.

"That must be ancient," Charles said, looking at the floor-length portrait of a cavalier, resplendent in a metal breastplate and short cape, to the right of the fireplace in the parlor.

"My husband's ancestor," Mrs. Carley said, coming into the room. "He died in the Battle of Langport."

"Your husband is from Somerset?" Miss Hogarth asked, proving the quality of her historical education.

"As am I. We're distant cousins, in fact."

Now that Charles thought about it, he could see that all members of the family had the same small eyes, set deeply beside their long, narrow noses. He wondered exactly how distant the cousinship was.

"I am glad to hear Miss Carley is feeling better," Miss Hogarth said, as a maid brought in a tea service. "I have been so eager to see her again, after what we went through together when her dear friend died."

"She has been quite prostrate with grief," Mrs. Carley announced.

Charles recalled Miss Carley's violent sobbing that night, even though at that early point in the evening, her friend may have been thought able to recover. He also remembered that, while life had gone on for him, it had only been three weeks, and for those who loved Miss Lugoson, the loss was very fresh. He made clumsy remarks to that effect.

"Indeed," Mrs. Carley said. "Tea?"

Charles and Miss Hogarth sat on opposite sides of Mrs. Carley. He felt a sense of déjà vu when the tea was passed out. "Your teacups are the same in both houses?"

"I bring this set with me," Mrs. Carley said, holding up her distinctive shell cup. "It is like traveling with my mother."

"Very sweet," Miss Hogarth murmured, cupping the warm vessel in her hands.

The parlor door opened again, setting the fire to fluttering, and Miss Carley entered the room. She wore an unflattering dress patterned with brown and gold flowers. Her sleeves were heavily flounced from elbow to wrist, though the end result, given the woebegone state of the girl, was not the fashionable look she'd been attempting.

No, Miss Carley, though she had a good complexion, would never be the domestic angel her friend would have been. She looked only a step above a governess.

Without speaking, she took a teacup from her mother and sat at the edge of her chair next to Miss Hogarth. Her back was straight, yet her shoulders still seemed to slump. Her hair lumped unflatteringly along the back of her short neck.

"Are you well?" Miss Hogarth asked sympathetically, lifting her hand as if to pat the other girl. "Such a dreadful time you must have had recently."

"I cannot think of my dear Christiana without crying yet," the girl admitted.

Her handkerchief, unlike Fred's disgusting cloth, was pristine and edged with lace. When she lifted it to dot at her nostrils, Charles saw they were red and sore. She really had been ill. Or crying.

"Let me say another name," Miss Hogarth said. "Marie Rueff. Did you know her?"

Miss Carley blinked slowly, then shook her head in the negative.

"She was a fellow parishioner at St. Luke's?" Miss Hogarth clarified uncertainly.

"We worship in London," Miss Carley said. "Almost never out here."

Charles noticed that she had not quite answered the question. "I see. Do you know anyone French?"

"What an odd question," Mrs. Carley said. "One does meet French people from time to time."

He tried again. "I apologize. The Rueffs are French."

"Clearly," Mrs. Carley said.

Charles decided he'd better take a turn in another direction. "We've been told that Miss Lugoson was in love, but the name we were given for her suitor seems to be wrong."

"Why, that's no business of yours," Mrs. Carley said.

"It was Horatio!" Miss Carley shrieked over her mother, tears welling in her eyes.

Miss Hogarth raised her eyebrows. Charles spoke quickly, not wanting to lose the chance in case the girl descended into hysteria. "Mr.—?"

"Durant. Horatio Durant." She let out a keening sigh, then blew her nose, the tears freely dripping. "We were both in love with dear Mr. Durant. But she was winning his love. Christiana was everything I am not."

"You must have hated her," Miss Hogarth said in the most conversational of tones.

"No." Miss Carley's small eyes widened, tears dotting her stubby eyelashes. "No, no. She had sparkle, and such dreams. No interest in a conventional life. If she had her way, she'd never have married a man like Mr. Durant. But she liked to pretend they were engaged. She said it was to keep other suitors away from her."

So Miss Carley stayed doggedly with her friend, hoping to take this man on the rebound? Charles admired her tenacity. "Who is this gentleman?"

"A young man of wealth and connection," Mrs. Carley said, shaking her head. "With a good future, given his political bent."

"He is a protégé of Father's." Miss Carley caressed the words.

"Miss Lugoson was in love," Charles said carefully. "But you thought she would not accept his suit if it were offered."

"She wanted to be an actress." Miss Carley nodded to herself and took a sip of her tea.

"Her mother would never have allowed that," Mrs. Carley

said, laughing lightly. "Oh, the ideas these girls have as they end their time in the schoolroom. But thoughts soon turn to more sensible things when they come out, and as a mother, you learn not to worry overmuch."

"Now Christiana never will." Miss Carley applied her handkerchief again. "Be sensible, I mean."

"There is some thought that Miss Lugoson met her end by foul means," Miss Hogarth ventured.

Charles noticed she had set down her teacup and was clasping her hands quite tightly in her lap. Not quite as bold as she wanted to be.

"Oh, good heavens," Miss Carley said, her voice muffled by her exertions with her handkerchief, as her mother shook her head. "Don't be silly."

"You don't think she had any enemies?" Miss Hogarth asked.

"She was everything that was good," Miss Carley declared, closing her hand around her soaked handkerchief. "I'd never believe such foolishness."

"This is what comes of spending time with theater folk," her mother declared. "Such dramatics."

Of course, these people did not seem to know Marie Rueff. They might have thought differently if they knew how similar the deaths were. But Charles suspected they'd come to the end of what they could learn. When Miss Carley sneezed loudly, he paid his respects one last time and removed himself and Miss Hogarth from the parlor.

Twenty minutes later, they were halfway returned to mutton stew and Mrs. Hogarth's warm fire. Charles had been mired in his thoughts regarding the interview and Miss Hogarth had been quiet as well. He still had some irritation with her regarding the Pelham Crescent incident and did not know how to bridge the new gap between them. "How are we going to find this Mr. Durant?" he asked.

"I've met him," Miss Hogarth said.

"How? Where?" Charles stopped under a tree. One drip fell off a branch and slid chillingly down his neck. The temperature had dropped since they had first ventured out. Snow might be coming.

"St. Luke's, of course."

"And?" Charles demanded, swiping at his neck.

"Very handsome. He escorted his mother to a ladies' tea last year. She passed away at the beginning of last fall."

"Do your parents know him? His father?"

"I never heard of a father. I assume he's on his own, now."

"Pelham Crescent?" Charles asked sourly.

"Sydney Street. Quite a new house that his mother built."

"He's a gentleman?"

"Yes. I think I understood the mother had property in Dorset."

He considered her. "You seem to know quite a lot."

"I am of an age to learn things about people," she said, not quite meeting his eyes. "Even if they are the sort to consort more with a Miss Carley than a Miss Hogarth."

"You are fine enough for any man," Charles declared gallantly.

She touched his arm. "That is so very kind of you, Mr. Dickens. But I am afraid I am not simpering enough for the average man. I'd rather be out walking the streets, solving our mystery, than be sitting with some Mr. Durant's mother, sipping tea, hoping she finds me worthy of mention to her son."

"You like a challenge, I can see that. Perhaps you would prefer a man who is a project, rather than one who already has the world laid out at his feet?"

Cold breath puffed from her mouth in an egg shape. "The truth of that remains to be seen. But as to our business?"

He considered. "With Mrs. Durant being deceased, how does a Miss Carley come to a Mr. Durant's attention?"

"I'm sure Mr. Carley would bring him to dinner, or invite him to a party. Mr. Durant is very charming, a good guest."

"Without a Mr. Carley, or a Lord Lugoson, for that matter?" he inquired.

"Oh, I see. How would Miss Christiana Lugoson have seen him?" She worried at her upper lip for a moment. "Goodness, she wasn't out. Her brother is too young to have been his friend. Mr. Durant must be older than you are."

"A theater enthusiast?" Charles asked.

"I have no idea."

"I will think of something," Charles said, racking his brain for an idea. How did one meet respectable strangers without an introduction?

"I know you will," Miss Hogarth said.

The light went on. "I shall go to his house, collecting for charity," Charles said. "Anyone might turn up at a house doing that, and we will be dressed perfectly respectably. I'll take William with me."

She nodded enthusiastically. "What will you collect for?"

"Some charity to distribute clothing to the mudlarks, perhaps," Charles said, thinking of those ragged children he had seen on the riverbank.

"That sounds like a very nice charity. Do you know any mudlarks?" she asked uncertainly.

He winked at her. "I like all strata of society. If you can teach me about the upper class, I can return the favor with the low."

The rest of the way home, he regaled her with his story of Lucy Fair and the other children he'd met under Blackfriars Bridge.

When they reached her door, Miss Hogarth took his hand, very tenderly, and said, "They sound a very sensible cause indeed, Mr. Dickens, and it does you credit to think of them. We shall solicit my father, so you have a sponsor, and a letter of introduction."

"This charity will do wonders for getting me in any door," Charles declared, trying to sound like a man worthy of Miss Hogarth's hand.

She nodded. "You have the best ideas, Mr. Dickens. No wonder you are such a good journalist."

Charles's heart swelled, and the Pelham Crescent conversation seemed almost as far away as his humiliating life of a decade before as he spent the evening cosseted by the delightful family. By the time he left to walk home, he had a letter of introduction in praise of his charity from Mr. Hogarth and a series of radiant smiles from the Hogarth sisters that had his head in a whirl.

# Chapter 17

William Aga gleefully joined Charles as an officer of the newly created Charity for Dressing the Mudlark Children of Blackfriars Bridge. The pair hitched a ride to a public house on Kings Road, close to Sydney Street, on a newspaper wagon after they were finished at their office the next evening.

"Do you suspect this man of being the poisoner?" William asked, as they stepped into the Spotted Dog for a pint before heading north.

"Why would a gentleman murder two girls?" Charles countered.

"If they were expecting his bastard babes?" William set coins down on the counter as the barman appeared with their drinks.

"No one has suggested either girl had expectations," Charles said.

"What are you hoping to get out of the meeting, then?"

"At this moment, Lady Lugoson is the obvious killer. Though I doubt she killed Marie Rueff, that death would have inspired her actions. Although, Angela Acton is suspicious as well. I don't like that she beats Julie." He glanced at the barman when he came their way. "Do you have anything to eat?"

"Game pie."

"I'll take a slice of that. Do you want anything?"

"No." William had a look of confusion. "What do you mean, Julie is being beaten? That lovely sprite?"

"So she claims. I saw a bruise on her face."

William swore under his breath. "I hope it is Angela Acton then, so the old bag hangs for her crimes."

"That's harsh. Many a mistress has offered correction to a sassy servant, and Julie has a mouth on her."

"She's a darling," William said. "I won't hear a word against her."

"I find her troublesome. I never know when she will turn up, and I'm not convinced she isn't adverse to a bit of light-fingered action."

William shrugged. "She's got to survive. What's her story?"

"No idea. At least there's been no indication Percy Chalke is violent toward her. I'd be concerned about that."

The barman came back with a large slice of pie. Charles's mouth watered at the sight of the hot water pastry lined with bacon, and the thickly diced meat inside.

"That's enough for two," William said, but Charles mock-snarled and pulled the plate toward him, forcing his friend to ask for his own.

"You know we are in a fashionable area when the public house food is this good," Charles said a few minutes later, half of his pie already gone. "But back to our topic. Since Miss Lugoson spent time with this Mr. Durant, then he might have insight into her. In regard to Miss Rueff, we still don't know if she might have taken the fatal dose herself. There has been that suggestion of foraging."

"You cannot have wasted three weeks upon this death and not have it be murder," William said, his lips shiny with bacon grease.

"At least some good will come from it, for the mudlarks, at any rate."

"And Miss Catherine Hogarth," William said. "What is going on there?"

"She wants a fine house on a fine street," Charles told him. He glanced down and found only one last bite left on his plate.

"You don't think you can rise to that?"

"Not this year, certainly. I'll have to find the time to study the law to move up in the world."

"You're only twenty-two. You have time."

"She is obviously ready to consider a serious suit."

"And you are not?" His voice went up, as if questioning the truth of Charles's statement.

"Not in that manner. No, a girl who wanted to live in three snug rooms in Furnival's Inn, with the hopes of better things, that would be different."

"You are certain that is not her? After all, her father knows your prospects and introduced you."

"The father may not know what the daughter wants."

"If she likes you, even loves you, her expectations will learn to match your prospects," William said.

Charles set his fork down, thinking of what his father had brought his mother to, from a comfortable life to an unsteady dependence on her children. He didn't want a girl to lower herself to him, he wanted to raise himself to her, but pride forbid further discussion, even with William. "On to the matter of the moment. We had better take our begging box to Durant's home."

William finished his last bites as Charles paid the barman for the excellent pie and they left, enjoying the well-lit streets, despite the encroaching dark.

"We're looking for a new house, last in a row of five. Apparently, Durant's mother signed on to a scheme to build with four other families."

They walked along with the tide of men returning home from their labors. Carts went by, with tradesmen attending to sell off the last of their goods before families barred their doors for the night.

"This must be it," Charles exclaimed, stopping. "I didn't realize the house would be so near the burial ground." The last of the stucco-fronted terraced houses looked fresh and prosperous. A number of lights were on in the front of the house, so Charles had no concerns about calling.

He marched up the steps and rang the bell. Not a minute later, a parlormaid with a pretty, narrow face and very dark hair opened the door.

"Good evening. I would like to see Mr. Durant, if you please," Charles said.

"Who is calling?"

"Charles Dickens and William Aga of the Charity for Dressing the Mudlark Children of Blackfriars Bridge."

"Oh, Mr. Durant don't see people he don't know," she said, starting to push the door closed.

"We are from St. Luke's," Charles said, a quick lie. "I have a letter of recommendation."

"I'll take it," she said, clearly bored.

He handed her Mr. Hogarth's note and she took it, closing the door, leaving them on the step.

"Not a friendly household," William quipped.

"He might be inundated by charitable requests," Charles said.

"If we are barred entrance, it is not particularly bad for him. But I meant to tell you, Lady Holland has invited us around again tomorrow night for another of her salons. Are you game?"

How he was coming up in the world, to receive an invitation this desirable. "I cannot say no, though I am about ready to move out to this area. I spend much too much time to-ing and fro-ing."

The door opened again and the parlormaid gestured them inside, still surly. The house was not large and Charles saw a room made up as a study across the hall, which might have been a second parlor in another sort of household, before they handed over their coats and were ushered into the room to the right. A fire was laid but not lit, and the room had the damp air of disuse.

"The receiving room of a man who does not receive," William said, running his finger along a china vase and coming away with a dark trail of dust.

Charles picked up the lamp that the maid had left. Other than that, the only light was that of the gas lamp on the street outside the window. He held up the light source and walked along the walls. "Castles," he said. "Someone has collected amateur paintings of castles."

"Some ancestor did them," William said, brushing the dust off his hands over the fire grate.

Just then, the door opened. Charles turned with his lamp and saw a man with broad shoulders, a warrior's body, and the face of an angelic child. His hair, a brownish bronze, hung tightly ringletted around his soft forehead. Those Cupidish, puckered red lips opened. Charles recognized the man as the mourner he'd seen hanging back, glared at by Mr. Carley, at Miss Lugoson's funeral.

"Dear me, it is cold," said he, rushing forward to light the fire. "Drat that maid."

"You are Mr. Durant?" Charles inquired.

"Indeed I am. You are Charles Dickens?"

"I am, and this is my fellow member of the Society, William Aga."

Mr. Durant rose and shook both their hands. "I am sorry to hear about the plight of these children, but I'd understood that mudlarking was a source of income."

"An uncertain one, and this particular group of children is

very young," Charles said. "Ollie in particular pulled at my heartstrings."

Mr. Durant peered nearsightedly at them. "I do not think I have seen you at St. Luke's."

"I reside in Holborn at the moment, but I am considering a move."

"I must have misunderstood my maid," Mr. Durant said. "Will you sit? We shall draw our chairs quite close to the fire for warmth."

They nodded and pulled unornamented chairs of worn green velvet toward the fire, setting a loose circle.

"That's better," said their host. "I never use this room. Where did you acquire my name?"

"The Carleys are acquaintances of ours."

"I see." Mr. Durant's lower lip went between his teeth and he bit down, quite hard. "They are not often at St. Luke's either."

"I was at Miss Lugoson's bedside when she expired," Charles said gently. "I thought we might discuss her."

"Whatever for?"

"The truth is, sir, that Lady Lugoson has discovered certain mysteries in her daughter's life, and she commissioned me to find answers." When Mr. Durant nodded thoughtfully, Charles went on. "I saw you at her funeral. You knew her?"

"Yes, of course. Our fathers were friends, long ago. I am, or was, some eight years older than she, but Lady Lugoson asked me to dine when they returned, and I called on the family regularly after that."

"What about the Rueffs, also of the parish? Did you know them as well?"

The man considered. "The name is familiar to me, but not the family."

Charles sighed inwardly. He was beginning to think that no one person had killed both girls. The connection was so tenuous, and through the parents only.

"When did you last see Miss Lugoson?"

"At St. Luke's, the Sunday before she died," he said promptly.

"You were not at the Epiphany party?"

"A bad lung inflammation caused me to take to my bed for a few days."

"So you saw her two days before she died, then became ill the day before?"

"If you say so." Mr. Durant's straightforward manner had no hint of subterfuge or political thinking.

"Can you tell us the manner of your illness?" asked William, joining the conversation for the first time. "Perhaps it was the same illness that Miss Lugoson suffered from."

Mr. Durant looked up at the ceiling. "I was wracked by chills, and then by fire. A fever, obviously. Before that, a sore throat. After, a cough that kept me breathless for days. I thought I would never be well again."

"Very sorry," Charles said. "It was definitely not the same illness."

"It was very unpleasant, but I never felt close to death." He shook his head.

"If you don't mind me asking, did Miss Lugoson like to forage, or make her own herbal concoctions?" Charles inquired.

Mr. Durant laughed heartily. "No. She liked to read plays, and practice thrilling speeches, and dance. Never took walks, always the carriage, would not have known an elm from an oak."

"Do you think she had enemies?" Charles asked.

"Her aunt didn't seem to like her much. I escorted the family to the Garrick Theater a couple of times to see a play, then the panto, and met Miss Acton afterward."

"Do you think her aunt might have poisoned her?" Charles asked.

"Why?" Mr. Durant asked blankly. "Why would anyone kill such a girl?"

"Money," William said. "She was an heiress."

"I'm well aware of that, as a man must be."

"Were you considering offering for her?"

"I was in no way promised to her, nor had any affectionate words been offered. She was not yet out, and I am in no hurry."

"Would it surprise you to know Miss Lugoson claimed she was engaged to some people?" Charles was unsure of exactly the financial state of the Durant household. Dusty rooms were a sign of careless housekeeping, but were they a sign of relative poverty as well? He could not say, but perhaps Lady Holland might offer insight at her salon.

"She was a fanciful creature. Definitely not engaged. Tell me why you asked about the Rueff family," Durant said, seeming to sharpen.

"The daughter of that house, also an heiress, died in the same manner one year before. Her father came from the same village where the Lugosons lived until recently."

"Have you spoken to her parents?" Durant asked.

"No, she has only a father. We should solicit him for our Society as well."

"Yes, do that," Durant said slowly.

"Any other suggestions or insights?" Charles asked. "For Lady Lugoson's sake?"

Mr. Durant reached into his pocket, pulling out a handful of shillings. "For your Society, as I assume these mudlarks are real."

"Very much so," Charles assured him, placing the money in a little cloth bag he had bought for the purpose of looking official. "Any final thoughts on Miss Carley, for instance?"

"I see the Carleys often, as I have hopes of a political career myself," Mr. Durant said. "But we did not speak of Miss Lugoson."

"Why not? Miss Carley and Miss Lugoson clearly spoke of you."

Mr. Durant seemed startled by this. "The question always is, do you marry for connection, for wealth, for friendship, or for love?"

"Miss Lugoson had the wealth, but her father, who was the best connection, was deceased. Miss Carley has the connections now," William said.

Mr. Durant nodded. "None of this mattered because the girls were not yet out. I was focused on my career. Not standing for an election now, still learning, but in the next five years or so . . ."

"Very good," Charles said, tiring of the chilly, dark room, and this rather vacant gentleman. "Thank you for your donation and suggestion that we apply to Monsieur Rueff for additional support."

# Chapter 18

Charles arrived at Holland House with William the next night, somewhat more at ease than the first time he had been invited more than two weeks before. In these interactions he'd had with the political class, the Carleys, Mr. Durant and such, he hadn't found any finer humanity than that available at the Hogarth dinner table. He knew himself to be self-educated to the highest standard, and a keen observer of human behavior. He no longer felt himself unequal to such company.

Lady Holland seemed to be in something of a flutter when he saw her in the first drawing room. "Mr. Dickens," she exclaimed as he went to greet his hostess. She fussed with her skirts, then straightened her rope of pearls, from which descended a diamond-and-ruby pendant.

"My lady. What an honor to be remembered," Charles said, bowing over her hand.

"I thought of you especially, given the awkwardness of the situation." The corners of her lips turned down, deepening her jowls.

"What is wrong, dear lady?"

William winked and moved on to give them some privacy. She took Charles's arm and drew him into a corner love seat. Behind them was a triangular table with a stunning silver candelabrum. It held three deliciously scented beeswax candles. A spot for relaxation, but the lady's mood made him tense.

"It is Lady Lugoson," she said.

"Is she ill?" Charles asked, concerned despite himself, though he knew all too well that the woman might be a filicide.

"She is here," Lady Holland hissed.

"In your house? She came to your gathering? Less than a month after her daughter died?"

She nodded, jowls wobbling with the vehemence of her movements. "She is in the Gilt Chamber."

How extremely odd, Lady Lugoson was proving to be. "Whatever for?"

"I had a footman shut the door. He is standing guard."

"What will you do?"

"Can you escort her home, Mr. Dickens? She cannot see anyone. Just a penny short of distraught, I think. Ready to fly into a rage. I wonder if she had planned to find a second husband just before her daughter came out, and now all of her plans are ruined."

"Does she need money?"

"Not that I have heard."

He frowned. "Did she ask after someone specific?"

"Why?"

"She might have a specific marital target, though my thoughts incline in another direction. Do you know Jacques Rueff?"

"Yes, of course. He doesn't live far."

"You know his daughter died in the same manner as Miss Lugoson, and poison was suspected at the time."

"She was murdered?"

"It was thought she poisoned herself with something she had gathered. Herb, mushroom, something of that nature."

"I see." The lady played with her fan.

"Is it possible that Lady Lugoson took action against her own daughter? She could have had the idea from Monsieur Rueff."

"No." Lady Holland shook her head again. "He is not such a man. And if Lady Lugoson wants a husband, it was the wrong time to kill her daughter. I think you are wrong, Mr. Dickens. You are not in possession of all the facts yet."

"But the money," he said. "You were the first person to tell me that the girl was Angela Acton's daughter, not Lady Lugoson's."

Her hands stilled. "Was I right?"

Charles nodded.

"Still, Christiana was accepted as such. Now, Lady Lugoson cannot remarry this year." Lady Holland patted his leg. "I shall introduce you to Monsieur Rueff to satisfy your curiosity, then you will remove Lady Lugoson."

"Agreed," Charles said, helping her to rise. "He has a fiancée, I believe?"

"Or he did. That talk has died out, given his finances and his health." Lady Holland directed him toward her card room, pausing to introduce him to half a dozen distinguished men along the way, all Whig party members. Charles had seen half of them in political meetings over the past months, but had never met any personally. He didn't see William at all and wondered where he had gone.

Lady Holland nodded in the direction of a table. Four men were playing whist, glasses of port at their elbows. Charles took them in. All graying, evening dress in good condition, comfortable men. One of them, though, seemed to droop more than the others.

"Rueff?" he whispered, inclining his head toward the one whose head seemed too heavy for his neck to hold up. His hair held the remains of flame around his ears and neck, though it was grayed above, and his scalp shone through at the top.

She nodded. "After this, the Gilt Chamber, Mr. Dickens."

He waved his hand in a mockery of a handshake and they went toward the gamers.

"Gentlemen, if I may interrupt? I'd like to introduce you to my young friend, the journalist Charles Dickens." She went around the table, introducing each one.

"Very pleased," Monsieur Rueff said in a faded voice, with no hint of interest in Charles whatsoever.

Matthew Post, across from Rueff, a solicitor, was the only man who seemed to recognize his name. "A pleasure, Mr. Dickens. I take the *Morning Chronicle* and read it assiduously each day."

Charles glanced sideways at Monsieur Rueff, but the man, with deep bags under his eyes, his skin an unflattering shade with no hint of pink in it, didn't seem to have listened.

"I have some thoughts on one of the candidates," Mr. Post said. "Perhaps I can steer you to a certain fact that is sure to discredit the man in the eyes of your readers."

"Very good, thank you, Mr. Post." Charles allowed Lady Holland to whisk him away after a promise to call on Mr. Post at his offices in Gray's Inn sometime in the near future.

"Has Monsieur Rueff always been like that?" Charles asked.

"No. He slowly decayed after his wife died, and his daughter's death completed the process. Now, he only waits for death. I think something is eating him from the inside."

"Like an actual cancer, rather than guilt?"

"Yes. He did not kill his daughter. Either it was a mishap, or some greater mechanism you have yet to see. His former fiancée is perhaps the culprit? I believe she returned to France instead of staying to care for him."

With that, Lady Holland left him with the footman who guarded Lady Lugoson. He let Charles into the Gilt Chamber and closed the door. Charles's eyes were dazzled by all the gold decorations for a moment. Light flashed around the room, creating a dizzying aspect. When his eyes adjusted, he saw Lady Lugoson, regarding the bust of a man with long, curly hair.

"What brings you out on a winter's night, my lady?" Charles asked, coming up next to her.

Her profile was serene. She didn't seem startled by his appearance in the room. "I was restless. I thought Lady Holland a friend, but she seemed horrified by my arrival."

"It is very soon for you to be at a party," he said gently.

"One day passes like another, until I lose all sense of time. I used to vary the color of my dresses by the day, an anchor to reality. Now, all black," she said, gesturing down her ebony skirt.

"Lady Holland said you were looking for someone?"

"I had thought to find Charles Greville," she said carelessly, picking up a glass of wine. "He amuses me."

"I understand he is much sought after. Perhaps you could ask him to call on you in your own home."

"I am tired of it," she said, her sudden petulance reminding him of her sister. "I think I shall return to France."

"What about Lord Lugoson?"

"He is more at home there as well." She shivered. "What if my daughter's attacker comes for him?"

He wondered if she sensed a dangerous flaw in her own character, one that might harm her child, or in some other agent. "Have you come to any further conclusions, my lady? I am now led to believe that Miss Rueff's death was thought to be an accidental poisoning, therefore poison can clearly be suspected in your daughter's death as well."

"It is the Garrick," she said in a whisper. "Oh, my husband was capable of anything."

"Your husband, God rest his soul, is long deceased, my lady," Charles said. Was the lady in danger of losing her mind?

A candle, malfunctioning, flickered and went out to the right of them. Just the one light source vanquished, reflected in all the mirrors around them, seemed to leave behind an air of gloom. Of menace.

"Did he die like your daughter?" Charles asked.

She winced, as if her old head injury flared. "I still hear his voice. Oh, he didn't suffer enough."

"Did he tell you to take Christiana's life?" Charles said in a pregnant whisper.

She turned fully to him, and gripped his shoulders in surprisingly strong fingers. "Christiana was the daughter of my heart. She was light itself, perfect. I would never have harmed her, whatever it cost my son."

"Do you suspect your son then?" Charles asked.

Tears welled up instantly in her beautiful eyes, only slightly weathered at the far corners, running down her perfect nose and dripping onto her tender lips.

"Dear me, you do," Charles said. "And his father? Do you suspect the same?"

She didn't answer his question. "It wasn't Angela, how could she have given my poor dear poison?"

"I don't know, but she's a violent woman. She beats her own servant."

"An actress's drama," the lady said, not bothering to wipe away her tears. "You must find who did it, Mr. Dickens. I cannot live like this, wondering if my own child killed his sister for money."

Charles nodded, his heart swelling with pity for the beautiful baroness despite his lack of trust in her. "I promise you I will understand how your daughter came to die."

"Thank you, Mr. Dickens." She drew herself up, and removed her hands from his shoulders. "We shall drink this wine that was brought to me, and then you shall escort me home."

"Of course, my lady," he said, sitting across from her as she gestured and taking the very full glass of wine that she offered.

*   *   *

Charles spent the next morning with a decidedly thick head, courtesy of sharing a decanter of very rich wine with Lady Lugoson. They had stumbled back to her house after drinking the decanter dry, and he had forgotten about William. All caution had been lost as well, drinking into the wee hours with a possible murderer.

He forced himself to focus through the miasma of headache and stomach cramps, and managed to complete two articles before William came in from a political meeting, a cross expression on his face.

"What happened to you last night?" he demanded, pushing his chair next to Charles's.

"Lady Holland asked me to watch over Lady Lugoson, who had come to her gathering."

"I heard about that. Did you get anywhere with her?"

Charles ignored the question. "I want to go back to Dr. Keville. I wonder if I could get him and Dr. Manette into a room to talk through their patient histories."

William poked his index finger into the desk. "Either Miss Lugoson was poisoned or she wasn't. No one will ever know unless a killer confesses. You have two dead girls."

"Lady Lugoson has begun to suspect her own son."

William snorted derisively. "He wasn't in England when Marie Rueff died. But I guess she didn't confess to anything."

"No, not even facts about her husband's end, but I did meet Miss Rueff's father. He did not seem like a killer. Two different deaths, unconnected except through the parish and a link to Fontainebleau."

"Different doctors."

"Yes. I am missing something both girls had in common. It wasn't friends, or men, or hobbies."

"That you know of. Sometimes it takes time to uncover the truth. Will you give up?"

"No, too much of my personal self-worth is tied up in the tale now. I want the Hogarths to see that I can solve this puzzle. After all, there are young girls in that family, living in the same parish." He pushed back from his desk. "I'm sorry, William. I am too restless to do more than return to the doctor."

Charles waited in Dr. Keville's parlor for half an hour. Eventually, a very stout lady tottered out of his office and he was brought to the doctor by the same woman as before.

"Mr. Dickens," the doctor said, rising from his desk to shake his hand. "You look unwell, sir."

"I did not come for myself."

"Hmmm." The doctor peered at him. "Reddened nose, glazed eyes, and your waistcoat fits differently than when I saw you last."

Charles put his hand over his abdomen. "What?"

"You have the look of a man overly strained. Are you sleeping well? Bowels regular?"

"I have always been restless," Charles said. "The thought of Miss Lugoson keeps me up at night. And financial worries."

"Overimbibed recently?"

"Last night."

"Lay off the drink and the rich food for a few days," the doctor advised. "I'll take your pulse."

Charles drew back. "I will take your advice, sir, and pay your bill, but I am here to acquaint you with Dr. Manette and his examination of Marie Rueff, the girl who died like Miss Lugoson did a year earlier."

"What did he suspect?" The doctor took his wrist.

"Some natural poison, probably digested by accident. Miss Rueff was a forager."

"Like a mushroom?"

Charles nodded. "Or noxious weed."

Dr. Keville let go of him and steepled his fingers. "It took both girls at least sixteen hours to die. It is possible that is what killed her. I have wondered if there was an emotional disturbance. Troubled people seem to attract one another."

"What troubled person attracted Miss Lugoson?" Charles asked.

"I have treated a close friend of hers, who is very troubled emotionally."

"Who?" Charles demanded. "Mr. Durant? Miss Carley? Her own brother?"

The doctor stiffened, as if he'd realized he'd said too much. "I cannot tell you."

"You must," Charles said. "Lady Lugoson is afraid the killer is within her own family. This family must have peace or it will be torn to pieces."

The doctor sighed. "I will deny it if you use my name, but Miss Carley is not well."

"Miss Lugoson's best friend is emotionally disturbed. By her friend's death, of course," Charles countered.

"Even before that," the doctor revealed. "She suffers from terrible jealousies."

# Chapter 19

Charles stared at Dr. Keville from his position on the other side of the desk, though the face in his mind's eye was Miss Carley, of the bad hair and perfect complexion. Here was new information.

"She has bodily attacked her own brother several times," the doctor said in a low voice. "That is why he is away at school as much as possible, or traveling, to keep them apart."

"What causes these rages?" Charles asked.

"Some perception of his receiving special treatment, I believe."

Charles shifted in his chair. "I've never even heard the son's name."

"Bertram," he said. "I would not have expected Miss Lugoson's connection to Miss Carley, reformed by her return to England, to have lasted long."

"I know Miss Carley was jealous of her friend. I have heard her speak of it," Charles said.

Dr. Keville nodded. "Look there for your poison, rather than at the victim's brother."

"But he inherited a great deal of money from his sister."

"I do not think young Lord Lugoson is disturbed."

Charles was not sure he agreed with the doctor, but at least he had a new angle to pursue and confirmation that Dr. Keville could see a natural poison at work. "Thank you for your insight. It is reason to continue in my labors."

"Do not forget to exercise," the doctor said, as Charles rose. "It helps with the overconsumption."

Charles thought of all the many miles he had walked in recent weeks, despite the tightness of his waistcoat, a piece of clothing that seemed to squeeze around his innards ever more tightly as he departed the office.

He ignored the omnibus that went by, resolving to walk home, and to drink nothing stronger than ale for the rest of the week, and no pudding either. After he made these resolutions, he allowed himself a moment of satisfaction.

Who was likely to be a murderer? Why, a deranged person, of course. A deranged person who had never denied she knew Marie Rueff, who had been in the local area for both murderers, and who might likely be very jealous of Miss Lugoson, due to her love for the same man.

Why, of course the poisoner was Beatrice Carley! He had a skip in his step as he passed the bakeshop where he often bought dinner. While he contemplated not getting food at all, he needed to feed Fred, who was thin as a greyhound. He went inside and ordered a simple cut of meat with gravy, instead of pie.

Back at home, with his brother fed, he wrote an energetic letter to Miss Hogarth, detailing his case. Ink spattered from his pen, decorating his page with droplets, as he rushed to lay out his thoughts.

In the first, Miss Carley had emotional disturbances.

She was known to have bodily harmed her brother.

She resided near both girls.

She had been present the night Miss Lugoson died.

And last, she loved the same man as Miss Lugoson, a girl with more beauty and money than she possessed.

The killer was found! He implored that she and her sisters keep a healthy distance from Beatrice Carley if ever an offer of friendship was made and sealed his letter for posting, feeling quite pleased.

Charles had hoped to seek counsel from Mr. Hogarth later in the day about his next steps, now that his head was clear. At the very least, Miss Carley must be confined somewhere so that she would never follow through on her fiendish impulses again.

However, Mr. Hogarth had been called into editorial meetings all day, and by the time Charles left work, to fulfill his commitment to hunt coins with Fred that night, he had not seen his mentor.

When he arrived home, he found a letter from Miss Hogarth. He held the letter with fond regard, knowing she must have responded to him immediately to have had a letter back to him by the last post.

He opened it, expecting congratulations, but instead found words of gentle caution. Concern with the idea that they might destroy a young girl's reputation when there were plenty of other suspects was paramount in her mind. Irritation surged, even as he respected that she stood up for her own opinions. Still, she was wrong and he was correct.

To rebut her, he went to his writing desk and wrote a response.

> *Dear Miss Hogarth,*
> *In regard to my previous missive, I believe Miss Carley is indeed our murderess. Who else is likely? I have enclosed a list of motivations of all our candidates:*

1. *Beatrice Carley due to anger over Horatio Durant*
2. *Lady Lugoson due to a desire to have her son inherit*
3. *Lord Lugoson due to hatred of his half sister*
4. *Christiana Lugoson due to misadventure*
5. *Angela Acton due to fears over her daughter's theatrical career exposing her*
6. *Persons unknown or minor players in her life, including everyone who had been at the Epiphany party, persons such as Percy Chalke, Julie Saville, and the dance master who knew her, assorted parishioners*

*What, Miss Hogarth, do you think I should do next, given this extensive list, in order to prove my theory?*

Of course, she'd see his point clearly and come around to his way of thinking. Before he had folded his pages, he heard a knock at the door.

"Fred," he called, hoping his brother would answer the door, but he didn't appear. Was he even in the bedroom, as Charles had thought?

He pushed out of his chair and took his candle to the door. Instead of William, whom he always expected, he saw a tall woman, cloaked and veiled.

"Good evening, Mr. Dickens."

He recognized the soft, aristocratic voice with its faint hint of French. Lady Lugoson. Whom he had last seen two nights before, held up by her butler as Charles left her at her front door, even more cupshot than he had been.

"My lady." He heard the shock in his voice, saw her finger cover her lips in front of her veil, urging him to caution. Standing back from the door, he gave her room to come in, making sure his candle stayed well clear of her clothing.

As soon as he closed the door, he rushed to the waning fire and added coal. A titled lady in his rooms? Who might ever have predicted this? He kept warm enough with fingerless gloves and a muffler around his neck, but didn't expect a lady to tolerate a chilly room. Should he offer tea? Did he have any?

"I am sorry it is so dark, my lady. I was busy at my desk." He lit both of his lamps. When he had friends visiting, they knew to bring lamps of their own, if they lived nearby. He and Fred needed to sell their coins and buy more furnishings. Where was his brother anyway? He was supposed to be supervising the lad.

"It is of no concern." She drew off her cloak. Underneath she wore another mourning gown, this one a traveling dress, rather than the evening one she'd worn at Lady Holland's house, but equally new and stylish. Lady Lugoson's figure had not been damaged in the least by childbearing. The gathered material of her bodice displayed her tiny waist. Her more than thirty years did not show on her body, and in the flickering candlelight, did not show on what he could see of her face, either.

Only good sense kept him from thinking she'd come here to attempt an assignation. He was much too far below her, and she, far too beautiful to need to play in lesser ranks. "Has something happened? With your son, perhaps? Some new development since I saw you on Tuesday night?"

She lifted her veil, sharing the full effect of her marblelike face with him. "We did debate the school question, but he begged me not to part from him. Instead, we discussed returning to France."

From the standpoint of a grieving mother, he could understand why she would want to leave the scene of such unhappiness, but might she also be a poisoner attempting to escape the long arm of justice? Or removing her son from it?

"I see," he said. "Are you going soon?"

A handkerchief appeared as if by magic. She dabbed at the corners of her eyes. "Not soon enough, there is no soon enough unless I might have saved her."

Charles, wordless at the delicacy of her speech, gestured her to one of the chairs pulled up next to the deal table. The coins were still out.

She glanced down at them. "Elizabeth?" she asked, fingering one as she sat. "This is an interesting hobby."

He stood over the table, too uneasy to sit. "A project, with my younger brother. Fred is a bit younger than Lord Lugoson." And seemingly not at home.

"I see. History is a wise occupation for a young scholar." She tilted one coin on its side and attempted to spin it, but it was far too battered to do so. It fell over, exposing its shield back. She shivered.

"Are you chilled? Shall I put a kettle on?"

"No. I don't expect refreshment at a bachelor establishment." She crossed her hands over her waist and bent forward slightly.

He wondered when she'd had cause to be in one before, but didn't care to inquire. "Then what purpose brings you here, and without companion?"

"My maid is downstairs in the carriage," Lady Lugoson said, after a long sigh. "But I must know. Have you made any progress?"

At this time of night? She could have sent a note summoning him to Lugoson House upon her convenience. What other plans did she have for this evening? "I had another interview with Dr. Keville, and as a result, I have come to the conclusion that Beatrice Carley is responsible for your daughter's death. She would not deny knowing Marie Rueff, and she was jealous of your daughter's success with a Mr. Durant, a young, aspiring politician."

"I doubt Miss Carley knew Marie," the lady said, after a considering pause. "Monsieur Rueff is not political, and the Carleys are only interested in political people."

"Miss Rueff had a lover," Charles said. "She tried to run off shortly before she died, but was stopped."

The lady's feet shifted audibly on the floorboards. "I know nothing of that. Perhaps she killed herself out of despair at being thwarted. That age is so dramatic."

"There is no doubt of poison in her case," Charles told her, watching his guest closely.

"I am sure you are right, but Beatrice Carley is a stupid girl."

Why was Lady Lugoson so sure? "What if Miss Rueff won her lover away from Miss Carley, in the same way as Miss Carley might have felt your daughter won Mr. Durant away from her?"

The lady's fists closed, then opened again. "What poison could a foolish young girl obtain?"

Was she irritated? "Anything an apothecary might carry. Anything that might be in the home. Poison is easy to obtain."

"It takes planning to poison." She shook her head. "Beatrice is not a planner, not like her parents. She and her brother did not inherit their parents' mental acuity."

Now he understood. She wanted to press him to some agenda. He gave her an opening. "Then who is your first suspect?"

"It is still my sister."

"Not your son?"

"No, I cannot look upon my dear boy and think that. My fancy was merely the effect of the wine that night. It gave me strange ideas."

"Then your mind is changed in no way despite the fate of Miss Rueff?"

"It was in the papers. My sister had to come to her idea from somewhere. She is obsessed with youth."

Charles regarded Lady Lugoson's lovely hair. Her maid had

spent a great deal of time curling the front into tight clutches of blond ringlets. Not a hint of disinterested dishabille was evident on the lady's person. He did not see her going gently into her middle age.

"You believe your sister is not well?" he asked.

"We shall see her in Bedlam before the end," she said, then twisted her lips together tightly. "I would like to resolve the situation very quickly."

So she could return to France. Charles had the feeling that Lady Lugoson was willing to sweep the entire Marie Rueff story under the rug in order to have her sister put away. Why? Did she need whatever possessions her sister had? If her money was sunk into the Garrick, surely there was not much. Or was this the result of some deeper rivalry, something to do with the late Lord Lugoson, perhaps?

Was the lady protecting her late husband? What was the complete and true story there?

He was cast onto the waves of his thoughts. Who might be able to tell him more? The Carleys were too closely involved, in his opinion, to be of use, and he could not think to access Lady Holland on his own. Mrs. Decker came to mind. Would she allow a return call?

He heard a key in the door. Relieved that his young brother had turned up, he went to the door and welcomed him heartily. "Fred! Where have you been? I thought we had plans for tonight."

"Here I am," his brother said, droplets falling from his coat, his hair damp where it hadn't been protected by his hat. "William asked me to help him rearrange his rooms. But the weather is too foul for anything other than a game of draughts by the fire."

A chair creaked and when Charles turned around, Lady Lugoson had already repinned her hat. Quickly, he fetched her cloak and dropped it over her shoulders, careful not to touch her.

As she fastened it, she inclined her head, but said nothing, and swept out the still-open door.

Fred didn't speak until the footsteps had ceased to ring on the stairs. "What was that about?"

"I'm not sure," Charles said soberly. "But I want to find out. Set out the draughts board and heat up some cider while I dash off a quick note."

Charles had decided not to request Miss Hogarth's companionship this time, as much as he'd like to see her since she admitted he was right in his ranking of murder suspects. While she had been an asset on his first call to Mrs. Decker, he recalled that she had said some things weren't fit for certain ears. Perhaps she would say more if he came alone.

Late Friday afternoon, he made his way to Mrs. Decker's home, following the note he'd sent that morning. There had been no time for her to respond. Thankfully, she agreed to receive him, and as the sky rapidly darkened outside, he found himself on her settee, drinking tea poured from that same silver teapot as before.

Mrs. Decker, however, was transformed. She wore a new hairstyle with curls along the side of her face, rather than the formerly severe one. Her dress looked fresh and pretty, a striped fabric that was kind to her expansive figure.

"You must forgive me," she fluttered, touching her curls. "Mr. Decker requested a new miniature for me and I had the painter in today."

"It's a wonderful thing to have a strong marriage," Charles said gaily.

"Are you thinking of marriage yourself, Mr. Dickens?"

"My position in life has improved," he said. "It is not out of the question."

"That is well done for such a young man. I've heard it said you show promise." She said this in such a tone of cheerful enthusiasm that he felt none of the discomfort he'd had from Lady Lugoson's call.

"Thank you for the compliment." He noted there was a new chair in the room, too, upholstered in a rich red velvet fabric. Perhaps she was going to pose on it. "I came today to follow up on our previous conversation. I had the sense you were unwilling to discuss certain indelicate matters in front of Miss Hogarth, who is of course a few years younger than I am."

"You feel you need to know these things?"

"I had begun to believe that Beatrice Carley might have poisoned her friend, and Miss Rueff as well, over possible slights of a romantic nature," he admitted. "But Lady Lugoson is intent on her sister being the murderess, though the evidence seems slighter. You had some enthusiasm for the poisoner being even closer to home. I am afraid I am in the thrall of a poisoner, madam. I wish not to act on anyone's behalf if the possibility exists that they have been a party to this tragic death."

"What is your deepest thought on the matter?" she asked.

"That Lady Lugoson might have some secret agenda to punish her sister for the facts surrounding Christiana Lugoson's birth in the first place. Is there any chance Lord Lugoson was murdered?"

"I don't believe so." Mrs. Decker stared at the floral-patterned carpet. Her skirts rustled against the wool. "I have never heard there was the slightest question. He had been short of breath for years and ultimately died of a lung infection."

"That doesn't sound like poison," Charles agreed. "Would Angela Acton truly kill her own daughter simply to hide the mere possibility that having the girl around would show her true age?"

"I've never met her."

"She can be violent," Charles admitted.. "I've seen the result of a blow on the face of her assistant. But a poisoner?"

"That is a more subtle art, so they say," Mrs. Decker said with a toss of her black curls. Then she touched the silver at her temples self-consciously, as if realizing she was not of the age to make such a coquettish gesture.

"I implore you to share the complete truth with me," Charles begged. "I appeal to your good sense. If I am wrong about Beatrice Carley, I need to stop impugning her character."

"I don't think it is a very good one," Mrs. Decker said frankly. "But she's a child, as Christiana was, rest her soul."

"And the Lugosons?"

"It is a terrible story. Lord Lugoson was Lucifer's own devil, I'm afraid. We still shudder to think of him." She picked up her teacup and drank heartily.

Charles glanced down and realized his own tea had cooled entirely. He polished off the entire teacup at one go, waiting for her speech to begin.

"I've been told he shot himself," Mrs. Decker said, not offering him more tea. "That is the truth."

"He was a suicide?" Charles said, startled. "What about his lungs?"

"That is the public story, and he did have trouble with them, so it was believed." The lady leaned forward, her curls dangling like a spaniel's ears. The release of a secret seemed to energize her. "A long life of misdeeds culminated in a rape even he could not live with, or so I'm told."

Charles could scarcely believe his ears. First one story, then another. These Lugosons were a tragic puzzle. "Was that someone his own daughter?"

"Might that be why they fled to France after?" Mrs. Decker said with a gasp.

His eyes widened as he remembered the slim, angelic girl. "You think Miss Lugoson bore a child?"

Her eyes rounded. "If she did, I did not hear of it, but even in the parish, you don't hear everything."

"Her figure had recovered, if that is true, but it would have been over a year by the time I saw her," Charles ruminated.

"He was a very bad man, and the Actons were so intimidated by his rank that they gave him everything he wanted."

"Is the son the same as the father?"

She put her hand in front of her mouth. "He is very young, but this business of not sending him away to school makes me wonder."

"Lady Lugoson wants to keep him close. Of course." Charles's mind whirred. "What if it was Christiana Lugoson herself who was the bad seed? Might she have been poisoned to save her brother, unpleasant as I find him?"

"That points to Lady Lugoson then, not Angela Acton."

"The lady is deflecting," Charles said gloomily. "How I wish one could see evil on a face."

"One may not see evil, but one can see unhappiness, and no one in that family is at peace." Mrs. Decker straightened. "Unlike your Mr. and Miss Hogarth, who seem two very contented people."

"They are everything that is good," Charles said. "I thought to throw myself on their mercy for dinner this evening, since I am so close."

"Did I help you at all, Mr. Dickens? I cannot be sure."

"Does rape twist a woman's mind?" he asked. "Lord Lugoson defiled Miss Acton, while elevating her older sister."

"And none of them ended up happy."

"Is there any way Miss Acton benefits from her daughter's death, from her sister or nephew being blamed for it?"

"Revenge?" Mrs. Decker suggested.

"For what? Lady Lugoson was a victim of this man, too."

"If the father raped his daughter, Miss Acton might want revenge on the woman who didn't protect her," Mrs. Decker said with a sigh.

Charles closed his eyes. Yes, of course. That did make sense.

"What a murky world. I can imagine these women as innocent children, until destroyed by the beast who desired them."

"A great deal for you to consider. If all of this happened within the family, it is best you leave it alone."

Uneasily, Charles took his leave. He would agree with Mrs. Decker, if not for the conundrum of Marie Rueff.

He had trouble opening the Hogarths' front gate, as if the horrors clouding his mind were preventing him from entering such a clean, wholesome place. Forcing himself to stand up straight, to paste a smile on his downturned mouth, he lifted the gate until the latch loosened, and marched up to the Hogarths' door.

Miss Hogarth herself opened it. She looked surprised for a moment, then broke into a smile. "Mr. Dickens! What a pleasant surprise."

He had expected some apology from her, some realization that he'd been right in his theories, but discerned nothing of the sort in her manner. "I've been to see Mrs. Decker."

"Without me?" She gestured him inside.

He shook the rain off his shoes and squelched in. "If you recall, she indicated there were things she wasn't willing to say in front of you."

She frowned. "Such as?"

He gave her a superior smile, rather catlike. "Certain theories and rumors regarding the Lugosons."

She didn't seem to recognize the slight. "Oh, dear. Well, take off your coat and come sit down. Father isn't home yet but the little ones are going to have their tea now."

Charles sat with the family for half an hour, eating bread and butter and drinking tea, speaking mostly to Miss Mary Hogarth on the subject of her parents' furnishings, until Mr. Hogarth arrived by bus. The family bustled around him, fetching slippers and dishes and any number of comforting things. Charles imagined coming home to this, instead of a cold flat and a brother who didn't have any more knowledge of housekeeping than he did.

He sat next to the fire, a little separate from them, and imagined what it would be like to be master of such a household.

"Are you coming to the table?" asked Mrs. Hogarth, appearing in the doorway. "I have a meat pie for us."

Charles rose and pulled his chair back to the table as Mr. Hogarth entered, bringing in the cold scent of the outdoors. "Thank you."

"What is the state of your investigation?" Mr. Hogarth asked, when they were all settled around the dinner.

With a thought to tender ears, he explained that he suspected one person, but that everyone else seemed to still be focused on the lady herself, while she pointed her finger in different directions as it suited her.

Mr. Hogarth took out his pipe at the end of the soliloquy. Mary rushed up with a tin of tobacco, and Miss Hogarth lit a taper from the fire for him. He puffed away, considering what Charles had said.

Finally, he spoke. "You need to rule out Miss Carley and Miss Acton. If you can do that, then justice may be served."

"In what fashion can justice be served?" Charles asked, stung that Mr. Hogarth did not agree with his theory. "There is no proof of poison, no matter what anyone might think."

"The family will be shunned if they are responsible. No one will receive them, or do business with them. They will leave London and not return," Mr. Hogarth said.

"Lady Lugoson did not kill Marie Rueff," Charles said. "No one seems to have seen her for close to two years, until four months ago."

"We must know if there is a poisoner in the neighborhood, Mr. Dickens," Miss Hogarth said.

"Or more than one. I agree. Either way, I am very glad Lord Lugoson is not in the neighborhood. What a dreadful man."

Miss Hogarth bent her head over her hands.

"I am sorry you have had to hear all these things," Charles said. "But not all men are bad. Many, like myself, treat women with the gentleness they deserve."

"For the first time, I found myself very glad I am not an heiress," she said, still looking troubled. "And neither is Beatrice Carley, for which I am sure she should be grateful."

"There are more important qualities than the size of one's purse," Charles said. "A good, honest heart is the most important. Of that, I am sure you have."

She smiled at him for so long that her father cleared his throat. Charles stayed calm as he said his good-byes and redressed in his damp outerwear and left the house, but if he did a little jig in the road as he went to search in the dark for a bus to take him back into London, nobody was there to see him dance.

# Chapter 20

Since it was Saturday and Charles didn't have any political meetings to attend, he spent the morning editing the second part of his Watkins Tottle sketch in front of the parlor fire.

Fred had stayed in the bedroom, studying one of Charles's legal books, but he came out just as Charles was becoming sick of his own words. He resolved to sort out the mystery of Angela Acton for once and for all. He had no hope of understanding Lady Lugoson otherwise. Her fate was too intertwined with her sister's.

"Would you like to walk to the Garrick with me?" he asked Fred.

"To see a play?" Fred straightened his waistcoat, grinning widely.

"To see an actress." Charles noticed that his brother's clothes were too tight. He had grown again, and would need new clothing soon. "The one that Julie works for."

"Is she a real poisoner?" Fred asked eagerly.

Charles put down his quill. "Her sister seems to think so."

Fred lost his smile. "Makes you wonder what kind of child-hood they had."

"I have no idea, but anything good must have died away when Lord Lugoson came into their lives." He had spared his young brother much information, but he had heard certain details.

They bundled up and went out together, staying close for warmth, a bit of good luck when Fred skittered on black ice, invisible on the road, and nearly fell. Charles managed to hold him up, and the lad pretended to skate after that, swinging out his arms as if to balance, as he took long, gliding strides. While too grown up to join in, Charles enjoyed the sight of his mischievous brother's antics, until he accidentally knocked a package out of an elderly passerby's hand.

Before braving the Garrick, they had cups of hot cider in a public house to fortify themselves. Charles made mental notes for his sketch on the topic. Eventually, they arrived at the stage door of the theater.

The unlocked door and empty back hallway made Charles think someone must be present, but no one greeted them as they went through the warren of rear corridors and out a door that led them into the pit. Onstage was just one figure, dressed in a brown robe that had a tree design appliqued on it. Percy Chalke's voice rang out.

> Full fathom five thy father lies;
> Of his bones are coral made;
> Those are pearls that were his eyes:
> Nothing of him that doth fade
> But doth suffer a sea-change
> Into something rich and strange.

"Ariel, from *The Tempest*," Charles whispered.

"He's terrifying," Fred whispered back, staring at the creeping figure on the stage making broad gestures at the floor, as if peering into a storm-tossed sea.

"The character is telling a lie," Charles explained, as someone read the next lines from the wings.

When it came to the part of Miranda, Julie, as might be expected, did not appear, but Angela Acton, gliding from stage right, dressed in a black mourning dress. Unlike her sister's fashionable new gown, Miss Acton's dress might have been the lady's castoffs from Lord Lugoson's demise, the elbows shiny, and an obvious mend at the hem. Her first lines were nothing special, but when she said,

> I might call him
> A thing divine, for nothing natural
> I ever saw so noble . . .

Charles could see the adoration in her face, an image of youthful fascination for an ancient being. Could this be how Miss Acton had seen Lord Lugoson, once upon a time?

He and his brother watched, enchanted, as the two actors worked through the scene, Chalke playing two parts—throwing off his robe to be Ferdinand, Miranda's lover. But the two transcended what they wore. So seamlessly did they perform, that Charles began to believe that the two must act together in all things. Even murder?

Abruptly, Chalke stopped speaking. Miss Acton screeched, "Julie!"

Fred's mouth hung open as the girl dashed onto the stage, her body in a blue dress so slim and pliant, her every gesture so graceful, that she made Miss Acton look like an aging crone. The spell the actors had created vanished as the actress berated her protégée about something.

Julie went back into the wings and came out with a bolt of

fabric and another woman. They attempted to drape a rich blue robe over Miss Acton, tacking it in with pins.

Miss Acton cried out, then lashed out with her hand, striking Julie on the cheek.

Fred gasped and made as if to move forward, but Charles held him back. The woman, however talented, was a devil.

Julie put her hand to her cheek and stared forward. Charles knew the instant she saw them, but his gaze redirected at Percy Chalke, who had his arm around Miss Acton, comforting her for all the world as if she had been the one wronged.

A moment later, and Miss Acton was saying lines again, back in character, while the seamstress gathered material at her waist and tacked it into pleats.

Julie's hands dropped to her sides. She stood there, a noble, forlorn creature, the red mark obvious on her cheek.

Charles took his brother's arm and turned away. Would a woman so prone to violence be capable of subtle poison? He might better believe that Percy Chalke would poison someone who tormented his beloved. The question remained if Miss Lugoson's becoming an actress would be enough to make her mother crazed, but given how little it took for the woman to fly into a violent rage, perhaps, just perhaps, Lady Lugoson had a point.

They left the theater by the main door. Charles blinked in the daylight, limited though it was.

"I'd heard theater folk were crazy, but I've never seen anything like that. Did you really want to be an actor?" Fred asked.

"A couple of years ago," Charles said.

Fred snorted. "I'm hungry. Can we go eat?"

"We'll fetch something on the way home." They made their way through the crowded streets. The air had warmed just enough for people to be out about their business, gathering food to prepare for Sunday, and catching up on errands. He saw brisk business at a secondhand clothing stall, a clothesline of women's half boots rocking dangerously over a child's head as a gust of wind roared through.

They stopped in at a bakeshop, purchasing loaves for the next couple of days, and cakes as well. A butcher in the next street had stew meat, and Charles knew they had potatoes put by, so they could make something over the fire. Not the cozy domesticity of the Hogarths, but a way to stay out of the biting wind if it kept up.

They had been home some twenty minutes, and Fred had only just come in with fresh cans of water, when a hearty knock rang at the door.

Charles went to answer it, already hoping for an invitation to dine in some less labor-intensive manner, and found a most unexpected person upon opening. "Lord Lugoson?"

The lad was swallowed up by a heavy coat more fit for a coachman than a young man-around-town. His top hat was much too high, and his muffler covered his mouth. He spat it out of his way and spoke. "There has been a most dreadful development."

The way he delivered the line reminded Charles of a stage play. "What is wrong? Has someone confessed to making your sister so ill?"

"No, it's Horatio Durant. He's dead."

"But I just saw him a few days ago and he seemed to be in blooming health," Charles said, then felt like an idiot, for saying the obvious. "Was he poisoned?"

Lord Lugoson shook his head, then coughed. "Could I trouble you for something to drink?"

"Why did you come for me? Shouldn't your mother have sent a servant?" Charles stepped aside and called to Fred. "Pour out a cup from the kettle for Lord Lugoson."

"It isn't hot yet," Fred said.

"No matter," Charles said, as the young lord coughed again. "Have you been ill, my lord?"

"Weak chest," the boy sighed, then bent over as the force of the cough took him again.

Just like his father, Charles recalled. Fred poured out a cup of the liquid he had just brought up the steps, and Lord Lugoson took it. After a minute, his coughs subsided.

"My lord?" Charles asked.

"I wanted to see your rooms. I never see anything in London," said the lordling petulantly.

Charles sighed and brought him to the fire, then he and Fred opened the inner doors of the apartment to show Lord Lugoson how a young journalist lived.

When they were done, he smacked his lips with satisfaction. "I have a carriage waiting downstairs. We should go to Mr. Durant's house."

"How did your family learn of this death? He told me no words of affection had been exchanged between your sister and himself. I admit I am flummoxed," Charles said.

"Don't you want to see how he died?" Lord Lugoson asked, ignoring the question. "His body is at his house."

"Can't you tell me yourself?" Charles couldn't see how viewing a dead body would tell him if the man had been poisoned or not. He was no doctor.

"I don't know." The boy stamped his foot. "I'm terribly curious."

"Very well." Charles, not wanting to take more than one ghoulish youth in hand, told Fred to stay behind. He considered taking part of a loaf with him, but decided that a dead body might bring his dinner right back up again. It was better to go hungry.

They met William Aga in the corridor. He saluted. "Well met, my lads. I was just coming to discover your dinner plans."

"Horatio Durant is dead," Charles said.

William's mouth dropped open. "You don't say," William said, after he recovered.

"This is Lord Lugoson," Charles explained. "He came to tell us, and now we are going to Durant's house."

William felt his head, and discovering a hat there, said, "It is a pleasure to meet you, my lord, despite the circumstances."

Lord Lugoson nodded politely.

William's expression went stern. "I'll come with you. I might have to cover this for the *Chronicle* anyway."

A few minutes later, they sat in a comfortable coach with the young lord, speeding to Sydney Street as fast as the icy streets allowed. Charles leaned his head back against the squabs, listening to William's gruesome tales of London deaths, calculated to thrill their young companion.

"How did you learn about the death?" Charles asked again during a lull in the conversation.

"A boy came with a note," the young lord answered. "I was with Mother. She looked confused when she read it and then asked Panch to investigate the situation. He sent a stable boy to Sydney Street and found the house in chaos."

"Was the message boy from the Durant house?"

"No."

Charles wondered if it had been one of the boys who watched his rented horse that day. Probably. "What did the note say?"

The boy looked solemn. "It said 'I miss her. I'm sorry. HD.'"

The pulse in Charles's throat leapt. "A confession?" He turned to William. "An admission of guilt? Perhaps there really was a secret engagement, despite his claim of innocence."

His fellow journalist fingered the wispy moustache he had started. "If so, it is a very obscure admission. It could mean anything."

"Did he kill himself?" Charles asked.

"I think he must have killed himself." The boy's voice squeaked. "I will see the body and decide for myself. I'm a man, not a babe in leading strings."

Charles saw the marks of uncomfortable adolescence on the

boy and remembered he had not been allowed to see his sister in her mortal distress. But did not the mother have the right to keep her only child safe?

They arrived on Sydney Street. Though nearly dark, rainy, and cold, people milled about, too curious to remain indoors like sensible folk. This time, they had a driver to mind the horses, so they went past the crowd and to the house without interaction.

The bored parlormaid was not in evidence, but a house-keeper of middle years, frizzy graying hair trailing from her cap, opened the door. "Lady Lugoson received a note from Mr. Durant," Charles explained. "This is her son."

The woman stepped aside after a sharp glance at the young lord. "What does he think anyone can do now? Him without female relatives to lay him out. No one to care."

"Has a constable been called?" William asked.

"No, sir. It's a shameful thing, but there's no one to be in charge. I've called for his man of business to come."

"I know he was disinclined to marry just now, but perhaps he had some kind of steady relationship?" Charles suggested.

The housekeeper blushed. "I'm a decent woman, sir, and you've no right to be asking me these things."

Lord Lugoson gnawed at his lower lip, pulling the very cor-ner of his mouth to the center of his teeth. He had a bright-eyed, eager look about him. "Did he quarrel with his mistress?"

"I didn't say he had one," she snapped.

"This is Lord Lugoson," William reminded her.

The woman colored further. "I'm sorry, my lord. I don't know who she was."

Ah, so there had been a mistress. "Did you merely not know her name, or did you never see her?"

"Never saw her, sir," the woman answered. "But." She sniffed. "A person knows, when she is taking care of a gentleman."

"You saw the evidence," Charles suggested.

She looked away as she nodded.

"Where are the earthly remains?" Charles asked.

"In his room. He called for a bath in front of the fire, must have been about three hours ago."

"He died there?"

She nodded.

"Is he still in the tub?"

Her eyes welled with tears and she sniffled. "Joe and Billy pulled him out. He's on the bed. Who is going to clean up the blood, I ask you?"

"Blood?" Charles frowned.

"It's a right mess, sir, how he done it."

Not likely to be poison then. Had Durant shot himself? William frowned as Charles felt his old side pain flash white heat in his abdomen. He fought to gain control of himself as a knock came on the door.

They hung back as the housekeeper answered it. "Good evening, Mr. Post, thank you for coming."

"Such a dreadful occasion," said the man. "This is Mr. Dawes, the undertaker."

Charles recognized Matthew Post from Lady Holland's house. The solicitor, of middle years, had a prosperous look about him. He seemed a likely sort to have a client like Durant.

"Are you Mr. Durant's executor?" he asked.

"I do have that honor, yes. It is Dickens, isn't it?"

"Yes. Doesn't Mr. Durant have the social standing to require a funeral furnisher, rather than an undertaker?"

"There are a number of considerations, Mr. Dickens," he said. "Are you here as a friend of the deceased or as a reporter?"

"We were sent for, in a way," Charles explained.

Post sighed but didn't ask any further questions. "Please, allow these gentlemen to do their work."

The housekeeper stepped back, and a tall, thin man stepped in, followed by two younger men in smocks, carrying a stretcher.

Charles and William shared a glance. They let the men go ahead of them on the stairs, but they followed directly upon their path. Charles wasn't willing to let the body go unseen.

The housekeeper directed them into the main bedroom, where they found Horatio Durant on his bed, a sheet pulled over his lifeless body.

The undertaker's men began to confer. Charles ignored them and removed the sheet, William at his side.

He heard a strangled noise and turned to see Lord Lugoson swaying on his feet.

"Get him out of here," Post said.

The housekeeper took the boy's arm and gently pulled him into the corridor.

"What a waste," Charles muttered as he stared down at the marblelike body, again having that impression of a man in full strength, with the face of an angel. A gray angel now, with no animation of features. His eyes were slitted and his mouth hung open, but he had not lost his looks, and his hair still flopped over his brow in lazy curls that had not lost their spring.

William exhaled sharply and pointed to Durant's arms. Charles saw the deep cuts on the man's inner wrists.

"Suicide," William breathed.

"We'll lay him out and put him in his coffin at my parlor," Mr. Dawes told the housekeeper.

"Have you contacted his cousin?" she asked.

"It will take weeks," said Mr. Post. "He is traveling on the Continent. I will notify the rector tomorrow, then arrange the funeral on Monday, but it will all have to be done without a family representative."

"As long as you are doing what he wants," she said. "Poor boy."

One of the undertaker's assistants gave Charles a dirty look. He moved out of the way and perused the room, looking for what Durant had used to slash his wrists open.

The hip tub was still in evidence, the water so putrid that he had to hold his handkerchief over his nose. The fire had gone out. Trying not to gag, he searched the area around it for a weapon, but found none.

William had followed him, and pointed to the floor. Lying next to the head of the tub was a brown bottle, uncorked.

Charles bent down and picked it up. Tan paper, glued to the front, notified the holder that it was LAUDANUM POISON.

"How helpful. The antidote information is right on the label," William said, reading over his shoulder.

"He must have taken it to dull the pain before he sliced," Charles said, turning the bottle over. No liquid was left to drip out.

"But where is the knife?" William asked.

Charles shook his head. "Don't see it."

William pointed to a door. "I'll bet that's the dressing room." He vanished inside.

Charles knew they'd never be back here again, so he did his level best to memorize every little detail. The candlesticks on the fireplace, the towels on the rack. A tray that contained a bottle of wine, half-empty, and one glass. A plate with crumbs on it. No clothing. No scent of perfume or pomade in the air, but the odor of blood hung cloyingly in the air, along with the darker smells of human waste.

He felt positively dizzy and nauseated by the time William reappeared.

"No sign of a knife, other than a razor."

"Clean?"

"Yes, put away in a cupboard with shaving things. No disorder."

"Discarded clothes? Nightwear?" He heard a grunt and turned around. The undertaker's assistants had Durant lifted onto the stretcher now, neatly covered with a sheet. Dawes looked winded. He must have helped.

"Yes, it's all there. No way to know if his decision was sudden or preplanned."

The assistants moved out of the room, the heavy burden between them. Mr. Dawes conferred with Mr. Post in a low voice about clothing.

Charles responded as the housekeeper took the solicitor into the dressing room. "Of course it was preplanned. He sent a note to Lady Lugoson."

"Do we even know if it was in his handwriting?" William lifted a brow.

Lord Lugoson reentered the room once the body was gone. Charles moved to block him. The body might be gone but the tub and its ghastly contents remained.

"If he killed my sister I'm glad he's dead," said Lord Lugoson fiercely.

"I thought you hated her," Charles said.

The boy's mouth trembled. "There were moments when I did not."

Charles risked patting his shoulder. "Losing a lifetime companion is terribly painful, I am sure."

"Maybe we should go back to France," the boy said in a small voice. "Dreadful things seem to keep happening here."

Charles doubted that murder was unknown in France. "Did you see any sign that Mr. Durant was distraught due to your sister's death?"

"I didn't take much notice of him," he said. "He called a couple of times a week last autumn, but he's only come once since Christiana died."

"Did he seem emotional?"

"He was conventional," the boy said after a pause. "I wouldn't have thought him to have much sensibility, but my sister and her friend Miss Carley sighed over him like he was some romantic poet."

"Just over his looks, or his personality as well?" William asked.

"I don't know," the boy said. He scrunched up his nose. "Silly girl talk. Honestly, I'd be more likely to believe he'd lost all his money and that was why he did it."

"Then why send your mother that note?"

"Maybe his last thoughts were sentimental?" the boy suggested. "Knowing my mother would grieve for him as well, after knowing him for several months and his possibly becoming part of the family in the future."

"A pretty notion," William said. He scratched his temple.

"I think we should go," Charles said. "I would like to confer with my employer. Do you mind if we rode with you, sir?"

"Very well," the boy agreed.

The trio went downstairs. They made their good-byes to the housekeeper, then returned to the carriage, all three lost in their own thoughts. Charles looked forward to discussing the matter with Mr. Hogarth. And Miss Hogarth.


Mrs. Hogarth chuckled heartily at the sight of the two journalists, the carriage having driven past Lugoson House in order to leave them at the Hogarths before Lord Lugoson, coughing and pale again, returned home. "We see ye so often that ye need a room of yer own, Mr. Dickens!"

He grinned at her. "Do you know William Aga? He writes for the *Morning Chronicle* as well."

"I recognize the name. Come in, the pair of ye. We've eaten, but I can toast ye some bread and cheese."

"Thank you," William said.

Charles's stomach roiled at the thought of eating, after what they'd seen, but his fellow journalist was a good five years older and more hardened than he.

"Mr. Dickens!" Miss Hogarth exclaimed, coming down the

hallway in her everyday gray dress as he was in the process of removing his coat. "You look quite pale."

She took his arm, steadying him as he plucked off his hat and gloves. "What is wrong?"

"Horatio Durant is dead," he explained. "We've just come from viewing the body."

Her mouth puckered into an O. "Poor thing. And him, bless him. What happened?"

She led him to the fire, her soft fingers clutched around his forearm. William followed behind, but Charles scarcely noticed as she made him sit in a love seat and then perched at his side, so close that he could see each individual blond eyebrow.

"Mr. Hogarth should hear the tale," William said to Mrs. Hogarth, as he took the chair closest to the fire.

She nodded. "I'll fetch him and then find ye some food."

Charles ignored the sight of William munching on bread, melted cheese, and stewed apples as he told the family what they had seen and been told.

"Ye don't suppose the boy had some kind of relationship with Lady Lugoson, do ye?" Mr. Hogarth said, then paused to light his pipe.

"It's not impossible, under the circumstances," Charles said.

"I think he killed the girl," William growled, then bit savagely at his bread crust.

"But you met him. He was a mild sort," Charles protested.

The journalist set his empty plate on the armrest of his chair and glanced over at Charles's untouched plate. "Could have been an accident."

"Not after Marie Rueff's death," Miss Hogarth said.

"Could he have killed Miss Lugoson when he found out she wasn't who the family claimed she was?"

"She was still an heiress," William argued. "Are you going to eat that?"

Charles passed him the plate of food. Miss Hogarth took his hand in hers, placed her other hand over his, and patted him. He felt a jolt of fire run up his arm at the tender touch. When her mother saw what she was doing, Miss Hogarth colored and let him go.

"I don't think Horatio Durant killed Miss Lugoson," Mr. Hogarth said.

"He claimed he'd been very ill around then," Charles said, wishing he could stroke his cheek with the hand Miss Hogarth had touched so sweetly, but he didn't want anyone to notice his sentimentality.

"Maybe he'd been poisoned as well," William said. "But survived, due to his larger size."

"What an idea," Miss Hogarth said.

" 'I miss her. I'm sorry,' " Mr. Hogarth said thoughtfully, repeating the words from the note. "If Lady Lugoson killed the girl, perhaps to make sure the money stayed in her control, is it possible it was because Mr. Durant had agreed to marry Lady Lugoson instead?"

Charles remembered the angelic face and winced. "His last thoughts were of Miss Lugoson. It's true that her mother is not old, but she has a son who will soon reach his majority. Why would he prefer her?"

"She was restarting her political salons, or at least she had intended to. An experienced political wife, instead of an untried young girl with a lot of ugly rumors surrounding her?" Mr. Hogarth suggested.

"I see your point," William said, wiping his mouth on the back of his hand. "Yes, I rather like that theory."

Charles felt a flash of heat at the suggestion that Lady Lugoson had killed her daughter in cold blood. He stood and left the dining room, not able to take the fire or the conversation for a moment longer. When he reached the entry hall, he sat down on the bench above the shoes and let his head drop to his chest.

A few seconds later, Miss Hogarth appeared and sat next to him. "Aren't you well?"

He lifted his heavy head and looked at her. Really looked. The tender concern in her eyes was a balm to him. He instantly felt better. "We live in a great city. So many people, and one does see dreadful things. But the sight of that man, dead like that. And even worse, the place where he had died." He shuddered. "I need to toughen myself. I am too tenderhearted."

"You care about people," she said. "You liked him. I appreciate your sensibility more than ye know."

"I appreciate your kindness," he told her. "You are the best of girls, truly."

Her eyes glistened as her cheeks colored. "What a lovely thing to say."

"Someday, Miss Hogarth, I—" The words that had not entirely formed in his head were not born, for their fellow trio of conversationalists were heard in the corridor. The Hogarths appeared at the door into the entry.

"I thought ye were going to faint dead away," Mrs. Hogarth said, passing her fingers over his forehead. "We should put ye to bed for the night."

"I can't," he said. "I have to go to Sudbury tomorrow so I'm ready for Sunday's political meeting."

"I don't think that is wise," Mr. Hogarth said, "if ye are this ill. William, can ye go to Sudbury instead?"

"No," Charles protested, fearful of losing his job. "I will go. I just have to be in a coach for most of a day."

"As if that is relaxing," William jeered. "I will check on you in the morning. If you are still unwell, you can take my meeting in Woolwich on Monday instead."

"How are you getting back into town tonight?" Miss Hogarth asked.

"I think we should ask at Lugoson House next door for a carriage," William said.

"I'm willing to brave Panch," Charles said. He was deeply weary, but elated in parts.

Miss Hogarth flashed him a smile, giving him the energy to stand and take his coat from the hook. "When will we see you again, Mr. Dickens?"

"As always," he said, "sooner than either of us probably thinks."

# Chapter 21

Charles and William successfully talked Lady Lugoson's butler into sending them home in a carriage. Charles nodded off on the drive home and felt quite peckish by the time he arrived. He ate the remains of dinner and shared the Durant story with Fred, as his brother paced in front of the sputtering fire.

"You look green," Charles said. "What's wrong? Are you coming down with something?"

Fred fussed with his blanket. He'd been asleep when Charles arrived, but came into the parlor when Charles stirred the fire. "I'm not going to be able to sleep after hearing that. Let's go coin hunting."

"I doubt I will sleep well this night either after seeing Horatio Durant's sad mess, so why try to rest?" Charles said equably. "But you didn't answer me. Are you ill?"

"No, but I wish I hadn't asked about Horatio Durant," his brother said frankly. "Tales of the macabre are one thing, but this was actually someone you knew. This isn't a game, all these people dying. None of them much older than me or you, either."

"I know," Charles said, picking up his bowl and taking it to their washbasin. "It needs to stop. Let's bundle up and go out, shall we?"

"Fresh air," Fred said, going to his shoes. "Just what we need."

They went down the stairs and reached the street before they'd even finished tying their mufflers, equally ready to get out of the stuffy room.

"We won't be able to see much," Fred fretted as they turned up the street, a small trowel that he'd purchased at a stall leaning against his shoulder. "New moon tonight."

"Yet you wanted to go out?"

"I could see you have one of your headaches," his brother said. "The fires make it worse."

"London makes it worse. Besides, it turns out seeing the body of a suicide is a very hard thing." Charles pushed that gray skin with those horrible cuts far to the back of his mind. "I'm sure it made it worse that I knew the man. And I should stop talking about it, for your sake."

"No doubt. I'm glad I did not go with you." Fred patted his arm and Charles smiled sideways at his little brother.

He ruminated on the subject while they walked through the quiet streets toward their personal tree bank. He spread a length of toweling over the wet ground to spare their clothes and they knelt down, Fred with his trowel and Charles with his spoon.

"How do you imagine the coins came to be here?" Fred asked, as they worked by the light of their lantern.

To amuse them both, and to distract himself from sadder thoughts, Charles spun a story of the tempestuous Elizabethan age Countess of Derby, and her affairs with both the Earl of Essex and Walter Raleigh. She'd had assignations with both of these men under this very tree, when it was a mere sapling, and coins had dropped from the men's purses during their passion.

He'd just come to a thrilling bit about Essex's arrest for treason right under the tree when he heard female laughter. Fred scrambled to cover the lamp. Charles leaned against the tree and turned his face away. At least they had yet to find anything that night, so they had nothing to hand over to a watchman.

"*A Midsummer Night's Dream* is rumored to have been performed for the first time at the Derby wedding," she said.

"Julie Saville," Charles groaned. "Why are you following me again?"

"This is where I find you," she said simply, as she reached them. "You pirates."

Fred opened the lamp and struck a pose, as if he were standing at the wheel of a mighty ship.

Without speaking, Julie pulled off her lacy knit shawl with dirt streaks around the edges and revealed her torn bodice. The marks of fingers bit into her upper arm just below her shoulder. Charles took the lamp from Fred and examined her face as his brother exclaimed. She had a cut at the corner of her mouth.

She stuck her tongue in her cheek. "I think I have a tooth loose. Can you help me, Mr. Dickens? I need to find a new position before she kills me."

"With poison?" he asked bluntly.

She wrinkled her nose. "She's not clever enough."

"I doubt that. She's held on to her theater all this time."

"Maybe all the gin is damaging her mind," Julie snapped. "You know how hard they work me. You're the only person I know who is out and about at this time of night."

"You can sleep in front of our fire," Fred offered, before Charles could shush him.

"Don't worry," she simpered, looking at Charles's expression. "I won't damage your reputation, and surely you can't hurt mine."

"Only for the n-night," Charles stammered. "But you have to be gone in the morning. I leave for Sudbury before noon."

"Please don't leave town," she said, taking his arm. "I can't go back there. I'm afraid of Angela and Percy."

"You're an actress." He didn't wrench his arm away for fear of hurting her.

Tears dripped down her cheeks and nose. "I hurt." She worked her mouth. "I swear to you, I don't know what to do."

"Don't you have any family?" Fred asked, his forehead wrinkled with concern. He took off his muffler and tied it around Julie's neck, hiding the worst of the rips.

His brother had always had that for support, unlike Charles himself. He'd never have asked.

Julie shook her head. "They took me directly out of a workhouse two years ago. My father died when I was young and my mother when I was twelve."

"What about becoming a maid of all work?" Fred carefully rewrapped Julie's shawl around her. "You could afford that, couldn't you, Charles?"

"She's too good an actress to waste her time as a maid." Charles unwound his muffler and handed it to Fred. He tied it around Julie's neck over the shawl.

She wiped her eyes with the edges and sniffed. "Do you know anyone who can help me?"

"I'll think about it," he said, still unsure of her.

"What are you doing?" she asked.

"Hunting," Fred said. "For pirate treasure."

"A simple amusement," Charles added quickly.

"You'd better not get caught. All these lawyers in the surrounding buildings will have your head on a pike," she said tartly.

"There's the Julie I know." Charles beamed, entirely restored to good humor. "Come, kneel on the towel and help us look for lumps. You should be warm enough now."

"She ought to be indoors," Fred insisted. "I can make her a cup of tea."

"I'm fine. Lumps?" Julie knelt next to Charles, hiking her shawl up on her shoulder. Then she fussed with his muffler, covering her hair. She poked experimentally in the dirt.

"You don't want to get your mittens dirty," Fred cautioned.

"Dirt comes off," she said, removing her mittens and burying her hands in the muck.

They worked in silence for half an hour or so, ignoring Fred's sighs of impatience, his urge to be a knight rescuing his lady ignored by Julie, finding nothing but pebbles. Charles began to yawn, the day catching up with him. Then his spoon stopped on something hard. He scratched around it. A rock? A coin? "Stop for a moment," he told the others.

Fred handed the trowel to him and he used it to scoop up his lump. "Do you think you've found something?"

"Here goes nothing." He took off his glove and began the slow process of crumbling the hard-packed dirt.

After a minute, Fred grew impatient and held up the lantern so he could see what Charles was doing.

"Is that gold?" Julie's breath brushed against Charles's cheek as she stared into his hands.

He spit on the dirt to loosen where the first hint of the coin was emerging.

"Be careful," she urged. "You don't want to bend it. Gold is soft."

Slowly, he worked at it, spitting until his mouth was dry, but by then, one side had emerged. "A shield back."

"That's a proper gold coin," Fred crowed. "That must be worth something."

Charles slipped it into his pocket. "We'll clean it up and take another look tomorrow."

"I can take it," Fred offered, holding out his hand.

"I have it safe," Charles insisted. He'd keep it close even in sleep, not wanting it to disappear. Hearing teeth chattering, and afraid that it was his jaw doing the rattling, he called an end to their evening. "Fill in the hole," he instructed, handing the trowel back to Fred.

"If this blasted rain would stop, we'd get further," his brother muttered.

"It keeps the top of the ground soft," Charles countered.

"Do you think all the trees have coins buried underneath?" Julie asked, standing up.

"Probably not."

"Why did you start looking?"

"It was an accident. I found that one when I was with you, not gold, and I thought I would look again." In the dark, he couldn't glare at Fred to make sure he kept his mouth shut, but thankfully his brother was too busy shifting dirt to say anything.

"It's worth trying again," Julie said, "if you're going to turn up gold coins."

"Sleep is good too," Charles said. "This isn't the sort of thing you can do in the daylight."

"Eventually someone will catch you," she agreed. "But finding a gold coin was fun."

They walked back to Furnival's Inn, more slowly than they had set out. Charles felt pleasantly tired, though anxious. Also, he was sneezing with increasing regularity. Julie slipped on a patch of ice and grabbed his arm to keep herself upright. They slid around together, trying to rebalance, as Fred danced around them, trying to figure out where to latch on to them. Julie moaned in pain as Fred caught the bruise on her arm when he grabbed her, but by the time they were safely upright, all were laughing, the echoes bouncing off buildings.

Charles shushed them as they went up the stairs. Inside, the fire had gone out and the rooms were cold. Fred went to relight the fire and put the kettle on while Charles took Julie to their water can to wash her hands and see to her wounds. A ring must have caught just under her eye, for there was a spot where a scab had formed.

"The first time she just hit your face. Now it's your face and your arm," he pointed out as he handed her a cake of soap and poured clean, cold water into their washbowl.

"I can't go back there, but I need a character. The theater world is a small place," she said.

"People must know that she's a violent woman," Charles said. His hands now clean, he opened a cupboard and pulled out a small box. "This is our sewing kit. You can fix your dress."

"Thank you." She dunked her hands into the bowl of water until they were clean, then dried them and took the box.

"I'll find you a blanket and you can sleep in front of the fire."

"Thank you, Mr. Dickens," she said. "I'm happy to clean and cook in order to pay my way."

He didn't want to formalize anything, to find himself with her in his employ. Any expectations could be dangerous. Also, he didn't want any other women in his life. He wanted his private thoughts to be filled with Miss Hogarth, not Julie, not Lady Lugoson. How complicated it all was when so many people wanted something of him.

He sneezed. "You'll need to make other arrangements, but for now, you can fix your dress, get some rest, and tomorrow, I have a little acting job for you."

Julie handed him the towel. "What?"

He wiped his nose. His words came out muffled. "We'll talk about it then."

"So you aren't going out of town?"

"William didn't seem to mind going for me. I'll trade with him this time." It seemed best.

"Thank you," she said. "You won't regret it. I'll take good care of both of you."

"Just for a day or two," he cautioned, then sneezed again. He put his hand to his forehead. "I'm going to bed," he called to Fred.

"I'll join you after the tea is made."

Charles stumbled from the room, half-blind with fatigue, but once inside, he carefully slipped the still dirty gold coin into a ripped seam on his pillowcase. It would be safe there, and he hadn't wanted to remind Julie of its existence by cleaning it in front of her.

Charles felt like a carriage was driving back and forth over his forehead when he woke, digging its wheels into his sore skull, but Fred and Julie were both bright-eyed and eager when he left the bedroom the next morning.

"What is your plan?" the actress asked.

"Clean yourself as best you can. I need you to look very respectable."

Fred swallowed a piece of bread. "Where are we going?"

"To St. Luke's for services, and then hopefully to Marie Rueff's house. I have an idea to get us more information," Charles explained.

"You just want to see the Hogarths." Fred had deep circles under his eyes, as if he were thirty-four instead of fourteen. "I'm not going all the way to Brompton. I'll go to a closer church."

"Then what?"

His brother shrugged. "I have friends."

He didn't like the idea of showing up in Brompton with just Julie Saville. It looked too much like courting. "No, Fred, you are coming with us."

"I'm not walking that far," he whined. "It's too bloody cold."

"I need you," Charles snapped. "We have a lady present."

"Sorry," Fred mumbled.

Julie glanced between the two of them. "I didn't have any brothers or sisters that lived. How amusing to watch you together."

Charles heard church bells toll. "There is an omnibus coming soon. If we leave now we can catch it."

Three hours later, they had survived the service. He, Fred, and Julie had huddled in the back. He'd wanted to see Miss Hogarth, to bask under her warm smile, but he knew he couldn't expect one with Julie in tow.

She had seen them, though, when she'd taken one of the twins out after she had started to fuss, loudly. He had agonized under her puzzled glance at them as she walked by.

Julie put her hand on his arm and smiled at Miss Hogarth, sensing with some feminine wile that she was important.

Miss Hogarth had turned away, stone-faced when she'd caught sight of the gesture. Charles jerked his arm away from Julie, hoping Miss Hogarth had seen that too, afraid she'd think he had rejected her in favor of courting the actress.

And maybe she had seen what he'd done, because she had greeted his party politely enough after the service, in the vestibule.

"That is the actress Julie Saville," he explained to her in a low voice after he raced ahead of his brother and Julie to speak to her privately for a moment. "I hired her to enact a plan."

"Oh?" Miss Hogarth smiled politely at an older woman who brushed by, her lips turned down as she saw them together.

"Yes." He leaned toward her ear. "I didn't see Monsieur Rueff today."

"Neither did I." Her bland tone wounded him.

How could she think he'd want the actress? What did he have to do to prove himself worthy of a decent woman? "I thought I would have Miss Saville pretend to be a friend of Miss Rueff's and see if we could obtain any information from the household."

"Oh." A wrinkle that had appeared between her eyebrows cleared. "An excellent idea."

"I hope someone is home," he fretted, as Fred and Julie reached them.

Miss Hogarth's eyes roamed up and down Julie's figure. "You should trade your shawl for my cloak," she said. "Yours is dirty and you don't look like someone who would have a friend in Pelham Crescent."

Charles winced.

"Are you sure?" Julie asked with a little smile. "It's the mud of honest work. The Dickenses and I were digging for treasure in the wee hours."

"What?" Miss Hogarth asked, but then her sister Mary came up to them.

As Mary fired questions, Miss Hogarth whipped off her cloak, gesturing impatiently at the shawl. Julie reluctantly traded them, still smirking.

At least, Charles noticed, she'd done a good job with the repair to her dress. He'd found his little sewing kit that morning. Fanny had given it to him at Christmas but he'd never used it. Julie had talent as a seamstress. Unfortunately, that was no way to earn a living. The wages paid to women who worked sewing clothes was abysmal. She'd be a fool to do anything but act, given her talent.

"Can I go home now?" Fred asked, bumping his shoulder against Charles.

"May I present my brother Fred?" Charles asked. "This is Miss Hogarth and Miss Mary Hogarth, Fred."

"How do you do," his brother said politely, exposing his dimples as he took an extra-long look at Mary. She took no interest in him, though both girls responded appropriately. Fred was a mere child to Mary, who was a year or so older than he.

"Who is this?" Mary asked Charles, indicating Julie.

"She's our maid of all work," Fred piped up.

"Very temporarily," Charles said. "Due to irregularities in her employment."

Mary's clear gaze moved up and down Julie's dress. The pink-and-black-striped fabric was discolored in places and the sleeves were not current, probably a hand-me-down from Angela Acton. Julie looked like the youngest daughter of an artistic family or a parlormaid on her day off.

"You'll have to keep the cloak on," Charles said. "If we want to get into the Rueff household."

"Why aren't you taking Kate?" Mary asked.

"She's already been on the street with me." He cleared his throat and gave Miss Hogarth a last, long look, noting that today her ribbons were bright green. She'd worn green before, but not quite that shade. "We are planning a little deception to see if we can access Miss Rueff's letters or any other sources of information, to see if she ever named her lover. Enjoy the rest of your day." Miss Hogarth did not respond.

He escaped with his two charges after he greeted the rest of the Hogarths, feeling like the ringmaster of a circus, leading his acts. They made fast work of their walk to Pelham Crescent, Charles in his best hat, Fred in a hand-me-down topper, and Julie in a bonnet that was the nicest part of her wardrobe.

She caught him looking as they crossed the street. "Retrimmed from leftover bits," she said, touching the velvet self-consciously. "I didn't steal anything."

"I never said you were a thief, just that you were dealing in black market goods," Charles said. "Now, there's no point changing your name, but you should emulate Miss Lugoson in voice and manner. That might make you seem more familiar to the household and get us in."

"What about Fred?" she asked.

"No help for it. He's obviously my brother," Charles said, patting Fred's cheek as the boy crossed his eyes.

"What do I need to know?" Julie asked.

"An excellent question. Here is all the background I have for your role." He outlined everything he knew about Marie Rueff.

"I hope I don't have to recognize any flora or fauna," Julie said sourly. "Mushrooms make me sneeze."

"That's strange," Fred said. "I hate sparrows."

The pair of reprobates exchanged increasingly bizarre, probably fictitious facts about themselves until Charles spotted the correct street and directed his charges there.

"There it is." Charles squared his shoulders and marched onto the porch of the Rueff home. No sign of activity in the house next door this time. He rattled the door knocker and settled in to wait.

After a couple of minutes, the door was answered by a footman. The family indeed had money if they were spending it on a man to open the door. Marie Rueff's money being spent again, not that the poor girl had any use for it now. "Yes?"

"I am Charles Dickens, an acquaintance of Monsieur Rueff, and this is Miss Saville," he said. "Miss Saville was a friend of Miss Rueff's, and she's just returned from a long stay in Paris. She only just became aware of the tragic death."

When Charles turned to indicate Julie, she had a handkerchief out and was dotting her eyes. He couldn't help but recognize the "CD" embroidery on the corner. His mother had given him new handkerchiefs for Christmas. So much for Julie not being a thief.

The footman's gaze swept the threesome. He stepped back from the door and allowed them entrance. Shocked at the ease of his deception, Charles kept a straight face as he ushered Julie ahead of himself.

The footman directed them into a large reception room with bowed windows and a marble-fronted fireplace. Ice-blue walls gave the room a cool, frosty feel. A few watercolor paintings dotted the walls, not enough for the space. "I will see if Monsieur Rueff is at home."

After he left the room, Charles surveyed the trio's dripping clothing and said, "Don't sit on anything."

"Why not? That's what it is there for," Julie said.

"The fabrics are very fine, and the footman did not take our coats. We aren't welcome to make ourselves comfortable." Charles walked along the walls, investigating the watercolors. He was struck by one picnicking scene. The man depicted might be Monsieur Rueff in happier days, which might make the young woman his late wife and the adolescent girl the late Marie Rueff.

Before Julie could argue further, the door opened and Monsieur Rueff stepped in. He must have been right down the hall. Given his appropriate dress for services, Charles wondered if the man had planned to go, then felt too ill to leave his house.

He looked even thinner than when Charles had last seen him at Lady Holland's salon, and even more gray in the face.

Glancing at them in confusion, Monsieur Rueff said, in a fading sort of voice, "What is this about?"

Julie strode to him and held her hand out, not seeming to notice that she was approaching a man who seemed little more than a specter. "My dear monsieur! I did not know my friend had perished! How many splendid hours we have spent picking mushrooms and herbs in Fontainebleau Forest. My dearest wish when I returned was to see my sweet Marie again."

She had even managed to add some French inflection to her voice.

"How very like her you are," said Monsieur Rueff in a surprised tone, inflection coming back to his voice. "You could be my Marie come back to life."

Charles glanced at the picnic scene painting again. The girl and the woman both had red hair, but that was about all he could determine.

"Oh, la, sir," Julie said with a melodious chuckle. "She was so much more beautiful than me."

Monsieur Rueff stared at her, eyes wide. He licked his thin, colorless lips. "You must be her twin," he said with flat emphasis. "I remember she had a friend like you, but I never knew her name."

"I am Julie. I am so pleased that she spoke of me," Julie simpered. "Please, monsieur, might I have the letters I sent to her, as a remembrance? I lost hers in a fire." She pointed down to the hem of her dress. She was taller than Miss Hogarth, and the pink-and-black stripes showed at her ankles. "I have very little left."

"How dreadful," he exclaimed, almost sounding like a normal man with years left in his lifespan. "I shall have her casket fetched. You can look through them. No one has separated her correspondence. We will not need them much longer."

Charles took this to be a reference to the cancer Lady Holland suggested.

"How delightful," she exclaimed. "I am so grateful to you."

"Are you here with your family?" he asked, staring at Charles with confusion, his hands shaking slightly as he opened and closed them.

"Perhaps you cannot place me, monsieur," Charles said. "Lady Holland introduced us. You were with Matthew Post, the solicitor, at her salon?"

"Ah," he said slowly. "Please forgive me. I am not well. You are a relative of my Marie's *sœur jumelle*?"

"It is a tangled tale," Charles said. "Mademoiselle is seeking employment in the theater, but she has had a most difficult time with her possessions being destroyed."

"I have been reduced to selling what little I have left," Julie said. Like magic, she produced the Queen Elizabeth gold coin from her mitten. "See? This should be a treasure to pass to my children someday, but I must sell even this."

Monsieur Rueff exclaimed as he looked into her hand. His expression became almost tender as he stared at it. "What a lovely coin. I collect coins, as I'm sure my Marie must have told you."

The footman appeared in the doorway and said something in French. His master gave him a brief set of instructions in the same language before the footman asked for their coats and, taking them, departed again.

Charles applauded Julie's skill even as he felt horror at her duplicity. He suspected he'd never see their coin again. Fred met his eyes and shook his head slightly, his lip curling. Somehow, the actress had even had time to polish the coin, probably while the brothers had barricaded themselves into the kitchen, attempting to wash up before church.

"Come, come, my dear," Monsieur Rueff said, gesturing to a sofa. "Sit with me and speak of Marie."

Julie smiled politely, too into her role to even glance at Charles, and gamely launched into an anecdote about favorite dolls. Charles held his breath, hoping the story was too generic to possibly be wrong. The bereaved father seemed to accept every word as gospel, and even laughed at one point, though he then began to cough so harshly that Julie patted him on the back. It was positively eerie how animated Julie had made him, but then the clear signs of illness would resurrect.

Some ten minutes later, a maid entered with tea. Another ten minutes passed and the footman reappeared with a small casket and a canvas satchel.

"I shall look through the documents for your name," Charles said, taking the casket while Julie continued to amuse in what sounded like the most rudimentary schoolroom French, albeit with an accurate accent. He noticed that she touched her bonnet, which she had not removed, from time to time. Perhaps she was concerned that Marie Rueff had a different hair color from her "twin."

Showing all due reverence, in case Monsieur Rueff ever took his eyes off Julie, Charles opened the casket and began to read through the letters. Schoolgirl stuff and in large handwriting, he didn't see any names that he recognized. Nothing about the Lugosons, or Horatio Durant.

He glanced up and saw circles of feverish red had appeared on the sick man's cheeks. He hoped they weren't injuring the bereaved father with their deception. No longer knowing if they had done the wrong thing or not in coming here, he kept going, just wanting to be done with this situation. But then, a few more letters in, the name "Carley" jumped out at him.

# Chapter 22

So Miss Rueff had indeed known the Carley family, though it was just a casual mention of a garden party in their Brompton garden some eighteen months before, that was, six months before Miss Rueff's death. Why had Miss Carley tiptoed around the question? He flipped through the rest of the letters, randomly pulling out three with no obvious attribution that he could claim had come from Julie.

Julie glanced at him. "Did you find my letters, dear Cousin Charles?"

"I did, yes."

"You can put them in here for safekeeping from the dreadful weather," their host said, pushing the canvas satchel toward Charles with his foot. It shook.

Charles stared at Monsieur Rueff, who despite his obvious frailty and possible fever, looked genuinely happy. Charles opened the satchel, his guilt diminishing. Inside was a great deal of green silk fabric. "There is something in here."

"It is a dress. It was sent by the seamstress just the day after." Monsieur Rueff's voice broke before he could finish his sad words. "It was never worn. Dear mademoiselle, I wish for you to have it, as a remembrance of my daughter. Her favorite color, no?"

"Oh, *oui*," Julie said, her eyes filling with tears. She took both of his hands in hers. "*Merci, monsieur. Je suis désolé pour votre perte.* I am so very sorry for your loss."

As soon as Charles could manage to extricate Julie, they departed. His daggerlike glares at her, out of sight of their host, prevented her from promising that she would visit again soon. Charles had a thousand questions for the man about his daughter, but could ask none of them. He was simply too ill. Besides, if the girl hadn't kept letters about her lover, at least nowhere her father could find them, what would her father have known? He couldn't ask the sick, grieving man if his seventeen-year-old had had any enemies.

Though he rather suspected that, if Marie Rueff had been like Julie Saville, she might very well have had one or two.

"Give it back," he snapped, as soon as they had reached the main road.

"What?"

He glared at her. "The coin, Julie. And my handkerchief, and whatever else you've stolen."

"Charles!" Fred exclaimed, putting his hand on his brother's arm.

She sniffed. "I just borrowed them. I thought they might be useful and they were. An actress needs props."

"I don't believe you."

She touched her cheek with her index finger. "I require one kiss as payment for their return."

Fred choked out a laugh. "How about you kiss me instead?"

Indignant beyond speech at her attempt to manipulate and embarrass him, Charles held out his hand, a basilisk glare in his eyes, until she huffed and looked away after a two-minute standoff in the rain. She gave up the coin and the cloth. He knotted the queen into the handkerchief and shoved them deep into his waistcoat pocket. "That's quite enough stealing. Once more and Miss Acton or not, you are out on your ear."

"What about my new dress?" she pouted.

"You can have it. I hope it helps you find a new theater."

She snatched the satchel away from him. "Did you get any good information from the letters?" she asked, as if nothing untoward had happened.

Only the fact that Fred was also listening made him answer. "It held confirmation that she did know the Carleys. We hadn't been certain of that before. Nothing about Miss Lugoson, or any member of her family."

"Maybe she communicated with her lover through some person, rather than through letters," Julie said. "I don't think that footman likes girls. He looked at Fred more than me. You need to get a person into the household, or at least talking to the servants."

Fred growled and kicked a rock across the street. Charles heard a rumble of thunder, then rain clattered on the rooftops, sounding like hail, and they were hit by sharp pellets of rain. He pulled his brother close.

"Can we take a hackney?" Julie said, a hand protectively over her velvet brim. "I don't want my bonnet ruined."

"I'm not made of money," Charles told her. "If we see a bus, I'll pay for that."

Charles sneezed the entire way back to his office from Greenwich the next day, grateful that William Aga had made the trip to Sudbury on his behalf. He wanted nothing more than a towel on his head and a hot rum punch in his hand, but first he had to write his article on the very dull political meeting he had sat through.

As he walked into the large room, hacking and coughing, he

heard his name being called. Mr. Hogarth had his head out of his office door and beckoned him in.

Charles wiped his streaming nose and came toward him. The room swam around him when he saw Miss Hogarth seated in a chair in front of her father's desk. He clutched his damp handkerchief. Was she an illusion, this neat figure in a bonnet and coat? What penance would he have to pay to receive Miss Hogarth's forgiveness?

"Oh," Charles groaned. Why couldn't he be at his best in front of Miss Hogarth? "You want your cloak back, of course. I'm afraid I forgot it in my rooms. I'll fetch it back for you."

Always assuming, of course, that he could get it away from Julie Saville.

"It's no trouble, Mr. Dickens," Miss Hogarth said, smiling sweetly from her father's office chair. "I think Miss Saville needs it more than I do. As you can see, I have a new cloak myself." She pointed to a peg on the wall, where a new blue wool cloak with a cape and a velvet collar were draped. While a masculine design, it was cut down to a woman's size.

"How nice," he said, and sneezed.

"Oh, you poor man," she said, rising.

He watched, tunnel-visioned, as she came to him and touched his forehead. "He doesn't have a fever," she told her father.

"I need to eat, that is all," Charles said. "The water was very choppy on the way back from Greenwich."

"So you could go to see Beatrice Carley with me this afternoon?" she asked anxiously. "She has requested a meeting with us."

She moved to the desk, under her father's watchful eye, and poured a cup of tea.

"Where did the cloak come from?" Charles took the cup gratefully, still stuck on that point.

She spoke while Charles drained the contents of the cup. The still-warm liquid was such a contrast to his chilled body that he could feel the heat of it going down his innards. "Lady Lugoson sent that maid Agnes over with a selection of Miss Lugoson's wardrobe. She enclosed a note that said she'd chosen a few special remembrances for herself and Miss Carley but she thought my sisters and I might like the rest."

"That was very generous to you, if not to Agnes," Charles said, remembering how plainly dressed the lady's maid had been. Often the maid herself might have expected to gain her mistress's wardrobe.

"I was rather surprised to see her, to be honest," Miss Hogarth said. "It's been nearly a month. I wonder that she is still employed."

"Maybe she knows something and they are afraid of what she will say if they turn her off," Mr. Hogarth said. "Now, Charles, why don't I have one of the boys fetch you something to eat? That hot potato seller is usually in the street about now."

"Thank you, sir."

Mr. Hogarth departed, leaving them alone.

"Can you use her wardrobe?" Charles asked, recognizing the mark of favor even if he wasn't quite in the best state to impress the editor's daughter.

"Mary is slender enough. There are a few things I can let out," she said, blushing.

"Miss Lugoson was still just a girl," Charles said. "The size of a child really. I picked her up, you recall."

"Yes, I remember. She had a great number of white dresses. So impractical."

"Maybe it is the style in France."

"I don't know. Definitely not Edinburgh or London. Will you sit and rest? I hope Father can get you that potato. There will probably be cake at the Carleys, but we can't count on it."

"If we turn up at the right time. If Mrs. Carley is at home she might have something nice. She seemed proud of her tea service."

"She did have lovely tea but I crave something exotic. I can't help remembering that lovely Epiphany tart we made."

"Ah, the strawberry jam," Charles said, nearly licking his lips in remembrance. "Well, it is February now. Strawberries are only a few months away."

"We have a strawberry patch."

"You must send me a note when you see them growing. There is a coffee stand near Lincoln's Inn that has shockingly good cake. Some cream, fresh strawberries, and that cake. Nothing better for a picnic."

She giggled. "I will let you know."

He grinned back at her. "Since we are speaking of February I should tell you that it is my birthday this week."

"How nice," she said.

"Yes. I will be twenty-three on Saturday. I thought to have a little flare-up in my rooms. Now that I have a maid, however, temporary, I ought to be able to not embarrass myself." He shivered, wishing he was tucked between his blankets at home.

"Can Miss Saville cook?"

"Oh, we'll bring in food," he said. "I hope she knows how to clean. She's got to earn her way somehow, until she finds another theater job."

"What will that take?" Her tone had gone frosty.

He had to do something. Glancing behind him, he made sure the door was very nearly shut. He leaned forward, intimately, and spoke into her ear, making sure his warm breath fell on the delicate shell. "Speaking to managers. I'm sure most of them will know of her. She has quite a following from the pit. Also, Monsieur Rueff gave her one of his daughter's dresses yesterday. He said they were practically twins, and it had come after she died."

She shivered. "He didn't return it to the dressmaker?"

He shook his head, feeling her hair against his nose. "Maybe he had forgotten it. After all, it was still there after a year."

"I imagine an actress can impersonate a great number of people," she said thoughtfully, turning toward him, so that his nose brushed her cheek.

They were so close now. He could feel her breath, too, but he gamely kept the conversation going. "I don't know that Julie would have met the Rueffs, but of course she knows the type. I told her to act like Miss Lugoson, but she even used a French accent. Shocking really. I wanted to be an actor myself when I was young, but her natural talent far supersedes mine."

Miss Hogarth started to ask another question, but then one of the boys popped in with a bundle of potato wrapped in newsprint. Charles stepped away so quickly that the room spun. Miss Hogarth poured out the rest of the tea, cold now, and Charles wolfed down his food.

Her cheeks were quite pink when she finally dared look his way a couple of minutes later. "Are you better?"

"Quite restored," he assured her. "I'm not even sneezing."

"Your skin is hot," she said.

"Being near you makes it so," he returned.

"Mr. Dickens," she whispered. "You're being very forward."

"You aren't stopping me."

Mr. Hogarth returned before she could respond. "I have a hackney waiting outside." He took his daughter's new cloak from the peg as she stood, and he draped it over her shoulders.

"Thank you. I will write my article when I return," Charles assured him.

Miss Hogarth sat very close to him in the carriage. Her new cloak didn't smell like her yet. The scent of rosemary and cedar clung to the wool as it brushed against his arm.

"Do you think my mother should have accepted the clothes,

when we suspect Lady Lugoson of having killed Miss Lugoson?" she asked, plucking at the fabric.

"There are so many other possibilities, no less Horatio Durant," he said, wishing her fingers were plucking at him instead. "I think the question is more whether Miss Lugoson herself would want you to have them. The answer to that, I think, is yes. You tended her in her final illness more than Miss Carley or Lady Lugoson did."

"I didn't have the sense that either of them knew what to do," Miss Hogarth admitted. "Thank you for setting my mind at ease, Mr. Dickens."

The carriage stopped in front of the Carley home in London and the driver said he would wait nearby.

"I'm to go home right after this interview," she said. "But I'll take you back to the office first. I'm sorry you still have to write your article."

"It's fine. I'm used to working hard. It is how I have moved ahead in life, and will go even further." Also, he didn't want to spend any more time around Julie than necessary. She was all kinds of trouble. He had to resign himself to the fact that, with free rein and no one home, she could find and pocket what little money and valuables he had.

"I know, Mr. Dickens. You have a very good reputation." She nodded at him.

"I want you to understand me," he said in a low voice.

Outside the carriage he heard the driver shout something to the horses and the conveyance lurched before stopping again. "We'd better go," said Miss Hogarth.

The Carleys' butler showed them in, but instead of taking them to the main reception room, brought them to the first floor and showed them into a small room, furnished as a girl's sitting room. The walls were hung with rose-and-ivy wallpaper and the furnishings were plush and undersized. A large doll-house rested on a table angled across a corner of the room.

Charles felt uncomfortable, though Miss Hogarth had a small smile on her face as she examined an inexpert charcoal drawing of a handsome boy with a sulky expression.

"I don't think he wanted to sit for the artist," she said.

Charles stared dully at a white-painted rocking pony with what looked like a real horse's mane, in the opposite corner from the dollhouse. In between, a small fireplace blazed away, overheating the room. He reached for his handkerchief but he must have left it in his coat. Instead he sniffed and looked around for books, but all he found was an old Bible on the tea table.

A maid they hadn't seen before brought in a floral tea service. Pretty iced cakes were set on a matching plate.

"That ought to please you," Miss Hogarth said. "Shall I pour?"

Before he could answer, Miss Carley appeared at the door. She clutched a handkerchief and her eyes were reddened. Her dress had a mismatched floral ruffle at the bottom, as if it had been lengthened from a dress belonging to a shorter girl. "Oh, Mr. Dickens," she cried, rushing toward him, mousy sausage curls fluttering like oversize dog ears. She had a nasal voice, as if pushing all the sound she generated through her nose.

He stepped back in alarm, but she bumped into him, then dropped her handkerchief and grabbed his hands before he could set her aside.

"Tell me you were with him at the last," Miss Carley moaned.

He smelled something hot on her breath and suspected she'd stretched her fingers around a decanter of sherry. Pulling away, he said, "Mr. Durant, do you mean?"

"My poor Horatio," she groaned, extending every "O" to nearly comedic effect. Her hands went to her draping lacy collar, which seemed to be an attempt to make over an old dress of some equally unfortunate cousin, much larger in the bosom.

The way the sound reverberated made Charles's forehead hurt. Her voice assaulted his skull.

"First Miss Lugoson, and now Mr. Durant," Miss Hogarth said, a calculating expression coming over her face. "You must be quite bereft."

"A new Romeo and Juliet," Miss Carley said in dramatic tones, reaching for and squeezing Charles's hands so tightly that his flesh pressed uncomfortably against his skin. "How sorry I feel for them, poor lambs."

In the face of so much discomfort, his body rebelled. He sneezed harshly, not having even the control of his hands to block it. Wrenching away, he bent down to pick up her handkerchief and used it to blot his nose, deciding it was the lesser crime compared to letting something noxious hang off his nose.

"Oh, all the trauma has made you ill," Miss Carley cried.

"Indeed," he agreed. "You do understand how Mr. Durant died, do you not?"

She shook her head. "Of grief?"

"Or guilt," he suggested. "It was a scene to indicate self-harm, Miss Carley."

Her skin went blotchy. "Will there be an inquiry?"

"When we were there, there was no indication that the police were being called in to investigate, as should probably have been done, if he had been murdered, and someone made it look otherwise."

"How would that have been possible?" Miss Hogarth asked, collapsing onto an overstuffed chair.

"If he'd been drugged first, someone could have done the rest. I had plenty of time to think about it on the way to Greenwich and back," Charles explained. "Not that I know for sure."

"Should you go to the police?" Miss Hogarth asked.

Miss Carley began to sob, huge, gulping noises that seemed to take the air out of the room. Already overheated, Charles saw the roses on the wall spin. He sat down abruptly on a small, lyre-back chair, his knees folding to his waist.

Miss Hogarth glanced between the two of them. She pulled out her handkerchief but then seemed to think better of it, probably because Charles had already borrowed it.

"Might you ring your maid for more handkerchiefs?" she asked Miss Carley. When the girl just sobbed harder, Miss Hogarth used the bellpull herself. "Does your mother know how distressed you are?"

"I cannot believe someone would have murdered sweet Mr. Durant. But why would he have harmed himself?" Miss Carley gasped, reaching for her collar again, and pulling the fabric away from her throat. "He had me to live for. I could have mended his poor broken heart."

"He was not marriage-minded," Charles said, seeing that her throat was reddened where the lace had scratched her. "I am sorry, Miss Carley, but he wanted to establish himself first. Perhaps the road he had to climb seemed too great in his distress. He had just lost his mother, too."

"No," she said, suddenly calm. She blinked hard, dispelling tears. "I think someone killed poor Horatio, like you said. Someone is killing all my friends."

"Your friends," Charles said slowly, trying to focus. "Why? Lady Lugoson is certain her sister killed your friend. What connection did Horatio have to the Garrick Theater?"

"None. Horatio had no connection to the theater," Miss Carley said. "He preferred the opera, though he hadn't had a box since his mother died."

"Financial difficulties?" Miss Hogarth said, glancing at Charles.

"He had an excellent future in front of him," Miss Carley said, beginning to cry again. Her lace was entirely askew by now. "I'd have been a good wife to him."

"Had you spoken since Miss Lugoson died?"

"Of course not," she snapped, before resuming her sobs. "But once I was out, this spring, we'd have seen each other."

"So you have no idea what has been going on since the last time you saw him, which was when?" Charles asked.

"New Year's Day," she said. "My parents had a card party."

"Which means you never saw the illness that kept him in bed around Epiphany."

She paused. "No. It seems I've been kept from many of the little details of his life."

"Any other form of communication?"

She hiccupped. "No."

The maid reappeared and Miss Hogarth asked for handkerchiefs. By the time they arrived, Miss Carley seemed drained, though Charles felt better after eating a couple of the iced cakes.

"We have learned that Marie Rueff knew your family," he said, remembering another point he had wanted closure on. "We saw it in her letters."

Miss Carley blew her nose in unladylike fashion after snatching a handkerchief. "Yes? I suppose so, but I didn't know her much at all. She had a heavy accent. I never could understand her. Since she had no mother we never called."

"But she did come here?" Charles persisted.

Miss Carley waved the damp piece of cloth. "I think her father had business with mine, or wanted something. I can only remember seeing her a couple of times. She was very quiet."

"Any impressions?" Miss Hogarth asked.

Miss Carley's nostrils flared. "Beautiful, but in a young way. A round face. Very French."

"Red hair?" Charles guessed, thinking of Julie Saville.

"Yes." Miss Carley nodded. "Red gold."

"Pointed chin?" he inquired.

"I don't remember. My brother said she looked interesting and I should speak to her, but it was too hard." Miss Carley began to fiddle with her lace again.

When Charles and Miss Hogarth escaped the house and were back in the hackney, he said, "I can't imagine Horatio and

Miss Lugoson having much of a future. She wanted to be an actress and he didn't even like the theater. That makes no sense."

"No wonder he wasn't interested in marriage to her."

He chewed on his lower lip. "He probably never even met Angela Acton."

"It could have been a suicide," she suggested.

"Over Miss Lugoson?" Charles scoffed. "No."

Her fingers danced lightly over his sleeve. "I see your point. But that suicide note?"

" 'I miss her. I'm sorry,' " Charles said. "The only 'her' is obviously Miss Lugoson. None of it makes sense."

"If he was the young man in Miss Rueff's life, he'd probably have killed himself last year, when he lost access to her after the failed elopement."

He leaned forward so he could look more fully into Miss Hogarth's face. "We have no idea who that young man was."

"I meant to ask Miss Carley more about that," Miss Hogarth said. "Do you think her brother could have been Miss Rueff's runaway lover?"

"We don't know anything about him," Charles mused. "I shall send a letter to him. Assuming he lives at his family's home."

"How old is he?"

"I don't even know that. He can't be much older than twenty, given's his mother's presumable age. Bertram Carley might be a dead end, or be very useful. It is impossible to know."

Miss Hogarth's lips flattened. "All we have are three dead bodies. Two girls who died the same way a year apart, and one young man, who died suspiciously, and who no one really cares about."

"Except Miss Carley. The curse of having no family," Charles said. "His executor just wants him buried and forgotten."

"I wonder if there are financial problems. From what you said that night, I wouldn't be surprised."

Charles nodded as the hackney stopped in front of the

*Chronicle* offices. "You said you wanted a mystery. I have certainly given you that. I will see if I can get that interview with young Mr. Carley and see where that leads us. Meanwhile, I have to deal with Julie Saville."

Her tone went cool. "You don't want a maid of all work?"

"She's meant to be onstage," he said, not wanting to admit the full truth. "Thank you, Miss Hogarth, for taking care of me today. It meant a great deal."

She smiled at him with genuine warmth. "My pleasure. I am sorry you are saddled with that actress, but you have such an air about you so that you are a natural person to turn to for help."

"How kind of you to say." Flushing, he opened the carriage door, leaving her to return home.

Charles saw William coming down the street as he swung down from the carriage, a complicated maneuver involving dropping off steps while avoiding being tangled up with the driver and the reins.

"How was Sudbury?" Charles called to him with an effort, due to his scratchy throat.

"You get to go there tomorrow," William said, tucking the hem of his coat closely against his body, trying to avoid the splash from Miss Hogarth's hackney as it moved away.

"Why?" Charles asked, feeling his nose prickle again.

"Today's meeting was canceled. I managed to speak to a couple of candidates, but the debate will be tomorrow night."

"Sod it," Charles muttered. "And I still have to write the Greenwich article."

"Lucky you. I guess I'm free for the night." William rocked back on his heels.

"Can I ask you a favor?"

He pulled out a cigar. "Another one? It will cost you."

"Not Sudbury again," Charles said. "But I wonder if you have any thoughts, of something that might be done for Julie

Saville. Angela Acton has been hitting her, and Percy Chalke has her receiving smuggled goods."

"Really?" William stuck the cigar into the side of his mouth.

"Yes. I've had her at my rooms these past couple nights, but she's a bit of a thief, and she's asked me to kiss her, and it's a disaster."

William guffawed around the cigar. "Sounds like you are in over your head."

"Yes. I don't want a dalliance with her." Charles rolled his eyes.

"No, you want Miss Hogarth." He grinned, clenching his teeth to keep his cigar in his mouth.

"Maybe," Charles admitted. "Do you have any ideas?"

He sneezed as William put his finger to his chin. "You had better get out of the rain, my lad."

"Yes," Charles agreed.

"Is Miss Saville at the inn right now?"

"Probably," he said sourly. "She's likely spent the day going through my things looking for any small portable items to turn into funds."

"Then she might be off to the pawnshop already." William chuckled. "But if she's there I will speak to her."

"Thank you. You've been a good friend today." Charles clapped William on his very damp shoulder and opened the door. He hoped his head stayed in one piece long enough to get his article written, and his note to Bertram Carley, which he would post to the Carleys' London residence. Then he'd have to get home and pack for the early stage. With any luck he'd find a few hours to sleep.

Charles wrote by lamplight, finally turning in his story at ten thirty. He had his ticket for the stagecoach and would have to leave about five for his trip to Sudbury. A boy had run out to get that and a meat pie for him a few hours before.

He stumbled home, utterly exhausted by the effort of drying his nose and writing his story at the same time. Hopefully he had something clean to stuff into his carpetbag. He had a chance of getting home late the next night, instead of having to stay at an inn. That was some comfort.

When he opened his front door he had the immediate sense that something was wrong. It was much too late to call for Fred but as he closed the door something flew at him in the near dark, striking him in the chest.

# Chapter 23

❧

"How dare you!" a woman screamed, pummeling Charles.

Charles grabbed for arms, but they were moving fast and he was disoriented by the suddenness of the attack. He reached lower, dropping his head down, and attempted to grab her around the waist. He smelled greasepaint? Alcohol?

"Julie?" Had William done something? He'd thought he could trust his friend.

No answer. The woman kicked back, striking Charles's calf with a booted foot. She put too much force behind the blow to be slim-bodied Julie.

He swung her around, slamming her against the door. Julie had never reeked of gin and greasepaint. As he fought to keep her against the door, pressing his body against hers, her bonnet came loose. He blew hair out of his eyes and risked pulling off the bonnet.

In the dark, he could just see that the hair wasn't red. Probably blond.

"Miss Acton?"

"Where is she?" Angela Acton demanded. "Where is my Julie?"

"Where is my brother?" Charles demanded. "If you hurt him I'll see you hang for it, you mad bitch."

She snorted. "He's left."

"When?"

"He said I could wait for you, then he went out."

"Smart boy."

She shifted, and he pushed her back against the door.

"I won't hit you again," she gasped.

"You belong in Bedlam," Charles growled. "I don't trust you."

"Where is Julie?" she said in an eerily calm voice.

"What did Fred tell you?"

"Just that she wasn't here."

That eerie voice again. The calm before the outbreak of fresh rage?

"I have not been here all day," Charles protested.

"Was she with you?"

"No."

She grunted. "You're hurting my arm." Her head twisted and he could smell her foul breath.

"If I let you go will you promise to leave?" he asked.

"What if that jade is hiding in the bedroom with your brother?"

"When has Julie Saville ever hid from anything?" Charles asked. "She's more likely to come at your eyes with her fingers."

"That's what you think," she said with an air of satisfaction. "She's got my fire in her, and the inheritance of her father's hair proves it."

Had he heard her correctly? Hellfire and damnation, his head ached so. "Her father? He had red hair? I've never heard who her parents are."

Miss Acton made an unsuccessful attempt to pull her arm away. "Julie's father doesn't know her. My parents sent me away because of Christiana, and even after my sister took her, they left me there."

"Where?" He tried to make sense of her words.

"In Fontainebleau. There was a place they sent girls like me, like a convent school for sinners. Madame Rueff would come to see me sometimes. The Rueffs were in business with my father, fine cloth makers."

He felt sick. The pie turned over in his stomach. "And Monsieur Rueff?"

"He was a fine figure of a man back then. Just a dozen or so years older than me." Her arm moved. "Such beautiful hair."

"Marie Rueff was also a redhead," Charles said. His brain felt too full for his skull. He stepped back from Miss Acton, releasing her. "Did you kill the girl, hoping to give your daughter with Monsieur Rueff Marie's life?"

Miss Acton turned around. He heard the fabric of her clothes slide against the door. With enough sense of self-preservation to move away, he grabbed for a matchbox and lit the candle that was in a holder on the mantelpiece. Once he had sufficient light, he added coal from the hod to the fire.

The woman moved toward him, looking like a monster out of a fairy tale, her hair a tangled mass around her face, her various shawls and cloaks transforming her body into a dark lump.

"I didn't kill anyone, Mr. Dickens," she said. "I love my daughters, and I had no objection to Marie, either. After all, she was my Julie's half sister."

Two daughters lost to her. No wonder she was mad. "Why doesn't Julie know you are her mother?"

"My parents removed me from France for obvious reasons. Julie was fostered there, then brought to England when she was six or seven."

"Too young to remember much." But he remembered how convincing her accent had been. Something had remained of her childhood experience in France.

"My parents fostered her with a cook of theirs who had married to an innkeeper years before. Julie was there until she was twelve and the cook became ill. I took her after the woman died and taught her my craft. She likes to make up stories about herself but that's the truth."

"Why?"

"I knew Christiana would never be mine, buy why not Julie? No one cared about a servant girl."

"But you didn't tell her you were her mother."

"No. No one suspects, not even Jacques." Angela laughed, a gentle tinkle. "I never see him anymore. He's too ill to care about much of anything these days."

"You have been Monsieur Rueff's mistress in recent years?"

She fingered the trim of her sleeve, and gave him a coy expression.

Charles knew she was playing a character now, as surely as he knew she was telling the truth about Julie.

"Who killed Marie Rueff?" he demanded.

"I don't know."

"Who killed Christiana?" In the same harsh tone.

Her voice shrilled. "I don't know. On Julie's life, I don't know."

"Was it your sister?"

She sobbed once. "She could not have killed Marie."

"Why not?"

"She's too weak. She loved Christiana. I don't know why, I'm just sure of it," she screeched.

"What about Horatio Durant?"

"I don't know who that is," she cried, pushing at his shoulders.

He skipped back. "Christiana loved him, hoped he'd court her in earnest. In fact, she seems to have claimed to a couple of people that she had a fiancé. He died a few days ago, after sending your sister a note saying he missed her and was sorry."

"Was my sister his lover?"

Charles blinked. He hadn't considered how deep that friendship went. "I don't know."

Miss Acton lifted the candle and held it to her face. "I do things that shame me. I have a terrible temper. But I am not a murderess."

"If you weren't an actress that tone of voice might convince me," he admitted.

"Someone is killing young people," she said. "But I do not benefit from any of these deaths. Neither did Julie, or Percy."

"Your sister benefited."

"Not from all of the deaths. Marie Rueff could mean nothing to her."

If Miss Acton had thought Julie might benefit from the Rueff girl's death, she had not taken advantage of it in the past year. "Does your sister know about Julie?"

"You might think so, but no, I really don't believe she does. Much too self-absorbed. Why would a servant actress interest her? My parents would not have told her. I had all the shame and my sister had all the reward. Her son inherits many thousands of pounds and my Julie is wandering the streets at night."

"That is Mr. Chalke's fault."

"I need to keep Julie away from him. Now that I am aging and she is fully in bloom." Her voice was as soft as a rose petal. "I worry. She's just sixteen, you know. Where is she?"

He had thought Julie older, though she looked so young. Hadn't Julie even claimed to be older? He rather thought so. Maybe she believed it to be true. But he had never guessed who her parents were. Why had it not occurred to him at the Rueff house? Perhaps because it had not seemed to occur to her own father. "I do not know."

"You had better keep her safe, Mr. Dickens. If you think I am a murderess, think of what I might do if Julie is harmed." She cackled.

He stood, his feet rooted to the floor, ready to protect himself from the madwoman, while she walked away. The door opened and closed, but he still stood, a creature of stone, so many thoughts whirling in his head that the rest of him would not function.

Charles stumbled up the stairs at Furnival's Inn at eight the next night, fresh off the stagecoach. He knew he didn't have it in him to go to the office and turn in his story. While he'd scratched out his article during the time the coach had been empty enough to allow the elbow room, he'd decided his headache and the concern for Julie's whereabouts were enough to allow him the rest of the night off.

Aside from his physical complaints, he felt positively ill that he'd sent William to deal with Julie, not having any idea of what the girl had been through in her young life. Shuffled from one country to another, from one family to another, never knowing the affection of a decent parent. Not knowing her friend Christiana was her half sister, never meeting her other sister, Marie Rueff. No wonder she had become what she was.

And both of the other girls were dead now. What if someone came after Julie? He'd never forgive himself.

He leaned against the wall as he pulled out his key, then shakily inserted it into the lock. His legs felt like raw dough, all flesh and no hard structure, as they moved him inside.

"I didn't think I'd see you tonight," Fred said, jumping up from the hearthrug as Charles closed the door.

"Where were you last night?" Charles demanded, fresh concerns rising as he caught sight of his brother. "I was worried. We had a break-in."

"I visited with Mother," his brother said. "Boz has a cold so I stayed up with him. I did wonder what had happened."

Charles checked Fred over. No sign of anything to disprove the story. He calmed down a fraction. "Angela Acton came looking for Julie. I wonder that you let her in, then scampered. I came home so late and left so early I wasn't able to check our possessions and see that you took anything."

Fred looked confused. "You can't expect me to know that a woman alone might be dangerous."

"Use better judgment," Charles snapped, then sneezed mightily.

"Your nose is all red," Fred observed. He held something up.

Charles's eyes focused on the slice of bread and butter. He reached for it. "I have a cold, too. Please leave a note if you aren't coming home. I was worried."

Fred chewed on his lower lip. "It doesn't sound like you had time to worry. What happened with the actress? And where is Julie?"

"I did worry, Fred. I'm responsible for you, you know that."

"I'm old enough to manage myself."

Charles leaned over him and fluffed his hair. "Sometimes. Anyway, I am glad you left, I suppose. Miss Acton attacked me, but we came to terms, after she told me Julie was actually her daughter."

"What?" Fred gasped.

"I don't know that Julie knows. I rather think not. I shall have to check with William Aga. I told him to talk to Julie and I haven't seen either of them since. Blasted Sudbury." He bit into the bread. Creamy butter soothed his sore mouth.

Fred pointed to the table as he stood. "You have quite a lot of mail. Maybe the answer is there."

Charles set his hat on a chair and poked through the mail while he chewed. Nothing looked interesting until he found a letter addressed to him in an unfamiliar hand. He read it, Fred attempting to follow along over his shoulder, then dropped it to the table. "I shall have to go out again. What time is it?"

Fred rubbed his eyes. "Why? It's before nine. I haven't heard the bells yet."

"He said he'd remain until ten," Charles said. "Will you check with William? Make sure he knows where Julie is? Someone's got to make sure she's safe."

Fred puffed out his chest. "Yes, you can count on me, but where are you going?"

"The Royal Oak. Bertram Carley is waiting there for me." He picked up the letter again, and his hat. Fred followed, locking the door behind him, and walked down the corridor to William's rooms while Charles returned to the street. At least he'd get something warm to eat, and the floor wouldn't be moving under his feet.

Thankfully, the public house was in Leather Lane, nearby. Bertram had chosen well. Charles arrived in front of the windows within minutes. He ducked inside the door. While he had never been there, he liked the look of the place. Situated on the ground floor of a two-story building, the inside was a pleasant mix of darkened beams and whitewash.

He glanced around, hoping to find some mix of Carley features that would send him in the right direction, but he saw three young men sitting alone at different tables and none of them had any obvious sign of Carley.

"Do you have any food left?" he asked the barman.

"Stew."

"I'll take a bowl of that and a brandy and water," Charles said, his voice scratchy. "Do you know who Bertram Carley is?"

"He's at that table to the right of the fireplace," the man said, scratching at his huge whiskers. "You must be Dickens. I've seen you about."

"That's right. If your stew is good you will see me again," Charles said, setting coins on the counter.

The man whisked them away and poured his drink before disappearing into the back. Charles took a long sip, swallowing gingerly around his sore throat. He hoped the brandy would kill whatever was lingering there.

Peering through the gloom, he could just perceive the outline of the young man the barman had indicated. He walked slowly in his direction, hoping to form an impression before he announced himself.

Eventually, he made out more definite features from the light of the fire. A strong Roman nose, firm chin. Hair probably the same color as his sister's. Having said that, he appeared tall and strong, not so different than Horatio Durant.

"Bertram Carley?" He took another drink and swished it around his mouth.

"Mr. Dickens?" The young man bounded from his chair and held out his hand. "Thank you for coming."

"My pleasure." Bertram's movements showed him to be young indeed, as did his face full-on. Younger than Charles, he had the same excellent skin as his sister, but the hair did not detract from the high, noble forehead. Fortune had favored one Carley offspring but not the other. Features that were too masculine on Miss Carley's face were perfect on her brother's.

Bertram pulled out the opposite chair and Charles sat, grateful to have the warmth of the fire at his back. Cold and damp from the long day in a stagecoach still needed to seep from his bones.

"I'll get you another of those," he said with a nod to his almost empty glass, leaving Charles to remove his coat and hat.

The barman set a spoon and bowl down on the table, then another brandy and water a few minutes later. Bertram took his seat again. "I am surprised I do not know you, Mr. Dickens. I understand you are reading law as well?"

"In theory, but I have a busy life as a parliamentary journalist, and recently I have begun to write sketches."

"How wonderfully industrious," Bertram exclaimed. "I am merely doing what I can to follow in my father's footsteps. After some foolishness last year, I have dedicated myself to my studies, but of course I have years of training left."

"I was thrown on my own devices from a young age," Charles replied. "So earning a living has been paramount."

"You've found a good one," the other man said, taking a drink from his tankard. "It is better than being dependent on your parents. I had a small legacy from a relative, and spent it all on scheming."

"What kind of schemes?" Charles asked.

"I fell in love with an heiress," Bertram said frankly. "At eighteen, when I could not have known less about me or her. She was seventeen and I spent a great sum of money on presents and plans, renting a carriage and rooms, so we could hide away while the banns were read. You know, all that romantical novel sort of thing."

"What happened?"

"We were caught. None of it ever happened. I have three rooms' worth of furniture moldering in some warehouse, and no money to spend, and no heiress wife." He laughed as if he found it genuinely funny now.

"Who was the girl?"

"I thought you knew," he said, his open expression conveying surprise. "It was Marie Rueff."

"You were her secret lover?" Charles asked.

"Yes." One shoulder jerked. "Such a tragedy that she died. I hadn't seen her in some time before that. As you can imagine, she was basically a prisoner after we were found out."

Charles stared closely at him, trying to discern his level of distress. "Her father doesn't seem very aware."

"I understand he is dying," Bertram said frankly. "But when I saw him last, he was still well. So angry. Barred me from the house, said I would never marry his daughter, even when we were of age, because I was untrustworthy."

"Are you untrustworthy?" Had Bertram flown into a rage after, decided to kill what he could not have?

"We were impetuous, dramatic." He shrugged. "But Marie was

wealthy, beautiful, unhappy. It made sense to me to give her what she wanted, which was her own establishment, her own life. Her father had planned to wed someone she disliked, you see."

"I met a Mrs. Appleby, who told me that a party was going on before Christmas, with lots of French people at it, and that was the night Miss Rueff attempted to escape with you."

"It was the night her father was having a party, yes," Bertram agreed.

"You said you hadn't seen her in some time before she died. Christmas is not that long before Epiphany. All of this happened, what, a couple of weeks before she suddenly died, presumably of poison?"

Bertram let go of his tankard and let his hands fall to his lap. "No, it was right at the beginning of December."

"So your aborted elopement was about five weeks before she died?"

"I suppose so."

"And you do not see any link between the two events?"

"I did not poison her. I loved her." His hands moved to the table. He folded one across the other. "I thought she might have harmed herself in despair."

Charles couldn't decide if he believed the young man. "Were you still engaged at that point? Were you hoping to marry her when she was older?"

"I had no contact with her after that fateful night," he said in a calm voice. "I know nothing about her from then on."

Charles thought he detected some small heat under the quiet words. "Would her father have killed her?"

"With poison?" Bertram snapped. "Of course not."

"Then what is your theory of her death?" Charles asked.

The young man shook his head. "I don't have one. I fought with my parents. They said I was too young to marry. I pointed out that she had money, and my father said she had no connections, which were just as important in politics. He counseled me to wait three or four years before I locked myself into matrimony."

"Did you agree with him?"

"I knew that there was no hope of seeing Marie again until she was out, which was about a year away." He shrugged again. "A year is a long time. Would I have tried to see her at parties then? Yes, I suppose so."

Charles narrowed his eyes. "Unless you had fallen in love with someone else. Christiana Lugoson, for instance?"

"Are you trying to link me to multiple dead girls?" Bertram demanded. "No, I was not in love with my sister's friend. My sister irritates me. I'd be unlikely to even like any of her friends."

"What about Horatio Durant?"

His eyes widened. "What are you accusing me of?"

"He is dead, too, and your sister was in love with him."

He sighed. "My father said that Horatio Durant was financially embarrassed and he believes the young man committed suicide because he was ruined."

Charles played with his glass. "Since your father was mentoring Mr. Durant, I assume he would know these things."

"Yes," he said. "I believe you are right."

"So, we have a girl in love with you who was poisoned, perhaps by her own hand, a girl who was friends with your sister who was likely poisoned, and a man whom your sister was in love with who committed suicide."

"You want my sister to be a murderess," Bertram said slowly. "Because you think she is connected to everyone."

"Angela Acton is more connected to both dead girls than I realized," Charles said. "I don't know about Mr. Durant, but your father's theory may be sound."

"It makes sense to me," Bertram agreed.

"What is your opinion of your sister?"

He looked down his nose at Charles. "My opinion is, that if my sister is a murderess, both my father's career and my own are over," he said, standing up. "I know you are a journalist, but I hope you do not attempt to print any salacious information about my family. You have no proof of anything, and multiple suspects. I would caution you to be very careful."

"I have nothing to attempt to put into an article," Charles assured him, standing as well. The room seemed to rock and sway in front of his feverish, dazed eyes. "The *Chronicle* did print information about Miss Rueff's death last year, and certainly all of these deaths are news, but we have supposed nothing. That is not at the heart of this. Lady Lugoson asked me to uncover the truth, as has her son."

"She wants to know if her sister is a madwoman," Bertram said. He fixed Charles with a stare, then turned and left.

Charles reseated himself, smiling. Bertram Carley was a fool. He'd just admitted to a lie. He knew very well who Angela Acton was. Charles had never mentioned her madness. And lies, well, they led to truths.

Charles stood up and ran out the door. He saw Bertram on the street, a few feet away. "Wait," he called.

"What?" Bertram walked back toward him, adjusting his hat.

"Look, my intentions aren't bad. I'm having a little party on Saturday night. It's my birthday, and people are coming to my rooms in Furnival's Inn. Why don't you come and see that I associate with honest people?"

He crossed his arms. "Why do you care what I think?"

"Because Lady Lugoson asked me to understand her daughter's death," Charles said. "And I might still need your help."

Bertram sighed. "I'll think about it."

"You never know who might help you in your career," Charles said.

The young man nodded. "You'll have my answer in my attendance, or lack thereof."

He walked away, and Charles ducked back into the public house. He'd left his coat on his chair, and his food on the table.

He considered another brandy and water, but finished his stew instead. It tasted wonderful, though he had trouble swallowing some of the meat. After that, he walked the short distance to his rooms.

He felt much better upon returning home, warm and fed, than he had just off the stagecoach. Confusion struck him though, when he saw the cozy domestic scene in his sitting room.

Fred, Julie, and William all sat around the deal table. Charles could see they were examining the collection of Elizabethan coins. So Julie hadn't absconded with them. Even the gold one winked from the table. And she was safe. He had the sensation that his blood ran through his veins a little more smoothly now.

"Did you find your friend?" Fred asked, still puffed up, proud of himself for his little party.

"Yes, and I see you have found ours. Where have you been, Julie?" Charles demanded.

"She slept in front of my fire last night," William said. "I apologize. She fell asleep and I didn't want to wake her by going out of the door."

"You can dock my pay," Julie said with a saucy grin.

"Your— I mean, Miss Acton was here looking for you," Charles said. "We are going to have to deal with that situation, but I need my bed, so please keep the noise down." He escaped before he did something foolish like tell her who her mother was.

# Chapter 24

❧

Hard at work the next morning on his article about the debate at Sudbury, he didn't glance up from his pen until he saw the long, black skirt. Muttered comments from the reporters around him drifted through the room as he said a confused "Good morning" to the skirt. As she greeted him he recognized the voice.

*Lady Lugoson.*

He pushed back his chair and stood. "What brings you into London, my lady?"

"I had some business at my husband's bank," she said, looking as lovely as ever despite the mourning attire. "Is there somewhere we can speak?"

"Let me see if one of the editors' offices can be borrowed." He went down the aisle, hissing to one of the boys to bring tea to Mr. Hogarth's office, then poked his head into the room. It was empty and he could see his mentor bent over Thomas Pillar's desk in the alcove past the offices.

He darted down the hallway. "Excuse me, sirs. May I borrow your office? Lady Lugoson has arrived unexpectedly."

Mr. Hogarth blinked through the puff of smoke that rose from his pipe. "I'll be there in a few minutes."

Charles nodded, then went to retrieve Lady Lugoson. She was entirely out of place in the newsroom, but William was speaking to her intently. He heard the name "Rueff."

"Did you know Monsieur Rueff has died?" William asked.

"No." Charles turned to Lady Lugoson. He had looked as if his days were numbered, but this was very soon. "Such sad news."

"Not unexpected, poor man." She sighed.

"I have a private office for us, if you'll follow me," Charles said.

When he had her seated and the tea had arrived, he closed the door and sat in Mr. Hogarth's second chair. "Is that why you came? To tell me about Monsieur Rueff's sad demise?"

"I'm not sure how sad it was. He has followed his wife and only child into eternal bliss."

"Only ch-child?" Charles stuttered.

Lady Lugoson frowned.

"What about Julie Saville?" he asked.

Lady Lugoson tilted her head and blinked. "What about her? She is Angela's maid, and does some acting herself."

"You don't know that your sister claims Julie Saville is her daughter with Monsieur Rueff?"

Lady's Lugoson's chest jerked as she let out an inaudible cry. "Are you serious?"

"Yes, ma'am," Charles said in a sober voice. "Miss Acton claimed Julie Saville is her daughter."

The lady's nostrils worked, as if she couldn't take in enough air. "Good heavens. She is so very debauched."

"I think she is unhinged," Charles said. "But not lying in this case. Monsieur Rueff said Julie could have been his daughter's twin. That made me think your sister was telling the truth, though Rueff didn't recognize her as such."

"He met her?"

"Yes. I brought her to him, pretending Julie was an old

friend who had just heard about Miss Rueff's death." Charles cleared his throat awkwardly. His cold was much improved, but not entirely gone. "I wanted to find out who her secret lover had been."

"Who was it?"

"Bertram Carley, as it turned out."

"How odd. I would not have thought either of the Carley children had the ability to take action to go with their ambitions," Lady Lugoson said.

Charles changed the subject. "I don't know if Miss Acton killed your Christiana, but she shouldn't be walking the streets."

"She's a very sick woman, but she's also unmarried and has money. It is hard to harness a woman like that."

Charles knew the same thing to be true of the woman sitting next to him. Another sister, same issues. "Would you like to pour?"

As Lady Lugoson complied, he asked, "What do you think? Is it possible that Julie is your niece?"

"I would believe anything right now. But with poor Jacques dead, we will never know. Julie will never get a penny from the Rueff family." She spoke with a surprising lack of interest, given that Julie had been friendly with Christiana, never realizing they were half sisters.

Charles spoke slowly, hoping to engage her attention. "I would like to remove Julie from Miss Acton's employ. She doesn't know who she really is, and there can be no doubt that her mother has hit her multiple times. Do you have any ideas?"

All Lady Lugoson said was "She is a good actress?"

"Yes. I wish I had better connections in the theater. I have written letters to those managers whom I know, but there has been no time for a response." Guiltily, he realized he hadn't even sent those letters yet. He looked at the lady expectantly.

"Why not send her to Carley House?" Lady Lugoson suggested after a long pause. "Mrs. Carley called on me yesterday with Beatrice and was complaining that she couldn't get good help in Brompton."

"Does she often call?" Charles wondered if Bertram had come to see him after the rest of his family had left for Brompton.

"When she is out our way. I rather think she's keeping an eye on my son for Beatrice."

"Really?" Charles found that hard to believe. Miss Carley seemed too eager for love to wait so long.

Lady Lugoson shook her head, keeping her gaze locked on Charles. "But that's a long proposition. It will be a decade or more before he is ready to wed. Beatrice will be firmly on the shelf. They need to look elsewhere."

Especially if Miss Beatrice Carley was a mad poisoner. "Have you had any more thoughts about poor Mr. Durant?"

Lady Lugoson pulled a handkerchief from her delicate silk bag. "He must have loved my Christiana more dearly than we knew. I am sorry for it. It would have been such a comfort if she had known."

A comfort to know a young man of promise would kill himself if you died? Charles wanted to shudder. "I have had word that he was ruined."

Lady Lugoson dotted the corners of her eyes with her handkerchief. "I am not surprised. His mother was the one with the business acumen."

Mr. Hogarth came into the office, apologizing for his absence. "How nice to see you, Lady Lugoson."

She forced a smile in his direction before replacing her handkerchief in her bag.

"We were just speaking of Monsieur Rueff's passing," Charles told him.

"I am sorry to hear that. I never knew him well, but of course did see him at St. Luke's." Mr. Hogarth put his pipe on his desk.

Thin smoke trailed from the nearly extinguished tobacco, covering the scent of ink and paper.

"A sad loss," Lady Lugoson agreed.

"Do you think you could write a character for Julie?" Charles asked her. "Since she was a friend of your daughter's?"

"Oh, I can write something."

Charles jumped up from his chair and grabbed a quill, ink, and a piece of paper. "If you do it now, perhaps Mr. Hogarth could take Julie with him when he returns home this evening, and bring her over to Carley House, since they are in Brompton presently."

Lady Lugoson nodded. "I suppose we had better get the girl out of London before Angela finds her." She bent her head over the paper and dipped the quill into the ink.

"We will give ye a moment to yourself," Mr. Hogarth said, rising.

Charles drew him into the corridor. "I told Lady Lugoson that Miss Acton claims Julie is her daughter. Which would make her Christiana's half sister. But Lady Lugoson scarcely reacted."

"It's a shocking notion."

"She must be used to shock by now," Charles said. "She said Mrs. Carley might have a staff opening in Brompton. At least this would get Julie out of London and my rooms."

"It really is not a good idea to have her there," Mr. Hogarth agreed. "I will take her. Why don't you go to the inn and gather her things? I will say our good-byes to the lady."

With no regrets, Charles dashed to the row of pegs on the wall, found his coat and hat, and left the building. He walked home, whistling, trying to decide what he could afford for his birthday flare-up, only three days away. Some excellent refreshments were required. His birthday, and Miss Hogarth would be coming. Of course he needed Julie out of there. He'd seen no sign of her doing any actual work, like cleaning the place.

When he burst through his front door, he could smell the delicious meaty scent of sausages. Cabbage wafted through the air, too, less enticing but hearty and filling. Laughter bubbled in the parlor, his brother's and Julie's.

"Julie and I have cooked dinner," Fred announced proudly. "We didn't think you would be here in time."

"I can eat Julie's portion. You need to gather your things," he told the actress. "You are going to Brompton this evening."

Julie untied the towel from her waist. "I am? Why?" She brushed strands of hair, fluffed from the heat of the fire where they had cooked their makeshift meal, back into place.

"We think we can get you work with the Carley household. It removes you from the area for now, and you'll be next door to Lugoson House and two doors down from the Hogarths."

"I've never been to Christiana's home," Julie said, a little wistfully.

"You need to eat," Fred protested.

"I'm not hungry," Julie claimed.

"Lady Lugoson wrote you a reference," Charles said coaxingly. "Mr. Hogarth has it. Get your things and I'll take you back to the office."

"What things?" she asked, a hint of temper appearing in her voice. "I fled the theater with the clothes on my back."

"Servants have their clothes paid for. We'll make sure they promise to give you time off to audition if we can find a theater who wants you. It's just temporary. Miss Acton needs time to calm down. We need time to sort out who the real murderer is."

"I don't want you gentlemen hurt." She clasped her hands together. "I suppose I have to go, if Miss Acton is searching for me here."

"You can't continue to sleep on William's sofa," Fred said, wide-eyed and earnest. "It isn't proper."

She laughed. "I'm not proper. I'm an actress. But I am hungry, can we eat first?"

Charles gave in. "Quickly." They split the food three ways,

and sat on the hearthrug, a battered, stained affair taken from the Dickenses' kitchen.

"Who is going to cook for your birthday party with me gone?" she asked, sucking on greasy fingers.

"I'll bring food in from a bakeshop. No one expects food really. As long as I get some good drink," Charles said. "We'd better go."

She took Miss Hogarth's cloak from a peg and wrapped it around herself. Charles saw the Elizabethan coins were stacked on the mantelpiece. Whatever thieving instincts she'd initially come with seemed to have dissipated. He couldn't quite understand her, but then, she was just a girl, not a proper young lady like Miss Hogarth, and raised indifferently, no less.

He took her arm on the wet stairs, then they walked, side by side, to the *Chronicle*. Mr. Hogarth greeted her kindly enough at his office door, and said he'd let Charles know what had happened the next morning.

"Where will I go if the Carleys don't want me?" she asked, betraying anxiety for the first time.

"We'll find you a bed for the night. Don't worry," Mr. Hogarth told her, as William passed by, on his way from Thomas Pillar's office back to the newsroom.

"Hello, Miss Saville, what brings you here?" His gaze seemed unusually intent.

"I'm going to Brompton," she said pertly. "Moving up in the world."

"I'll tell you about it in a moment," Charles said. "Fancy a brandy and water? I have a new public house for you to try."

"Lead on," William said, as Mr. Hogarth led Julie out of the door, where he had a hackney waiting. Charles could see his friend's gaze following the girl.

The next morning, Mr. Hogarth sent a boy to fetch Charles into his office. Charles perched on the edge of a chair in his mentor's office, watching pipe smoke wreath Hogarth's gray head.

"Took Miss Saville to Mrs. Carley," Hogarth said.

"Did you find success?" Charles asked.

"Yes. She agreed to take the girl on when she read Lady Lugoson's recommendation."

"What is she going to do?"

"I think the better question is how is she going to do? Miss Saville told me she considers the position a lark. As far as she's concerned she's acting the part of a maid to humor ye."

Charles sighed. "Thank you for taking her there, at least. I do need to keep my promise and send those letters to theatrical managers. William and I scratched out a few more last night. I did go to the theater almost every night for three years, and I made an effort to get to know people, but he knows more of them."

"Have them send word directly to Carley House," Mr. Hogarth advised. "Ye need to be done with the situation."

"Why? I feel somewhat responsible."

Mr. Hogarth pulled out his pipe, shaking it for emphasis. "I have come to the conclusion that Angela Acton killed Christiana Lugoson. Her own daughter. That means Julie Saville is a murderess's daughter, brought up under verra low circumstances."

Charles didn't want to hear it. "I know, but—"

"I helped ye rescue Julie from the awkward situation at your rooms." He reached for his tin of tobacco and opened the lid. "If she stayed there, I believe Julie would have expectations of ye, Charles."

"I have no interest in that way," Charles protested. "I never made any move in her direction. She's an actress, not a proper young girl."

"But did she make a move in yers?" He fixed Charles with a hard-eyed gaze before packing his pipe.

"Once," Charles admitted. But he drew himself straighter instead of shrinking before those fierce Scottish eyes. He'd done nothing wrong. "But it did not please me. What could I do? She was injured. She needed help. I had nothing better to offer." He lifted his hands.

Mr. Hogarth made a very Scottish noise in the back of his throat. "How do ye feel about my daughter? It is not kind to my Kate to have a vivacious young girl in yer home, badly raised and supervised."

His old side pain flared. He kept his expression calm. "I don't disagree with you, sir. I am most humbled by your criticism. I honor your daughter and would never want her to think my help was less than entirely innocent."

"Then ye are done with Miss Saville?"

"I—" Charles hesitated. "Yes."

"Good," Mr. Hogarth said, his tone going casual, "because Kate is coming into town this afternoon, and I know she would like to see ye."

# Chapter 25

That afternoon at his desk, Charles had his head buried in a selection of old issues of the *Chronicle*, attempting to come to terms with Walker Ferrand's political history and the recent Peterborough election, which had caused so much uproar with stories of irregular practices among the candidates. He had puzzled his way through a few of the more insulting claims when he heard a feminine voice, which stood out in this masculine bastion. Looking up, he saw Miss Hogarth at the door to the newsroom, and had the rare opportunity to regard her without her noticing.

Standing next to her father, she looked very fine in a close winter bonnet that allowed her blond curls to frame her face. The blue color accentuated her heavily lidded eyes, even from several feet away. Rosy cheeks and lips made the cold day obvious, and demonstrated how a little wind suited her. He admired her curvaceous figure, clad in the Scottish tartan dress he'd seen before, while her father helped her remove her cloak, then they both came toward him.

He forced his gaze back to the pile of papers, not wanting to be caught staring.

"Charles," Mr. Hogarth said. "My daughter finds herself with some hours to spare this afternoon."

"How delightful," he exclaimed, keeping his expression neutral as he heard William snickering softly behind him. "I'm happy to accompany her. Did you have some shopping to do, Miss Hogarth?"

"I thought we might go to Cecil Court," Miss Hogarth said as soon as her father, smiling vaguely, had moved out of earshot, humming a tune.

"What is there?" Charles asked.

"Rooms to let," she said with a mischievous grin.

Charles stood with alarm as William guffawed. He turned and stared down his friend, who coughed an apology before returning his attention to his work.

"Oh?" Charles asked.

"I know where Percy Chalke and Miss Acton live," she told him. "I had the address from young Lord Lugoson. He was out walking in the orchard yesterday and shared his theatrical enthusiasm with me."

"Oh dear. Does he want to be an actor now?"

Miss Hogarth put her tongue in her cheek. "I believe he is more of a theatergoer than a participant, but he is also a hero-worshipper of his aunt."

"I have hoped to avoid them, rather than interact," Charles told her. "She is a dreadful termagant."

She raised her eyebrows. "Lord Lugoson also told me they are considering joining a traveling circuit. Sending some production out on the road with their theatrical troupe."

Charles lowered his voice. "So they aren't home?"

Her tone matched his. "Right. They went north to investigate the possibility. And my father is certain that Miss Acton is, well, responsible."

He drummed his fingers against his upper lip. Did Mr. Hogarth realize his daughter wanted to drift into a possible murderess's path? "What do you think we could find?"

"I don't know, but what an opportunity." Her eyes twinkled. "You're up to a little mischief, aren't you, Mr. Dickens?"

He shook his head, but said, "Not always." Not with her present. Hadn't he tried to uncover the mysteries behind Christiana Lugoson's death because he was worried about the safety of the Hogarth girls?

"I dare you to come with me," she said with an encouraging smile.

"Your father would not approve."

"He did. He asked you to entertain me." She smiled encouragingly. "This is how I want to be entertained."

"You are certain they are not home?" He stared hard at her, while William laughed softly behind him.

"Yes. I am as sure as I can be."

"Very well." He went and took his coat and hat from its peg, and then walked out onto the street with her, impatient now to have the adventure over with as quickly as possible. "So where do they live?"

"The street, where, my father was happy to tell me, Mozart once lived."

He had to strain to hear her over the noise on the street. Two carriages had collided and the drivers were shouting at each other. "He would know where a musical genius lodged."

She stood on tiptoes to speak into his ear. "Yes, he had to play some music for me."

He found it hard to speak with the tingle of her warm breath in his ear. Had she no idea what that did to a man? Of course not, she was an innocent. Though he had played the same trick on her not too long ago.

He saw a coffee cart and pulled her in that direction. They both refreshed themselves before they continued their walk. He needed the warmth of a hot beverage in his belly to counteract the chill wind and the attractive girl.

"Are you looking forward to your birthday?" she asked, taking his arm as they navigated past the odiferous remains a horse had left on the street.

"Oh yes. I'm glad to be moving into the most productive and useful phase of life."

"I have the sense that your childhood was difficult," she said softly.

"Not my childhood, no. Quite idyllic. We lived in Portsmouth. I often think of those times. But there were difficulties later on."

"Oh?"

He chuckled. "I would like to have a life of steady progress, rather than these wild upswings and downturns. We moved more than I would have liked when I was young. For different business reasons, of course, but that wasn't always why."

"We came all the way from Scotland," Miss Hogarth pointed out as they turned onto the court, a long row of shops on each side with apartments overhead. "I do miss our family there, but here we are."

He turned in a circle. "What number?"

"Eleven. Just over the bookseller there." She pointed to a red brick building, heavily darkened by smoke.

"Let's see if we can get in." Charles had no idea what to do. Should they talk to neighbors? Try to break in? He was distracted by the sight of a coin shop down the block but Miss Hogarth towed him toward the bookshop.

Instead of bright coins, rows of books were stacked inside the wide, tall windows, anonymous in their leather bindings. Charles could see dust at the top of one stack as Miss Hogarth opened the door.

She poked her head in the door. A bell tinkled. When they stepped in, a hush fell over them. No customers were in the shop and all the paper seemed to insulate the walls from the noise of the street.

"Do you know Miss Acton or Mr. Chalke?" Miss Hogarth asked the gray-bearded proprietor, who was cutting pages in a leather-bound book on the countertop.

"Never heard of 'em," he said, glancing up as he wiped his hands on his apron. "Why?"

"They live upstairs," Charles interjected, describing the pair.

"Oh, I seen 'em," the bookseller said agreeably. "But they never come in 'ere."

"Which door do we use to go upstairs?" Miss Hogarth asked.

"On the right. It's never locked at this time of day." The man fingered his beard. "Can I interest you in *Rookwood*? We just had in a new shipment."

"Oh," Miss Hogarth said, but Charles shook his head.

"Just the stairs today, thank you," he said.

They went back outside of the shop. "Have you read *Rookwood*? It's quite the runaway seller."

"I've perused it. We passed a copy around at the newspaper," Charles said. "Your father must have it?"

"Yes. Do you remember this line at the very beginning?" She quoted, " 'Before a terrible truth comes to light, there are certain murmuring whispers . . .' "

"There have been a great many of those in this story," Charles agreed. "But I am more concerned about your safety than pursuing whispers when you are present."

He pulled open the boot-marked door to the right of the bookshop. "This doesn't look like the home of a flourishing manager."

"Theater management is a difficult way to make money, I believe," Miss Hogarth said. "And I am not worried, Mr. Dickens. You shall protect me."

"Indeed I shall." Charles smiled at her. "But I do love the theater. It's a secret fancy of mine, I must admit."

They walked up the narrow flight of steps single file. It smelled of onions and spilt ale, but the atmosphere was surprisingly peaceful for an environment where Angela Acton lived. Perhaps the peace of the bookshop pervaded the place.

They found four doors on the landing. "Number three," Miss Hogarth said. "According to her nephew."

Charles, not knowing what else to do, walked to the door and knocked. For all he knew it would cause the other three doors to open, if this was a floor of voluble types rather than people who kept to themselves. Instead, the door itself opened.

A woman, black-haired, overripe, and in her forties, wiped her hands on a stained apron. "Sorry. Just doing the blacking."

"I thought Julie Saville worked here," Charles said.

"Oh, that Julie is an actress. She earns her bed and board by caring for Miss Acton's clothing, but I haven't seen her around lately. Not sure where she's gone to," the maid said.

"My name is Catherine Hogarth," Charles's companion announced. "We've been sent by Lord Lugoson. Have you worked for Mr. Chalke very long?"

"Mary Contadino," she said promptly, eyebrows flying up at the name of a lord. "Three years now, but Mr. Chalke isn't here today. I don't think he'll be back until tomorrow."

"Milord had some questions," Charles said.

"Oh?" The maid wiped her hands again and glanced about nervously, as if the young lord might be lurking in the corridor.

"How do you find Miss Acton?" Charles asked. "We were friends of her niece Miss Lugoson, and I imagine the death of her niece has hit her very hard."

Mary Contadino wiped her hands yet again, smearing the black mess she'd been using on the stove deeper into the wrinkles on the sides of her fingers. "Such a sweet lady. I've heard her cry many a tear since Epiphany. They had been so busy with panto season that they'd been sleeping at the theater before. Just work, work, work."

"Would you say she is sweet to Julie?" Miss Hogarth asked, a minute amount of skepticism in her voice.

Her words tumbled over each other with increasing speed as she spoke. "They are dramatic with each other. Very much alike, really, but Miss Acton is a perfect angel to me. Never an unkind word, and ever so neat. Makes keeping up these rooms so much easier."

"Did you ever meet Miss Lugoson?" Charles asked, since the maid seemed willing enough to chat.

Mrs. Contadino leaned against the door frame. "I did, yes, but never in December, because of the panto. Very dedicated to the Garrick, are my players. It's a very relaxing month for me. I just deliver them a bit of food, and take the washing back and forth."

"What about Horatio Durant? Did he ever visit?" Miss Hogarth asked.

Mrs. Contadino frowned and rubbed her nose, leaving a faint stain of lampblack and grease on her skin. "I'm not familiar with the name. Is he an actor? That's all that comes here."

"No," Charles said. "Not an actor."

"If he wasn't wanting to be in the theater, Mr. Chalke wouldn't have time for him," Mrs. Contadino said. "It's all theater with those two. No talk or interest in anything else."

"Do they do research for their parts? I know Mr. Chalke specializes in *Richard III*. Do they do things like research poison, for instance?"

"Poison?" Mrs. Contadino laughed. "I've never seen either of them read anything except a script or an accounts book. What is Lord Lugoson after, anyway?"

"It is a very long story," Charles said. "I don't think we are going to find his answers here."

"Thank you for speaking to us," Miss Hogarth added.

As soon as the maid shut the door, Charles took her arm, reversed their path, and went back to the street. "I suppose I can't take you into a public house for a conversation," Charles said.

"No, there really isn't anywhere a young lady can go," Miss Hogarth said, leaning against him. "But we can return to my father's office and speak there."

He didn't want to lose her touch. "Let's walk slowly." He looked at the overcast sky. "The rain has let up, and the version of Miss Acton that we heard described today did not sound like the one I've met."

"It is possible that Julie Saville merely drives Miss Acton crazy," Miss Hogarth said, moving them past the bookshop toward the street corner. "I sense you've had your troubles with her."

"I don't trust her." Charles pressed his arm against hers. Her cloak had started to smell more like the Hogarths' scents of hearth and beans than the rosemary and cedar of the chest where it had been before. "I never know what to expect. She's unsettling and I'm glad she's gone to the Carleys."

"So no insight into poison, or any connection to Horatio Durant," Miss Hogarth mused. "And one had the sense that Miss Acton wouldn't have had time to poison anyone around Epiphany."

"No, panto season seems the wrong time for an actress to murder anyone," Charles quipped.

"We have a hole in our murder plot," she said with a sigh. "Now what do we do? Father was so certain."

"Let us go through our list of suspects," Charles said. "If we leave out Chalke and Acton, there is Horatio himself."

"Dead," Miss Hogarth said. "Oh, there is another of those carts. Maybe they have broth?"

Charles kept her arm in his hand as they crossed the street, careful on the slippery, malodorous cobblestones. They stopped in front of a cart holding metal urns. The proprietor was happy to sell them cups of beef broth. They stepped under a nearby overhang on an old building, and stood against the wall, holding their tin cups.

"So you think death exonerates him?" Charles asked.

"There are better candidates. Lady Lugoson, Beatrice Carley."

"Her brother," Charles said in the same spirit, having lost his pique that she hadn't accepted his deliverance of Beatrice Carley as villain. "Though he did not seem the murderous type."

"But you'd believe it of his sister or of Lady Lugoson?"

"I want to say it is a woman, poison being a womanish weapon, but with Lady Lugoson it makes little sense, unless we assume she needed her adopted daughter's money for her son."

"Horatio would have acquired it. He might have changed his mind about marriage for the sake of the money."

"Yet he didn't, a point in his favor. We know the Lugosons couldn't have killed Marie Rueff because they were in France."

"I don't like that. So Beatrice Carley killed Christiana out of jealousy for Horatio Durant's heart, and Marie Rueff because she tried to run away with Beatrice's brother?"

Charles finished his broth. "Monsieur Rueff had no reason to kill his daughter that we know of. Much less Miss Lugoson. Beatrice Carley is a better candidate."

Miss Hogarth took his cup and returned both of them to the broth seller, then they continued on their way, dodging puddles and other effluvia. "That's not much of a reason for Beatrice to kill Marie Rueff."

"We don't know what other relationship they might have had. After all, Miss Rueff knew the Carley family."

"Very true," Miss Hogarth sighed. "What about that dance instructor that we thought was in love with Miss Lugoson?"

"I had no sense he was involved," Charles said. "No passions invoked there."

A carriage slowed next to them. Mr. Hogarth stuck his chin out of the window.

"Father?" she gasped, separating from Charles by a couple of inches.

Had her father been spying on them? Charles felt overly supervised by his mentor, and didn't think Miss Hogarth much cared for the interruption either, but was glad they had been behaving fairly appropriately.

"There's a storm coming in. Time to go home. I was coming to look for ye," he called.

Charles pressed her hand. "Good-bye, Miss Hogarth, and thank you for the conversation." He helped her into the carriage and watched it drive away, then decided to go home and get dry. Why not take the rest of the day to work on a sketch? They were an excellent source of income for him.

The next morning Charles had to go to another political meeting, and worked late at the office, writing his article. He'd consulted with Fred and they had decided to fund his birthday party with one of the coins. He took the least fine of the silver coins to the coin merchant he'd seen in Cecil Court, upon his return to London, and sold it for enough to invite his mother and sisters to preside over quite a nice bachelor birthday party the next night.

"We're going to be busy all day shopping," Fred said, writing a list of what he needed to purchase.

"Just the drinks, and the drinking vessels," Charles said. "I wrote Mother with instructions for what I wanted her to cook for the party, and I'll pay her for the ingredients."

"I had better take the money to her in the morning."

"Yes, I suppose you are right. She might not have enough."

Charles divided up the money he'd received from the coin sale and pushed half across the table to his brother. "I'll go out for a box of glassware in the morning and bring it back before going to the wine shop in the afternoon."

"I will probably have to stay with Mother until she comes with the girls."

Charles glanced around, feeling the slightest bit disheartened by that. "It's difficult to clean by candlelight, but we'd better. Didn't Julie do anything other than go through my possessions when she stayed here?"

"Ate what little food we had put by, used an enormous amount of water." He reflected. "She did empty the chamber pots."

"Filled them up herself," Charles muttered. "Oh well. Do you want to tidy the tables or wash the floor?"

"Wash," Fred said. "The kettle is full. Won't be any trouble to mop the floor."

Charles nodded. "If I put everything on the tables into my carpetbag, it should do, then I can dust the surfaces. It should still be fairly clean tomorrow, if we don't burn too much coal."

"We'll be gone all day," Fred pointed out.

He grinned and punched his brother's shoulder. "An excellent point, dear boy."

They worked merrily away, singing tunes they knew. Fred danced a hornpipe with his mop and Charles sang a moving Scottish ballad while holding his carpetbag to his chest, in mournful imitation of a man about to leave his lady love.

He put it down once the deal table was dry of the wet water wash he'd given it, and he pulled out a bowl of beeswax polish his mother had made so he could shine it up.

"Are you going to buy any chairs?" Fred asked, squeezing out his mop as he finished mopping the bedroom floor.

"I might have the money for another secondhand one. I'll

see what is available in the stalls if I have time. Hopefully, William can lend us his, but we won't have time to help him carry them here."

"Someone will go over for you."

"Sure. Whoever comes first can do a bit of fetching and carrying for the cause," Charles said, rubbing the leftover polish into his hands. At this time of year, he could polish up his fingers every day, just to keep them more mobile in the cold.

He'd heard the church bells ring ten times before the rooms were cleaned to his satisfaction. They'd used too many candles, but the work was complete.

"Is there any ale left in the jug?" he asked. "I could stand to wet my whistle."

"I'll check," Fred said, and went to the cupboard just as a knock came at the door.

"That will be William," Charles said. "Maybe he'll bring the chairs tonight." He went and opened the door to find Julie Saville, cheeks red and panting visibly.

His heart sank. Why was she back? "Are you in some distress?" His thoughts tumbled together. What was she doing here? He'd thought her safely out of the way of the Hogarths.

As if to mock him, she wore Miss Hogarth's old cloak. He checked the passage, saw it was empty, then jerked her inside, before dropping her arm like a hot poker. When she unfastened the cloak, Charles saw the neat uniform of a parlormaid.

"Very nice." He added a faint touch of sarcasm. "Didn't have to start in the kitchen? They must really have needed help."

"I'm about ready to say good-bye to those bloody Carleys," she growled. "I've hitched a ride as far as the Strand on the back of the wagon and walked the rest of the way."

She wouldn't have already given notice, he hoped. Not with the Hogarths coming to his party. He couldn't take her back in. "It can't be worse than Angela Acton."

"Can't it? The servants only get meat on Sundays. We aren't allowed to leave the house except on our half days." She kicked out of her shoes and dumped them in front of the fireplace, as if she lived here. "I'm like you. I have to take walks."

"Watch it, the floors are clean. Aren't you being a bit familiar with my parlor?" Charles asked.

"You found me the work in order to get rid of me," she said. "I figure if I leave I'm your servant again."

"Hello, Julie," Fred said cheerily, hoisting the jug. "I'm off to fetch some ale."

"Thank you," Charles said as his brother reached for his coat. He waited until Fred left before starting with Julie again. "Now, look here. This was only an emergency measure until we could find you a new spot in a theatrical troupe. As far as I'm concerned, I'd like you off playing the provinces."

"Oh, you'd like that, wouldn't you," she snarled. "But I'm not bad, Mr. Dickens. I could have stolen that gold coin off you and sold it too. I know people. But I didn't do it. I didn't take anything."

"That's the very least you should do in someone's home. Besides, I was trying to be your friend, not your employer. Like I said, this was because it was an emergency, that was all. You need to go back to the Carleys until I can find you something else . . ."

She dropped onto the sofa. "Actresses are paid much better than parlormaids, that's for certain."

He winced at the tortured squeak of the springs. "It's a proper trade. But if you work your way up to housekeeper, that's a fine career as well. Good money. My grandmother was a housekeeper for an important family."

"And look at you now," she mocked. "Charles Dickens, gentleman journalist, who wishes he was an actor."

He felt wounded. What did she know? "I don't now, not really. I'd rather be a playwright."

"I don't believe you. Everyone wants to be an actor." She put her hands on her hips. "Isn't anyone going to offer me a cup of tea?"

"You'd better go back to Carley House before you are discovered," Charles insisted. "There's no use being dramatic when you're a servant. Have a rest and be ready to go when I get you an audition. What is your half day?"

"Monday," she said glumly. "But not next week of course, since I didn't work a full week."

He hid his irritation with enthusiasm. "That gives us time to set up auditions. Monday week, that's the thing. I'm sure we'll have something for you by then. William Aga and I both wrote letters."

"He's a nice man," Julie said. "Let me sleep in front of his fire, and not an inappropriate word. Not that I'd have minded a bit of courting. He's a handsome devil."

"Is he?" Charles yawned. "I hadn't noticed. Look, you had better go. It's a long walk, as I well know, having done it a number of times."

"Can't I hire a hackney?" she begged. "Spare me a few coins?"

"No, I need everything I have to fund my party tomorrow. It's my birthday. Did you really come all the way here to whine for a few minutes?"

"No." She frowned. "At least give me a cup of tea first." She pulled off her gloves. Her fingers looked red, and there was a streak down her palm that looked unhealthy.

Charles frowned. Was there something wrong with her hands?

"There was something I meant to tell you." Julie poked at the tight bun at the back of her head. "Goodness but my head hurts. The way I've had to pin my hair to meet requirements. That Mrs. Carley."

Despite his better judgment, he lit a candle and held it over her hands so he could see them clearly. "What happened?"

"They're burned," she said sourly.

"How?" He set the candle aside before hot wax dripped on her sore fingers.

"That's what I meant to tell you. It's about Mrs. Carley and her bloody tea service."

"What about it?" Charles asked. "Did you pour hot tea on yourself?"

"Of course not," Julie huffed, sitting on his sofa and rearranging her skirts as if she meant to stay for a while. "I burned them with a cleaning solution. Who uses chloride of lime to clean fine teacups?"

Who indeed? Charles filled the kettle from his water can, and moved the kettle over the fire to heat for tea. "That seems extreme. Were they stained?"

Julie nodded. "Mrs. Carley personally gave me the instructions. She wants them bleached clean after every use. What if I make a mistake? I'm afraid I will poison someone. She's an MP's wife. What if some important lady takes sick, and I'm to blame?"

"Poison someone?" Charles repeated, sitting down next to her, feeling quite limp. The wheels turned in his head. "With her bleaching solution?" Could that be it? The solution?

"Yes." Julie pulled her hands away from her skirts and put them to her temples. "Look at my hands. It burns my skin and she uses that tea service every day. I won't be pretty enough to be a parlormaid for long with that as my duty."

"It's a dangerous thing to do." Charles didn't want to look at her reddened hands again. It felt too intimate.

Julie wiggled her fingers, forcing him to see how red they were.

He glanced away. "Yes, housemaids don't have nice hands,

Julie, but think about what you are saying. Think about Miss Lugoson."

Julie stared at him, then thrust her fingers into her hair, dislodging pins and a hank of red that fell down her cheek. She blinked, twirled her hair, then her mouth dropped open. "You don't think Christiana died from chloride of lime, do you?"

# Chapter 26

"I have to wonder. I must speak to a doctor." Had he finally figured it out? Had chloride of lime killed Christiana?

"Christiana's doctor?"

"Yes. I'll go to see Dr. Keville tomorrow."

She stared at him. Charles arched back, afraid she would try to kiss him again, but she didn't move. Instead, she seemed lost in reflection.

"Just be patient for a little longer," Charles told her.

"Certainly, until the chloride of lime kills me." She stared down at her hands, her hair hiding her face. "What if you cannot find me work? What if I only had my position in the troupe because of my special relationship to Angela?"

"What is that special relationship?" He wondered what she knew, or suspected.

"Her parents had some connection to my family. I'm not entirely certain what. When Miss Acton saw me, she was enchanted, so the story went, and said I must be onstage. So I was brought on as a child actress."

"I saw you in *Richard III* and other parts last month. I know how the lads in the pit cheered for you. I can assure you that such charisma that you possess is sufficient for your chosen career."

"You don't like me," she accused.

"I don't trust you, but I think you will go far."

"Because of the coin, I suppose."

"That and the fact that you did no cleaning when you were supposedly my maid," he retorted.

She pushed her hair back and grinned impishly at him. "You have so many books. I was distracted when I started to dust them."

"Don't get distracted at Carley House, or you'll be out on your ear before we can find you better work," Charles advised. "And don't drink out of any teacups."

"Do you think you'll ever uncover who killed Christiana?"

He chewed the inside of his cheek. "Everyone who has died is connected to the Carleys or Miss Acton."

"How?"

Charles ticked them off on his fingers. "Miss Lugoson was friends with Miss Carley. Miss Rueff attempted to run away with Bertram Carley. Miss Carley was in love with Horatio Durant."

"And Angela?"

Fred came back in. He hoisted the can in triumph. "Ran into William Aga. He gave me some of his fresh supply of ale, because it's simply bucketing rain out." He poured steaming water from the kettle into their teapot.

"He's a nice man," Julie said dreamily.

"Miss Lugoson was Miss Acton's daughter. Monsieur Rueff had a tryst with Miss Acton," Charles said, in an attempt to regain her attention.

"He did?" Julie interrupted.

Charles winced. He'd said too much, but at least she was paying attention. "So I've been told."

"Goodness. I hadn't heard about that, but then I never knew the Rueff family. I heard the name, of course, but they were wealthy. I had a neighbor whose daughter worked in their kitchen. What about Mr. Durant?"

He watched Fred set cups on the table. "He connects back through the Lugosons to Miss Acton."

"But what about Lady Lugoson?"

"Her adopted daughter dies, Miss Rueff is the daughter of her friend, Mr. Durant contacted her last before he died. She can't have killed Miss Rueff herself. Do you know anything about their life in France, any connection there?" Other than the girl herself, sitting next to him.

"No." She reflected. "I don't see that Lady Lugoson killed Christiana. I've never thought that. She loved her mother. It seemed a close and affectionate relationship."

"What about Miss Acton?"

"She isn't one who schemes," Julie said.

"She's mad though. Still, I lean to Miss Beatrice Carley, since the doctor says she's unbalanced, and because she could have done it, and might have thought she had a reason to kill."

Julie shivered. "I have to go back there."

"Maybe you shouldn't." Charles had never laid the case out quite like this. Bertram had no reason to kill Christiana that he knew of, but Beatrice had some cause to attack all three of the dead.

"No, I want to find out the truth. I want to know who killed Christiana. I will watch Beatrice for you."

"And see what?"

"If she goes into the housekeeper's quarters, where the tea service is kept, or the kitchen."

"Miss Lugoson did take tea there before her mother's Epiphany party."

At the mention of tea, Fred poured, and handed out the cups.

Charles yawned and breathed in fragrant steam. "I might see Bertram tomorrow at my flare-up. Here, I'll write you a note. See if you can get it to him. Maybe he can bring you with him."

She mimicked a fine aristocratic lady. "The young master escorting a parlormaid to a party?"

Charles shrugged. "You're an actress, yes? This is all just a ruse to get you away from the Garrick troupe. Maybe he will be amused."

"Maybe he will kill me," Julie said.

Charles blinked, but she put a hand on his shoulder before he could sound an alarm. "I'll be pleasant," she said.

"I find myself in agony for your safety." Was he doing the right thing, sending her back?

"I am an actress," Julie repeated. "I am playing the part of the parlormaid, in order to determine if Beatrice Carley is a mad poisoner."

"Just remember this is real life, not a stage," he cautioned, lifting his cup to his lips in tandem with her. "Don't be foolish."

The next morning, Charles went to Harley Street directly after breakfast, assuming Dr. Keville lived above his consulting rooms. When he reached the street corner, he passed a man smelling strongly of oil paint. As he walked past, he saw a paintbrush, still damp, sticking out of the man's overcoat pocket. Scaffolding had been erected around the front of the building.

He rang the bell for patients and visitors. The same pleasant woman greeted him by name. "I wonder if Dr. Keville could spare me a few moments on the same matter we discussed previously?" Charles asked.

She brought him into the doctor's office and said she would see if he was available. Charles went right to the anatomical drawing on the wall, tracing the path the chloride of lime might have taken as it burned down into poor Miss Lugoson's stomach. He shuddered.

The housekeeper brought tea. "Dr. Keville said he can be down in a little while."

"Thank you. That's very kind." Charles took the cup with its filling of dark liquid, and wondered how many times he had taken, and would take in the future, a cup of tea with someone, never knowing if the intention was simple hospitality or something much darker. People read tea leaves. If only they could read the tea as well.

He smelled his tea. If it was adulterated, wouldn't he smell something over the familiar brew? The scent of chlorine, perhaps?

His thoughts drifted to Miss Hogarth. He'd have to warn her and her mother to never take tea with Mrs. Carley again, or at least not to do so without smelling it first. Also, he'd ask Mrs. Hogarth tonight if she had any suggestions for what Julie could apply to her hands to protect herself against the bleaching agent. She kept a tidy house and must have some thoughts on the matter.

By the time Dr. Keville arrived, natty in checked pants, a blue waistcoat and black frockcoat, Charles had been scribbling thoughts for a sketch about schoolmasters on a scrap of borrowed paper.

"Hello again, Mr. Dickens." Dr. Keville looked keenly into Charles's face.

"Once again, not here for me," Charles said cheerfully. "I'm here because of something I learned from the new parlormaid at Carley House."

"Ah, Beatrice up to her old tricks again?"

"Not that I'm aware of." Charles paused, hoping the doctor would explain what those "old tricks" were, but he did not, merely went to the teapot and poured himself a cup.

"The new parlormaid told me Mrs. Carley insists upon treating her entire tea service with chloride of lime after every use."

"Strange." The doctor picked up his cup.

"Yes, I thought it was unusual. No one in her house seems to have an infection or anything like that. And I thought about accidental ingestion of a toxic dose of the stuff, since Miss Lugoson was at tea there the day she died. Or even, I suppose, Beatrice could have deliberately put some of the powder into the tea."

"That won't do," Dr. Keville said, polishing off his cup. "You'd smell it, for one thing. I suppose if they habitually use the stuff, they might become accustomed to a faint scent of chlorine."

"Interesting," Charles said coaxingly.

"Still though, there was no burn damage to Miss Lugoson's mouth."

"I didn't see any," Charles agreed, disappointed.

The doctor warmed to his theme. "Also, if it burned through her stomach then she'd probably have bled to death internally. I saw no sign of that."

"What would the signs have been?"

"Confusion, cool skin, rapid heartbeat."

"How long would it take?"

"You could die from blood loss in perhaps eight hours or much less, or an infection could start and it might take three days to kill a person. Neither matches Miss Lugoson's unfortunate demise."

"So not chloride of lime, then."

"No, but a good suggestion. I'm amazed you haven't given up yet. You're a tenacious young man."

He took that for praise. "Could you please tell me more about Miss Carley? May I tell you some things in confidence?"

"Of course."

Charles lowered his voice. "I now know her brother was the lover of the late Marie Rueff, who died the same way. And Horatio Durant, a recent suicide or murder victim, was the beloved of Miss Lugoson and Miss Carley."

"Gracious," the doctor exclaimed. "No wonder you haven't given up with all of that learned."

"The situation refuses to resolve itself. Who will die next? Miss Carley is hardly an attractive girl and she's bound to be spurned again."

Dr. Keville rubbed his chin. "You want me to tell you that Miss Carley is a murderess."

"Yes, I suppose I do." Charles waited, breathless.

After a long pause, Dr. Keville shook his head. "She is narcissistic and hysterical. I cannot deny it. I could see her attacking someone bodily in anger, but I don't see her as a keen planner. Women aren't, you know. They act on impulse. As can be shown by the irregular disorder of Miss Carley's body, her mind is disordered as well."

Charles attempted to ignore the cruel generalization in favor of the specific. "She is ill?"

Dr. Keville scratched his chin again. "She suffers from a peculiar, unusually unregulated condition of the blood vessels of the uterus. This cannot help but lead to a mental disorder."

Charles noted the doctor seemed to be suffering from an inflammation of one of his hair follicles. His chin became redder every time he scratched it.

"So you can see her becoming violent," Charles asked. "But she would be more likely to pour some poison into a cup of tea on impulse?"

The doctor shook his head. "I have revealed all of this to you so that you can understand her better. I do not point my finger at her, not for this. It does not sound like anything she is capable of. She would have to obtain the poison, and put it into the tea, and only manage to serve it to the victim. That does take some planning."

"Do you treat any other members of the family?"

"I can assure you that Miss Lugoson didn't die due to an overly enthusiastic disinfection ritual," the doctor said.

"Why would Mrs. Carley want such a disinfection ritual?"

"She might regularly offer tea to people who are ill, I really couldn't say. She is not my patient." The doctor rose to his feet, fingering his chin again. "I do have certain commitments today."

Charles rose as well. "Of course, Doctor. Thank you so much for your time."

After the doctor left the room, presumably to tend to his chin, Charles let himself out, irritated that another theory had proven worthless.

Mr. Hogarth's violin rang through Charles's rooms with the mellifluous rendering of a Mozart sonata as Charles finished shaking hands with all the people at his party. He was terribly flattered that so many had come, even Bertram Carley.

"Have a glass of champagne," Charles urged everyone, striking a pose, his fingers under his black velvet lapels. Fanny had made sure each of the eight buttons down the front were tightened and shined. "My brother will make a glass of hot brandy and water if you want something warm, and there is wine for the ladies."

As Mr. Hogarth moved into a more sprightly part of his song, Fred grabbed for Miss Mary Hogarth's hand and spun her around the room, gathering everyone's attention. Charles's mother seemed delighted at the sight, so he took her hand and danced her, laughing giddily, around the center of the room, where the sofa had been before they moved it, then took a spin with his sister Fanny, her light brown ringlets dancing around her cheeks.

"You've never looked so well, dearest," he whispered in her ear.

"I think I might be in love with Mr. Burnett," Fanny whispered back.

"Isn't he the religious one?" Charles asked. His words were lost under a flourish from the violin.

William Aga bowed to Miss Hogarth and they joined the fun. Seated on the sofa with the *Chronicle*'s under-editor, Thomas Pillar, Bertram Carley watched Mary Hogarth closely, but didn't find a partner of his own.

Everyone laughed and clapped as Mr. Hogarth finished his piece, his hair flapping with the exuberant violence of his playing. Charles hauled professional musician Fanny over to Mr. Hogarth and demanded they perform together. "A treat for us all," he promised, as the two decided on a tune.

"'Cherry Ripe,'" Fanny announced, as Mr. Hogarth put bow to string.

Charles then took his sister Leticia's hand, to give her a turn at dancing. Everyone who was willing regained the floor. He saw that Bertram had managed to obtain Mary Hogarth's hand this time, and his wide smile gave evidence of being the happiest man on the floor.

It seemed everyone had come to his party, with the promise of good drink paid for by the recovered coin. Or at least, everyone but Julie Saville, who not unexpectedly, hadn't managed to sneak out of Carley House for an impromptu half day.

After a bit of light opera, Mr. Hogarth talked Fanny into performing some traditional Scottish tunes. After a number of these, the crowd was so breathless they all, by mutual consent, broke to drink everything Charles had left in his rooms. While they drank, Charles and Fred put on sailor caps that his brother had found at a thirdhand stall and danced a hornpipe of their own devising. The crowd clapped delightedly when they had finished, Miss Hogarth loudest of all.

A few minutes later, parched, Charles had upended the last of the champagne bottles. "I hadn't expected it to be so hot in here," he said to William.

"I'll go to the local public house for ale," his friend offered. "Can you spare Fred to help me carry the jugs?"

"Happy to get out of the heat for a few minutes?" Charles asked his brother.

Fred nodded.

"I'll join you," Thomas Pillar said.

"Very well, but don't stop to drink," Charles ordered. "Just bring back the jugs." He reached into his pocket and handed Fred all the coins he had left.

"Even a February room warms with this many bodies in it," Bertram said, sidling up to him. Mary Hogarth had deserted him to chat with Letitia and Fanny. "The crushes I have been in at political parties with Father, you cannot imagine. I've seen ladies swoon more times than I can remember."

"In London?" Charles asked, always eager for political tidbits for his articles.

"Certainly," Bertram agreed. "And in Somerset. I'm glad I came tonight, in fact. This is much more amusing than political parties."

"Thank you. Somerset?" Charles vaguely remembered hearing mention of the county before. "Is that where your family estate is?"

Bertram followed him as he went to open the window in the room. It stuck a bit, given that it hadn't been opened in months, but finally a chill air swept into the room. "Yes. It is in the Somerset Levels, near Glastonbury. Old, old country. My father's family was around to greet the Normans, they say, before the family became wealthy speculating on draining projects about a hundred years ago."

His mother led a round of applause as the room began to cool. Charles took a bow. "A long history."

"Yes. Our family has always loved the moors and marshes. We enjoy the outdoors, the good hunting and foraging."

Charles's ears fastened on the word like a hunting dog. "Foraging? I understand Marie Rueff learned to forage around Fontainebleau. Is that what you had in common?"

"Indeed, yes. We were both country-bred and happier for it. Not that we had exactly the same interests. For myself, I'm more interested in archaeology than say, mushrooms or herbs."

"Did Miss Rueff like to gather mushrooms?" Charles asked. Mushrooms could be spectacularly poisonous.

"Wild herbs, mostly," Bertram said. "Bless me, but that wind is chill."

Charles pulled him out of the direct path of the breeze. He stayed nearby, wanting to close the window before the point came when he would have to light the fire and use up all the coal he had for the next couple of days.

Bertram kept speaking. "My mother loves to hunt for mushrooms, though. Beatrice and I have gone foraging with her since we were children. My father was often away, and she didn't like us to stay with our nurses and governesses and tutors." He laughed. "Father could never understand why we learned so little when he was gone. I never did get any Greek."

So Beatrice knew her poisonous mushrooms and herbs, then. "Your mother and sister must be expert foragers. I've always understood it is best to avoid mushrooms unless you really know what you are doing."

"Oh yes." Bertram grinned conspiratorially. "My family tree is very unusual. Father is descended from a famous Somerset witch pricker, and Mother is descended from Maria Stevens, the last arrested Somerset witch from over a hundred years ago. Or so it is said."

"Your mother learned witchcraft?" Charles asked skeptically.

"Oh no!" Bertram laughed. "But she learned the crafts of wild women. You know, what to pick in the light of the moon and that sort of nonsense. She has old books, and the women in our family are always trained in the arts of the stillroom."

"Fascinating. Do you think your sister considers herself a wise woman?"

"She isn't nearly as good as Mother. Has trouble sticking to things," Bertram reflected. "She worked hard on a freckle cream three years ago. That was the last time I saw her really trying to perfect anything in the stillroom. Do you think Miss Mary Hogarth would enjoy my witch stories? Some girls love to be frightened."

"Miss Mary Hogarth seems the practical sort to me," Charles said. "But you can give it a try."

"Close the window," Mr. Hogarth called. "Your sister is shivering."

Charles closed it as Bertram moved toward Miss Mary Hogarth, a predator intent on the prowl. Well, it had been a year and more since Marie Rueff died, but he didn't think Mrs. Hogarth would appreciate him allowing a flirtation between her fifteen-year-old daughter and a man who had tried to run away with an heiress.

Marie Rueff had been just a bit older when they had fallen in love. Bertram liked young girls, and he didn't know if they could trust him.

He lifted his chin in Miss Hogarth's direction and she came to him. Drawing her into the shadow of the doorway he whispered in her ear about Bertram Carley's interest in her younger sister and his concern that the man was both a bit of a cad and a bit of a fortune hunter.

"No point in wasting Mary's time then," she said. "Thank you, Mr. Dickens. You greatly improve upon me every time I see you." She gave him a sweet smile, even while those heavy-lidded eyes of hers made him think of other things.

When she left his side to attend to her sister, he went straight to the room they used as a kitchen, hoping some water was left in the jug so he could douse his head.

The jug being empty, he took it and left his rooms, going downstairs to the common tap. He met William, Fred, and Thomas on the landing.

"Did Julie come?" William asked, setting his stoneware beer jug on the wood floor. The others kept tramping up the stairs, leaving the two alone.

"No, but even if she'd been able to exit the house, she might not have found a ride. Last night she came in on a cart."

William shook his head. "I'm nervous about her. She does not like her new mistress according to Fred."

"I am not quite at ease, myself," Charles admitted. "Bertram Carley was telling me his mother has trained as a wise woman, and is descended from witches. Can you imagine?"

William folded his arms over his chest. "They sound like they all belong in Bedlam."

"I have the sense Miss Carley's doctor thinks so," Charles agreed. "But more to the point, have you had any response from theater managers?"

"No. Even with Julie's experience, she's just another pretty face trying to find work. She'd have had better luck a couple of months ago when the pantomimes were being cast."

"You are absolutely correct," Charles agreed. "This is the worst time of year to look."

"We could go to Percy Chalke, and ask him if he can force his mistress to be reasonable in her treatment of Julie."

Charles lifted his brows. "I don't know that she has it in her to be reasonable. Now, if everyone understood that Miss Acton was Julie's mother, it could lance the wound, get all secrets out in the open. It does seem like one secret builds on the next in that family."

"She is Julie's mother?" William exclaimed.

"With Jacques Rueff," Charles confirmed, knowing his fellow reporter would keep the information to himself.

"Bloody hell," his friend muttered. "I had no idea. No, if Julie is Miss Acton's daughter, I don't see anything improving. She's better off away. If a mother cannot treat her own daughter with a natural tenderness, there is no hope for her. And she doesn't like the new mistress. Aren't you concerned for her?"

"I'll tell you what," Charles said. "The Hogarths will take a hackney home because of the late hour. We'll go with them and knock on the tradesmen's entrance to Carley House. Perhaps someone will still be in the kitchens and can check on Julie for us."

"Can we manage that?"

"If we had an excuse." Charles snapped his fingers. "I will speak to Bertram." He hunted through the room for the young man, William in tow, and found him holding his hands over the fire in the kitchen.

"Gentlemen," Bertram exclaimed. His hands went to his unbound neckcloth, and he quickly retied it.

Charles's keen eyes detected a rash on the lad's throat. "You don't look well. Would you like us to convey you back to Brompton with us tonight?"

Bertram blinked slowly. "You're going to Brompton?"

"We want a quick word with your mother's new maid, actually."

"Why?" He rubbed at his throat.

"I am responsible for having her hired," Charles admitted. "And I want to check on her."

Bertram had dark shadows under his eyes. "It's after midnight."

"I think enthusiasm is waning," Charles said. "The beer is gone again. We'll be there and back before you know it, no trouble to the household."

"I've seen yawning," William added.

"I'll send Fred to fetch a hackney for us all," Charles said. He went for his brother, before Bertram Carley could think twice about the sense of getting the new family maid out of bed late at night.

Miss Hogarth joined him when he came back into the room after sending Fred to find the hackney. "Do we need to get our wraps?"

"Yes," Charles said. "I'll fetch them for you, and we are all going to escort you home."

"You are?" She tilted her head. "Why? Something to do with our murders?"

# Chapter 27

❧

Charles put his mouth to Miss Hogarth's ear. "William is worried about Julie Saville. We have a scheme to check on her, since she didn't turn up tonight." He explained his plan to visit Carley House.

"I can simply check on her tomorrow," Miss Hogarth offered.

Charles moved to stand behind her, and said in a low voice, "Look at Mr. Aga."

Indeed, the reporter was shifting from side to side as he spoke to Bertram Carley, clearly nervous.

"Goodness," Miss Hogarth exclaimed.

"I begin to think he's in love with Julie Saville," Charles said. "I don't see the reason for such anxiety. It was never likely she would come here tonight."

"Nor even proper," Mr. Hogarth said, appearing at his side. "A parlormaid at Mr. Dickens's party?"

"One hopes she will be able to call herself an actress again someday soon." Charles felt the need to defend the girl.

"I look forward to escorting these gentle ladies home," Bertram said, coming toward them with a beaming smile at Miss Mary Hogarth, in conversation with Charles's sister near the window.

Miss Hogarth and her father said nothing, but made sure that Miss Mary Hogarth was at the far end of the coach from the hopeful lover as the six of them seated themselves in the hackney coach a few minutes later. The fact that Miss Hogarth had listened to his concerns and made arrangements, trusting his judgment, despite the fact that Bertram, cad or not, would in many ways be a catch for a Hogarth, warmed Charles's heart.

Nonetheless, Bertram attempted conversation on the jolting ride back to Brompton, despite frequent sips from a flask he'd attempted to pass around unsuccessfully before drinking the contents himself. Charles, unable to see much of Miss Hogarth in the limited lantern light, gave up and closed his eyes, drifting sleepily, wondering how irritated Julie would be by three slightly sozzled men coming to her place of employment in the middle of the night to make sure she was well.

The coach stopped in front of the Hogarths' house first. Charles came to full attention when Miss Hogarth pressed his hand good-bye, her breath gentle on his cheek. Mary, a saucier creature, patted his shoulder and gave him a wink he could just see in the dim light.

"I look forward to a closer acquaintance with our families," Bertram said, his words slurring.

"A pleasure to meet ye," Mr. Hogarth said, without making any commitment to the young man. He joined his daughters on the path to their door.

"You know," Charles mumbled as the horses began to move again. "You aren't the only one with a rash. Your new maid, Julie, has complained of such an ailment."

"That's not the same at all," Bertram said.

"No?" William asked. "Why not? Maybe there's a problem with your water supply."

Bertram belched. "I don't know what's causing mine, but the maid is probably reacting to the cleaning solution Mother likes."

"Something unusual?" Charles asked, waking up fully.

"Mother likes her tea service to be dazzlingly white." Bertram fell back against the seat since he hadn't held on to the strap.

"Doesn't every proud keeper of her home?" William asked.

"Not like her. I remember she slapped the maid we had around the holidays this year because there was a brown stain on a cup."

"Did a guest complain?"

"No, it was right after she gave tea to Lady Lugoson and her daughter. They wouldn't complain. Miss Lugoson and my sister were bosom beaus." Bertram snorted drunkenly.

"What happened?" Charles asked, trying to blink his way back into full sobriety.

"The maid gave notice. She was a local girl."

"I meant, what did your mother say?" William said intently. "About the stain? One dousing in tea on an otherwise clean cup should not leave brown stains."

"If it was badly cleaned?" Bertram said uncertainly.

"Was the maid a lazy girl?" Charles asked.

"Not that I heard."

"What do you think happened?"

"Some kind of grit stained the cup really b-b-badly?" Bertram ventured.

"Bad tea leaves?" William suggested. He jerked his head toward the window and drummed his fingers on it.

"Maybe." Bertram yawned.

"Did your mother teach you about poisonous mushrooms?" Charles asked, putting one idea together with another, hoping to get information out of the young man before he passed out. "When you were a child?"

"Of course. Some of them can be quite deceptive."

"How?"

"Some have red tinges or other obvious signs. You have to be careful." He warmed to the topic. "In Somerset we have death caps and other poisonous mushrooms."

"Did you ever see your mother pick any?"

"Once I thought she did, but she laughed and said she knew what she was doing."

"When was that?"

"I was maybe twelve. I assumed I had just mistaken the yellowish cast of the fungus."

"What about your sister?"

Bertram's head tilted drunkenly. "Never saw her picking the poisonous ones."

"Did anyone around you die shortly after your mother picked them?" William said, an edge in his voice.

"I remember the mushroom because I was afraid to eat the mushrooms at breakfast the next morning, but no one who ate them became ill," Bertram said, then giggled.

"What time of year?" Charles asked.

"Autumn, of course." Bertram stared up at the smoke-stained roof of the coach.

Charles made an encouraging noise. "Oh?"

"That might have been about the time my father's mother finally died."

"Was it sudden?" Charles asked.

Bertram closed his eyes. "She had been slowly decaying for years. A blessing that she went."

William lifted his brows in Charles's direction, but how could they know if one fact could be joined to another?

The hackney went past Lugoson House, all the lights extinguished at this time of night. The late hour and the country road meant all they could hear were the horses clopping along, the jangle of the reins, the coachman's winter wheeze.

Bertram coughed and burped up a vent of beery breath that scented the coach. Charles felt queasy and turned his head to the window in the hope of picking up the draft through the improperly fitted glass. Then he saw the row of houses, Georgian structures, probably built from white stone, but badly yellowed and chipped around the edges. Unlike the baroness's home, the Carley house was well lit, not as if for a party, but as if it were some four hours earlier, the family and domestics still about their evening routines.

"Are so many candles always lit at this hour?" Charles asked.

"Is your mother doing witchy rituals at midnight?" William joked.

"No. I don't know what is going on." Bertram thumped the roof and the coachman pulled to the side of the road.

Charles jumped out, followed by the other two men. "Should we go in through the front?"

"Of course, you are my guests. I'll have our butler find the maid for you and then—"

Before he could finish, a scream radiated from the house, the sound chilling Charles to the marrow. A different sort of cry than Epiphany night, more terrifying.

"Julie!" William yelled, and rushed up the steps. He pulled the bell and banged on the door.

Bertram stared, at a loss with the confusion. They heard a cry, a different female voice this time. "That's Beatrice."

Charles joined William at the door, Bertram a few steps behind. While it was secured, it began to open after he rattled it. William pushed through, ignoring whoever was behind the door, and ran across the front hallway, his shoes leaving damp marks on the oriental red fabric.

At the back of the hall was a dark wood staircase with a red runner, leading up to a balcony landing, then the next floor. But the stairs didn't draw Charles's attention, nor the figures at the landing.

A girl lay crumpled at the base. At a dead run, he reached her just as William flung himself to his knees on the ancient carpet.

Dangerously still at the foot of the staircase, Julie Saville wore a black uniform dress and white apron, her red hair still contained in a tight bun. Her eyes were closed, and as Charles took a close look, he saw her bodice rise and fall. Still breathing. He muttered a prayer of thanks and leaned forward, looking for obvious wounds.

Above them, he heard a cry, recognizing Beatrice Carley's irritatingly nasal voice, but the shriek confused him. As he touched Julie's wrist and William spoke into her ear, he saw a blur pass.

Bertram leapt over Julie's feet and climbed the steps two at a time, the first occasion Charles had seen him move with purpose.

His attention pulled back to Julie when her head shifted. William glanced at Charles, wild-eyed, then bent back to the girl. "Help me pick her up," he said, and slowly, so slowly, slid his arm under her neck so he could cradle her head.

Charles sat back on his heels and took the lower half of her body. Together, they carried the just-stirring girl into a room with a low-burning fire in the grate, and deposited her on a sofa that, while not exactly long enough for the purpose, was an improvement over a lightly carpeted marble floor in February.

Outside the room he heard shouts and cries, then footsteps on the stair again. Ignoring the commotion, he found two candelabras on the mantelpiece and lit them to increase the room's illumination, then returned to the sofa with one of them. Julie's eyes opened, her gaze snapping to William, then to Charles.

"She pushed me," Julie whispered.

"Who? Miss Carley?" asked William.

"No. *Mrs.* Carley," she corrected.

"Did you complain about the chloride of lime again?" Charles asked, confused as he set the candles on the table in front of the sofa.

"I asked her why she was crying over a miniature painting of a young man." Julie's voice sounded a little stronger now.

"Enough," William said. "Julie, can you move your hands for me?"

Nothing happened for a moment, then the fingers of her right hand, which had been clenched into a loose fist, spread and then tightened again.

"What about your legs?"

Her knees were bent to allow her to fit on the sofa, but Charles saw one leg bend slightly, then the other.

"I don't see any blood," William said, letting out a breath. "I think you'll be fine." He patted her shoulder.

"Where was she looking at this miniature?" Charles asked. "How did you get to the stairs?"

"Balcony. Chairs there. That's where she likes to sit. She chased me down. I fell."

"Must have just been from the landing," William said. "Or you would have died."

"Probably going to be terribly bruised," Charles agreed. "We'll have to carry her to the carriage."

"Where to from there?" William asked.

"We'll take her to the Hogarths," Charles decided. "That's close. Wait a moment, let's check your left arm, Julie. You haven't moved it yet."

Julie moaned as she shifted, her arm trapped between the sofa back and her body. Her elbow bent and her hand came into view.

"What's that?" William plucked something round from her hand.

Charles fetched a candelabrum and stood over William's shoulder. He saw the handsome face on the miniature. His eyebrows rose and his suspicions sparked to life. "That's Horatio Durant."

"Give it to me," said an angry female voice.

The air shifted. Skirts rustled, then William's arm was jerked back.

"Mother!" Beatrice Carley shrieked as more Carleys ran into the room.

Bertram reached his mother, grabbing her around the waist.

Charles lifted the candelabra from the table so it wouldn't be pushed over if one of them were attacked again, and put it on a table by the wall. He grabbed the miniature from William's hand, holding it out of reach.

"Why do you have this?" he demanded of the wild-eyed woman.

Beatrice started to cry. "She killed him. She killed my beloved."

"What?" Charles demanded.

"He wasn't a suicide?" William asked.

"She loved him," Julie said drowsily behind him. "Big tears running down her nose. Slobber and snot. A right mess."

"The laudanum," Charles said, realizing the truth had been before him all along. He stared coldly into Mrs. Carley's eyes. "You drugged him, then slit his wrists."

"He was naked in a bathtub," William said.

"They must have been bathing together," Charles said, blushing.

"He had a headache," Mrs. Carley said, matter-of-factly, fussing with the cuff of her black dress. A mourning dress. It looked too tight, as if the fabric had shrunk or she had gained weight. "He drank it himself."

"Why?" Charles asked, not entirely believing her. "Why kill him?"

"I watched him do it," Mrs. Carley said.

"Then what?" Charles demanded.

"I helped him with the knife," she said in the same calm voice.

That dress continued to bother him. Mourning, yet an evening dress as well, that left her fleshy arms and weathered décolletage on view, in early February chill. He could see no sign of goose-flesh on her arms, however.

"Why?" Charles asked. "Because of his finances?"

She glanced at him, as if noticing for the first time that a real person was speaking to her. "He hurt my daughter. My husband found out about us. Horatio was ruining everything."

"Who else hurt your daughter?" Charles asked. "Christiana Lugoson?"

"She won Horatio's affection away from Beatrice. Christiana was a whore like her mother. She didn't deserve him." Mrs. Carley spat on the tattered-around-the-edges carpet under her feet.

What a thing for an upper-class gentlewoman to do. That, and the lack of jewelry that might also indicate her place in the order. She was half one thing and half quite another. How had he not seen it before, this light of madness in her eye? Had it only appeared when her husband sent her out to Brompton?

"And Marie Rueff hurt Bertram?" Charles asked, not quite believing how reasonable he sounded as he pieced together the chain of events. But he didn't want her to fly into a rage again. He wanted answers.

"Terribly," Mrs. Carley growled, a crazed, dark look in her eyes.

"I bet she put something in the tea," Julie said from the sofa.

"You had the tea service bleached every day, so you'd only poison the people you wanted," Charles said. "You, the mushroom expert, the wise woman, would know how to kill with a cup of tea."

"My grandmother taught me that," Mrs. Carley said.

The room stayed transfixed, horrified, as the woman began a monotone recital of her family tree, going back three generations before that famous last witch tried in Somerset.

"Surely these are old wives' tales," Charles cried.

"No," Mrs. Carley said, in a slightly more triumphant voice.

"My great-grandmother killed three to get her daughter the man she wanted. I even know their names, John Mill, James Smith, Alan Barber."

"What did she use?"

"Death cap mushrooms," the madwoman revealed. "Ground up, just like I learned, like we all learn. Into tiny little bits, just like tea leaves."

Charles caught a candle flicker from the corner of his eye, some defect of the wick. When he turned his head, he saw the bellpull, and swiftly took two steps to the wall and yanked on it.

"Her name was Margery," Miss Carley said as her mother finished speaking. "Oh, Mother. I didn't want Horatio to *die*. Our family doesn't do anything like that anymore. Not in generations."

# Chapter 28

Miss Carley had said the word "die" with such emphasis that Charles was brought to wonder what other punishments the young wise-woman-in-training might have considered acceptable.

"The old ways are best," her mother said complacently.

"You killed my friend!" Miss Carley shrieked.

"I did it for love," her mother insisted. "You'll understand when you are a mother."

Charles sidled to the door along the wall as Miss Carley sobbed, making sure William stayed in front of Julie, protecting her, as Miss Carley broke into noisy tears and embraced her mother.

Slowly opening the door, he saw a male servant in the hall. "Run for a constable," he ordered. "Fast as you can. Send someone on a horse to the Kensington police station if needed."

He didn't know if Mrs. Carley belonged in Newgate Prison or Bedlam, but he wouldn't leave this house until the proper authorities had her in hand.

* * *

Charles felt more than a little worse for wear as he thanked Mrs. Hogarth for his brushed clothing the next morning. He and William had spent the night in the Hogarths' parlor, cozy in front of a warm fire, but a party followed by a late night of capturing a killer and rescuing a friend, then a night on the floor wrapped in one's cloak, was not ever going to make a man's attire suitable for calling on a baroness.

Mr. Hogarth had offered a dressing gown and both unexpected guests had in turn donned the garment so that Mrs. Hogarth and her maid could do what they could to repair their coats and cravats. Fortunately, both men had worn black cravats and were spared the embarrassment of visibly unclean linen.

William set his teacup on the dining table. Charles looked at it with a shudder and his friend laughed. "Come now, very few teacups ever have poison in them."

"I wonder if Lady Lugoson will feel guilty for taking her daughter to Mrs. Carley's home that fateful day," Charles mused. For himself, he felt bad for questioning Lord and Lady Lugoson's possible hand in the girl's death.

"How could she have known?"

"I would feel guilty. I would imagine, given that Lady Lugoson raised the girl from earliest infancy, that she loved her as much as her own child. Or so I can hope."

"A child of that father?" William shook his head. "I only wish Julie Saville might have had some piece of either fortune, from either of her parents."

"At least she isn't dead. She survived what her half sisters did not," Charles stated.

"There is that. And a beautiful girl can always get ahead in life."

Charles heard a note of tenderness in William's voice. "She has stolen your heart?"

William raised his eyebrows just as the door to the parlor

opened and Mr. Hogarth poked his head in. "Ready to go, the pair of ye? We've had a note from Lady Lugoson and she's ready to see us."

Charles nodded. He'd taken the time to pen a few lines earlier, explaining how Christiana had died and at whose hand. The Hogarths' maid had delivered it.

William rose, and they both followed Mr. Hogarth into the entry hall to pile on their coats and hats. Mr. Hogarth would, of course, accompany them, and Julie was still in Miss Hogarth and her sister's room, being ordered to rest in bed for a day or two by Mrs. Hogarth, but the welcome sight of Kate Hogarth appeared just as Charles had buttoned his coat.

"Are you joining us?" he asked, drinking in the sight of her neat, rounded figure in gray, those sleepy eyes enhanced with a matching blue ribbon around her throat, and shining hair.

"If you don't mind," she answered.

"Of course not. You are most welcome." Charles felt a silly grin break out on his lips.

"Since she aided ye, I thought it appropriate," Mr. Hogarth explained.

Charles disagreed, given the unsavory details he would have to share, but surely it would be a learning experience for a girl who one day would have to shield children of her own from the world.

They left the house and began their tramp through the apple orchard. Unlike that late-night voyage more than a month ago, weak sunlight lit their path, a much muddier one than before. The ground, no longer frozen, was damp with wet earth, and the scent of decaying leaves was heavy on their nostrils.

A black-and-white cat darted across their path, probably on the trail of a smaller animal. The reminder of predators and prey set Charles on a philosophical bent as they came up to the French doors they had entered that Epiphany night.

Panch opened a door for them and let them in. Charles wondered if they were being brought into the large drawing room where they had first seen Christiana Lugoson suffering for effect. No sign of what had happened January sixth remained on the carpet. The room gleamed with beeswax polish and the air was fresh.

Lady Lugoson was seated in one of the furniture arrangements. She greeted them gravely, William being the only newcomer.

"Thank you for your note of explanation, Mr. Dickens. Panch told me there was a great deal of activity at the Carleys' late last night," she said, her voice shaking. "I cannot believe I watched my daughter drink that tea and had no idea of the evil present. My poor girl."

"I am so very sorry," Charles said. "So much has been revealed as we have tried to understand what happened to your daughter."

"We had some concerns about Julie Saville," William interjected. "Do you remember who she is?"

One of Lady Lugoson's eyes closed. The other squinted. The expression looked pained. "Yes."

"You thought it wise to turn your own niece into a servant?" William demanded. "When she came from two wealthy families and had a good trade of her own?"

"I simply thought she would be safe in a household, both from herself and my sister." Lady Lugoson lifted a handkerchief to her eyes. "She has a tendency to roam."

"She did so even after taking the position," Charles admitted. "Now she is resting at the Hogarths', a victim of an attempt on her life."

Lady Lugoson's hand flew to her mouth. "Who tried to kill her?"

Lord Lugoson entered the room. He had a new air of confidence since they had first seen him here, though he possessed the same spindly limbs. When he sat next to his mother, she took his hand and clutched it tightly against her heart.

"Mrs. Carley," Charles explained.

"Another victim?" Her hand fell to her lap, the fashionable mourning gown much less startling on her than it had been on Mrs. Carley. "Until your note, Mr. Dickens, I would have thought Beatrice to have done it, in that family at least."

"Julie realized all too quickly that something strange was going on with Mrs. Carley's tea service. But it was when she found that lady in a black dress, crying over a miniature of the late Horatio Durant, that she became suspicious, and Mrs. Carley chased her down the central staircase in a rage."

"She fell," William said flatly. "And of course, is out of a job again, and injured. What are you going to do about it, Lady Lugoson?"

"William," Mr. Hogarth chided, but the lady's gaze fixed on the reporter.

Lady Lugoson spoke in tender tones. "She must be badly hurt. Of course she can come here, and we will tend her."

Lord Lugoson nodded. "It is right that we help."

Charles imagined the young lord's love of the theater prompted his enthusiasm.

"We are happy to care for her at my house," Mr. Hogarth said stiffly.

"I'll send for Dr. Keville," the lady insisted. "Panch?"

The butler had been silently waiting against the wall. He nodded and went out, leaving them alone in the room.

"Please explain everything, Mr. Dickens," Lady Lugoson said. "I am most confused, despite your note. And my son hasn't read it. Surely Mr. Durant killed himself. How was he involved?"

"Mrs. Carley was clearly involved in the Durant tragedy," Charles said. "She has admitted as much."

"Why?"

Mr. Hogarth glanced at his daughter, then shook his head at the baroness.

She colored and looked away. "You said something about the tea?"

"Yes," Charles said. "While Mrs. Carley was justly famed for her afternoon tea service, she did, upon occasion, add one ingredient, dried and ground death cap mushrooms, gathered from the family estate in Somerset."

Lord Lugoson leapt to his feet. "What?" he gasped.

"I am so sorry to relay this tragic news to you both," Charles said. "She killed both Marie Rueff and Miss Lugoson with her special mushroom tea."

"Why?" Lady Lugoson said, the word sounding more like a keen than before. Tears welled up in her eyes, proving Charles's theory that the girl had been loved by her adopted mother, if not her half brother.

"Mrs. Carley believes she is a wise woman, like her long-ago ancestress Margery before her, who killed those who hurt her children," he explained, feeling the strong gaze of interested eyes on him. He warmed to his topic, gesturing along with his words. "Miss Rueff's death was necessary a year before because Mrs. Carley didn't want a lower-class girl marrying into the Carley family. Mr. Carley is a Member of Parliament with designs on even higher office. While the lovers were caught and separated, Mrs. Carley took the opportunity to invite Marie Rueff for tea, to discuss the matter."

"She put lethal mushrooms in the tea?"

"Powdered by her private family methods," Charles agreed. "But it did leave a residue, which is why she always had her service cleaned with chloride of lime. A daily routine, so her servants would not know when she had used, er, extra ingredients in her brew."

"And my daughter?" Lady Lugoson asked.

"Christiana had to die because Beatrice wanted to marry Horatio and he was more interested in Christiana. Mrs. Carley had been hoping Horatio would propose to Beatrice if Christiana was out of the picture, but instead, he seduced Mrs. Carley herself," Charles said. "He had no real interest in marriage, but he was around the Carleys a great deal. He must have seen the bored wife as easy prey."

"I don't understand why he died," Lord Lugoson interrupted.

"Because the husband found out," William interjected. "Banned his wife and children to Brompton, as if he doesn't have his own private amusements, the hypocrite."

Again, Mr. Hogarth glared, but Miss Hogarth seemed composed.

Charles went back to the subject. "Horatio Durant did commit suicide, but was assisted in some fashion by Mrs. Carley, who wanted to punish him for ruining her daughter's happiness and damaging her marriage."

"I cannot believe I trusted such an evil woman," Lady Lugoson said. "Not only to take tea with her, but to send Julie to her household. I am ashamed. I will take Julie with me when we return to France. We will go as soon as she is well enough to travel."

"Take Julie to France?" William cried. "But she has not lived there since earliest childhood. She doesn't even remember living there."

"Can you think of a better place for her?" Lady Lugoson asked.

William blinked and sat back. "Perhaps, my lady. May I call upon you tomorrow to discuss her future?"

Charles's head snapped toward his friend. Did he want to marry the wild, impetuous, charismatic actress? He must not want a quiet home.

"What will happen now?" Lady Lugoson asked after agreeing to William's request.

"The constable came, then policeman were sent for," Charles

said. "That is why we are seeing you so late in the day. We were up much of the night waiting for them."

"Where is Mrs. Carley?"

"Newgate Prison, I imagine. There will be a trial."

"Her husband? Her children?"

"Her husband was sent for but never came," Charles said. "Bertram may be in charge of his sister now. He will have to come to some kind of agreement with his father, but neither he nor Miss Carley did anything wrong."

"Are you certain?" Lady Lugoson asked. "Beatrice is innocent?"

"A difficult case," Charles admitted, "from what I've heard from Dr. Keville. But never did her mother implicate her in the crimes and she seemed as shocked as Bertram, or indeed, myself and William."

"I am glad for that," Lady Lugoson murmured.

"You must be most pleased to know your sister is entirely innocent of the deaths," Charles said pointedly.

Lady Lugoson nodded. "I hope she can find some peace, now, with both daughters out of her life." She put a shaky hand to her face. "I am sorry I didn't offer you any refreshment. I need to lie down, I'm afraid. My head aches. But Panch can bring you something."

"We can do without, my lady," Charles said. "I hope you feel better soon."

"We must offer them something, Mother," Lord Lugoson said. "For all their troubles. Don't you have a charity, Mr. Dickens?"

"Mr. Aga and I are the founders of the Charity for Dressing the Mudlark Children of Blackfriars Bridge," Charles said, somewhat confused. "The children need help, of course, but I was very happy to fulfill your mother's request despite the irregularity of it. I'm a reporter, not a Bow Street Runner."

Lord Lugoson's chest rose in mild amusement. "Our banker

will visit you at your place of business tomorrow or Tuesday," he stated. "Something good must come out of this miserable situation."

"Julie Saville," Miss Hogarth said, speaking for the first time. "I second the notion that she deserves some recompense for her suffering."

Lady Lugoson, eyes glazed with pain, nodded. "I will not take her out of her position in life, but I will settle something upon her."

"We are your witnesses, my lady," Mr. Hogarth said.

"A dowry, I think," she said. "Cash, not a building. I'm not sure my father's giving my sister a theater ever did her any real good. Five hundred pounds? That should allow her to establish a household."

"That is very kind of you, my lady," Mr. Hogarth said.

William drew a breath and let it out noisily through his nose as Lady Lugoson rose, assisted by her son. Mr. Hogarth took her other arm, and William followed them behind.

Charles had been lost in contemplation of five hundred pounds and did not rise. A delicate clearing of the throat reminded him that Miss Hogarth remained.

When he glanced in her direction, she said, "I wish I could have been there for every thrilling moment of this investigation, but alas, I am under my parents' supervision."

"Yes."

"They are very good, my parents, but I know enough of the world to understand more than they realize," she said.

Charles thought there had been parts of the case that she yet did not know, and he hoped she never would understand some of the foul doings attributed to the late Lord Lugoson.

"I am glad it is over," he said.

"Yes. You have worked very hard for the lady. I am glad someone will benefit."

"Julie Saville and the mudlarks," Charles said, a wide grin

spreading across his face. "I can't wait to see their faces when we are able to buy them new clothing."

They both stood, since her father and William did not appear to be returning.

"I would do it all again," Miss Hogarth whispered, "in order to spend more time with you. Though I am in awe of how you uncovered the truth. I hope I played some small part in helping you."

"You did," he assured her. "I admit, that at the time, I was irritated by your refusal to accept my pronouncement that Beatrice Carley was responsible, but in hindsight, that makes me trust in your judgment more. You make me dig deeper."

"I would like you to trust me." She twisted her hands together. "I believe we could uncover great things together, that you would bring me more adventure than the average life might."

*I could truly love this girl.* He leaned over, still grinning, and kissed her on the cheek. As she blushed, he said, "I have to go out of town tomorrow for another debate, but I will find an excuse to see you very soon, Miss Hogarth."

"Perhaps someday I will give you permission to call me Kate," she said shyly.

"W-will you?" he stammered. "I mean, would you?"

"Yes, Mr. Dickens. After all, you gave me the mystery I requested, not just the lovemaking." She took a step toward him, her eyes sparkling, then went to her tiptoes and pressed her soft, pink lips against his.

Charles tasted tea on her breath. He closed his eyes and leaned into the touch of their mouths, not daring to deepen the butterfly touch, his body and heart in full agreement. There had never been a kiss like this before and there never would be again.

"It is a far, far better idea for us to have experienced this together, than I would have ever dreamed," he sighed as she pulled away.

She put her fingers to her lips, eyebrows high on her forehead. "Oh, Mr. Dickens."

"Kate." He grinned.

"What—"

The door opened before he could hear her question in full. Panch stood in the doorway. They walked out, so close to each other that their arms nearly brushed.

Mrs. Hogarth gave William permission to see Julie before he went back into town, but Charles declined, since he had a bag to pack for his next meeting.

He had to rise quite early for the stagecoach, but when he walked out of his front door the next morning, he discovered William outside.

"Have you slept?" Charles demanded, looking at his friend's unshaven face.

William, despite the February early morning, did not wear his coat, gloves, or hat. Still, he did not seem to feel the chill of the hour. He offered Charles a madcap grin. "I have proposed to Julie and we will wed as soon as the banns can be called."

"Congratulations," Charles said heartily, offering his hand. He and William shook. Though he thought he could pull his exhausted friend over in one swift motion, the handshake was firm. "You should return to your rooms and warm yourself. I would go with you to celebrate, but I have to catch the coach."

"Mr. Hogarth kindly allowed me a day away from my duties to speak to Lady Lugoson," William told him. "I need to bathe and dress and then go back to Brompton to make arrangements both for Julie to be removed to Lugoson House and for the dowry."

"You'll see the rector at St. Luke's?" Charles reached for his muffler and began to unwind it to hand to his friend but William shook his head.

"That is a good plan. Julie can claim to be a parishioner since she did just move into the area a few nights ago."

Charles moved toward the steps as a laundress came up them, holding a bundle of clean linen. "Does Julie understand who she is?"

The woman put her head down and angled past them. "No," William said. "She is still dizzy. Her eyes don't quite focus. It is one thing to assure her I want to be her life protector, and another to explain all the details."

He'd have to take William to his rooms, or risk the man freezing to death outside. Grateful that he had not yet heard the bell marking the hour, he took his friend's arm with his free hand and pulled him down the corridor, following the scent of clean fabric. "She needs to know, in order to grieve properly. Why, she lost two sisters."

"I'm well aware," William said. "But you saw her. She needs time."

Privately, Charles disagreed. Julie had seemed quite sensible on the sofa at the Carleys' house, and that was right after returning to consciousness. But it would now be William's duty to guard and protect his young bride, and he hoped his friend would not think it a poor bargain.

"What will you do about her mother?"

"With any hope, she has gone to the provinces," William said as they reached his door. "Time will tell if Julie and Miss Acton have a relationship or not, or if they even should."

"It is to her credit that Julie was never abandoned," Charles said. "Her aunt is providing for her. If only these women could have protected the other two girls."

"I feel sorry for Beatrice Carley as well," William said, pulling his key from his pocket. "There is not much hope for a girl with a mad mother, but I can, at least, save Julie."

"And make her a mother?"

William grinned. "Time will tell."

For himself, Charles would prefer a girl whom he could trust in all things, a girl of refinement to balance her gambler's heart. For all women gambled on the men they chose, and their children either reaped the benefit or paid the price.

As William waved and opened his door, Charles clambered down the steps toward the street. He could not help thinking of the delights of a wife at home, if not one with Julie's nonexistent domestic capabilities.

Kate Hogarth, however, would make a wonderful companion. With that quick mind, those sterling domestic skills, that pretty face, what a pleasure their marriage could be. He whistled merrily as he reached the road, swinging his carpetbag at his side as he walked past a stream of carters, readying their wares for the day ahead.

He'd uncovered the truth behind the deaths of three young people. His experiences were exciting enough to turn into a novel. Though he had too much imagination to ever take anything directly from life.

An hour later, as he sat inside the stagecoach taking him to yet another parliamentary meeting, he pulled out a pencil stub and a scrap of paper. He decided to write his sister Fanny, to order his thoughts after everything that had transpired. *"Dearest,"* he wrote, holding his paper over his satchel to keep it steady in the jolting coach. *"I'm going to set down a tale of two murders, and the sad death of a promising young man. . . ."*

# Acknowledgments

Thank you to my father, David Hiestand, for allowing me to use yet another family name as my new pen name. We're not entirely sure who his grandfather "Redmond" was since his appearance in family history only lasted two months, but that just makes Heather Redmond a more appropriately mysterious name!

Thank you to my beta readers Judy DiCanio, Ransom Stevens, Julie Mulhern, and Madeline Pruett. Many people read early drafts of the first few chapters in their various incarnations, including Delle Jacobs, Eilis Flynn, Mary Jo Hiestand, David Hiestand, Stand Hiestand, Peter Sentfleben, and my agent, Laurie McLean at Fuse Literary. Thanks so much to Peter and my Kensington editor, Elizabeth May, for championing this book.

The works of Charles Dickens have stimulated fiction of mine over the years, but I never thought I'd be using his actual life in a novel. Not that I think he was ever an amateur sleuth. My plot is entirely fictitious as is most everyone in the book, though I did attempt to be faithful to Dickens's career and lifestyle as I understood it to be in his early twenties. More and more, as I did my research, I found myself inspired by his wife, Catherine Hogarth Dickens, and I hope I did her credit. Much information about her has vanished, but I imagined her at age nineteen based on what little I could find in letters and biography. Any mistakes or fabrications are my own, and made with reverence. Thank you to the biographers Lillian Nayder, Claire Tomalin, Michael Slater, and Hilary Macaskill, among others, for their works on the subject. I sincerely appreciate the efforts of Dickens-related institutions and the Dickens family for keeping this history alive.

# BOOK CLUB READING GUIDE for
## A Tale of Two Murders

1. Charles Dickens's novel *A Tale of Two Cities* inspired aspects of this novel. What similarities are shared between these two books? Does reading this book make you want to read or reread the classic Dickens novel?

2. What did you know about Charles Dickens before reading this novel? Is it hard to picture him as a young man before he became the international celebrity, and the tired middle-aged man he appears to be in the extant photos? Based on Charles as described in this novel, are you surprised he became such a great and enduring success?

3. What do you think of 1830s courtship as described in this novel? Is it strange to you that Charles and Kate don't call each other by their first names? That there is almost no physical contact between them? Do you think love and trust can grow when a couple is so rarely alone together? Would you pursue a romantic partner who lived five miles away if you had to walk through winter weather each way to get to them?

4. What do you think of Kate's challenge to Charles? "Give me a mystery, Mr. Dickens, and a solution, and I will follow you into places I should not." Do you think a woman of Kate's time might really have said something like this?

5. Do you think Kate and Charles have an equal partnership? In a time when men primarily found friendships with one another, do you think Kate really would have been able to share an interest in mysteries with her significant other?

6. Given how Christiana Lugoson died, would you have suspected murder from the start?

7. The author left some aspects of Charles's relationship

with Lady Lugoson up to the reader's imagination. What do you think their relationship was?

8. Julie Saville is a character who complicates Charles's life. What did you think about how he handled her? Did you think Mr. Hogarth's concerns were appropriate?

9. In the 1830s, there was quite a bit of take-out dining as many Londoners didn't have kitchens as we think of them today. Water was also not available directly into many homes. How would these things affect your daily life?

10. Some of the characters in this novel are real, like Lady Holland and John Black. What kind of research interests do you have after reading this novel? Will you do further reading to discover who and what was real?

11. Which of the supporting characters are you hoping to see in the next books in this series?

12. According to Wikipedia, "A genius is a person who displays exceptional intellectual ability, creative productivity, universality in genres or originality, typically to a degree that is associated with the achievement of new advances in a domain of knowledge." Do you think Charles Dickens meets the criteria? Why or why not?